THE TERAS TRIALS
Lucien Burr

Cover Art by Clown Saint
Internal Art by M.E. Morgan

print ISBN: 978-0-6455494-6-1

Category (Adult Fiction)
Genre (SFF/ Dystopian / Romance / LGBT)

Content Warnings:

Homophobia, homophobic slurs, substance abuse, familial abuse, ableist attitudes, class issues, religious themes, religious mockery, body horror, dysphoria, gore, violence, graphic deaths, lifechanging injury, medical talk, explicit sex scenes, suicide

"*You're not a monster,' I said.*
But I lied.
What I really wanted to say was that a monster is not such a terrible thing to be. From the Latin root monstrum, a divine messenger of catastrophe, then adapted by the Old French to mean an animal of myriad origins: centaur, griffin, satyr. To be a monster is to be a hybrid signal, a lighthouse: both shelter and warning at once."

Ocean Vuong, On Earth We're Briefly Gorgeous

LESSON ONE: NOLI DORMIRE DUM IN SPECULIS

The snow has been falling for weeks; a heavy bone-white swathe that blankets the little market town of Watford.

I scan the place, breathing short with my body low against the snow. It's impossible to tell which of the fallen stone structures have crumbled due to disrepair and which have fallen from the force of beasts.

Maybe if I'd come just a few days earlier, I would have seen it happen.

But now, in the flickering gaslight of a streetlamp, all I see is carnage.

"Stinks," I mutter, yanking a cigarette out of my pocket. I lean forward to shield the flame from the wind and breathe a little gratefully once it's lit.

"God, really?" my brother Thaddeus mutters. He's angry about it and tries to swipe it from my fingers. I swat back at him. This is a small pleasure, and I will take it. Thaddeus glares at me and gestures around. "Now?"

"I figure there are worse vices," I hiss back. "Certainly not like drinking on the job." Thaddeus stares at me. He's deeply unimpressed, but then, what's new?

I take another drag and let the smoke settle in my lungs. "Besides, it calms my soul, Thad. And in a place like this, you can hardly blame me."

We're both crouched in snow and blood. I know the technicality of what I'm seeing. I know it's limbs, blood, gore— but the reality of it is snagging in my periphery, caught on the thorn of my willpower. I *know* I'm squatting in people, but if I just refuse to think about it hard enough, maybe I can pretend it's all ok.

Thad snorts once at me and turns back to stare at the streetlamp. I watch him for a moment, watch his breath swirling hot in the air, this even-paced drum that makes me forget where we are and what we're doing.

"There," Thaddeus whispers after a while. He nods seriously into the roiling dark of night, seeing some shape only a graduated Hunter could pick out.

I'm not about to dispute. All I have are very boring, very human eyes, so if my brother sees something, I decide I better get ready to kill it. I shrug nonchalantly, but anxiety is clawing at the edges of my mind. "If you say so."

I get to my feet and ignore the way my body shakes. I dust the snow off my pants. I walk. It's all very mundane and proper like my body isn't aware of what it's about to do— though my heart seems to know.

Trying in vain to keep my heart at a reasonable pace, I step out into the street.

The streetlamps must have been lit days ago. I can tell because their gaslight is a muffled, muted blur. It makes the street seem fuzzy. A crumpled, disembowelled body is slumped against one of them—perhaps the lamplighter himself. I make a point of not looking at it. No one survived this. No one remained alive to relight these lamps. I have to make do with the light available.

I walk, feeling eyes on me. I don't know if I'm imagining it, but the darkness feels loaded and heavy like a thousand bodies are crammed close and tracking me. After a moment where nothing happens, I feel my knees buckle. Instinct tells me to lower myself to the ground; something about standing tall sends my guts spinning. I am too exposed here, and the darkness is a curtained vignette around me. It hides all manner of things that crave the warm flesh on my bones.

Calm, I tell myself. I peer into the shadows, hoping to spot the same shapes my brother did. Nothing solidifies. The night remains a swirling mystery, and that only makes me more tense. I force a breath to settle myself when a gust of wind nearly throws me to the ground. Hands up, I shield my face against the sharp whipping wind, squeezing my eyes against the onslaught. Too late I realise the mistake.

I snap my eyes open.

Squinting through the snow, I see movement. Out of the smudge of night, something speeds along the cobblestones. It weaves through all the open, broken bodies and throws its head back; the dead town echoes with a wide-throated howl.

Then I see a red mist gurgling from its mouth. Blood and gore and saliva spray out with its scream. Its head resolves into a sinewy, hard skull, dog-like and terrifying.

For a moment, I am frozen. In my periphery, I see my brother. He starts gesturing silently, then more urgently, and then it's my own insistent voice in my head telling me to take the gun out—*for God's sake, man, get out the damn gun*—my heart throwing itself into that unnatural, anxious flutter.

I realise I'm not going to move. I realise this is it. I am going to stand here and let the beast rip open my belly. In half a moment or less, Cassius Jones will be little more than an indecent smell and a red mark upon the snow.

"Move!" Thaddeus yells.

His rage makes me blink. I get over myself. Some shift in me, some will to live overrides my fear. Everything in me clicks and I turn, squaring myself against the incoming assault.

I shove both hands into my coat.

Howling, high-pitched clicking rises in the air; maybe it had been a *gryphon* once, or a wolf — long-necked, long-faced, bounding forward on unnatural haunches. Black talons beat against the cobblestones, this scattering percussion of scratches. Black pits for eyes. It takes everything in me not to shift.

I wrench my hands free of the coat. In my left, under my tight grip, I raise my flintlock pistol and pull the hammer back. In my right, I have the sparker. Long as my finger, fat as two thumbs, it could pass as a lighter to an untrained eye. I shoot my hand forward with it.

"Hold," I whisper to myself, to my nerves. "Hold, hold."

The beast squeals and leaps.

I close my eyes tight and flick the sparker open. A hot ball of white light flares from the silver column, so bright I can see the flash of it through my eyelids. The beast screams, momentarily blinded. Whipping around, I open my eyes, aim the pistol, and fire.

The silver bullet buries itself in the beast's head. My body is so full of adrenaline I see it all happen in slow motion. The bullet moves like a corkscrew, ripping through its flesh. I squeeze my eyes against the splatter of blood and gore, and the *teras'* strange, inhuman keening echoes through the cadaver of Watford itself; a self-made graveyard for the beast to die in.

It thumps to the ground, dead.

I stand panting, staring over the barrel of my smoking gun at the prone, limp thing at my feet.

Three hollow claps are all Thaddeus gives me. They echo out over the snow. I turn to look at him, my vision slightly obscured by the flutter of smoke from the pistol.

Three claps. The bastard.

"Not good enough for you?" I say quietly. Bile rises in the back of my throat.

"For me?" Thaddeus looks affronted. Then he tuts. "It's not me you have to impress, Cass."

I resist the urge to turn and stare towards London.

"A *teras* like this dead before you've even set foot in the University — you won't be riding on my coattails in there. I estimate it's at least a C tier. That reputation will be good for you."

I put the gun away and flick my brother a look of quiet disbelief. This is all his idea. I don't know much about the University. Graduates are forbidden to speak on it. But the admission trials in particular are a well-guarded secret. I prompt him in the hopes he'll tell me more. "Will it?"

Thaddeus's expression shifts darker. "People might stare in London, but that's a hell of a lot easier to manage than getting eaten. And if you stick out as much as we do, and you've managed to kill one, that's the kind of reputation you want to spread."

I say nothing to that. A layered exhaustion is filling me up. We were not born in London. We only got a spot because of him. Some families have been behind the walls for generations, and they won't let us forget it.

Instead, I look down at the beast and say, "It's not the first one I've killed."

Thaddeus shrugs and opens his coat. He unstraps a thick, wide blade from his side and hefts it towards me. "First one whose head you'll be taking for a trophy."

But before he can hand the blade over, Thaddeus shudders to a stop. His brows twist together.

"What the fuck?" he whispers.

I follow his gaze. He's staring at the dead *teras*, a look of confused fear blooming in his eyes.

"What is it?"

Thaddeus kicks the thing's head. "Never seen this thing before."

Up close, I see he's right. I study *teras*, because my whole life has been training for the University. I know every anatomical drawing, every genus, every category. Thaddeus is right. There's not a neat class to drop this one into. It bears the qualities of a horse and a dog, but its talons suggest something else entirely.

"*Gryphon* class?" I offer weakly.

Thaddeus shoots me a look. "No. But not a *cerberus,* and not an *arion*. Not fully, anyway."

"*Chimera?*"

"Something like that."

I frown, a little horrified. I know what it is, but I don't know what it means. "A hybrid?"

Thaddeus doesn't answer me. "Get the head," he says, thrusting the hilt of the blade into my hands.

I know better than to argue. Thaddeus' brow is twitching. I note the way he sets his jaw. If he gets angry, I'm the only one that will cop it, now that the *teras* is dead, and I'd rather not have to lie to our mother about how I got a bruise.

Still, I curse to my heart's content in the quiet of my mind. I shuck the long coat from my body, roll up my sleeves, and greatly regret wearing white. Then I go to my knees to saw off the beast's head.

Every time I'm close to one of these, my body reacts instinctively. An ingrained human response to something unnatural to our world. I start sweating almost immediately. There's something about the eyes, the beady blackness of them, the void, the eternality—I might throw up. It's fear, the

6

true kind, the one that makes me want to run. A shake starts in my hands as I'm sawing through bone. I can't stop it.

"Oh, God, you look pathetic." Thaddeus comes and pats me on the shoulder. "And bloody tense. Listen, we're London-based now. Not like before."

Before. Instantly, my childhood floods me. Just impressions of a panicked life, my mother clutching her smelling salts on the fainting lounge, my father watching from the window with a shotgun aimed at the air. When you lived outside of London proper, without any of the University's wards, expecting an attack was the best defence. Perhaps the only defence, without a Hunter nearby.

But Thaddeus was admitted to the University, and admission was all it took for London to open her arms to you. Crowded and foul-scented arms, perhaps, but hers was an embrace no one would turn down.

Not when London's wards kept the *teras* at bay.

"You're nineteen. A man proper. You won't have me to hold your hand—"

I spit at my brother, "Oh, like I'd want to hold your sweaty hand—"

"But the trials aren't a joke," he says over me. "You better keep your head." Firm. A touch of scolding beneath it. I feel myself flush, and Thaddeus makes it worse by saying, "None of that God-damned hesitation. So, tell me, Cass. What's the first rule of being a hunter?"

"Never let your guard down," I parrot. The motto of our father: *noli dormire dum in speculis*—never fall asleep at the watchtower. The fear leaves me. I put down the blade. My hands are covered in gore, and my brother can be so *God-damned righteous* — but in the end, Thad is right. It's not just my own reputation I have to worry about, but my family's. It means all the more to them, now they've made it to London.

My admission to the University will cement the Jones

family in London society. No more talk about where we've come from. We'll be useful members of society. Thaddeus won't just be a fluke; the ability to graduate will be in our blood. And that's all that matters, in the end. For the city to be indebted to you is to live a life of safety.

I pick up the blade again. Thaddeus watches me saw away at the *teras*'s neck. I will my brother out of my mind; let the glow of the gaslight lamp swallow him and obscure his image, ignoring his persistent stare. I put my whole body into severing the head, whacking desperately at the bone, and when it finally cracks free it's a shock. I stare at the gap between the head and body for a moment. Then I throw the blade across the snow for Thaddeus to deal with and heave the head up. Black blood and stringy tendon slop to the ground. I lift it to head-height and give a mock bow before it.

"Good evening, kind *teras*. You do me a great honour by dying."

"Cassius," my brother says. It's a warning.

"What?" I turn the head towards Thaddeus. "He does."

The humour only takes me so far.

The ride back to London is long and silent. I stare back at Watford for a moment. Looking at it fills me with a gnawing sense of dread. The *teras* brutalised this town. They are getting brazen.

All the while as we move closer and closer to home, I squint through the dark for the tall spires and domes of the University, hoping to spot it rising out of the city. A beacon calling to me, promising safety.

But the clouds hang low this evening and show me nothing.

LESSON TWO

With my trophy in tow, Thaddeus intends to bring me before the dean of the University. I pretend like I don't know it's practically a bribe: we're begging the University to take me without having to go through admissions. It's easier this way. My pride can stay protected. This dead *teras* will at least prove I have some ability, but I know Thaddeus has set up this meeting because he doesn't think I can make it. I'm too weak. Too brittle. An embarrassment to his legacy.

When I wake in our shared bedroom, Thaddeus is already up. I take the time to pull myself from sleep, even when his frustrated voice calls from outside the door. I stare at myself in the mirror. Thaddeus is strong, with visible muscle and a sturdiness to him that makes him seem grounded. I'm a wispy, lanky boy. Muscle clings to my bones in thin ropey strips. I look about as sturdy as the books I've wrapped myself up in all my life. My hair is long like a girl's—I am teased for this constantly—but I plait it up and lay it over my shoulder and dress in the very best clothes I have. I wear high-waisted black pants, an open-necked white shirt, and my long black duster coat.

The hybrid's head stinks in a way I can't explain. I half expect to find it decaying already, but when I exit the room and see its haunting, vacant stare, I find its neck has only congealed with blood. Its putrid smell permeates our small apartment. I gag as I walk past and try to hide it before Thad sees, but he notices and scoffs at me, rolls his eyes. It's not the worst reaction, but I know how easily he tips towards anger, and I don't want to push him there; he wants me to bear the masculine apathy our father pushed upon us, but I feel too much to ever be very good at that.

My brother revels in his role as Hunter. Even at breakfast, he sits in his beautiful black Hunter's coat, full of pride. The mantle is bright with silver thread, all of his conquests embroidered in tiny detail so a lifetime of hunting could fill it out.

It's the most prestigious class the University has to offer. These are the brave souls who leave the safe wards of London and cull the *teras* that terrorise the rest of England. I know Thaddeus will judge me when I choose another class. I am an obvious candidate for Scholar. I've read every book I could get my hands on that had any detail on the *teras*. I know their types; I know many of their weaknesses. I know Latin to a decent extent. I would love to wrap myself up in the books and the scrolls and the tomes and let a century of knowledge seep into my skin.

Thaddeus will judge me, but it's what I'm cut out for. He is a strange and inconsistent man: he doesn't think I have the skill for a Hunter, but he'll think me weak if I do anything less. I think Hunters are brutes. Violent, ungovernable, reactive people—they are good soldiers and nothing more. To me, it's the Scholars that run this place. The Scholars that run the University itself.

I keep all this to myself and pretend I don't see the look on his face.

We eat porridge and share a handful of berries between us. We eat in silence. Our mother comes in, sliding back the curtain she uses to divide our parent's room from the rest of the apartment. I catch a glimpse of my father, catatonic and as vacant-stared as the severed *teras* head on the table.

"Do you have to keep it there," she whispers, flinching at the sight.

Thaddeus ignores her. He has little time for our mother.

I ignore the question, too, and say instead, "Do you need help with father?"

She silently shakes her head and divvies out a small bowl of oats to spoon-feed to him. She won't look me in the eye. I try to pretend that it doesn't sting, but I've noticed this nervousness in her for days. It's been brewing up, gaining power, as if she's too frightened to speak about what might come to pass if I fail her at the trials.

I scoff down the rest of my breakfast, eager to get out of here, to leave behind the stuffy oppressiveness of my mother's desperation. I put on my boots and yank the head from the table.

"Let's go," I tell Thaddeus.

Something flashes in his eyes, the first bit of respect I've had from him in a while.

"Good man," he says with a nod. He gets up and slaps my back twice, an intimate gesture. "Let's get you a spot."

LESSON THREE

"What the fuck is that?" Dean Drearton exclaims when Thaddeus slams the severed head of the *teras* onto his desk. Red-faced, flustered; I feel like I'm seeing something I shouldn't. I want to go prostrate before this man, bow to him. He is more than a celebrity. He is a saviour. He runs the University that gives the men and women who fight and protect us from monsters. It feels like being close to God.

But this image of mine is stained by the way Thaddeus speaks to him. He is casual. Flippant. My brother is close to the dean in a way only graduates can be; there is a shared sense of passage, a journey they have experienced together. Only they know the true secrets of this world.

The dean gestures wildly. "Thaddeus, what in God's name—"

"Cassius killed it out in Watford," Thaddeus grunts, step-ping back from the horse-dog hybrid with a Hunter's caution. He puts himself out of its range like it might come alive and chomp through his hand. "Had the feet of a gryphon, too. A full hybrid. I can't think of a single Greco-Roman class that it could fit in. Nor anything British."

We're standing in the dean's office, in the heart of the University. I've never been here except in my dreams, and it overwhelms me. This room alone has arched ceilings, windows, all manner of trinkets and books. It's luxury beyond luxury. For a long time, our tiny London home was the most beautiful room I had ever been in, but I know it's small for a family of four. This office is almost half its size.

It's clear Thaddeus wants to say more. He slammed his lips together after the word *hybrid*. I look between him and the dean, thinking I've missed something. The dean stares at Thad, completely unhappily, and then he casts that scrutinising gaze onto me.

My stomach drops. Coming here was a mistake. He looks at me and sees something that makes his lip curl off his teeth in disgust.

"Out in Watford?" the dean clarifies. He's a stout, round old man, with a permanently angry look in his eye. Rubbing the coarse whiskers on his chin, the dean stumbles over to his desk, scrunching up his face at the sight of the butchered head.

"Stinks, doesn't it?" I whisper, trying to make conversation.

Thaddeus spins to me so quickly that I'm almost certain he's snapped his neck. Fury burns in his eyes, his nostrils flare —it might've been comical if I didn't know it meant I truly overstepped.

The dean glances at me, brows pinched together in pity. I feel like dying, then—that's the kind of emotion he elicits in me. Shame makes my face burn. Then the dean carries on like I said nothing. He reaches down to a drawer, groaning through the stretch, and pulls out a pile of paper. With his face impassive he gives it a cursory glance before slamming it down on the desk. "Watford." He prods the page with a fat finger. "You were assigned Watford, Thaddeus Jones, not your brother."

Ah, so that's it. Thaddeus overstepped, not me. I glance at my brother and see him flinch; I watch the anger catching like flint in his blood. He takes a breath so deep his chest begins to puff up.

"Dean—"

The dean's red face looks set to burst. "You think a trophy will be enough to get him in? I thought we taught you the dangers of idealism, Thaddeus. Christ. What a disappointment." A tense minute of silence passes where no one moves. I can feel every nerve in my body tighten up. I worry that I'm visibly shaking, that I'll lose the last bit of respect from both of these men.

To my surprise, it's the dean who blinks first, not my brother. Dean Drearton deflates a little and sighs, turning back to the desk. "Would you get the fucking thing off my desk?" he mutters. I leap forward to take it off. A crusty patch of dried blood snows down as I remove it, and I try to wipe it clean with my sleeve. The dean raises a brow and I regret everything. I regret every breath I have ever taken until now. I am not made for this. My time in London should have taught me everything is politics, especially life and death, and I have no graduate class. Why should a man like the dean give me respect? I realise I am being memorable for all the wrong reasons and step back with the head in my hands.

The dean says drily, "I was sending this out this evening, but I suppose there's no harm in teaching you both a lesson early."

The dean walks around his desk and rips open a set of drawers. I wait rigidly while he rummages through them, not daring to look at my brother. The air is thick, suddenly, sticky with tension. I can almost feel it seeping out of Thad's pores. The instant we leave this place, I know I'll cop the lot of it.

Clearly, Thad had been in the wrong to drag me out for *teras* hunting before I'd even been confirmed in the University, but he will find a way to make this all my fault.

"Here," the dean grumbles. He slaps an envelope into Thaddeus' hands. "Case out Watford again. Try to follow your orders this time."

Thaddeus takes the letter far more gently than I assume is possible for his big, calloused hands. Then he turns on his heels without another word and leaves me alone with the dean.

I chance a look at the door, give the dean an awkward half-bow, and make to leave.

"This is the place ego comes to die, Mr Jones," the dean says. I stumble to a stop and turn back to him. "There are far too many risks in this world for the University to select men and women for its cohort who cannot follow the basic rules of our society."

"Yes, sir," I mutter, standing straight. If I had any fire in me, I might have talked back. But all I can think about is my family. A shared name, a shared fate. Ruining my reputation means ruining theirs, and I cannot do that to them. I give a little bow of my head and hope the dean can see the real depth in it, the deference, the defeat. "Sorry, sir."

"We shall see you next week. Prepare for enrolment, Cassius—once you've read that letter."

THADDEUS SLAMS the letter down on the table. I jump harder than I mean to, body reacting to memories of anger and preparing early for a strike that doesn't come. Sweat prickles at the back of my neck. I try to settle myself like I don't care.

But there is anger in the air so thick I can feel my hands start to shake with it.

Thad had been a storm blazing through the streets of London as he walked home. I'd exited the dean's office to find him fuming, letter half-crumpled in his hand. And without uttering a word he'd burst from the University's grounds and stomped through the near empty streets, sidestepping other graduates and sneering at the Working Class with far more venom than usual.

"Christ's sake," Thaddeus says. Now at home, he runs his hands down his face. Despair is new to Thaddeus, as well as that frightening hint of desperation. I haven't heard this kind of tone from his mouth for a long while. "They can't do this."

"Well, they're the University, brother. Pretty sure they can do whatever they damn well please." I try to keep my hands steady as I light a cigarette, body turned away from my brother's scorn. Thad doesn't even try to rip it from my grasp, and that says plenty about his state of mind. He just stands there, catatonic like our father.

"Will you let me read the bloody thing now?" I mutter, exhaling smoke. Thaddeus doesn't move, though it seems the fight has left him. I seize the opportunity and edge the letter closer to read it.

At first it reads like a plain invitation, willing me to apply for the University and take part in admissions. But it's more than that.

It contains a threat.

Thaddeus throws his fist on the table. I jerk away again, picking the letter up to save the crumpled thing from my brother's rage. I read it over again, holding the smoke in my lungs until they burn. The cig is good but not enough to stop the dread. It creeps up my back, prickly tingles edging up my spine.

I let the cig burn away. I'm barely smoking it now.

I don't know what I'm going to do.

"What is it?"

I flinch again because I recognise the voice, and more than anything, I don't want her to know. But my mother edges into the room. She's been out in London, and she closes the door behind her, smoothing down a hoop skirt. God, she looks awful. She looks exhausted, melancholic. I'm not sure what's done it. The state of my father always makes her sad, but so does half the people who claim to be her friend. Londoners know we aren't really one of them—even if Thaddeus' graduation earned us a place here. We are new money.

I exhale, knowing that whether I tell her or not, her day is only going to get worse. I still can't bring myself to say it, so I lie and say, "It's fine."

My mother is too smart. The exhaustion leaves her, and she perks up, purses her lips. She sees the look on Thaddeus' face, the sheer anger, and wraps her shawl tighter around her. Thaddeus is unapproachable, so the onus is on me. My mother drops her eyes. "Cassius?"

I can only shake my head. I feel the helplessness bubble up in me, but I can't let it devolve into anger. I chance a look at my father. The old man is propped up in the lounge room and staring vacantly out at the dreary London sky. This is his every day. I stare at him and see everything our life will become if the threat in that letter comes to pass.

University admission means you can live in London, and graduation means your family can, too. And all of London is safe behind the wards. There is no saying where they came from—the massive crystal wards that protect us—or who made them, though a dozen London-based families claim a generational link to their creator. Or founders. The stories say God blessed this city and made it his bastion to protect us from the evils Satan unleashed upon the world. But many families resist the church's input, and claim scientific genius, or a stroke of luck. There is no single story; like every myth, there are variations. Numerous accounts. All this to say that, in the end, does it really matter? As much as the scholar in me craves their origin, the basest human part of me is grateful enough for their protection.

They stand taller than any man; wide and imperfect crystal structures that are placed at each gate around the walled city. The protection they offer is invisible to the eye, but it is there. Somehow, they guarantee safety from the *teras*.

There is, of course, a price. For those who live in London, it comes at the cost of a member of your family dedicating their life to fighting the threat. It is one of the only ways to get into the city long-term, unless you are descended from the Working Class which keeps the place running.

Thaddeus didn't mind it. He revelled in it, really. Hunter. Saviour of the Jones family. Some of that joy is innocent; I know my brother is glad for the knowledge, the lessons on how to defend himself, and I remember hearing Thaddeus crying with relief the night of his graduation, guaranteeing our safety in London so long as he was a practising Hunter. But the darker side is that Thaddeus loves the glory. The power he has over our family.

That's why he's angry now, I think. Everything is suddenly out of his hands.

"What is it?" my mother says again. Thaddeus comes forward to block her, but she shoves past him and snatches the letter from my hands.

She can read but not well. I wait for her to parse it. I lower myself into a waiting chair and focus on the cigarette, on the burning smell, the aftertaste in my throat. Out of the corner of my eye, I watch her. She reads it slowly, hovering on each word. Then she reads it frantically, then again. I squeeze my eyes shut, feeling like all the air has been knocked out of me, like moving will exhaust me. Then I hear my mother sob.

My heart twists. The sound is a hollow thud that warps into a high keening, and she crumples to the floor in front of me, and I don't know what to do. I hesitate, my hand close to her head, and then I look up at the ceiling, blinking, trying to make out the delicate patterns in the cornices to keep my mind off what is happening. My mother grabs at my pants, hands desperately clawing at me.

"Cassius," she cries. She screams it like I'm dying. Like she is dying. Her voice breaks halfway through and makes my name a whisper. A prayer. She is praying to God with every syllable. "Cassius, please. Please."

My father doesn't react. Thaddeus presses his fist against his mouth. But my mother is on the floor hysterical, pulling at my clothes. I have never seen her beg before.

"Stop it." My voice cracks. I hate it. I hate sounding weak. I try in vain to gently shake her off, prying her hands away from my pants, but she holds them tight and pleads. The letter scrunches up in her fist.

I feel like my insides are cooking. My chest is heavy. I'm nauseous and sweating. "Stop it," I whisper again, over the sound of her cries.

"Please, you have to—"

"Stop it!"

"Cassius, if you don't—"

"*I know!*" Furious, I bolt to standing. My mother whimpers before me and I regret the anger. She's been like this before, crumpled on the ground before the anger of men. My father. My brother. Now me. It feels like the ultimate betrayal. Perhaps it's an anger I have inherited, but it's no excuse. I sink down to the floor next to her and calm myself. "I'm sorry. I know. I know what I have to do."

I don't know, not really. The letter is a threat. Not just for me, about to enter the admission trials, but for our entire family.

London is overcrowding. There are simply too many people riding on the coattails of a single graduate in their family, and London has decided she can only protect her protectors.

Family no longer counts. Thaddeus' performance as a Hunter is not enough to secure the Jones' family continued safety. But the dean has offered us amnesty. If I'm admitted. . . if I manage to do this, then our family can remain. But if I fail, only Thaddeus can stay behind London's wards. The rest of us will be back to roaming England or braving the beast-infested seas to another country.

The letter does mention I'll have the opportunity to apply for the Working Class—the hereditary caste that services the city. It feels like a jab. My remaining pride wonders if any London-born applicant has the same clause tacked onto the end. But I can't linger on this for long.

The life of my family rests on me.

The trials are brutal. I know this from Thaddeus, even if I don't fully understand what they are. Thaddeus has never told me the details. Then again, he didn't need to: he'd been a different man when he returned and that told me everything.

The University screws with you.

"It'll be fine," I say, patting my mother's head. I try to be casual about it, to smoke at a regular, calm pace on the floor beside her. "I'll be fine."

"We can't go back out there. Your father..." She trails off. The three of us turn to stare at the hollow and catatonic man in that chair.

"Cassius knows what to do," Thaddeus says, nodding along to convince himself. "He was good out there in Watford. A natural. Takes after me. He'll be fine, and we can stay."

Tears gather as the mounting pressure behind my eyes becomes too much. I swallow hard, willing those tears to stay back. Part of me wants to voice how lost I feel. How young. I am nineteen, and my life has been running and reading. Cortisol is permanent in my blood. I don't think I've ever known anything but stress.

I can't say anything, of course. My mother will weep if she knows there's any chance I might fail. I had fourteen years in the wild. She had every year until five years past.

I can't fail. I can't do that to her.

"It'll be fine," I say again. I try for a smile and gesture to the page. "Did you read the end of it?"

She peels away from her hands, staring at me with smudged kohl-lined eyes. Her braided hair is frazzled. I bite my tongue and help her to her feet. She looks down at the crumpled letter in her hand, sniffs back tears, and smooths the letter out.

After a moment, she only shakes her head. "I don't understand."

I put a pitying hand on her head. "I'm not going to fail. Not when it's an Open Call."

Her eyes shoot up at me. The effect of relief is instant. All her limbs unfold and she half collapses onto me, weeping.

"An Open Call!" she cries like a wailed prayer to God. "An Open Call!"

And to her, it might seem like God is smiling on us, like fate has finally been kind and given the Jones family a break. After all her years of praying, after what her husband has been through, what Thaddeus has done for us — maybe in a world where the universe owes us something, she would have been right.

But I know the truth of it. When I lift my eyes to meet my brother's, it's clear the older man knows, too.

Thaddeus' face is hard and solemn. The expression is knitted into his skin, the years-old worry in his brows surfacing now to comment loudly on my future.

An Open Call means anyone can apply for the University. Londoners, xenos, Working Class. Any year the University's Calling reaches humble doorsteps, it means they're expecting a bad one. A bloody one. A year filled with a hell of a lot of death.

None of the usual restrictions apply. Usually, you require connections, good words. . . Thaddeus had gotten in because our father had a cousin in London—now dead. To accept *xenos* outright, those Englanders born outside London's protection, is rare.

I hold my breath. I know there must be a darker meaning. That hybrid thing I shot in Watford, the number of calls my brother has been dragged to answer recently—some unknowable thing is happening. The *teras* are growing stronger.

Thaddeus snaps a finger in front of my face. "You train for Hunter. You hear me? Not Healer. Not Artificer. Not a God-damned Scholar."

Our mother gasps softly. Always shocked by blasphemy. "Thaddeus. . ."

I bite my tongue. He stares at me, jaw clenched. I wonder if he'll hit me if I try to say no. I will die as a Hunter. I know I will. I throw up my hands, pretending to be calm. "I'm not even in yet."

Thaddeus' fist comes down hard. The wooden table echoes the anger dully, reverberating it; I feel it in my feet, my heart. Both my mother and I jump. Thaddeus points to me, seething.

"Hunter," he says.

If I became a Hunter, a good one, London couldn't afford to kick us out. With an Open Call, they are clearly more than desperate—for candidates in every field. But there is no doubt the class that would go out and kill the *teras* is more in demand. Hunters die all the time. London always needs more of them.

I squirm but I know Thaddeus is right. I need to be in demand.

I swallow and consider my brother. He is always shifting. One moment he is my brother, and a good one at that. A man who clearly loves me, or at the very least respects me. The man who'd taken me to hunt in Watford was that version of Thaddeus.

Then, in other moments, he is this. Vicious. An animal cornered and lashing out. It makes sense—this life does that to you—but the knowledge never stops the sting.

I let it fester for only half a second. Then I close my eyes and stop the feeling at the source, hardening my heart against my brother's disdain. Right now, in this moment, I am a liability. If the Jones family had had one fewer child, perhaps the University would have looked the other way. But I tip the balance. Now I'll be the deciding factor on whether my parents can live out their days in London or die in the wilds of *teras*-infested lands.

I roll my shoulders and flash Thad a toothy grin. "Hunter," I say with a brightness I don't feel. "If I make it in at all."

"You will," Thaddeus says.

It's not encouragement. It's barely support.

It is Thaddeus' command.

LESSON FOUR

The Calling starts that afternoon.

A whining, high-pitched drone; a siren calling out to England. The wind stops, the rain quietens. The whole world seems to pause and listen. The keening is a cry and an invitation all in one, sent out from the very core of London. It reverberates past the city's wards, the curious, massive stones that give London its impenetrable barrier. The sound travels past that and out into the open, vulnerable heartland. It rings out on the hour, every hour.

That night, I pray.

I also wallow, in a sense.

Thaddeus is on call, so I have the room to myself. I get down on my knees and clasp my hands and whisper a pleading and desperate prayer to a God who rarely thinks of me. I do it with every bit of vigour and faith I can muster. I offer my complete devotion. I offer whatever it takes. And once I'm done, I sit there, locked in place like a statue, and I wait. I wait for the sign that I've been heard.

I don't know what I'm expecting, but I am not filled with relief. I want to be a saint at that moment. I want to be

touched by God's light. But I'm just a boy and I'm unremark-
able. I am probably filled with sin. I am not like my brother. I
am not like my father. I know I take after my mother. I know
all of them think that I'm feminine and soft, and I know my
mother is sending another prayer to God this evening, that I
will wake up a brute. Whatever it takes to stay in this city.

For some reason, that's the thing that makes me cry.

I feel like a freak for crying at all. It's not something the
men of London do. It's certainly not something a Jones man
is meant to do. But my father hasn't been more than a vacant
watcher in years, and Thaddeus is gone. I'm alone and I let
myself cry. And then, when it starts to hurt, when I start to
really feel it, I fumble under the bed for a bottle.

It's laudanum. I won't pretend there's anything good
inside that bottle, but it's numbing and freeing and it's what I
need. The doctors gave it to my father, but he's beyond it
now like he's beyond this world. He hardly blinks. He hardly
breathes. He does not need this golden substance as I do.

I shudder in revulsion as the bitter thing slides down my
throat. And then I wait for the magic of it. Laudanum.
Laudanum. From the Latin *laudare*. To praise. When the first
bit of swimming delirium hits me, I praise God. I roll the
Lord's name around my tongue as I swim in His ecstasy, His
freedom.

I don't know if I sleep or if I just slip somewhere between
waking and unconscious, but I welcome whatever it is. The
liminality of oblivion. Wrapped up in the flimsy embrace of a
white cotton sheet, I watch the lamplight flicker on my
eyelids, and ride the throbbing euphoria until it dissipates.

When it's out of my system, the sadness hits me. Barely
an hour has passed; every awful thing has stayed the same.
Whenever the high drifts away, I am left with the remains of
something heavy and unsettling. My body feels absent. My
skin feels wrapped around the wrong bones. I can feel every

tendon working like an old and rusty automaton, everything squeaking and on the verge of breaking. To put it simply, it leaves me feeling wrong.

I like to imagine there's something to it: if laudanum is holy, if its highs bring me closer to God, what's left over when it's gone is something of the Devil. Perhaps it's me—the real me. The dregs at the bottom of your tea. When everything else is stripped away, here I am, a pile of shit to be scraped off your boot.

I know self-pity is not a good trait. After a few minutes of wallowing, I haul myself up. There are only a few days until the admission trials. I'm not even sure what they are. But suddenly Thad is in my ear, crowding against me, hand around my throat.

Hunter, he screams, *you fucking choose hunter*.

I recall the sound of the beast at Watford, the curdling cries of something not of this world. Unbidden, every genus and class of monster in England comes to me, crawling forward to attack. I feel too young for this. Too unprepared. I am grateful for Thad's absence, then, because I know the way he'd look at me. With shaking hands, I light another cigarette and throw on my coat and my boots. I bring my flintlock gun, my sparker, and the tag that tells the guards who I am. That I belong here. Without it, I won't be able to get back in.

I don't know what I'm doing but I leave the apartment. I hunker down in my coat, huffing away, barely tasting the tobacco. The motion is a tic now; raise up, inhale, exhale, down, repeat.

London is safe. There are no crimes in these streets, not unless you want a hanging and your family cast out. Maybe it's the lingering laudanum in my bloodstream, a phantom of paranoia above my head, but I feel exposed. Eyes watch me stalk through the lanes. I know my feet are heading to the wards, but I don't know what to do when I get there. I've been out before, of course, but never alone. Thaddeus always leads, and the guards know his face alone. We've never had to show our identification, never been scrutinised by the guards. They see the Hunter insignia and Thaddeus is lifted from every grounding shackle I endure; my youth, my desires, my very nature.

I am so focused on smoking I don't realise how far I've walked until I'm there.

London has seven gates. The Romans built them, and once there was talk of tearing them down, growing the walled city to accommodate the influx of people. The *teras* meant it never happened—and I thank God for that, or we'd all be dead.

The entire city is backed against the River Thames which is consequently the last thing enveloped by London's wards.

I've walked to the east of London, to the big gate there.

Aldgate flickers with torch light and the eerie and supernatural glow of the ward stones, so that blue-and-orange light warps over the gate. Two circular towers sit on either side of the gate which is fortified with portcullises and chains. Usually, it's busy, but night slows down the traffic. The most exciting thing is a few members of the Cult of the Rift, those who, in the last decade, have started to worship the very tear that let monsters from myth spill into our world. They mill about at gates, waiting to worship the carcasses or *teras* if Hunting parties ever return with trophies; every act driven by a prophylactic aim to avert destruction. Worship of the threat is instituted to avert it.

The church lets them, but only because it spins tales about their order as an extension of God. Individuals called to a higher purpose. No matter that they wish to propitiate the *teras* themselves, like how the Romans would bribe mildew to avoid blighting their crops.

The procession pulls my gaze. There are six of them, in

strange yellow robes. They look like priests on feast days, though they are markedly more excessive with their decoration. They wear embroidered robes, wide-brimmed hats. Some wear patchwork cloaks made from the scales of *pythons* or *hydra* - D or C-tier *teras*. One wears the skinned skull of a *python* as a headdress. It looks gaudy, like a trophy, but the cult believes this is a form of worship. They won't waste the *teras* bodies. I watch as good Christian men and women sign the cross as they pass.

Some of London think of them as devil-worshippers. But they are baser than that. More human. More ancient in their practice.

I turn my gaze back to the gate and wonder if the cultists expect a Hunting party to return.

I think about walking out beyond the wards. I have my tag, and I have the sadness that spurred me here, but I don't truly have the guts. Nerves get the better of me. I veer suddenly to the right to a bustling taphouse and think about drinking myself to oblivion. But God has other plans.

The first step I take, before I'm even across the threshold, is apparently condemned by the heavens. A bell rings. There are shouts. For some reason the first thing I think of is the *teras*. They're attacking, I think. I reach for my gun. Then there's commotion at the gates. A stream of guards run in and out of the circular towers like panicked ants. Hastily, the portcullis is pulled up and then shudders down. I don't know why I feel nervous about it, but I press myself against the wall of the taphouse, hiding in the shadows to spy. Horses are braying outside. A high moan creaks from someone's throat. Gooseflesh erupts over my skin as I shiver, right hand closing tightly around the gun.

But it's not *teras*. A group of mounted Hunters stream in, with three riderless horses. I see several bodies strewn over their mounts' backs. City guards run to pull them free. I watch as two men haul a young woman off a horse, only for her stomach to burst apart. Black, sloppy entrails hit the ground with a wet squelch. She's dead. One of the guards drops her with a surprised shriek. It's chaos. I don't see Thaddeus. My stomach twists.

I don't see Thaddeus.

I run from the shadows. For the second time that night, I start to pray.

"Thaddeus Jones!" I howl. No one is listening. People are crying, people are panicked. A crowd trickles out from the taphouse to watch. The horses are so terrified one rears up as I run at it. I sidestep and tug on the mounted Hunter's arm. "Thaddeus Jones!" I say again. She shakes me free with a yell. I move to the next one.

"He's a hunter!" I say, stumbling between the horses. "He was on patrol. Where is he? *Where is he?*"

Someone grabs me. I can barely make out his face in the shadow.

"Son," he calls me. I try to wrench myself away, but he holds me fast. "Son, I'm sorry."

"No." Thaddeus isn't here. They didn't retrieve a body— maybe there's no body at all. I spin for the nearest horse without a rider and try to haul myself into its waiting saddle. The Hunter puts himself between me and the gate.

"You can't, son," he says, too calmly. Far too calmly.

"Where?" I shout. "Where did it happen?"

"Road to Southend," someone whispers. "Huge thing. Could barely see it."

They trail off. I imagine the *teras*, some hulking thing tearing the Hunters limb from limb. And then I see Thaddeus. We are children. Nothing bad has happened to us. Thaddeus is calm and sweet, and our father is at sea and his anger is never around to seep into us. No one screams at us. No one beats us. I am six and Thad is eleven and he tells me he will always look out for me. He will be the man who protects the Jones' family.

I know Thaddeus is no longer this boy. He is angry and violent, but he has given his whole life to protect me. I am softer than him because he took the brunt of it all—every bad thing in this world has always gone through him first. Am I meant to leave him to die? I can't. I won't. We share the trauma of being the sons of Mr and Mrs Jones. There is no one else in this world who understands.

"Is he dead?" I scream. The Hunter stares at me; he doesn't know. They just fled. They left my brother in the snow.

I think he sees it in my eyes because he steps out of the way. The ward stones are still down, but their field is flickering as they power back up.

Now or never. I choose now.

It is my turn to save him. I ride.

5

LESSON FIVE

The sky is red as the rising sun bleeds across the horizon. The sunrise here is not bright but gloomy and unsettling. Night still clings to the sky.

I make the horse gallop until it tires. The road we travel is one long stretch of pale upturned earth. Sprigs of grass suffocate at its edge under a growing pile of snow. Sometimes there are no trees for many minutes. Other times they are bunched together and peppered with white. Always, a sturdy breeze howls, an ocean wind carried far to reach me.

When I see the first bit of blood, I slow the horse to a trot. There's a long trail of it, leading through a snowy, tree-lined road. A dismembered foot lies further down the path. I ready my gun. The horse refuses to go any further; she stamps beneath me, breathing hard. I dismount and tie her to a tree. Before sense or nerves get the better of me, I force myself down the path. I stay low and quiet. My footfalls are a half-muffled crunching. After each step, I tense and wait for a sound. Nothing comes but I don't feel alone.

I am just starting to breathe easy when the Calling sounds. Another wail goes out, pulsing and waning. Then, somewhere in the distance, I hear a response. A waking moan. It echoes out over the plains, the hollow cry of some ancient thing waking up to stretch. I freeze and search through the trees for the shape of it. Nothing. No sign of anything slouching towards me.

I don't know whether to run or not. I whisper Thad's name, but I can't bring myself to shout it. Instead, I creep forward until the metallic smell of blood is everywhere. I see bodies. The smell has already settled in the snow, dug deep, made roots there. A foul and lingering thing, like fish that's been long-forgotten and half-cooked in the sun. I gag and pull my shirt high over my nose, but it does little to suppress the stench.

And then I see him.

"Thad. . ."

He's half collapsed against a tree. Sweat pools on his brow. Just by looking at him, I know he has a fever; skin scalding as his body panics over the wound. It doesn't quite hit me, what I'm seeing. I must stand there for a full minute uninterrupted before it registers that he's clutching his gut. I see the blood. I know his stomach is open. Holes puncture his shoulder. He is alive, but he is dead at the same time. Only a matter of time.

I don't know what to do.

When I stumble forward, he rouses. It's not an easy waking. He cocks the gun and aims it at me in a rush.

I wait for his eyes to soften in recognition, but he doesn't budge. My skin goes cold.

"What the fuck are you doing here?"

I frown. There's no relief in his voice. He sounds angry. Disappointed. Even in this, he's found a reason to hate me.

My hands are shaking. I long for a cigarette. Scoffing, pretending like he doesn't affect me, I say, "Your party came back decimated. No one could tell me if you were alive or not." After a beat when he says nothing, I move towards him. "What did you want me to do? Leave you here?"

"Yes!" he hisses. "Yes, you fool. I'm dead already."

"You're alive."

He pulls his hand away. I see a bloody intestine and flinch. "I am dead," he says slowly. "And you have condemned our mother to this very same fate."

I freeze at that. "You're a bastard." It comes out a whisper.

"And you are barely a man."

Part of me wants to leave, but how will I live knowing those are the last words he says to me? "I came out here, didn't I? I came to get you, because I know you think I won't pass admissions. And if I don't, you'll be around to take care of mother."

Finally, emotion breaks through. His eyebrows twist up. He blinks rapidly. I hate it. I hate seeing this. When he's like this, he is not Thaddeus the man. He is eleven, and I am six, and nothing bad has ever happened to us.

"Cass, we both know I'm not going to make it."

"Get up," I say. I go to loop my arms under his to pull him to standing. He groans in a way that sounds like a creaking ship. I hear the pain in it. He is biting back a howl. A rush of blood dribbles from between his fingers and I drop him with a cry not of pain but of despair.

"Please," I say. I don't know who I'm saying that for.

Over the high howl of the wind, we hear something that makes us go silent. A deep, booming cry: it echoes in my bones, shakes the very core of me. I feel the thunderclap of a heartbeat in my chest. Thad tells me to run, and I do, because I'm weak. I dart to the other side of the road and press up against a tree to watch.

Something comes crashing through the bushes beside me. I go still as it passes me. Either the blood of our conversation drew it here. In the growing light, I catch sight of the curved edge of its body. It is a serpent, as high as my navel. On either side of its head protrude two ram-like horns. *Cerastes.*

Thaddeus trains his gun on it, but it doesn't strike him. Instead, it starts to bury its head in the dirt.

That is a strategy, I remember that much from my books. The *cerastes* often acts as prey, as a way to kill its food — but also as a defence.

Something isn't right. I feel it, feel the wrongness of it knot in my stomach. That haunting drone of a howl couldn't have come from this creature. A *cerastes* couldn't have torn apart Thad's party.

Something else is hunting it.

The thought crystallises just as another creature bellows overhead. I drop to my knees, hands over my head. The creature screams, a satisfied, excited sound, and when it lands the ground shakes.

An odd ticking sound fills the air. Peering through my fingers, I watch as the *cerastes* reels out of the ground to face its enemy. But there won't be a fight. The *cerastes* doesn't stand a chance.

The ticking noise sounds again; I see a scorpion tail whip over the new *teras'* body and impale the *cerastes* in one smooth motion. The *cerastes* throws its head back and screams loudly, a high-pitched squeal that fetters out to a soft, squelchy squeak.

I start to shake. Its killer is a giant. We're both dead. Thaddeus stares up at it and the fear drains from his face. He is resigned. That expression is so much worse.

The *teras'* head sits high—two or three tall men stacked upon one another—and its body is sturdy and wide. It walks forward and easily crashes through the trees. Great feathered wings are folded neatly against its muscled flank, flaring only slightly when it jumps. It has the hulking body of a lion.

Massive paws pelt the ground. The scorpion tail ticks back into place as it walks.

And in the growing light, I see the sunlit edge of a human nose and lips and it turns to inspect my brother, its prey.

Manticore.

I hold my breath. The *manticore* opens its mouth. Its face is oddly generic, its skin a pale brown. This androgynous mix feels familiar, as if the creature is the cousin of every living human. As it opens its mouth, its jaw unhinges unnaturally wide, revealing three rows crammed with sharp teeth. First, it scoops the dead *cerastes* into its mouth and cranes its head back to gulp down the snake-like creature whole.

But the *cerastes* is tiny. It won't satisfy the *manticore* for long.

I reach for my gun. I don't know what the point is. I can see the thick hide from here. Will a bullet even make it through?

Thaddeus shoots first. He stares it down and pulls the trigger: one, two, three, *click, click, click*. Silence. He throws the pistol aside as the *manticore* howls in anger. A tiny trickle of blood leaks from a wound in its shoulder. That is all.

Thaddeus is going to die, and then it's going to be me.

I see him sitting there resigned to it and I want to scream. If dying here is what fate has in store for me, then the Greeks have been right all along. Sophocles said fate has a terrible power.

And with my father's voice, I hear the quote. *"You cannot escape it by wealth or war. No fort will keep it out, no ships outrun it."*

With Fate hanging over me like a guillotine waiting to drop, I run. As I run, I scream.

I sprint out of the bushes onto the road, running towards Southend, further away from the safety of London's wards. Coattails flap madly around my legs, the wind screams in my ears. My brother is shouting furiously. I think I hear him cry. No, he says. Cass, no. But I scream and wave and hope the *manticore* loves the chase more than prey that's prone.

I don't look back. Not when I hear the growl. Not when I feel the vibrations of something heavy chasing me. My throat burns. My mind runs black. The only thing moving me is the thrum of adrenaline, some embedded desire to live that is knitted into my very core. It is a drumbeat sound in my head.

Run. Run. Run.

The trees fall away again and leave me exposed. Behind me, the *manticore* bellows. The deep bass sound rumbles in my belly and I dash forward with renewed speed. Then my foot jams against something. All at once I'm tumbling through the air. I land badly. The air is knocked out of me. Pain throbs up my spine, the back of my head. I give a pathetic, wheezing cry—I am ashamed. I can't even do this for him. I can't even die far enough away to give him a chance. I look up in time to watch the *manticore* dive over me. The warmth from the underside of its belly spreads over my face and I stare at the white ribbed belly, the wingspan as it flares and blocks out the moonlight, the massive paws outstretched as it leaps. It lands beyond me with a crash, skidding to a stop and turning to face me.

I lay splayed in the snow, too terrified to move. If I run, it will eat me. If I stay, it will eat me. Slowly, I drag myself to my knees.

I hear another voice somewhere. It's not Thad's. But I can't pay attention to it.

The *manticore* growls and steps closer. It takes up my entire vision. No pinch of hope can save me now. That ticking sounds again. I'm dizzy, scared. I barely see the shape of the creature's scorpion tail being raised slowly over its impassive human face. The strange human eyes stare at me.

Pre-emptively, the *manticore* begins to open its jaw. I stare into black void behind the rows of teeth.

Tick, tick — it is getting ready to strike. I pull my gaze to the edge of the tail.

It whips forward. I dive to the side, and then roll again as the sharp tip comes striking down towards my new position. I scrabble to standing and throw myself aside. The scorpion tail crashes into the trunk of a tree behind me. Decimated pieces of bark explode through the air. I flinch to the side immediately and use the momentum to keep running. The *manticore* makes an odd noise of annoyance and lunges after me.

You can't outrun him, my brain tells me, but my legs ignore that and keep me sprinting at full speed. A bellow. That ticking sound again. My head snaps around and I watch the sharp point hurtle towards my eyes. Panicked, I drop to the ground and roll on to my back. The tail retracts and the *manticore* is standing over me. I watch in horror as it quivers, readying itself for the final strike. The jaw opens once more.

Something whizzes through the air.

The *manticore* screams; not the happy hunting sounds it had been making, but a terrible, outraged cry of pain. It rears onto its back legs. A glint of sunlight illuminates its flank, now slick with blood. Two feathered arrows jut out of its sternum. The *manticore* lands heavily and barrels forward. I barely roll in time to avoid being crushed.

The trees obscure it, but both parties are vocal. I imagine the strikes; the intermittent ticks of the scorpion's tail thudding into snow, into trees, into something that might have been flesh. I hear a gurgled grunt, a scream of outrage — both terrifyingly human. And then the *manticore* howls. Great heavy footfalls rush away.

I am tense and waiting. Is it dead?

I stay flat on my back, fingertips pressed into the snow. I

try to calculate the odds of surviving if I'm wrong about this. The *teras* is fast. If it catches sight of me, I'll have no time at all before my head is in its jaws. But if I am right? If that howl was a death cry? Staying here will be death, too.

Carefully, I push to my feet.

A crunch sounds in the bushes and I freeze. The adrenaline is making me more fearful than brave. I press against a tree, frightened to move, as if the *manticore* could play this kind of trick. The shadows shift. They resolve into a face, then two, then three: a young man and woman walked together, the man's arm slung around her neck. Another man walks behind them, face blood splattered.

They are Hunters of a kind, but not graduates.

The pair stop walking. I hear tenor tones that are hushed by the woman. When she speaks, it's with a thick, Midlands accent. "You alive over there?"

I force myself to push away from the tree and stumble up the path towards them.

"Yes," I say. A wash of shame seems to come with the admission. "I'm alive."

The pair look like siblings. Both of their Chinese features are speckled with blood. The young woman has short black hair with a hint of a wave in it. She looks flushed standing in the cold and supporting the weight of the man beside her. He is lean but sturdy, with dark eyes. He clutches his side. Blood seeps through his fingers.

"God," I say, stumbling forward. As I move closer, I see a large gash through the young man's coat, shirt, and skin. Three layers peel away from the body and flap in the wind like paper. "Are you alright?"

"He'll be fine," the young woman says sharply. She slips her arms around his shoulder and the other man comes forward to help shift his weight.

"You're all right," he whispers, patting the boy's shoulder. Then he looks up at me. "Are you from London?"

I pause. He is nearly two heads taller than me, well over six feet. White but tanned from a life under the sun, with dirty blond hair, bloody skin. The blue of his eyes is so intense it seems fake.

I don't know how to answer. "Is my brother dead?" I whisper. No one says anything, so I start up the path.

The *manticore's* corpse is nowhere to be seen. "It got away?" I ask, because I need to hear my own voice.

"It was injured," the woman says. "It fled. But no doubt it will be back soon."

"I thought they were Persian," I murmur quietly. I don't know why—my brain is running in overdrive and latching onto anything that isn't the fate of my brother. Speaking is easy; speaking is a necessity.

The young woman slowly guides her injured brother to sit in the snow. "They are. Or they were."

"*Manticore*," I say.

"*Androphagos*," the other man amends. "That's the Greek, anyway. Man-eater."

I grimace at this. "I thought they were rumours. Something that hadn't quite slipped through from the mythos."

"No such luck," the man replies cheerily, though his face is stripped of any humour. "Whatever grand force decided to mess with the world, it made sure every myth was accounted for."

I stare at him. I can't work him out. He is full of muscle, bulky. He seems happy in a warped way, as if there is no other way to be. I catch the accent and figure he's from around here, perhaps Southend. I know the lot of them are here for the Calling, and then I realise that I'm stalling. That further up the hill my brother is waiting for me. I have to know if he lives, but I can't move.

I look down at my hands. My heart is racing. I consider vomiting into the bushes just to stop the nausea from rolling around in my stomach.

"Shit," I say. The others stare at me. "Thank you. Excuse me."

I head up the slope. I'm not sure if they follow. Thad is vomiting blood when I arrive. Blood and gore pour from a torn hole in his cheek. His nose has been shattered, and blood pours from that, too. Most of his guts are in his hands.

He is not dead yet, but soon.

His eyes widen when he sees me. He goes through surprise, to horror, to a daunting kind of sadness I've never seen in him before. He opens his mouth and I brace myself for whatever this final wish is.

"West. . . tower," he gurgles. "Trials. Get the. . . west tower room. Facing the gates."

I nod at him because I don't know what else to do. "Don't speak. It's ok. I'm here."

It's all hollow and automatic, but I can't think of anything else to say. It all just tumbles out of me, these simple and easy lies to soothe my brother's passing.

Very soon, I will be alone in this world. My father's mind is gone. My mother barely speaks to me. My brother will be dead.

"Never let. . ." he starts to say that old mantra but gives up halfway through. He shakes his head and tries again with a new word.

"Hunter," he says. He commands. It is his final word.

Hunter. Hunter. Choose Hunter.

He dies staring at me with glassy eyes, staring without his soul. His body is empty. I crouch beside him, sniff, and close my eyes.

I try to keep it together. I knew this was coming. But if I knew it, if I had time to prepare, why does it feel so raw?

I want to be a child again. I wish we had never come to London. I wish my father had never met my mother. I wish I was dead.

I stop myself from spiralling further by sinking my fingers into the snow. When I feel the tears press forward, I give myself the luxury of screaming—but only in my imagination. I envision myself bending over in the snow, ripping at my skin, the glorious pain of stinging scratches grounding this body to the world. I imagine beating the trees and howling, howling like a *teras* on a hunt. I revel in the imagined ecstasy and it's still not enough.

"I'm sorry."

I don't turn around, but I swallow my tears and stare dead ahead at the tree above Thaddeus' head. "Are you?"

"One less hunter means more *teras*."

I grit my teeth so hard my jaw asks. "Aren't you just brimming with empathy?" I whisper. I slide my hand into my pockets and get a cigarette, which I light before I stand.

"That was," he pauses, "cruel of me. I'm Leo Shaw," the blonde man says as I turn. "And—I really am sorry."

"Cassius Jones," I say after a puff. "This was my brother, Thaddeus. Hunter class. Graduated two years ago."

It all starts coming out. I regret speaking; I tell myself to stop oversharing, and yet I can't seem to do it. "Are you heading to London?"

Leo Shaw stares at me. "I do believe I asked you first."

He speaks in a strange cadence, like a tightly wound spring. I expect the same kind of sharp anger Thaddeus has— had. But even when I don't speak for several moments, Leo simply waits.

"I live there," I tell him, and gesture back to my brother, "thanks to this corpse."

I don't know why I'm being cruel to myself, or to Thaddeus, especially when he can't fight back. Leo does not question me. I turn fully to inspect him, eyes taking in the pale armour of his muscular body. "But now I may not live there for long."

Leo's brow twitches. I see he doesn't understand—hasn't heard about the changes. When he doesn't press me, I decide to drop it.

"I really am sorry about your brother," he says. I'm not sure why I don't quite believe him. There's something about Leo Shaw—about the other *xenos*, too—and I don't know if it's because there's already such a clear divide in the sand between myself and them, or if they're all wound tight and serious by virtue of a hard existence, but I am fairly certain everything I'm seeing right now is a mask.

Leo Shaw asks, "What do you know about the admission trials?"

I tell the truth, "Not a damn thing."

He squints at me, pursing his lips. I'm not believed.

"Help me carry him and I'll give you a cigarette," I say.

Leo walks forward and wordlessly steals my lit cigarette from my hands. His rough fingers brush against mine and he takes a long drag without looking away. I'm pulled to the endless blue of his eyes and immediately flush. Then he coughs and splutters, choking out, "Disgusting."

"New to it?"

He doesn't reply. His downcast gaze watches me, and then he replaces the cigarette, gently tucking its end into my mouth.

"Help me in the trials, and the lot of us will escort you back to London," he says easily. "How about that?"

I'm shaken. I don't know what to say. "Do you think I have an advantage because I've lived behind the wards?"

"Of course, you have an advantage." It's the young woman. She is leading her struggling brother and two horses up the slope.

Leo's brows come together. He inclines his head "You all right, Si?"

A grunt from Si, the injured boy, and nothing more.

I see Leo's gaze on Si's sister. He mouths *Will he live?*

The woman considers Leo for a moment, and he shifts under her gaze. It looks like she is about to pass judgement, a sentence that will determine if Leo Shaw lives or dies. Then she turns back to her brother and nods, dissolving that strange bit of ceremony. "'Course he will. It's barely a paper cut."

"I've offered to escort Mr Cassius Jones and his brother's body back to London," Leo murmurs.

"In exchange for what?" the woman asks.

"A cigarette," Leo says with a smile. I don't correct him. The woman's eyes slide to me, and I think for certain she sees right through me. Then she walks over and offers her hand. I take it.

"Winifred Lin," she says with a smile. "But Winifred is a stupid name. You'll call me Fred."

"I will," I say. I'd meant to ask it as a question. "Cassius Jones."

Fred nods towards the man slumped against the horse's flank. "That man over there is my brother Silas."

I calmly smoke the cigarette. "I almost took you for Hunters," I say, looking between them and the *manticore's* blood in the snow. Fred retracts her hand slowly, mouth quirked in a curious smile.

"Are you trying for flattery, Mr Jones?"

"Only speaking the truth."

She considers me for a moment. "Have you ever killed a *teras* before?"

"Yes," I say. I don't tell them I've only been behind the wards for five years.

She looks me over once and nods and then no one speaks.

They help me load Thaddeus' body onto my mare and we ride the hour back to London. At the gates I show them my tag, and the other three state their business. The guards won't let them roam the city; their details are recorded and the three of them are rounded up to be escorted to the University.

Leo Shaw looks back at me before he goes. "Do keep your promise, Cassius Jones. Cannot wait to see you again."

I say nothing as I watch him go. I'm left with Thaddeus's broken body bleeding into the mare's coat, and a gathering of muttering, sad guards. My mother is there, too; she gets up from a squat, wrapped tight in her shawl. Whoever found her must have told her I'd gone, and I'd like to think she came out here to wait for me, but we both know the wrong brother is returning. We make eye contact across the milling crowd. Dark circles, tear-stained cheeks, and a hungry look of fury bear down on me. I expect to be screamed at, but when I dismount, when she sees the state of Thaddeus, she just lets me walk into her arms. She doesn't embrace me back. She's not even looking at me.

"Hunter," she tells me, and my stomach drops. "You have to go for Hunter."

6

LESSON SIX

The University promises to make a stained-glass portrait of him for one of their chapel's windows. They tell me he died a hero. I tell them a *manticore* is still out there, killing not one hour from London's gates, but I get no response.

In any case, I have no time to mourn. A few days after my brother is mauled to death, I am standing in the University's entrance hall. It is a massive, grey-stone building. The University's crest depicts the four mantles it offers its graduates. In the top left is the flintlock gun of a Hunter, the top right Rod of Asclepius for the Healers. The quill occupies the lower left quadrant for the Scholars, and an anvil in the lower right for the Artificers. A ribbon encircles the shield, bearing the phrase: NIHIL SINE DEO.

Nothing Without God.

Just in case we could ever forget the *teras* are Satan's agents, and us God's chosen warriors.

The facade to the entrance hall has a haunting feel to it, like lives spanning centuries have settled in its stone. Columns in the Corinthian style line its perimeter. Two wide

46

arched windows sit either side of the massive doors, and smaller, high-set windows run the length of the walls. The entranceway looks like a temple; like entering is an act of worship for some ancient god of knowledge.

But I have been raised Christian, and I can't help but murmur God's name as I walk across the threshold.

I am hit by the brightness of candlelight on marble. Half of one wall is all books, though they are so high off the ground they clearly aren't meant to be read. A small cross is on one of the walls, like a sad but necessary nod to the church, which funds much of the University's costs. The other walls are lined with marble carved busts stripped of all their paint, in that sanitised adoption of Greco-Roman aesthetic, the eerie whiteness of them softened by candle glow. The entrance hall is circular, though two arched door-ways cut through the far end wall and lead further into the University itself. It is Rome as imagined by a fascist, white and pure and perfect. Despite this, I stand bewitched, and for a moment it's like I'm alone. All the milling bodies of the University's prospective students vanish. It is just me and this waiting future.

I know I'll need friends here. I already owe Fred and Silas Lin and Leo Shaw my life. I spot them in the crowd, but they're not together. I'm surprised Silas is here and on his feet after the *manticore,* but if I hadn't been there myself, I wouldn't know he's injured. He stands stock still with a straight back, looking strong. Fred doesn't see me, but Leo does—we lock eyes, and he stalks towards me—but he doesn't say hello. He hovers near me for a moment, then scans around me, and with a sly smile goes instead to a pale girl nearby; pretty in a fine blue dress. She is missing her right arm. It's been replaced by an artificer's work; marble, steel, and gold interlink to give her an arm that looks like delicately painted porcelain.

Leo doesn't even introduce himself. "How'd you lose the arm?" he asks.

The girl is startled he is talking to her. Leo's shirt is smattered with dried blood. Even if it wasn't obvious by his clothes alone, I notice Leo's forehead is marked with a golden cross. It marks him as *xenos*.

"This?" The girl looks younger than him, just over the cusp of eighteen. She scoffs a little, like the extremely delicate, artificer-made steel-and-gold prosthetic is not something worth staring at or asking about. "*Teras*, of course. A big one. Boar-shaped. Caledonian class, you know."

"Sure," Leo says through a forced smile. *For God's sake.* I'm sure he's seen plenty of *teras* — and whatever arcane act has manifested these beasts from the Greek mythos made plenty of those massive boars stalk the land. Leo continues, "I suppose you killed it?"

"Clean shot through the head, of course." And then, when Leo doesn't offer his own story of brilliance, the girl decides to voice the curled concern at the back of her head. "Are you *sure* you're meant to be here?"

Leo doesn't say anything for a moment. His eyes slide to me like he's disbelieving of the attitude. He gives me a wink. "Oh, I'm rather sure."

Leo makes to leave but not before the girl can say, "Quality's hard to find these days."

"Don't be so hard on yourself," Leo whispers as he slinks away again.

He slips past me. "Mr Jones," he says, and doesn't stop to talk. I don't know what he's doing or why, but I watch after him.

Again, I find myself wondering what it's like to have that kind of confidence. It feels like a natural armour for him. There are others like him—obviously *xenos*, or less well-off— but they lack the energy he exudes. The ease. The gravity.

I look around the room. Not as many *xenos* as I'd been expecting, but enough that they all stand out. They aren't the only ones to be shunned. There are London-born workers, or their children: the ones who make the city run, but who will never enjoy the same privileges and money as University graduates. They have come to try their hand. I also notice a smattering of other nationalities, refugees from a world ravaged by the same monsters. But they will be like me, the *xenos*, the Workers–overlooked in favour of London's own.

I edge my way through the crowd and prop myself against one of the hall's internal columns. I also try not to think about looking like a cornered animal, but I'm not sure I succeed.

An open call is rare. It means the University is desperate. They regularly take the siblings of graduates, their children, their friends. The University only takes the very best, and their testing methods are relentless.

I know all this but standing here makes it all that more real.

"Quiet down. Quiet down, now."

The dean walks out. He's dressed in a long robe with gold edges. He looks sadder than ever this evening, but truly, it's just his face. He climbs onto the dais at the end of the hall, half slumping over the podium as he waits for the crowd to grow quiet. A buzz of excited whispers continues even when most voices stop, a mosquito-squeal that sits my teeth on edge.

"I am Dean Drearton," he says with little ceremony. "It is my humble pleasure to welcome you all to the halls of the University, many of you for the first time. You have all taken up the Calling, determined to protect this country from the growing presence of the *teras*."

How many of them are here for patriotism, I don't know.

What I do know is, more than ever, I am here for what London can give to me—not the other way around.

I want to learn. But I also want to live. I covet the knowledge in the books, the way to protect myself and my family if it ever comes down to it. I want my mother to sleep soundly for the rest of her life.

But I am here for myself, and I'm not the only one.

The dean continues in a slow, rambling way, though I'm distracted by movement in the crowd. I'm drawn to it like the rest of the waiting cohort. The dean stops as the crowd parts. Four graduates walk in, one for each discipline and marked by their vestments and their hats. The Scholar, Artificer, and Healer peel off to the sides, and the Hunter steps up to shake the dean's hand. I recognise her from the other night; she was in the party where my brother died. A small part of my mind starts to wonder who decided to leave him to die.

She wears the mantle — a long coat that is beautifully embroidered in silver thread with *teras* scattered across it. A *teras* can only be embroidered on the coat if the Hunter has killed it and returned with a trophy.

She removes her tricorn hat and continues forward to the Dean.

Leo moves beside me.

"Oh, am I worthy of your attention now?" I whisper. He says nothing, gives me nothing to work with, so I turn to inspect him. I wonder at the furrowed look on his face. He must feel the burden of my stare, because he glances at me. I flinch too obviously and turn away, desperate to break the feeling.

"Scholar?" I hear him whisper. "Is that what you're going for?"

"Hunter," I reply, not looking his way. His silence is one of surprise. For whatever reason, it makes him step closer. I try to ignore the surety Leo has about him. He is an outsider, a *xenos*, but he walks like he belongs here. I can't understand why I feel so out of sorts beside him.

"I've seen you out there. Might be best to stick to the books."

"Hunter," I say again, more sharply. This time I do turn to look at him. I meet the hard gleam of his eyes. "Stay out of it, Shaw."

He puts up both his hands as if frightened, but a smirk taints the gesture. "All right, alright, Mr Jones." He is barely affronted. I know several London-born boys that would have drawn on me for the attitude alone. "Maybe you'll show me a thing or two, next time we meet an *androphagos*."

Someone shushes us. Another comments on our disrespect; we are speaking over the Hunter who's come to address us.

"This is a gift," the Hunter is saying, taking the podium from Dean Drearton. "What you have now is a chance to prove yourself, the very essence of you. But as much as it is a gift, it is also an exchange. *Kryptos Logos* endows something upon you. The Mantle you choose will define the rest of your life. But," a short laugh undercuts her words, "as per a personal habit, I'm letting myself get too far ahead. The choice of the mantle is an entirely different task altogether. Admissions should hold your focus. They are far more pressing — and it would serve you all to concentrate on them. Far better to worry on that which you can control than to fret over the imagined exams you might never have to take."

A polite chuckle ripples through the crowd. Neither Leo nor I laugh, but I doubt it's because he has a refined sense of humour.

I watch the Hunter. Something undercuts her tone. Not fear, exactly, which has a stench to it, and usually struggles to be so perfectly hidden. But an awareness. A weariness. Like being in the hall at all is setting her on edge.

It does not bode well for the trials.

The two great doors on either side of the dais shift and open suddenly. A great creak echoes through the hall.

"Through there," the Dean says, "you will begin your admission to the University.

It's a ceremony. I see all the marks of it. The people who'd opened the doors are wearing togas. Their faces are obscured by masks in the shape of bulls and leopards. Symbols of Dionysus—which makes little sense. Dionysian mysteries are all about control—or the lack thereof. Of losing it, of seeing every refined thing in you melt away. My heart begins to race. I want to know the meaning. I want to understand.

"Please proceed in an orderly fashion."

The crowd buzzes again in reaction, anticipation like needles underfoot, animating all their bodies. They split down the middle, the seam of the crowd unravelling them into two columns that funnel through each door.

My stomach opens up and I suffer through a terrifying, dizzying instance where I'm terrified of what's behind them.

"What is this?" Leo asks me, nodding to the Dionysian masks. "A Hellenistic fan club?"

Up close he is nothing short of godlike. Symmetry, warm golden tone beneath his skin, a gleam in his eye that conjures for me the whim of the fae.

Stop it. Christ.

"Or a cult," I offer. I'm relieved when Leo smiles at me, even though he was an ass earlier.

"Bet you know more than me," he says with a grin, and I know now why he's chosen to sidle up to me and not the Lin siblings. We cut a deal in the forest over my brother's body. Cigarette, and all the University's secrets. For that face, I might have spilt it all, if I knew any. I watch the pink flesh of Leo's tongue press against the back of his teeth. He's waiting for me to answer; I don't.

"Come on, Mr Jones!" He slaps me heartily on the back. He's all muscle and strength. I feel it reverberate through me.

I choke and play it off with a cough. "Why would I ruin the surprise?"

"I'd rather you ruin it than let me find out the worst." Still smiling, but something in the facade is cracking. I feel another gaze on me; turn and find Fred spinning away.

Just as I'm thinking I've found a friend, there's the truth of it. This is an intelligence mission. They're all in it together.

I play to his hand. My lungs yearn for a cigarette. "Well, Shaw, what happens if you go in and find out it is indeed a cult? That the reasons so few stories escape this place is because so few people do?"

Leo scoffs. He's grinning, but his eyes darken; a morbid turn to his energy. "I'd much rather know now so I can skip heartily back into the wilds and get eaten."

We're swept along. I find myself passing over the threshold, and there's a shift in the air, a tension that fills the small vestibule waiting on the other side.

We pass the threshold, both physical and metaphysical, and I whisper the name of what I'm seeing, Leo shivers at the sound.

"*Phlebotomia.*"

7

LESSON SEVEN

Bloodletting.

I can't hold back my surprise, even when I am the expert in Leo's eyes.

The aesthetic of this room is markedly different from that of the great hall, which had still felt like part of the University, a great entrance to a new life. But now we are funnelled into a much smaller, windowless room. The ceiling is squashed. Claustrophobia is like an ant in my shoe, making itself known through the smallest of bites. This new vestibule is made entirely of sandstone, and I can't imagine any other purpose to it beyond funnelling us into the University itself. I ignore the other curious bodies, and even Leo, who is apparently a mosquito. A handsome one—really, quite dazzling— but he means to suck me dry, and not in a fun way. So as soon as I cross the threshold, I decide not to speak to him again.

Instead, I look to the centre of the room where a squat marble repository sits. A young woman, a prospective student, holds her forearm over it. She is broad nosed, has a calm look about her even as a knife comes towards her.

Someone cuts across the girl's arm. They're dressed entirely in white and wearing a black mask — some priest?

The young woman bleeds a little into the receptacle, and then a small glass vial is pressed against her skin until that, too, fills with blood. It is taken very carefully and labelled at a short table in the corner. The young woman presses on her arm and waits until the vial is handed back to her. She walks with it around the corner and out of sight.

The line moves forward. No one bats an eye.

My heart is racing. I can see Leo staring at me for an explanation I do not have. I try to relax my shoulders, appear as calm as everyone else apparently is. But I am seeing snippets of things drenched in ritual, the markers of re-enactment. Not Greek, nor Roman — this is Celtic. I freeze at that. Most of Britain's native creatures have been driven back, overcome by the more powerful and abundant Greco-Roman *teras*. There is no explanation for that, or at least, none given to the public. To see remnants of an ancient faith here unnerves me, because it suggests some relevance for the ritual, as if those other teras are re-emerging and require propitiation of a kind. I don't think I could stand that, though—the Greco-Romance variety of *teras* are already too overwhelming.

As for the ritual itself, I only know a handful of stories, things I found in books. Priests in white, a sickle, the blood of sacrifice.

And this is a sacrifice—not of life, but a bond of sorts I am to make with the institution. A covenant.

I think of all of this and say none of it. I think of Thaddeus, and everything he sacrificed. What is a bit of blood against my brother's life, or my family's?

I know I have to move but it's like there's an anchor in my shoes. Leo is watching me. I feel his eyes and the weight in them, and he is analysing me, searching for answers. London is not his domain. It's mine. If I can lead, I'll have an ally. But if he sees me for what I am (pathetic, and fragile, and not built for this) I may have an enemy.

There's nothing else to be done. I step forward.

A bright, young voice curls from beneath the mask. "Name?"

They wear a theatre mask, though not a design I've ever seen before. Certainly nothing that's actually in the archaeological record, but maybe a bastardised version. The mask's expression is eerily neutral, mouth in a horizontal gape. I thought it was made from wood, but it's nearly black, flecked with a green-like rusted bronze.

A sigh. "Name?"

"Sorry," I startle. "Cassius Jones."

The masked priest pauses, tilting their head as if to appraise me. I see in that open maw everything from apology to disappointment. Then, shortly, "Of course. Roll up your sleeve, Mr Jones."

I waste no time. I shuck the coat and I know my way around buttons, so it's only a few moments before I have the sleeve rolled up.

I hold my arm over the marble receptacle. It's better not to look, but I look anyway. The open vat is filled with all this bright red, newly oxygenated blood. The blood of hopeful students mixed. Is this strange conglomerate part of the ritual? Some light trauma bonding before the stress of exams?

The blade slices across my arm. It is one sharp moment of agitated violence. Body tensing, I squeeze my eyes shut against the flare of pain.

There's a solid few seconds before I manage to collect my runaway breath, and another few as the logical part of me calms down that animal instinct telling me to bolt. I've stumbled into something dangerous, it's telling me.

This is magic, or an attempt at it. An ancient magic that isn't understood but has been emulated anyway. Now the consequences fall on me. I start to think, to truly think: why do they need our blood? But once that thought surfaces, the priest returns and presses the warm vial of my blood against my palm.

I step back to the line. Behind me I hear, "Name?"

"Leo Shaw."

I shuffle down the hall slowly until Leo is beside me. I tell myself I am waiting because Fred and Silas Lin expect him to follow me, for whatever reason—to learn what I know about this place, most likely. But even I can't hold up my half-hearted vow of silence: I know I am waiting because I like the company.

He stops when he sees me.

"You waited," he says. Not a question, but he sounds surprised.

"Should I not have?" I ask with a smile, and he gives me a flippant shrug. I wipe the smile from my face. Fine. I can't get a read on him. He's always shifting. I'm never quite sure where I stand in his presence.

We shuffle forward, this new vestibule tight and dimly lit. That catastrophic sense fills me again, but I stamp it down. I decide if Leo is playing a game, I should do the same, so I ask, "Are you regretting it? Coming here?"

I don't know why I say it. It's not like either of us have many choices. Leo speaks without looking at me, "Why do you ask?"

While he's not looking, I stare at his shoulders. He's broad. Strong. I think myself too soft. For a dizzying moment, I am thinking about my body, and its lack of beauty next to Leo Shaw, and my brother is not dead, and this world is not filled with monsters. But then I remember Leo is waiting for me to speak, and I break my spell.

"Well," I fumble for a cigarette and wave a hand around the place. "This is a whole other world for you, isn't it? The taking of blood, the University — both the building and the institution. The *magic* of it. You see people in masks playing at the ancients. I'm sure you can't help but ask yourself why you came."

"The *teras*, Mr Jones, are quite encouraging."

"I think there's more to you than that, Mr Shaw," I say, perhaps because I hope there is, and in part because I know for sure. Leo Shaw could be a brute if he wanted to be. The University might take him for that alone. The strength. The brawn. But he is here trying to make a friend of me because he's smart enough to know the value in allies.

"I'd hate to disappoint you," Leo says.

"Then don't," I smile up at him, and exhale. He doesn't move and lets the smoke curl around his face. His eyes soften, melting in a sense; the pupil expands, the emotion bleeds down into his cheeks and I'm sure that little twitch is a smile.

He tilts at the hip, bending down to whisper in my ear.

"Are you flirting with me, Mr Jones?"

I freeze, but only for a second. I let him catch my frown. "God no, Mr Shaw. What a thing to say. I'm a Christian, you know."

He's smiling genuinely now. "Of course. As am I." But as I turn to walk away, I hear him say, "May God lead us away from sin."

Buzzing, excited, I eat my smile the instant I turn back the way we're walking. At the end of the vestibule, someone is waiting for us.

She is a particularly tall, lanky Hunter, flared leather tricorn sitting low on her head. Her hair is a warm auburn sitting loose and long over her shoulders. A tiered set of brief-cases are flung open next to her, where an assistant is stacking the vials of blood from prospective students.

I sniff. "Blood Hunter," I tell Leo before he asks.

He spins to me, smile gone. "What?"

"They're trained to hunt via blood. Tracking, and the like." When Leo doesn't look away, I flush. I don't know the details, but I also don't want him to know that. Instead, I shrug and tried to play it off. "The University has its secrets. It intends to keep them."

"But she's here. . . to hunt us?"

He doesn't sound afraid, exactly, only cautious. Wary. There is nothing else to be done except to hand it to her, and so I do. Under the long shadow cast by her tricorn, the Hunter is hauntingly beautiful. She is porcelain white. Freckles dot a broad, straight nose, and beneath her green eyes. She says nothing to me, but when she opens up her palm, I feel compelled to give her the vial. If there is magic involved, I can't say; I do as she wants before she's asked it, and with it complete the ritual of this entrance.

Still, the echo of Leo's concern is in my head. I know he's right.

For whatever reason, if I leave and the University wanted me, she or one of her kind will be tasked with finding me.

When Leo is done, we walk to the next threshold. I spy what's beyond and lean into Leo, hoping to rekindle that spark we had earlier. Flirting is far more fun than bleeding into vials.

I want to sling an arm around his neck, but I've never been so forward in my life. And, of course, there is the matter of *why* Leo Shaw wishes to be close to me. I am useful. I have an advantage. So instead, I twist and shoot him a grin before we head inside.

"Welcome to the University," I say, and his eyes do that thing again, softening at the corners, locked somewhere between amusement and disdain.

He moves ahead of me, and I linger just over the threshold. Thaddeus is in my mind. Talking to this boy is like spitting in my brother's face. He never wanted me to have friends. Not even allies. Leo Shaw is a distraction. Maybe that's why I feel such a thrill about doing it.

Or maybe it's that other intangible thing I can't quite place. Something in Leo's eyes, the way he holds himself. He's seen plenty of *teras*, but no stink of trophy-glory wafts off him the way it does most Londoners. He is scrappy. Desperate.

I find myself liking it.

I head into the room. The initiation is at an end. Now it's time to feast. I raise my hand at the faces I pass: many I don't care for, but Thaddeus ran with their siblings or studied with them, and that means I must stay in their good graces.

Leo has moved on. His eyes are hungry when they land on bowls overflowing with fruits, cheese, and meats. Coffers of tobacco and wine are scattered, too, free for us to pull from. London might be overcrowding, on the brink of a famine, but here is another reason to join the University's ranks: all the best food lands here first. The luxuries, too. I steer Leo away from the first table he wanders to, because what I think is happening is this: there are around ten tables. Groups are forming. Who knows if this is a social game or a singular test, but I saw the way Thaddeus stuck to his friends. His fellow graduates.

If I'm to choose my allies, I will choose them wisely—and I will start now.

I scan the hall, not knowing what I'm looking for until my eyes land on them. Two people sit side-by-side picking at their meal. The girl is fawn-skinned, ample-sized, long brown hair thrown over one shoulder. The boy has dark curly hair, pale skin. I recognise them. They're good enough to ally ourselves with.

"Sit," I prompt Leo, taking him by the shoulder to lead him further down to the table in question. It is absolutely not an excuse to touch his shoulder—which is not only broad, but *firm* and well-defined beneath my touch.

Leo doesn't flinch, so I send up a prayer that his opinion on sinning changes sometime soon, and then I turn my attention to the table.

"Victoria," I say with a purr.

The girl stops mid-chew and delivers me a sly smile and dramatic touch to her breast. The boy shifts next to her and tuts under his breath.

He says, "Well, well, Cassius Jones. What have you brought us?"

"Prey?" Victoria offers with a purr of her own.

Leo says nothing. They want to make him squirm; he is marked as a *xenos*, and they cling to their Londoner titles fiercely.

"Be nice, Bellamy," I say, though I doubt Leo is even a little bit concerned. I urge him down with a gesture. "This is a friend."

"Well, your friend is covered in blood," Victoria says with a curious quirk to her brow. "But I suppose that won't be uncommon soon."

Bellamy's smirk slips from his face. I feel the shift as well, and suddenly Leo is staring at me, waiting for me to reply. I don't—deliberately. I want to keep him hungry. But secretly I'm interested, too. Victoria's acting like she knows. And how could she? The University is a secret place. People don't talk about it.

I shift my attention and focus on pouring Leo a drink.

"You like wine?" I ask

"Love it," he says, without looking at me. He's looking at Victoria now, that same look he was giving me. I grit my teeth, hot with a jealousy I have no right to have, and pour him a cup.

"Drink," I tell him. "But don't get too drunk."

He stares at his cup as if I've poisoned it. "Why?"

"Just trust me," I say, and I let our thighs touch beneath the table in the hopes that will distract him from Victoria.

Leo glances between me and the other two, and must see some seriousness reflected there because he sips at his cup in a cautious manner.

Introductions, then. I open my palm. "Victoria Bennet, Bellamy Taylor, I'd like to introduce you to Leo Shaw."

"Hello, Leo Shaw," Victoria says, deep Chicago drawl coating her words.

Leo frowns. "American?"

"Allegedly," she says with a grin. Then, as if recognising the insufficiency of her reply, "Egypt born, America raised. Until I was six, anyway. My family emigrated. My father's a scholar."

"And you?" Leo prompts Bellamy.

He shrugs. "My father and eldest sister came here. Both graduated."

"Family tradition, then," Leo murmurs. He glances down at his palms, picking at a scabbed callous on one hand. No doubt he heard the pride in Bellamy's voice. I can't tell if he's judging Bellamy, or jealous. I want to know what he thinks of me.

"Not much else for us to do," Victoria says with a tight-lipped smile. "And we have a lot of motivation this year." She gives me a meaningful stare, and I nod back. She relaxes a fraction, and so I do; we all got the same warning, I suspect. Anyone who fails this year will have their family removed from London.

Before Leo gets a whiff of this I say, "Leo's from Southend. Answering the Call."

"That's a given," Bellamy murmurs.

Victoria slaps his arm "Oh, he's not that scrappy."

"I wasn't talking looks, beyond the blood and the *xenos* mark." Bellamy raises both hands.

Leo stares down at himself with a frown, like the blood is a surprise. His face crumples and he shrugs, wiping the base of his nose with his forefinger.

Victoria is the one who asks. "Encountered some trouble on the way over?"

She doesn't realise it, but I think Leo's leading them on. This is all a game to him, and Victoria and Bellamy are already a little tipsy when they shouldn't be. They're so full of nerves that both are vibrating, but the superiority is palpable. Leo is no threat to them. Leo is cannon fodder at best.

Then he says, "*Androphagos*," so casually, sipping his wine, and I watch the other two freeze. I decide my nerves are shot too and light that cigarette I wanted earlier. Elbows on the table, hand scratching my forehead, I puff away as Leo drops, "Or *manticore*, as Mr Jones called it."

I don't want to talk about Thaddeus. Victoria and Bellamy were doing me a service, and they *weren't talking about Thaddeus*. But how many *manticores* are running around? They know, now, who Leo is and how I know him.

Bellamy is the one who breaks, and I hate him for it. He swallows heavily. "Cass, I am deeply—"

"In your glass," I snap, then smile to smooth the hurt. "It's not wise to get drunk, Mr Taylor, not when we don't know what's coming."

No one says anything. I've probably stepped over the line; the air is thick and uncomfortable.

Victoria motions for my cigarette and I give it to her. I've known her for years. We fucked a grand total of once, before I realised my interests lay elsewhere. At one point we were both pining over Bellamy. These two are the closest people I can think of, but it's still surface-level. Bellamy has lived in

London forever, Victoria was six when she came, and I was fourteen when I stumbled through the gates. I was too old. Victoria could slip in and assimilate, and can hide her accent with effort. London has been so much of their lives, and I will always be slightly tainted.

I met them in study halls where generations of Londoners have been dumped by their parents to absorb the histories of *teras*, if not to actually kill any. It is where I've studied most of my young life, but it's not practical the way the University is. The secrets beyond the trials are inaccessible to the general public, and I have a scholar's mind: I want those secrets for myself.

Victoria watches me and when I see the sympathy in her eyes, I turn away. I refuse to be Thaddeus Jones' living brother. I am my own man. I don't want to be known for his death.

Victoria, of course, knows none of this, so she says to Leo, "Did you kill it?"

A stab in my heart. She knows that *I* didn't kill it.

Leo hesitates again. Some decision deflates the man's shoulders a fraction.

"A no, then?" Victoria prompts.

Leo scans the hall and stops. "There," he says, nodding across the room to a far table. "Those siblings wounded it. Perhaps fatally. We never saw the body."

All three of us Londoners swing towards the pair. Bellamy coos under his breath — trying to work them out, or trying to determine if they really have dispatched a *manticore*.

This is Leo's game. I am the easy target, the one Leo can charm. Silas and Fred Lin are in need of allies too.

But I am under no false pretense. Whatever the trials are, *manticore*-wounders are always better to have on your side.

"Call them over," I tell Leo. "They look lonely."

Leo stands without another word. I wait until he's out of earshot to address the looks on the others' faces.

"What are you doing?" Victoria asks, voice curling sweetly.

"No offence, Cass, but he's..." Bellamy clicks his tongue but says no more. They are basically one person, now, I think; I wonder if they're fucking, and then wonder why I care.

I ignore them and glance around the room. The untrained eye might have seen nothing more than people talking. Awkward friendships starting to bloom, all entirely innocent. But I can see the strategy at play. Londoners with an inkling of what they are getting into shaking hands with other Londoners. Anyone new to the Calling is sitting alone engrossed in a feast or trying to make friends.

"Range is better," I say quickly. "All three of us have some idea what we're getting into. We need allies. Not friends, but allies."

I see Leo approach the table and send an encouraging nod back the way he'd walked. The girl glances between Leo and me, and says something back to him. Bellamy is still staring at me so I prod him with, "You think there's an advantage in only speaking to Londoners?"

"I do." Bellamy sets his jaw, clearly frustrated. He shifts and tries to puff his chest without making the boyish play too obvious, but Victoria gives it away with a roll of her eyes. "Everyone who's meant to be here has killed a *teras*."

I think again to those study halls, dissecting *teras* bodies dragged in my hunting parties, or facing an F tier *cerastes* with graduate Hunters on standby.

"In a controlled format, maybe," I say, moving my attention to her. I grab back my cigarette and lean towards them, both elbows spread on the table. In my periphery, Leo is helping the siblings stand. "I've only ever gone up against a *teras* with my brother on hand. When I went out there to get him, I'll admit they nearly got me."

Neither seems fazed by this. They should be. I owe my life to *xenos*, and I don't quite understand these two. They've lived in London for most, if not all, of their lives. They don't have the same taste of life beyond the wards.

"Well, there's isn't a Hunter in my family. My sister's an Artificer," Bellamy says, like the knowledge of how to craft a *teras*-specific armoury, or how to weaponize prosthetics, has done anything but put him at an advantage.

"My father's a Scholar," Victoria says with a raised brow. "And I've killed *teras*."

"And would you have known the first thing about them if your father hadn't read you their horror every night?" I splay both hands, but both of them are staring at me with pursed lips. I'm not swaying them. Perhaps I'm losing them. "Anyone who was born outside of these walls and has killed a *teras* without a lick of the University's influence is worth five of us the moment those trials start."

Bellamy's face contorts. He doesn't like that—hates it, actually. He spits over his shoulder. Briefly, when my brother's anger flares in my chest, I consider standing up and slapping him across the face. But Victoria and he are a package deal, and I like her too much to risk it.

"They've grown up surviving attack after attack," I try one last time before Leo walks into earshot.

"But a *manticore*?" Bellamy exclaims, oblivious.

"*It killed my brother*," I hiss. "Decimated a graduate party. And they managed to wound it."

I leave the rest unsaid: I owe them. I am grateful. You dumb bastards, they made it bleed, can't you see how *fucking valuable*—

There it is again: that anger. Leo twitches at the sound in the corner of my eye. Too late for speaking now—Leo and his entourage come to a stop. "This is Silas and Winifred."

"Fred," the girl says sharply. "Silas, sit down."

Silas is clearly in pain, but trying to suppress it. *Like a cat amongst larger predators.* He doesn't want to risk appearing weak.

Leo and Fred sit down either side of me. I am unashamed when Leo sits beside me again, and I put a too-friendly hand on his back.

"Did you bring a trophy?" Bellamy asks immediately.

Fred can't keep the scorn from her face. Her brother mirrors it, a contained snarl of disdain that curls his top lip. He is quiet, which is smart and dangerous all at once. Fred seems to have a personality large enough for the both of them.

"No," Fred says flatly. "Chasing the thing down after it had torn a graduate Hunter party apart didn't seem like a priority."

"Oh, well, of course not," Bellamy purrs. "Your poor injured brother took the cake there, I bet."

I kick him under the table and shut him up. The damage is done, though. Silas clenches his jaw, his expression darkening. I can't quite parse it. Shame, maybe? Something close to self-disgust? I don't quite understand. Is that a *xenos* thing? Some weakness in being injured that is worth shaming someone over?

In any case, I'm worried. There's no way Silas Lin is ever going to trust us.

You don't need his trust. I swear I hear it in Thaddeus's voice, but that part of my mind is right. Trust comes in buckets if you say the right thing. What I'll need is effort. Work.

"Room with us," I say suddenly. I cut over the silence and they all turn to me. Bellamy is angry, or disappointed. Victoria has a lick of something similar behind her eyes. But the others just wait.

"Don't," Victoria says softly.

It is a warning I immediately ignore. "This isn't altruism," I clarify.

"If it's not altruistic, it's strategic," Fred says. She's quick. She purses her lips, eyes scathing in their evaluation of me. "So what exactly is the strategy?"

"Survive the trial. Get admitted. Graduate. Three steps to it, but we're stuck on the first."

No one speaks. Bellamy's expression shifts from disappointment to outright anger. I fancy I can hear the growl of a cornered animal in the back of Bellamy's throat.

"Why do you need us?" Fred looks ready to bolt. I see her lay a warning hand on Silas' arm—they're getting ready to leave. They want secrets I don't have, but they won't trust me for any of them.

"I don't," I lie. "But Leo seems to like you. And surely you can see everyone here is making allies."

I give her a moment to assess that and she removes the hand from her brother. "What do you know that we don't?"

Now that she's asking outright, I feel like I have her.

"Nothing but rumours," I say before Bellamy can stop me. "Whatever it is, it isn't good."

Leo has both his arms crossed, and a dark look in his face. It makes me want to pay attention.

I lean over to him. "I'm not asking for anything. Nothing but a room. Maybe a day or so´ from now you'll decide us Londoners are worth talking to, or maybe you'll never feel the need. I won't push it." When he doesn't say anything, I whisper, "Unless you want me to."

Leo's eyes flicker towards me, staring at me from under his eyelashes. We seem to understand each other, then. He unfurls his limbs. "I'm in."

I can barely contain the swell of a smile. Fred and Silas stand in silence together. Silas tilts his head to the side and Fred seems to translate for him by saying, "Thinking on it."

"Fine," I put up both hands. That's good enough for me, maybe as good as I'll get tonight.

By tomorrow, by the first trial, the point of allies will come into stark focus.

We will need each other then.

8

LESSON EIGHT

We are left to our own devices in the hall for about an hour.

After that, the first signs of panic start to show in our cohort. I estimate there's two or three hundred of us, spread out through the hall's massive tables. Maybe a third start to get antsy. I watch as a few move back to the colossal doors we walked through, and rattle futilely at them. There's another door at the end of the hall, much smaller, but that's locked too.

I might have been amongst the ones growing panicked, if I didn't have to worry about my appearance in front of this little party.

Both the Londoners and the *xenos*—they've already seen me at my worst. Snivelling and weak. I couldn't kill the *manticore*. I couldn't save my brother. They know I don't have the skill they've had to hone everyday, so I can't afford to look any kind of weak now.

As for Victoria and Bellamy, their friendship has always felt conditional, as every relationship within the wards is. There is no true bond. There is only the game. And if both of them are going to sit stock-still and chat as if we aren't locked in a hall, so be it. I won't be the first to complain.

When the first cry sounds—"Oh, God, this is it. This is the first trial!"—the large doors swing open and a ripple of laughter sounds in the hall, all aimed at the poor sod who cracked first.

The dean walks in and summarily ignores the commotion. He has four people with him. They drip academia; they are snobbish, and disdainful, and old enough I know they're practically one with the University. It sounds excessive, but they are here as little more than trophies: things the University has produced. Things you could become if you dedicate your life to study.

I know without the dean's announcement these are the heads of the four departments; the specialties the University offers.

Over the giggling and chatter, the dean speaks.

"There's more than three hundred of you," the dean says. "To date, the University's largest cohort has been no more than a hundred-and-fifty."

Another jolt goes through the room, though this one is cautious and surprised.

"Hundred-and-fifty was last year," I tell Leo. His face twists, and I imagine he's worried about not cutting these trials. I pat his shoulder, perhaps overly-friendly. "Don't worry. The University's getting more desperate. Who knows, they might drop their standards."

"Oh, for a hundred-and-fifty-one this year?" Leo quips, eyebrow raised. I only muffle a snort.

"Tomorrow, we will begin the trials that must be completed should you wish to study at the University. These will be brutal tests of character, strength, and wit — those characteristics you will need to face the threat of *teras* beyond London's wards. As such, even this first trial will not hold

71

back. I should remind all of you standing here that you have agreed to be here. You have agreed to participate by the University's rules. You may not leave the trials once they are begun; that is what you agreed to by handing your blood to one of our resident Blood Hunters. Should you leave the trial without completion, you will be found and returned to campus."

"What?" Silas hisses. It's the first thing I've heard from him. Both he and his sister bristle, though Fred is more concerned with keeping Silas' brewing outburst contained.

Similar sounds of confused and fearful outrage resound in the hall. The dean lets it happen, but it doesn't quiet down.

He shoots his hands up. "Silence. I will have silence!"

Warily, everyone quietens.

"Be calm. The secrets of this University are many. Should you graduate, you will be charged with the highest of honours and responsibilities of this great nation: keep London safe, at all costs. What you learn here—yes, even from the trials— must be protected knowledge. We cannot have well-meaning citizens attempt to quell the *teras* threat. We cannot have undergraduates acting with their half-knowledge. The University is an institution that must protect its own. So yes. If you choose not to complete the trials, you will not be able to live within London's wards."

"What if we fail?" someone asks.

The dean casts his eye about, searching for the source. "As I said," he speaks slowly. "If you do not complete the trials, you will not be able to live within London's wards."

I expect a cry of outrage or fear. Nothing comes. We are all here for the same thing: if not for the safety of ourselves and our families, then for a chance to better ourselves, to give us all a fighting chance to survive the *teras* threat. No one is naive enough to believe the safety London offers would come without consequence.

The dean affords us one last salvage. "Should anyone have had a change of heart, you must leave before the first trial begins."

No one moves. An uneasy hush falls upon the crowd.

The dean tries again. "Leaving the grounds once the first trial has begun or been successfully completed will forfeit your position in the trials. You will not be able to leave the grounds. Do you understand? Once more I will ask: do any wish to leave now?"

Once again, no one moves. I pray away the rapid pace of my heart. This explanation feels. . .lacking. I rack my brain for any conversation I've had with Thad that might tell me more about these trials. Nothing comes. Not one thing. I only have the sense of grief and exhaustion that came after Thaddeus' graduation. For three years I had the peace of my own room whilst he studied here, and tough many graduates stay on campus, he returned for our mother's benefit. But he came back a different man.

Ahead of me, the dean continues with a gesture to the professors standing beside him. "Before we begin, I thought it might be best to introduce you to the professors you'll be studying under, should you successfully complete the trials. Everyone standing here are experts in the field and have studied under the four founders of the University, or their direct proteges. We are lucky to have them."

He points first to an overly tall and stern man with a large hook nose and flat brown hair that falls to his cheeks. He is forty-something, but the way he rounds his shoulders makes him appear much older. "For the Mantle of the Scholar, you would learn under Professor Siward Hardinge. This is the mantle for those of you who know the power in books, those who can take what you read and know how to apply it to this world."

The dean moves along to a lithe, sinewy woman who

looks to be in her sixties. She has stark white hair in a short curly bob, and tough, sun-darkened skin. Scars pockmark her left cheek and down the neck, thick, silvery streams disappearing beneath her collar. Her left leg is missing. A shining marble prosthetic takes its place. The dean puts a gentle hand on her shoulder and her hard exterior crumples as she flashes him a smile.

"This is Professor Bedelia Dexter. For our brave students who wish to take up the Mantle of the Hunter, Professor Dexter will train you well. She learned directly from Angelica d'Avore, the first Hunter, in her final year alive. You'll be in good hands."

"God, she's terrifying," Bellamy whispers beside me. "I'll be having nightmares of her classes for years, I bet."

"Aren't you the pansy," Victoria quips.

I ignore them and turn instead to Leo. I don't know why. I just want to see his reaction. His eyes are fixed on the professor, lit up and hungry. I take her in again myself. Years ago, I would have gone prostrate before Professor Hardinge, just to soak in every bit of knowledge in that man's brain. Thad could have held the mantle of Hunter alone. I would have been well within my right.

Now, I must declare for Professor Dexter—if she'll have me. With a cohort this size, and with the letter every one of my Londoner brethren received, I know mostly everyone will be vying for the Hunter mantle first and foremost.

I have to stand out in these trials. I have to.

The next professor we are introduced to is a larger, round woman in her early forties. She has long blonde hair. Half of it is tied up, but the rest falls over her shoulders. She leans against a cane, though there is no obvious injury. She smiles out at the waiting students, but there is something in her eyes that makes me reject that happy exterior.

"Professor Flyta Yoxall," the dean announces, "is our resident Healer. What she does is invaluable. Any who take up this mantle will join Hunters in the fight against the *teras* and make sure they survive the encounter. An incredible cause to dedicate one's life to."

Professor Yoxall gives a sheepish smile as the dean moves along to the final professor. He is tall and broad shouldered with a severe face. His strong jaw is covered by a salt-and-pepper beard. Thin spectacles rest on his face, and he clutches a thin book to his chest as he surveys the crowd. He wears a startling number of rings on his fingers.

The dean slaps him on the back, but the professor barely gives a smile. "This is Professor Wesley Wymane, who will teach all of you interested in the Artificer stream how to use your hands to best serve London. Our own Professor Dexter wears some of Professor Wymane's artistry."

Professor Dexter displays her artificer-made leg for us prospective students to a round of excited applause.

"And here ends the introductions," the dean says. "Room assignments will be announced soon."

It is such a quiet and unassuming end that I jolt when he finishes. I look at the professors and wonder if I am wrong about them; if they are older than they look, more ancient. If I consider London beyond this campus, and England beyond that, is there a way to quantify the impact of these four individuals? On how many lives they've saved?

Conspicuously, though, there is not a foreigner amongst them.

"Rooms are assigned," Bellamy spits. "Looks like we won't be playing house with your *xenos*, Cass."

I stand without thinking. "Don't count on that, Taylor."

I look from my little party, and then back to the dean. I'd like to think he owes me, and I tell myself he does because that's what it takes to spark some courage in me. The rules of this game are beyond me, but I don't believe for a second it's as simple as the dean suggests. We cannot leave here unless we pass.

What happens if we don't?

The dean is in conversation with Professor Dexter when I approach. They both turn, and there's an assessing look in the Professor's eyes as she looks over me. I find myself praying that she doesn't recognise me, but of course she does; I share Thad's large nose, and I have a more gaunt version of his filled-out face.

"Cassius Jones, I presume," she says. I'm surprised to hear a distinctive, upper-class accent, and have to wonder if it's been learnt. Of course, I keep that to myself, and drop down into what I hope is a deep and gracious bow.

"Guilty," I say. "My brother spoke often of you, with deep respect. It is an honour to meet you."

"I am saddened to hear of his passing," she says, without a single shift in her tone to suggest it.

A smile tugs at my lips, and automaton-like, as bland as I can make it, I say, "Thank you for your kindness. But I did not come here to lure well-wishes from you. I came to bargain for my rooms."

This gets the dean's attention. He raises a brow at me, and the way he considered me in his office—like I am a pathetic shadow of my brother—shifts a minuscule amount towards somewhere positive. "Is that right?"

Bargaining, it turns out, is damn hard when you have none of your worldly possessions and no more knowledge than anyone else about what's about to come. But it's easier than fighting *teras*, and for a moment I feel a whole lot less useless than the *xenos* who fought through an onslaught to get here.

"There are six of us. There's a tower in the west wing with six rooms." Thad's trial rooms, but I refrain from reminding them of this. "I saw it on the way in."

"And what will you give me for it, young Jones?"

I swallow hard, because all I have to offer is my life and that of my party. Part of me wants to turn around, but I stop myself with everything I have in me, because once I see them—once I recognise that they are people whose lives I am toying with—I know I'll falter. So I say, "At some point in time, the six of us will rid London of that *manticore*, should it still pose a threat. And if not that, the next S-Tier *teras.*"

Professor Dexter shifts and gives me another appraising look. Whether she decides I'm terribly smart or resolutely stupid, I don't know.

It is, perhaps, a ridiculous thing to offer in exchange for a nice tower view. But even if I know very little about these trials, I know at least this: Thaddeus used his dying breath to guide me there. Snubbing him is not something I have the strength to do.

"Why would I sacrifice fledgling, prospective students?" the dean asks; there's a twinkle in his eye that betrays this faux concern.

I see the truth laid bare and speak without snark. "Because you would rather sacrifice us than graduated Hunters."

I say no more, though I could confirm that the Hunter cohort is dwindling. Professor Dexter leans in to whisper something, and then leaves without waiting for the dean's final word—nor spares me another look.

"So be it, Jones," says the dean. He rummages in his robe and opens up a little notebook. He flicks through several pages. They're all stamped with the University's coat of arms and delineated rooms in gold. Conspicuously, they're also all blank. "Tell me the names of your roommates."

I list them out and he scribes. When he's done, he tears the page out and hands it to me.

I wait to see if he says anything more, or if he will

comment on the room assignments we were supposed to have, but of course, that's never coming.

When I turn, I spot someone hovering by our table, and my stomach curdles because of who it is. A Londoner; big, sturdy build about him. He has a dark set of curls that contrasts pale skin. The type you wouldn't want to meet in a dark alley at night. He looks like he'd beat anyone senseless, indiscriminately. One of his teeth is missing.

He's got Bellamy in a headlock, exposing a line of poorly concealed hickeys, and Victoria's cheeks are browning in shame, so I walk up and put myself in the spotlight.

"Peter Drike," I snarl, "thug and bully. How are you?"

Drike looks up, eyes flashing. He lets go of Bellamy. "Cassius Jones, ponce and sodomite. All the worse for seeing you here. I thought the *manticore* had ripped your guts out, but it was your brilliant, graduate brother who died, wasn't it?"

I smile and pretend like there isn't any fire in my throat. I let myself imagine punching him, and in this dream he falls like a sack of bricks. I punch him three times: once for ponce, once for sodomite, and once for Thaddeus.

"*Manticore* got your tongue, pervert?"

Leo shoots to standing. Upright, he's slightly taller than Drike. Standing there in his blood-covered clothes, *xenos* mark on his forehead, makes him intimidating enough I see Drike step back instinctively. Leo doesn't say a word. I watch Fred wrap her fist around a bread knife, tensing, like she's readying herself to jump up and defend my honour too. But Drike just sucks his teeth and spits over his shoulder.

It's a lot less fun to bully me when I have people in my corner.

When he's gone, Bellamy exhales. "Sorry, Cass."

"Don't be," I say, but I'm not looking at him. My eyes are on Leo Shaw who jumped up so quickly for me. I wonder if I've read anything between us correctly, and if he would ever subject himself to being labelled sodomite just for the chance to bed me.

Once again: I am getting ahead of myself. I am not here to fuck. I am not here for friends. I am here for a spot in the University. I am here to secure my family's future.

Everything else needs to be forgotten—and fast.

"Thank you," I say to Leo. Then I turn to Fred and repeat myself; her knuckles are growing white from her grip on the knife. She meets my eye and her brow quivers, so I say it again with as much sincerity as I can muster. "I mean it."

She wets her lips and shrugs, glancing away from me. "You act like that in the farms and you get beaten bloody. I've never—" she scoffs and looks at her brother. "Never encountered someone like *that*."

"Like what?" Bellamy prompts.

"Cruel for the sake of it," Silas says. He reaches over for some bread and clicks his tongue. "Nothing like backbreaking labour to stamp that out of you."

I look at the size of him and try to imagine either one of them working. They're thin, but sinewy, as if their bodies have claimed every bit of muscle they could with what little food they had. The farms that service London are protected; Hunters and Healers that get stationed to care for crops and protect from *teras*. But the labourers would get to take very little food from them.

"Hopefully the trials will stamp it out of him," I say. Then I flick up the card with our room assignment.

"Mad bastard," Bellamy grins. "What the hell did you offer for that?"

All our fucking lives. A really, really bad day sometime in our graduated future.

"Nothing to worry about now," I say, and mean it, because we have to deal with trials before all that. And this is worth it for my brother's dying wish. "Let's go."

LESSON NINE

The rooms are in a secluded section of the University's dorm building, which is a massive dark sandstone building near the hall we eat in. The University's building stretches deep into the campus grounds, but so far, we are not permitted there.

We barely have a chance to take in the wealth of tall, windowed buildings and conical roofs. Most of the view is blurred by the night and the rain, with only a handful of fire lamps lighting our way.

"The sunset will be stunning," Leo tells us. He is standing in front of a large triptych window in our small reading room. A small shelf doubles as a reading seat beneath it. He spreads his arms wide to encompass the length of it. I watch his shirt stretch over his chest, hardened muscle exposed as the buttons of his white shirt strain to stay together.

I know the flush is coming and look away.

"You look downright miserable," Leo tells me, slapping an arm over my shoulder like we are old friends. "You better save some of that awful depression for when the trials actually start."

I know I should quip back, but I don't. Leo Shaw keeps shifting from overly-familiar to darkly guarded. I can't trust him, I *can't*—but I keep getting pulled in. It doesn't help that he's beautiful. And as much as I tell myself I'm not here for pretty boys, I feel myself growing desperate for that kind of intimacy. Grief and the horrors of my mortal life apparently are best soothed by men.

Leo peels his hand away and walks away when I don't reply.

Large crates filled with us Londoners' belongings have already been dragged up. Bellamy and Victoria laid claim to two rooms already, right at the front of the wing like they're eager to jump out of their shared home-to-be at any given chance. It could be true. They aren't happy with the guests I've invited, but I remind myself I'm not supposed to care. They can stare daggers at Fred, Silas, and Leo, but so long as we work together in any trial that requires it, we'll be fine.

We'll absolutely be fine.

I have claimed the room next to the sitting room. Not too small, it consists of a bed, a study desk, an oil lamp, and a fireplace. Its large window shares the same view as the triptych window: the University's gates. Carved on the lintel are the initials *TJ*, which is why I snagged it: I suspect there's something here, something left by my brother, and once the door is closed I immediately drop to my knees. Like an insect, I am on the ground, feeling along the seams of the floorboards, on my knees as if in prayer before the stone wall. I press and prod and wait for something to give. One floorboard screams with my weight, and I pry it free.

Nearly six years worth of dust bursts out of it. No one has touched this since my brother was in admissions. There are several flasks, bandages. A gun with six rounds calls my name, but I leave it there and shift it aside. There's a sparker. I grab it and shake it; a tiny amount of fuel sits in it, and I doubt I'll be able to replenish it, but I pocket it anyway. For when I'm in a bind.

A dirty bit of paper sits underneath it all.

I open it. It reads:

1. Python. Gun's useless. Dead: 32
2. Use for trials 2, 4. Library in centre. Massive willow. Courtyard. Meléti helps for a price. Dead: 1
3. Plant from 2 is a **toxin.** *Be careful to*

THE LETTER IS BLACKENED, both from an immense amount of ink, and from a burning that has clearly destroyed the rest of it.

I take a flask out, take a swig, choke. I hear a floorboard creak behind me, and spin—no one is there. Before someone can come, I put everything back under the board.

I'll only share what I know if I need to. I don't know who to trust yet, and I remind myself I only need this team if it comes down to it.

I get to unpacking.

My case is mostly made up of tomes, and a few pieces of clothing to get me through. I quickly realise there is little point to them: a trunk at the end of the bed supplies me a uniform.

I tut and drag it out. Grey pants, white shirt, tie, blazer, vest. They've even supplied us socks, emblazoned with the University's crest. I grab the woolly pair of them to ask the other's opinions—who embroiders socks?—but I stumble out onto a sight that gives me pause.

Silas has taken a seat beside Leo. I watch as he edges a

book out of the shelf between his legs. He opens it up, frowns, and awkwardly tries slotting it back into place.

Leo inclines his head towards it. "What is it?"

"Latin," Silas says softly. He jerks his head to the side, and I flatten myself to the wall before he spots me. In an even softer voice he says, "Which I can't read."

This is a dangerous thing to admit. Some of the lessons they teach us should we be admitted will be entirely in Latin. Or Greek. They might even make us learn Armenian. Anything to keep the University's secrets protected.

Leo says nothing for a beat. I resist the urge to spin around the bend. Eventually he says, "Show me." I hear the shuffling of the exchange.

Here, I chance a glance around the corner. I watch as Leo takes the book; a short, red-bound volume stamped with the golden letters of the publisher.

Leo scans the page.

Leo stutters out, "Your honeyed eyes, Juventius, if... sorry. Hang on. If anyone should let me kiss... all the time, uh."

"It's fine," Silas says. His dark eyes are already darkening further.

I know it. *Mellītōs oculōs tuōs, Iuventī...*

A love poem. Catullus.

"No, no, I'll, uh." Leo clears his throat. "If anyone should let me continually kiss your honey-sweet eyes, Juventius—"

"—I would kiss them three hundred thousand times, and I should never have enough."

I finish for him without thinking. God, I don't know why I do it, but it's done, and I'm in the doorway with embroidered socks in my hand, and it's not like I can hide. I step back on one foot trying to hide my regret.

Leo turns. They both stare at me. The silence is so terrible I consider screaming just to break it. Instead of going completely insane, I say something even more forward. Some bravery flares in me as I murmur, "It's not very popular, that one, but I like it. The Romans weren't too shy about kissing other men and writing it down."

"Is that why you like it?" Silas says gruffly. I stiffen on instinct, body readying itself to flee. I can't tell if there's judgement in his tone, or something else, but I brace myself for another round of 'ponce', 'sodomite', 'pervert', which I can't say is a particularly fun game. I flash a look to Leo, who is considering me with a half grin. His canines are exposed and glinting like a predator's, which makes my stomach flip, so I glance back down at Silas.

"I always forget you Londoners are uptight about that," he murmurs, reaching over to pluck the book from Leo's hands. He closes the book stiffly and reaches back between his legs to slot it away, glancing up as he does. "I didn't— mean anything by it."

I stare for probably too long, trying to assess how near Silas and Leo are, and if there's more in that hand width of distance between them. Are they together?

Do I care?

Yes, idiot, you very much do. I give a lavish shrug but stay standing precariously between the room and the hall. "Am I interrupting?"

"Hardly," Silas says, and he stands to excuse himself. I feel him tense as he edges slowly between me and the doorway.

I turn back to Leo. "I scared him away."

Leo smiles, then kills it, turning his head. "That's the most he's spoken since I've known him."

So not fucking then. Not that you need words to fuck.

"Well, he clearly just needed inspiration." I drum my fingers on the frame. I want to say more, but I am this awkward, overeager beanpole hovering with too much interest.

Leo laughs, runs his tongue along his teeth again; like he's putting on a show just for me. "Sure. You're certainly inspiring."

I laugh, too. I can't help it. "Do I really look so desperate for flattery?"

I say this whilst still perched at the threshold.

Leo turns back to me, and there's that gleam in his eye, the one that makes me question whether what he shows me is ever the real him. "Will I hurt your feelings if I say yes?"

Now the spell is ruined, and I can pull myself out of whatever stupid direction my desire was pulling me. "Keep your head tomorrow, Leo Shaw."

I go to turn away, and he shouts after me. I stay paralysed waiting for his question.

"Do you think I can win these trials?"

It is not a question I'm prepared for. How the hell am I supposed to know? Glancing over my shoulder, I see him halfway out of his seat. "Leo, I don't know a damned thing more than you do about these trials."

"I find that hard to believe."

"I know," I say. Then I gesture to the size of him. "But, at the very least, you look like you can hold your own."

"Well, sure. But universities take smarts. I can muddle my way through Latin, and apparently I can hold a conversation, but when it comes to the trials—"

"I wouldn't worry about that." My reply is abrupt and sharp. "They change constantly. There's no real preparation for them."

Leo pauses to consider me. "But you clearly think you'll benefit from a team."

I don't know what to say to that. I truly don't know.

Leo gets on his feet and comes towards me. He's prodding. He thinks he's cornered me, made me slip up.

Leo crosses his arms. "The trials are group work?"

"I am telling you the truth when I say I have no idea. But

I can't imagine it will hurt to bind together. *Xenos* and Londoners. Two walks of life. Two sets of experience. Surely that can only serve us."

He stares at me. He isn't fully buying it. I feel a pang of something close to disappointment, and don't know what to do with it. I am exhausted. I am still grieving. But I can't let factions form in my own team, and I already know they exist. The *xenos* are one. Victoria and Bellamy another. I am the lone wolf, and without establishing myself as integral to this team, if it ever comes down to it, they will choose each other over me.

"Hold on," I tell Leo, and don't wait to see if he obeys. I go and gather the others. They stagger into the sitting room with cautious disinterest.

"Sit," I say. Victoria and Bellamy beeline for the window seat. Silas slowly lowers himself to the ground. His sister pulls a face and leans against the wall, arms crossed tightly over her chest. Leo does the same.

I pull the flask from my coat and hand it to Leo before I go and crack a window. Cold, crisp air and the smell of incoming rain breezes into the stuffy sitting room.

"Cigarette?" I ask, lighting it.

Fred pushes herself off the wall. "Go on," she says, holding her hand out for one. I grin and delicately place my lit cigarette in between her fingers. I light another one and rest my arm against my side.

"Alright," I say, "let's talk shop. We all want to get into the University. I'm not asking you for your reasons, but I want to know your desired field." I glance between Leo and the siblings. "You know what the University offers, don't you?"

Studying at the University meant choosing a vocation, taking up a mantle in the fight against the *teras*.

Silas makes a low, non-committal noise, which is enough for me to dart out of the room, fumble some yellow paper from the desk in my room, and return to spread a row of it onto the floor.

"Right," I say. A bottle of ink clinks on the ground. I place a quill next to it.

Bellamy clears his throat and slips a fountain pen out of his pocket, waving it in my direction. He's trying to get me to flush.

"That's beautiful," Leo says, in a voice that sounds nothing like him. I see him regret it instantly. He flushes hard, blood rushing to his face. Bellamy gives him a pitying look. Smug bastard. I leap up and snatch the pen from Bellamy's hand before lobbying it over to Leo.

Leo catches it mid-air between forefinger and thumb.

"Hey!" Bellamy starts, but I wave him away, resuming my squat in the centre of the room.

"Lay off, you have plenty," I remind him. He grumbles but doesn't push it.

I uncork the bottle of ink and write a word on each slip of paper.

When I'm done, I stand. "The Mantles of the University. Assuming we all make it through the trials, we have to choose this role before we enter. And there's no switching majors. This is a commitment."

The Mantles written out are: Hunter, Artificer, Healer, Scholar.

Leo asks me the question he already knows the answer to. "Will you be a Hunter?"

"Yes," I tell him, writing my name underneath the title. I put it in ink before he can make another quip about how I should declare Scholar. He might be right, but I won't show him that.

"Victoria?" I ask with a flourish.

She smiles, makes her eyes larger to me, nibbles at the corner of her lips. She always flirts with me, for the fun of it,

I think—because there is no way I will take her to bed again, for obvious reasons.

"Healer," she says. "Obviously."

"And you?" I tilt the end of the feather towards Bellamy, eyebrow raised.

The young man grimaces like he hates the question. "God, you sound like my father. I can't say it suits you, Cass."

"Just answer."

"Uh, Scholar, probably. I used to think Artificer, but the tech involved... well, it never quite called to me."

"And books do?" I prompt, eyes narrowed. I'd never pegged him for Scholar.

At my cynicism, Bellamy peers between his legs and yanks another red-covered volume out from the shelf. "Do they really only have Latin books here? Arabic's a classic too, you know, and it is a hell of a lot more useful than a language that's dead."

Fred and Silas exchange a withering, silent glance, but Bellamy continues unbothered, replacing the book in the open slot on the shelf.

"All that to say, *yes*, books, you bastard. I thought you would have declared Scholar, too."

"No," I tell him with all the conviction I can muster. "Hunter is my calling."

It's not exactly a lie, but I turn before I can be interrogated. "My darling *xenos*." I spin on my heel to face Leo and stand.

"Oh, I'm to decide my fate now, is that right?"

My gaze softens. "As best you can." I lean the quill forward until the edge of its feather brushes over Leo's jaw. Leo doesn't break with my gaze as he plucks it from the air.

Bellamy clears his throat. "Want a rundown of what they do?"

"If I'm writing down my future, that might be the best."

"Hm," Bellamy says. The noise tells me he doesn't like Leo's tone. The bench creaks as Bellamy stands. He walks to me and plucks the cig from his lips—really, a bastard—and takes two quick drags before he hands it back to me. Then, arms folded, he walks over and taps one of the pages with the point of his toe.

"I'd say that one's obvious." He nods down towards the Hunter page. "You go and you kill the things that hunt humanity. Very heroic, always lauded." Bellamy claps his hands towards me. "But they can't do this alone."

"There's Artificers," Bellamy continues. "Useful for when Hunters inevitably lose a limb or three. I'm sure you've seen some wealthy weasel in the Great Hall with a prosthetic limb."

"Made of marble," Leo murmurs.

"Made of whatever you can pay for," I tell him, between another drag. "Hunters get commission for whatever *teras* they kill. Sometimes wealthy Londoners buy a trophy, sometimes the fee is drawn from the grand sum left by the University's benefactors. Either way, the Hunter gets paid."

Leo frowns. "You know that just made me have more questions, don't you?"

"Plenty of time for those later," I say. "No need to rush a friendship. Bellamy?"

"Healers are self-explanatory, I think," he says. "They need the same training as a Hunter, because they get deployed just as often. But the focus there is defence. Of both the Hunter they're assigned to, and themselves."

"They move in pairs?" Fred asks. Silas' eyes shift towards her.

I nod. "They can do. Sometimes a larger group. A lot of Healers head to other cities. Sometimes they head to towns."

"Is that right?" Fred says. A fat lot of cynicism climbs back over her words. "I've never seen one."

89

What can I say to that? I have no proof. So I shrug and tell her, "Well, what would I know? I'm no Healer."

"What would you know indeed?" Fred flashes me a winning smile and folds her arms.

She really doesn't like me.

"Alright, alright," Bellamy grumbles over the top of us. His voice is low and full. It seems to ground the room. "Enough griping. Give me the cig, Cass."

Bellamy reaches for the dying end of my cigarette and moves to the last sheet. He taps his foot twice. "Last one. Scholars. The people who learn the stuff that Hunters use to take *teras* down."

"Whole lot of stuffy research," Victoria says, "but even I can admit it's a useful path."

"And a cushy life behind London's walls," I remind her. "Just ask your father."

It makes her smile falter. She seems to think for a moment, and I hope she remembers our earlier conversation, and what it will mean for us. "Perhaps I should declare Hunter," she whispers, before I wave her down. "Hunter might be best for you lot, too."

I silently curse. I don't want the *xenos* to know this vulnerability.

Leo picks up on it. "Why?"

No one answers him.

"Fine by me," Fred says. "You can put me down for Hunter. There's nothing else I'd rather do."

I jump to do as she instructs, if only to move the conversation on. "And your brother?"

"Hunter," Fred answers for him. "Or Healer."

"Artificer."

Fred's expression freezes. I clock her stopping herself from spinning on her heel. Silas looks up at his sister from the floor, then up at Victoria. "Unless there's a reason I should stick to Hunter?"

Victoria hesitates. She turns to me like I'm the man holding all the answers.

"No," I lie. "Ignore her."

I doubt anyone believes me.

Fred lays a steadying hand on her brother's shoulder. "Then let's sleep. Tomorrow will come a lot quicker that way."

Silas hands the flask back to Leo. The silence continues as the siblings walk out of the sitting room and it stays until the soft clicks of their doors are heard down the corridor. Leo drinks from the flask and offers it to the room. Bellamy grabs it off him.

"Christ," he complains after a swig. "Conversation with them is like pulling teeth. At least you're tolerable, Mr Shaw."

Leo frowns yet again. "Thank you?"

"Yeah, yeah," Bellamy says. He taps the ground with the tip of his foot again. "What were you going on about here, Cass?"

"Well." I stub the cigarette on the window pane. "I was trying to show there was a balance. That if it came down to it, we'd be a group of people with a variety of useful skills."

"God," Bellamy sounds exhausted. "I thought it would be something useful."

Victoria looks between us. "We shouldn't be making plans for something that may not come to pass."

I send her a look, but she ignores me.

"Trying to game the University is a sure-fire way for us to be eliminated."

"There's no game," I say. I can tell she's scared, but truly, I am not trying to outsmart the institution. Just stay alive. "There's logic, and reasoning, and the morsels of information this damn institution deigns to tell us. I am working with what I have."

Victoria stands and gestures for the flask. I think she'll take a tentative sip, but then she's gulping half of it down.

She sticks it against my chest when she's done. "You're trying to get ahead of something we don't even know the rules to. I get it: you're a planner, Cassius Jones. You don't like surprises. But you can't do a damn thing more than pray at this point, and I have better things to do."

"Do you?" I say. My voice sounds strained, because she's right. I am trying to get a handle on a group of people, and I don't even know why. I have already bargained with their lives just to get to my brother's stash. Why should I care whether they all come together?

"Yes," she says, and she grabs Bellamy by the front of his shirt and leads him away.

That answers my question: they are certainly fucking.

I plop myself down on the window seat and lean on the sill, staring out at the grounds. There's already an itch in me for another cigarette, but I ignore the feeling. I'm already too dependent, and I can't be letting my nerves run me down tomorrow. Leo is staring at me—I can feel his eyes boring into the back of my skull—but I don't turn around. I stare at the moon, half hidden by clouds, and let the freezing wind cut across my face. In the shadows and the muted moonlight, the University gates glimmer black.

Everything I do here is for my life out there. I must secure a spot in this University, or there will be no point to living. My mother will die from the shock alone. My father can't defend himself. So I have to be the one to graduate. To kill the *teras*. To kill the beast that took my brother. To keep the rest of my family safe.

It takes me a while to realise Leo hasn't left.

"What is it?" I ask. "Want a cigarette?"

"God, you'll have another?" Leo says in surprise. He sounds like Thad. I could scream.

"You try living in my head," I say. I don't light another one, and I don't offer him one.

"Oh, I don't know." Leo comes and sits down next to me. "It doesn't seem so bad in there."

Now I can't help myself. I look at him, but I bury half my face in my shoulder so I can pretend I'm braver than I am.

"I would tell you flirting would get you nowhere," I whisper, "but I'd be lying."

Leo's breath audibly catches. But he doesn't look away. Something passes between the two of us. Something more than an acknowledgement, and closer to a promise.

Though what we are promising, I can't be sure. And I'm too scared to do anything about it. If he tipped forward, I would let him kiss me.

Whatever is brave in me says I should do it. How can we be sure what tomorrow brings? But it is too much of a risk, knowing Mr Leo Shaw might pull away. And it wouldn't be the rejection itself that hurt, but the look in his eyes. The disgust. I don't think I can stand it.

My interests aren't so very illegal in a world infested with monsters, but I know people see monstrosity in it. A wrongness.

I clear my throat. "You sure you don't want a cigarette?"

"Tobacco's fairly rare," Leo says, changing conversations easily. "Never really had a chance to warm to it."

Indeed it is, and only getting rarer. I had a small stash upon entering, and the University has some small stores, but when would Leo have had the luxury of forming an addiction? I give him an awkward smile, feeling chastised. How quickly I forgot what life outside these wards is really like.

"What did you want to talk about, Mr Shaw? You sat

down here for a reason, did you not? Or are you here for more things to report back to the Lins?"

Leo face shifts, and gone is that sweet, inquisitive expression of his. He looks out at the room. "*Acta deos numquam mortalia fallunt.*"

I scoff. "I am no god, Mr Shaw—and I'm not sure flattery will save you this time."

"You noticed," he says, clarifying. "And you let us play you."

"Or perhaps I was playing you all along—and before you ask, it's for nothing nefarious. I truly think whatever these trials are, we all might benefit from each other's experiences."

He doesn't believe me. I don't need him to. I drum my fingers on the windowsill. A fine rain has started up and I breathe it in. In the distance, there's a screech, a faint cackling horror. Somewhere to the west I hear a chittering reply. I shiver. It doesn't matter how safe I am. It never feels it.

"Why are you still here?" I whisper when Leo doesn't move.

"I hope you don't think I sat here for them. The Lins, I mean. They helped me get to London, and I helped them back, but there's no loyalty beyond that." I don't reply, because it's exactly the kind of thing he's expected to say, and for some reason, I feel the brunt of my grief at that moment. I am my father's queer son. I am not the one he wanted. Their golden boy is dead, and I am all that is left, and here is a pretty boy showing me attention, and that is all it takes for me to want him.

Has there ever been anyone so pathetic?

"I think I should go to bed, Mr Shaw," I whisper. I decouple myself from the sill and from his gaze. Then he reaches out and grabs me by the wrist. My heart jolts. Heat rushes to my cheeks.

Leo stands slowly. He is so close I feel the warmth of his

body, and my own flesh reacts. Some haunting *teras* screams in the background, a horrible background orchestra giving voice to my internal scream. What is he doing? What am I doing?

Leo leans in. I do not move. But he doesn't kiss me.

"Do you want to go to bed with me, Mr Jones?"

I flinch out of habit, expecting to hear the floorboards creak behind me, expecting to be caught. The act of speaking alone is not carnal, but it feels like it. Heat rushes through me. Leo says it openly. Not in Latin, or Greek, or some other language that might be able to mask the true intent of his question.

There is no hiding what he is asking. How easy it would be to say yes, and be two young men taking pleasure in one another, and forget the true nature of the world we live in.

"No," I tell him, when I want to say yes. I don't even amend it with, "Not yet." I watch his face as it shifts. He pulls away a fraction. A storm is in his eyes; uncharacteristic and intense, I see something close to hatred flicker through him. Then he lets me go and steps away.

"I am too forward," he says, half bowing. "I apologise."

I say nothing. I am frozen in place. I manage to return the bow of his head, and he leaves without further comment. When I hear the door to his room close, I collapse onto the window seat and knock my head back against the glass.

That man is dangerous, I decide.

But that knowledge alone won't be enough to stop my attraction.

LESSON TEN

The room is filled with red and purple light, bleeding through a dozen stained-glass windows. At the sound of a gong ringing out, marking the first trials' commencement, we have been led out of the hall through a series of corridors. Now we are here: a chapel, I think. The ceilings raise high into a point, and a cold grey stone covers the walls and floors. Great portraits of God and Mary and Jesus hang, but they are not to be compared to the windows.

Everywhere I look, light leeches through the coloured glass in streams of purple and red, like a sunset haemorrhaging. Every corner of this chapel is filled with it, swarmed with it. Great suits of armour overlook us, sentinels against every wall. They are ceremonial, heavily decorated with embossed detail. I am overwhelmed by the feeling of godliness. The holy man in me, the one raised to fear my own existence, lures me down onto my knees. One or two students are already down and in prayer. But I do not go. I only whisper in my own mind, "Lord, whatever this is, preserve me. Preserve me for my mother."

Whatever sin I almost committed with Leo, my willpower

should reward me here. Or it better: I did not give up the embrace of such a man only to be punished now.

There is a sense of woe among us. The crowd of us are draped in so intense a veil of anxiety that we might as well become one great and fearful beast.

The tension could slice through me.

"There are seven doors behind me," the dean explains. He stands to the left, basking in the soft glow of the sunlight. Blood Hunters frame him on either side. "Only eleven left us last night. Now, the name of every remaining prospective student is in this bowl. One-by-one, I will call out a name from this bowl. Each person will stand in front of a door from left to right as they are called. Once everyone is standing in front of a door, they will open. The trial is thus: once in the room, you must exit the room from the opposite door. The task is simple, but the obstacles are not. There are several instruments in the room. You may use all of them or none of them to complete the trial."

A number of voices sound. The students turn to one another, shouting questions out to the dean. He answers none of them. I feel someone staring at me and turn to Leo. We hold each other's gaze. We say nothing.

I regret not taking him to bed.

All of this feels wrong.

The dean pulls a name and reads it out over the cacophony. "Sara Tull."

Part of the crowd quietens. Several people move away, exposing a pale-faced girl with brown hair pulled into a tight bun. She shivers and pushes her way forward to the first door. The dean reads out five more names, and each time my anxiety threatens to eat me alive.

Then: "Silas Lin."

Fred makes a strangled noise. She is gripping Silas' arm, eyes locked on his face. He stares impassively towards the dean for a moment before he turns to her and untangles himself from her grip.

"It's alright," he says softly, like he is cooing to a baby. "I'll be alright."

Fred sniffles, blinking back tears. "Good luck. Just... be careful."

He considers her for a moment and nods slowly before he makes his way to the final door. I meet her gaze, and there is a look of pre-emptive mourning. Her eyes are full of sadness. Full of fear.

I whisper, "What do you think is behind that door?"

She stares at me a long while before she glances away and shrugs. I grimace. Am I alone in thinking something is wrong?

The dean looks over at the students lined up and gives a stern nod.

"Let the trials commence!"

As if by magic, the doors swing open. I strain forward with the rest of the crowd, eager to see inside. But there is nothing. The room is pitch black.

One by one, the prospective students slip into the dark.

Silas looks over his shoulder once, and then is gone.

The doors close behind them. There is nothing for a long moment. Leo lets out a shaky breath beside me. The dean moves back to the glass bowl, but makes no move to pull names. He just stands there, waiting for something. And then it happens.

A scream.

The entire crowd reacts. Another, this one a horrible, strangled echo of the first; bright and high and coming from that first door. I spin to Leo and find his face wild too. Everyone of us is on edge. No one here had known what was coming.

Except the dean.

"What is this?" Fred is screaming. "What have you done? Silas? *Silas!*"

She shoves forward through the crowd and I lose sight of her. People push on either side of me, crushing me. Suddenly I am sweating, suffocating.

"What the hell is going on?" Bellamy barks.

I grunt a strangled, "I don't—"

"Calm down!" the dean is shouting. "Calm down!"

"*Calm down?*" Someone near the front of the group shouts. "*Calm down?! Are you insane! Are there* teras *in there?*"

The movement of the crowd stops, everyone waiting with anxious anticipation for an answer we already know deep down.

Of course there are *teras* in there. What else would make someone scream like that?

In the lull, another scream goes up, then a few furious, panicked shouts. Several people escape the crowd and lunge towards the dean, but the Blood Hunters launch forward. They wallop the oncoming attackers. They leave them breathing but clutching injured arms. Those panicking then dart back towards the crowd. The motion starts again, but this time I am shoved back against one of the suits of armour as people try in vain to get back into the Great Hall. They throw themselves uselessly against the door. A few brawny young men call for space and, once it is given to them, they run towards the door like human battering rams. The door doesn't give. It is made of stone—it obviously wouldn't give— but it doesn't stop them from trying. Peter is amongst them, a frenzied, wide-eyed look on his face.

I stand frozen, not quite accepting what is happening.

The University has *teras* inside the wards. If any one of these got loose. . .

"Oh, god," Bellamy shouts. He shoulders his way towards the stone door. "Peter. Peter!" He grabs the young man but

Peter throws him off and shouts angrily, hammering the door with his shoulder once more.

Bellamy looks shaken. Victoria is in tears next to him. He puts her behind him and approaches Peter again. "They have our blood, Peter," he says loudly, loud enough the rest of the room can hear him. Many people grow quiet. There is something about his voice; it communicates a certainty that feels heavy and inescapable. "Doesn't matter if you force your way out of here. They'll find you anyway."

"Can't have anyone spreading the University's secrets," I say. A few people turn to look at me, furious. But it is true. We were all told the same thing. We all agreed to the same thing; a phylactery of our blood, to be hunted if we failed the trials, or denied them.

Everything is a test. Staying in this room is one of them.

I curse Thaddeus in my head. He sent me here without a single warning. Nothing but a scrap of paper.

My shock is reflected around me. These people's siblings, their parents: anyone with a University heritage had been sent here without the proper training, where they could very easily be killed.

All to keep a place behind these wards.

A dread falls over the crowd. The desperate need to escape has vanished. Apart from a few strangled cries, the hall is silent. A horrified acceptance is starting to settle in.

I bite my tongue so hard I taste blood. This fear isn't new to me, but it's been so long that I have felt so utterly alone.

Leo comes to me and knocks our arms together; a little bit of stolen intimacy for two shocked near-strangers. I make myself take deep breaths. The dean steps forward, and reads out seven new names.

I stand there as if in a trance. I have no idea how much time has passed, only that the crowd grows thinner and thinner. The screams and shouts remain consistent, like a haunt-

ing, haphazard beat to this twisted song. As names are called,
I spot Fred again. Her eyes are blank.

Bellamy turns to me. "I keep imagining. . ." he starts.

"Victoria Bennet," says the dean.

Bellamy grows very still. Victoria turns to him so slowly,
doe eyes staring up at him, glistening and sad. He raises a
hand to her face.

"You've got this, honey," he says.

She tries to smile, but it falters.

We stand in silence when she enters the trial. I watch
Bellamy. He stays unmoving and unblinking for as long as he
can, completely locked in that moment when he touched her,
when she'd been by his side. Is he listening for her scream? Is
he expecting it? It seems to drag forever. When the dean
begins the next round without the sound of her cries, Bellamy
crumples in relief.

But it means nothing until we know she is alive.

"Leo Shaw," the dean says.

Leo turns to me, and I remember the note my brother
left. "The gun is useless," I tell him and Bellamy, and I don't
wait for them to question me.

Bellamy slaps him heartily on the back, full of bravado.

Then—of course—it happens.

The dean opens his mouth.

"Cassius Jones."

11

LESSON ELEVEN

The room is dark.

I stand perfectly still, waiting for my eyes to adjust.

I feel three things in that moment.

Dread sits in me like lead. I saw it reflected on Leo's face moments before he'd stepped through his own door to face whatever terror lay beyond. Guilt is another thing latching onto me. I should have shown everyone Thaddeus' note earlier. I might have been able to save someone's life.

The third thing I feel is betrayal.

Thaddeus betrayed me—potentially betrayed my family by letting me run blind into these tests. If I fail, the Jones' family will be thrown out of the wards. So why hadn't Thaddeus told me?

It is too messy a feeling, too heavy and too much for me to think about now. I shove it out of my mind just as a spitting hiss envelops the room. Along the walls, torches in sconces lit up with sudden fire.

The room is narrow. With a torch in each corner, most of the room is lit by dull fire light. But there are still pockets of shadow for a *teras* to hide in. The floor is cement. There is blood on it, just a few splashes, though I note large areas of the floor are drenched in water. A drain sits off to the side. I grimace and squint over towards my goal: the door I need to escape from is plain and wooden. Completely ordinary.

But extraordinary circumstances.

I know I'm being watched. I keep my breathing steady, even with my heart racing. To my left sits a short wooden table. I scan it haphazardly, too on edge to commit my full attention to it. It's covered in weapons. A gun. A knife. An iron bar. All manner of weapons are laid out on it. My breath sounds loud as I move closer to it.

Another hiss echoes in the chamber. I freeze, scanning the room for another torch. There is no new light. There is no *teras* waiting for me on the ground.

I don't look up. Not when I tune in to the wheezing breath. Not when saliva drips from the ceiling.

I brace myself, panting once, twice.

I move.

I launch myself to the table and wrench up the iron bar, spinning so my back slams against the stone wall. With my left hand, I pull one of the torches free from its sconce.

Raising the torch into the shadows above me, I reveal my enemy. A huge snake-like body slithers overhead. Its jaw cracks open, wider and wider. Venom coats pointed teeth in thick, dripping layers. I have enough time to clock its monstrously wide body before the thing drops.

I run. I haul myself onto the table. The *teras* snaps at my feet, rushing forward to nip at my legs. Like a fool, I stay jumping, trying to keep my legs out of range.

I am not fast enough.

The *python* bites me. Its teeth are fine and sharp; two little stabs that puncture my leg. But then I scream. The torch clatters to the ground. Intense pain burns through my flesh. I kick the air, wild and panicked. My foot slips. The table falls out from underneath me; a brief respite as it clatters onto the *python*. All the weapons fall with it, pipe rolling across the floor and out of reach.

"God. *God.*"

I stagger away and manage to scramble up just as the *python* bursts through the table. My torch is on the ground, fire snuffed out, so I rush backwards to another corner and pull another free. The *python* launches at me, but when I shove the flame in its face, it squeals. Hissing and spitting, it tries in vain to attack through the flames.

I try to control my breathing. *Think, Jones, think.* My leg hurts to stand on. I don't know if it's poisonous. I don't know if its breath or its blood holds venom.

That is the danger with *teras* and myth — there are a dozen variations in the world, and if you want to stay alive, you need to believe all of them at once.

But I don't need to kill it. I just have to make it to the door.

So I stab forward with fire, forcing it to retreat further back along the floor. Every step towards it is met with a vicious whip-like bite.

My hands shake. I can't quite feel it under the adrenaline, but I am panicking. More than that, more than my consciousness: my body is in fear. My body knows what happens to people when a *teras* wants to eat it. They simply get eaten. They get killed. I feel like I'm just a boy with a bit of fire against a monster torn from myth. And if I die here, will my mother ever know?

Suddenly, it lunges. I roll forward out of its way and lose the torch in the process. So screw this.

I spin on my heel and dart for the door. I am fast, but the *teras* still fills my periphery: a fat, dark worm shooting overhead to block my retreat. It drops with a thud from the ceiling so I drop too, rolling towards the pipe on the ground. Scale scrapes on stone as it comes for me, and I wave the pipe wildly, scrabbling up half blind.

One spitting hiss later and I realise I'm no closer to the door. I'm facing it, but the *python* remains between me and freedom.

The *python* slithers forward, assessing me. Up close, I can see its thick body is covered in burn marks and stab wounds. Nothing on that table has been enough to pierce the thick snakeskin. Not even the gun, if my brother is to be believed.

Shit, if I knew my mythology better, maybe I could—

The thought ends early as the *python* shoots forward with startling quickness. I skid back once, then again. The *python*'s fangs close over air, but the frustration only seems to aid it: it strikes faster with every failed attack. Just like that, I'm backed up against the door I'd first entered. There isn't time to think. I lunge forward with the pipe and whack it across the head. A dull thud sounds. The creature screeches and rears up, flailing in the air.

I don't fucking wait for the thing to recover. I bolt. It tries to get me as I dart by it and narrowly misses my shoulder, and I'm so stupidly surprised I let myself whoop excitedly—until the *python*'s massive tail picks me up and slams me against the stone wall. The pipe clatters out of my hands, rolling away out of reach.

New fear sparks in me. I'm on the ground. I'm weaponless.

The *python* hisses at me. With two torches blown out, half its face is thrown into shadow. It only looks more terrifying. Some great, bloated dragon from myth: my whole body seizes in growing shock. My life seems closer to the edge sitting there, entirely at its mercy.

I feel for the sparker in my pocket. The fear in me wants

me to use it. But the fear that I'll fuck myself by wasting my greatest asset in the first trial is larger.

You can do this, you bastard. Get up.

The *python* makes me move. It hisses and strikes down beside me again. I roll three times towards my metal pipe before I stand and dive, stabbing forward with it into the *teras'* tail. The *python* makes a startled noise and lunges towards me again. I roll, grazing my face on the rough ground and diluted blood of my fellow would-be students. I push myself to my feet and jam the weapon into the *python's* flank a handful of times, thudding into it. It snaps and writhes in fury.

Then I make the decision. I launch the pipe at it and run.

I hear it hit. The *python* gives an outraged cry, and over the top of its scream, I hear my weapon clatter impotently to the ground. But the door is there. The door to my freedom. I lunge.

As soon as my fingers graze the metal of the doorknob, a grate flies up and slams against the ceiling. I spin in time to see the *python* ram itself against the metal grate, gnashing and hissing uselessly through the close-packed bars.

I stare at it. This isn't the same as hunting with Thaddeus. This feels a little too close to sport.

The monstrous *python* slowly stops its attack, but it stares at me with the knowing eyes of a predator. It takes me a moment to realise I am not only shaking, but blood is pouring from a cut above my eye. I want to touch it, but something about breaking eye contact with the creature unnerves me. I have never been this close to a living *teras* before, not without either me or it launching an attack. But I stare at it, and in staring, I am shaken. Unnerved. A certainty fills me, greater than anything I have ever felt.

I know this creature is more intelligent than I'd ever thought a *teras* could be. More intelligent than I want it to be.

Perhaps that is why I am compelled to speak to it.

In the pulsing death throes of my adrenaline, I recall it. I can identify this *teras*: D Tier *teras*, *Delphyne* class.

"I remember you," I tell it with a nod. "Your myth, I mean. Apollo slays you. *Python. Delphyne.*"

The *delphyne python* draws away from the bars with a quiet, angry hiss. I don't want to think it understands me, but what other conclusion can I draw?

"Well, let's see," I whisper, scanning the *teras'* face. "Do you remember the stories you were ripped from? Did you experience the death every time it was spoken?"

The *teras* paces the cell, ignoring me, but I want to speak the line anyway.

"The Homeric Hymn to Apollo," I say, "I know there's something in there about you dying." I can't remember it. I don't know it. But screw this beast to hell. "The writhing, the screaming. Apollo stole your life. I can't wait for someone else to steal it again."

It doesn't react. I watch it a moment longer. Then I open the door and I am free.

OUTSIDE THE TRIAL, it is chaos.

One of the doors to my left swings open wildly and whacks the wall. Someone throws themselves out, screaming. The young woman drops to her knees and sobs. Blood pours from her shoulder. I catch sight of it; destroyed, open and sinewy and split apart by teeth. Someone wearing a white apron approaches her for healing.

"Show me."

The voice startles me. I jump, and turn to find a Healer there for me, too. His skin is a russet-brown, his eyes are kind, but there's a distant stare to him. He barely sees me. I see his lips moving as if in prayer, and then I register slowly that he is speaking to me. I hear none of it.

You're in shock, something tells me. *How fucking pathetic.*

That last bit, of course, is from Thad.

The Healer stops trying to speak to me. He tugs me away from the door and puts something on the swelling of my left leg. I look down, startled to see my pant leg ripped apart. Red pinpricks dot my lower calf, and there's a prickly numbness to it that makes it hardly seem like my leg. God, I am getting dizzy. My body feels wrong.

I blink, and then I'm sitting on a long wooden bench beneath a series of stained-glass windows. How long I have been sitting there, I don't know, only that a good hundred people are milling about in this room with me. One of the trial doors opens and another student I don't know steps out and collapses.

I don't see Victoria, or Bellamy, or Leo. I don't see the Lins. But then again, everything and everyone is a blur. I crane my head to search for them, but nausea swims into my head and makes the movement sickening.

There are too many people. It's an odd expanse of a room; a fat hall with several closed doors leading off it. A hundred steps away, it curves to the left.

I look down at my leg. The swelling has gone down considerably. An itchy, blistering spot is growing near the puncture wound. I close my eyes and take a deep breath. This is normal, I remind myself. A thick layer of shock that is blocking everything else out. But the longer I sit there, the thinner that shock becomes.

A latent burst of adrenaline floods me. I double forward, feeling everything all at once: fear, shame, and swathes of anger filling me up. I remember the *manticore*, how I'd lain on my back beneath it, close to death. And now, locked in a room with fire and weapons, I'd still barely managed to make it out alive.

What am I without Thad? Shame is in me, tugging at the corner of my mind, but underneath it all is a logical fury that is growing.

It is the rage of a man who had come so close — *God*, I had come so damned close to real purpose, real drive and satisfaction— and here is just another wretched place. I want to lie down. I have that sinking feeling in me, where lying down forever feels attractive.

But then there's an outraged bark from down the hall: someone is shouting madly. A few others and I swing around at the sound. It is so harsh after so much stiff silence.

Several people step away, like the anger is too much to hear after the trial. People are shaken. But I make myself stand. I make myself feel this; I soak up the rage and the anger and the weeping, and I step into the spaces other people are vacating. And through the crowd, once more, I see him.

Leo.

I stop walking.

Then I am moving without really thinking, and the crowd moves apart to accommodate me, and Leo is standing there like a stone in a river, and *God*, he's alive. He is alive. Relief douses me, and I shake with the ebbing adrenaline and this new joy. The current pulls me towards him.

Leo is one of several students, animated and shouting: "How could you? How could you! What damned evil is in you to think you can throw us to *teras* and we'll just take it?!"

And I realise the torment of what he has faced. I see these students, and I know they are not Londoners. They are *xenos*. They are men and women who have spent every day fighting for their lives, only to be drawn here by the promise of safety and learning and protection.

And there are *teras* here, too.

I see Leo jab his finger against someone's chest and have to shift my way through the crowd to better make out his target. I freeze.

Dean Drearton faces Leo with a placid, detached smile. This was a different man, I think, than the one who solemnly greeted us all. Who spoke to Thad in his office. Who comforted my mother for our loss.

But no. They are one and the same. And the longer I look at him now, the more certain I am that he feels none of it. None of the weight of this trial, of the loss, of the deaths. This is only the first one.

And I know what is happening now. I know the horror of the University and what they are trying to do.

They do not want us all to graduate. They will only take the best. And everyone else, and every member of their family, will be culled. Culled to make room in the tight and overcrowded city.

"Now, now," the dean says, in a tone that confirms my musings and his apathy. "You've had a long day, Mr Shaw. A long day. And you've done well. You've passed the first trial. You wouldn't want to jeopardise that with your anxious ramblings."

He pats Leo's shoulder, and Leo reacts slowly; a sad understanding blossoms on his face. His eyes are wide, like he's scared, but there's a fury in the quiver of his lip. He won't bite off the dean's hand after that threat.

But someone else does. I see a young man break away from the crowd. A *xenos*, bleeding from a cut on his face, left arm swollen beyond belief. He screams, some primal and sorrowful cry, and launches himself at the dean.

Leo sidesteps. I expect to see the dean run, or sprawl upon impact. But he whistles once, and out from the bend two Blood Hunters move to flank him. One draws a gun. A shot rings out.

Bodily, the boy crumples to the ground.

All of us are silent. The Blood Hunters swoop in and soundlessly pick up the corpse. In my haze, I wonder where the other bodies are, how many of them were lost, whether the *teras* ate them. I wonder what they tell the families.

Have I ever seen a funeral in London for the victims of the University?

When the Blood Hunters turn a corner, the spell is broken. Everyone is uneasy and quiet.

The dean steps away from Leo as if nothing happened, and goes to hover by the bend in the hall. Leo stands there, staring into space for a moment longer, before he drops his shoulders and collapses his head against the wall.

A few students watch him; Londoners, mostly. But most people seem caught up in their own shocked revelations to pay him any mind. I have one petty moment to reflect on their complete loss of bravado and confidence. For once, I feel all of us are on an equal playing field. But that won't last.

This was the first trial. Of how many?

I stop before my stomach can sink and go to him. Something about Leo Shaw lures me in. I want to touch his shoulder but stop myself. Leo is bruised. His hair is awry; he had to fight in that room, just like I had. Even with his experience, it wasn't easy.

"Are you alright?"

"Doing swimmingly, Mr Jones. How are *you?*" He turns to me with a sad smile and we look at each other, and I know without asking that it is okay to touch him. I do. I put my hand on his shoulder, and I suddenly have no words. I am exhausted.

Maybe it isn't Leo, but the touch of another human after

I'd come so close to death, but when he turns and puts his own hand on my shoulder, I feel alive again.

Then I look at him and turn so my back is against the wall beside him.

"Whoever makes it through will be either very lucky or very skilled," I say.

Which is the point, of course. Just because most Londoners were raised by graduates, it means nothing until they've faced a *teras*. Until they can prove they're useful to this place, in defending London itself, why should anyone be given the safety of the wards?

"There is no reverence to death anywhere," Leo whispers to me. "Do you know how disappointing that is?"

I think about how to reply. I want to tell him I agree, but maybe I am past all that. Maybe I lost the ability to feel the depth of that years ago. London is a political minefield. I shouldn't have been surprised that the University has *teras* on campus.

Something catches my eye.

"Oh, Christ," I say, launching myself away. Leo follows behind. Bellamy emerges from one of the closed doors along the hall. He is bloody and limping, with one arm slung around Victoria's neck. She is battered, too, with a large cut on her cheek that has been hastily patched. "Bellamy," I mutter, gingerly touching the other man's cheek. "Are you—"

"Where is he?" Bellamy growls. He shoves passed me and limps out into the hall, scanning desperately. When he spots the dean, his face twists. "You!"

I run in front, blocking his view with splayed arms. "Don't. Hey!" I block Bellamy's next obscene gesture. "Listen. They just killed a man. Shot him down. Don't. He'll only be amused, Bellamy, because this is how the University has run for years."

Bellamy turns his death glare to me and sneers. He opens

his mouth—and says nothing. I am right. They all know it. He looks at me, and I see reflected the same pain in Victoria's eyes.

Our families have sent us knowing how easily we can die.

Bellamy crumples against Victoria, who gives a soft whimper of her own. She seems to be in shock and is staring distantly through one of the stained-glass windows as she leads Bellamy to the long seat beneath it.

It looks like a pew, and when they sit beneath the orangey haze of the coloured light, they are like followers of Christ in mourning. They weep, and in weeping, they mourn the death of the son of God and with him compassion and all things good. I pray when I see it, but I cannot pray earnestly. I have forgiven God for too long for the horror of this world. I thought London was a bastion he orchestrated.

So why this? Why this?

"Well, you're alive."

When I turn, Fred is standing there. Her hair is frizzed and she has smears of dirt over her face. I crane for Silas.

"I sent him back to the rooms," Fred said. She sounds serious and drained. All the while she speaks to me, she is staring straight at the dean.

Leo goes to comfort her, but stops himself. Fred tenses at the approach of his hand. "Are you alright?" Leo asks.

"I'm alive," she says quickly.

Leo grimaces. "That's not what I asked."

"I'm alive," she says again. "Despite what I've signed up for."

Fred falls silent after that, even when the dean tells us to move out and rest, even as we pass him on our exit.

All of us are furious. All of us are burning with it.

This is only the first trial.

I don't know what to do.

12

LESSON TWELVE

We are given a day's respite. Or at least, this is what we are told. The dean gently reminds us to wear our uniforms for the next trial, and reiterates it will start two days from now. We're too exhausted and shell shocked to question any of this. I move in a haze, blood in my ears and my head. Everything is pounding. Everything feels unreal. *Teras* behind the wards. All the University spouts is a lie.

Every prospective student flees to their rooms, despite there being no order to remain there. By all accounts, we should have had free reign of the grounds—to an extent. The entire front half of the University seems unoccupied, save for us. I assume this means students in the later years are further into the campus, but Blood Hunters are the only indication of graduates here.

When we step into the tower, Silas is standing there with rum. I don't know where he's gotten it from and in all honesty, I couldn't care less. That glass is the best thing I have ever seen.

"You are a God-send," I murmur.

"You might not say that when you see I've maybe had more than my fair share," he says, raising the bottle high. I see the line of it is greatly reduced, but I can't fault him. He pours me a glass and presses it into my hand.

"Are you alright?" I ask.

His brow creases. "Are you?"

Neither one of us speak, because we both know the answer. So, I raise my glass to him and we each put back a shot, a toast to being alive, a toast to feeling stripped of any good emotion, a toast to getting drunk.

I welcome the alcohol's burning in a fog and sit by the window. Very soon, the sunset comes, and then the rain. A fire is going. Everyone sits together in a comfortable, necessary silence.

It might have been cosy if this obliterating betrayal wasn't sitting overhead like a fat guillotine. I throw another whole drink down my throat without really tasting it. The burn is good. I light a cigarette and go to pour another.

All of us drink and recover some sense of feeling human. I smoke, and inhale, and keep it in my lungs until I feel them burning. The act centres me, makes me feel tethered to my body even when my mind starts to slip. The shock remains, though it's softer. It's not sitting in my flesh so much as is the awareness of being lied to. There is horror at the institution, and at my family. At what Thaddeus had kept from me. Fear at what I have signed myself up for.

Then we all look at one another. Speaking will unleash all of our shared anger. Whoever speaks first will be lancing an ugly boil, and so another minute yawns wide between us as we wait for the first of us to speak.

It is Victoria. She slips her hand from Bellamy's back and brings it into her lap. Quietly but with determination, she says, "Can we leave?"

No one says anything. I had expected more questions,

more general outrage at what we had gone through. But the mood is morose.

I take another drag of my cigarette and sigh. "With those Blood Hunters? No."

Victoria makes a noise of protest and I stop her.

"You gave your blood the same as the rest of us. They'd hunt us down before we got anywhere. And besides, where are you planning to go? Back to your family? The lot of you would be thrown out of London by the morning."

It is obvious Victoria knows this, but a sadness settles over her face anyway. It makes her look like one of those painted renaissance ladies, the ones who demand an audience; who say *see me* with their glares. *See me.* I want to see more than fierce sadness when I look at Victoria.

But there is no freedom here except forward. I have to keep reminding myself.

"They lied to us," Bellamy says. It's the first time he's spoken in hours. A weight is in his voice, like his throat is filled with gravel. He stares into the fire and says again, "They lied to us."

Whether he means the University or us Londoners' families, it doesn't matter. He's right. But the longer I think about it, the more I am forced to accept it. What was Thaddeus meant to do? Warn me what the trials really were? Risk the family's position and his own standing behind the wards and as a Hunter?

I am here for people other than Cassius Jones. I am here for the family. To keep the Jones behind London's wards. Safe. Solid. *Cassius Jones* is not a person. *Cassius Jones* is a means to an end. Another piece on the board. What I want doesn't really matter.

Besides, I don't know myself well enough to have an ambition outside this place. The University has been my path for over a decade. Before that, I had no bigger purpose than to survive.

Fred stands and starts to pace. Her brother watches her carefully, quirk in his brow. I see him clutch his side and wonder if the wound from the *manticore* has worsened after the *python*. After a minute, he stops Fred and encourages her to sit, but she just yanks her hands away and runs them through her hair. "Home was better than this," she whispers.

Silas nods. "I know," he says softly. "How terrible is that?"

Leo Shaw says nothing. I fiddle with my falling-apart braid and try to catch his eye. But Leo just frowns into the fireplace, red flames reflected in his eyes.

I take a final drag of my cigarette, crack the window, and stub it out in the rain, sending the smoke into the night. "We need a plan."

No one deigns to answer, so I try again. "We need to—"

"Do they expect us to die smiling?" Leo speaks suddenly.

I freeze. There it is—that sharp anger I'd been expecting out of the rest of them. Leo is bursting with it. "What are they trying to do here? What are they trying to produce?"

"Soldiers," says Fred.

"*Teras* killers," says Bellamy.

"But they need us trained. They want professionals. Why?"

I look between them all. I'm not understanding his line of questioning. "What are you asking?"

Leo's anger slips. Some genuine, sad curiosity peaks through. "They put all this effort into training people. Not everyone who comes, but a select few. Why? Wouldn't canon fodder work more in their favour?"

I look to Victoria and Bellamy, and they stare back at me. We are all thinking of the same thing—the written threat we received before coming here.

There is only so much room in this place. I want to tell Leo, but I see the look in the other Londoner's eyes. As much as I want to trust Leo, I can't push Bellamy and Victoria away to do it.

So I think for a moment for a plausible lie and say, "Not if they need to protect the University's image."

Fred unfolds her arms. "You think this is branding? They'll kill every sub-par soldier for the prestige?"

Surprisingly, Silas follows up. "They only produce the best. And the people who get through the trials untrained will undoubtedly be the best, even before they receive the University's tutelage."

My hand itches to grab another cigarette, because what Silas has said sounds right, but ugly. Even without the threat of overcrowding, this has been the University's game for God knows how long. If the trials were always this brutal, they were always meant to weed out the weak.

"How did they get so many *teras*?" Fred asks. She sounds scared by her question. "Did Hunters trap them? Drag them back?"

"Or are *teras* living on campus?" Victoria whispers. "Breeding here."

That sinks the mood even further.

But when the entire city is designed around the concept of protecting a favoured few, it really isn't a shock. So what is there to do? Competing in the trials seems inevitable.

I flash a look to Leo. Leo, this newcomer, who makes me curious. I track the glow of the fire along his jaw, the way it dances down his neck. Leo catches my eye. I snap my gaze away and light that cigarette.

That was God's fault, not mine. If Leo hadn't looked so good lit up like that, I wouldn't have been staring. Still, screw God. I know without a doubt, if Leo asks me to bed tonight, I will go.

Leo smiles at me. Dazzling. "You said we needed a plan."

"I did say that," I agree.

Fred shifts and slumps against a wall. "I, for one, would like to hear it."

"You'd hear it if I had one," I tell them, unfolding my legs to sit upright. "I'm not sure how we plan around the trials. They could be anything."

"You were all for plans last night," Bellamy says lowly. His glass clinks as he takes a long drink from it. His mood is rough. "Yammering about teamwork and diversifying our ranks. So you better have something."

The way he says it... God, he can be an ass. I feel myself flush and hope the heat from the fire is enough excuse for the colour of my cheeks.

Teamwork was useless in this first trial.

I throw up my hands, inhaling the tobacco again, and I lean back against the cold glass of the window. I hear the comforting patter of rain at my back. "Well, alright. Let's collaborate, shall we? They want promising students, but they haven't made us choose a mantle yet. So no trial will focus solely on any of the four disciplines."

"Well, there will definitely be elements," Bellamy says in a tone that makes me want to slap him.

"That's why I said *solely*, Bellamy. Pay attention."

He shuts his mouth. The ice clinks in Bellamy's glass as he stirs it, avoiding eye contact. God, we will fall apart at the seams like this. This was only the first trial.

"More drink?" Victoria asks. She procures the bottle from the floor and takes a hefty swig before she passes it along. She rocks back to lean on her hands, the uptight London-raised etiquette seeping out of her along with the stress of the day. "How many trials are there? Four?"

"Five," I whisper. "Or at least there were five when Thaddeus took them."

"Four when my sister did it," Bellamy says.

"We'll assume five," Victoria says with a nod. Already there are so many assumptions. "Maybe the first trial was to test for the Hunter mantle..." she trails off, clearly realising there is no logic to follow here.

"Will they use *teras* for every trial?" Silas muses.

"Do they have that kind of access?" his sister asks. They stare at each other, probably understanding that, yes, in fact, a place such as this likely has access to whatever it wants.

"If the choice is yours, why do the thing? But if it is another's choice, what do you blame—atoms or gods?" Bellamy slurs from his place on the ground. They are not his words, but Marcus Aurelias'. I wait for him to finish, to say, "Nothing is without purpose," and draw the conclusion that even when we have no choice, we can own this. All of us here will fight, and either emerge victorious or dead, but he doesn't speak again. I hear one choking sob and then he rolls towards the fire.

I feel it, then, brighter and sharper than ever. The horror. The disappointment. I wait for the acceptance to settle in my stomach, but I only have anxiety.

I look at Leo, spy the hungry, vigilant look in eyes. I want to be beneath him. I want him to fuck me; I want to be a whore who thinks of nothing but the pleasures of the body, and the only pain I will ever feel is the thrill of taking a man inside me. There will be no death. No blood. No monsters in the night. I will lose the very sense of myself to tangled sheets and sweat.

I cannot do that. I cannot do that.

I jerk upright suddenly. My body is ripe and bursting with the poison of alcohol; I am tipsy, and ashamed. My thoughts are sin. At that moment, they feel as terrible as the University's truth.

"I have to—go," I say, stilted. I need a Bible and a cross in my hand. I need a priest to put an end to carnal wants and to remind me what I am doing here.

"Where?" Leo says. Leo, with that honey-thick voice, and scent like something dark and aged: by God, he smells like church, like incense and old tomes. But if I keep thinking about that, I will stay.

"To pray," I say truthfully. "To pray. I'll be back as soon as I can."

And then I am gone.

THUNDER SOUNDS IN THE DISTANCE, a constant rumble like a thousand *teras* charging on the horizon. My heart thrums. Part of me hates this. I love the fire, love the sound of the rain when I am wrapped up inside and safe, and maybe there is that *teras*-bred fear in me that associates the night with death.

But I cannot sit still, and I feel tainted by the day. I know there is a chapel somewhere, because Thaddeus once spoke of it, and because the church and the University are close brethren. Wrapped in my Mackintosh coat, I set out.

London and the University have stood for centuries. I forget how old the city is; old age is such a luxury. But as I walk through the grounds that night, letting myself be drenched in rain, I must consider it. I run my hands along the big stones of the buildings and look up at the sky. The gleam of the ward stones' barrier flickers in the rain.

Something dark flies through the air.

Instantly, I drop to the ground. The gun is in my hand, my sparker is out. I feel everything in me tense—a *teras* has gotten in. Somehow, somewhere, a tear in the barrier exists.

I look up, trying to scan the buildings for shadows in familiar shapes. Everything looks like an enemy suddenly, and

I force myself to push through. I have hunted before. I have sat in the bodily remains of victims. I can do this.

A scream sounds from a window that pushes me into a run. Something must be climbing up the building. I want to shout at them to close their window, to cut off its access, but I can't afford to draw attention. Back flat against the wet wall, I drag myself along with the gun and sparker raised, breathing hard, blinking rapidly as the rain clouds my vision. Edging closer, I make out the dark mass curled around itself on the grass. Faintly, I hear its wheezing groan. An echoed cry sounds above.

"Dean Drearton! Get the dean! Get the fucking dean!"

Commotion and rattling sounds in the apartment above. Heavy footfalls and a crashing ring out. A door slams open, but they don't come around. I pause, tense, waiting for the beast to rise up and stalk this new exposed prey.

There is no movement.

I hesitate, then gently lower the sparker. Gun still trained, I walk towards the wheezing form.

At first I don't know what I'm seeing. There's a mess of tangled bone. The bloody, meat covered end of a spine punctures through the black mass. I assume it's fur until I'm close, and I see it's a wax coat. And then it all resolves. Two arms splay at awkward angles. One leg broken, bone piercing through flesh. Gooey, red-black blood pooling from a head that's half caved in. The moaning, wheezing cry of a suicide still alive.

I gawk. God, I just stand there, because this isn't what I thought. I expected a monster, not a man, and I *don't know what to do*.

"H. . ." the man exhales. I get closer, because I'm a Christian, I'm a *good person*, I am not disgusted by the sight. I force myself to get down on my knees, as if in prayer, as if to propitiate his pain.

"What have you done?" I say, and I hate that I sound admonishing when I mean to sound sad. I put a hand on his shoulder which entices another gurgled sound. He won't have much longer left, but I can't imagine this pain. I cock my gun. I place the barrel to his brainpan. I do not squeeze.

Tears are in my eyes. "What have you *done?*" I say. "You made it. You passed the trial. You. . ." And I trail off, because who am I even talking to? I know why he's done it. I know what turmoil is in his heart. What I don't know is his name, or his family. Is he a Londoner? A *xenos?* A worker? Will his family ever know what became of their son?

"Good lad."

I hear grass crunching behind me. When I turn, the dean is stalking toward me. Some bereft person—a friend, a room-mate—vomits violently at the shadowy sight of the mangled man.

"Go on, go up to bed," the dean says, far softer than I thought him capable. "Have a good strong drink. Here, take this." He pulls a bottle of something heady from his coat and taps the crying man's shoulder. I watch the roommate take it and stagger back to the door, barely conscious. He manages to hold on, though. Keeps the bottle in his fingers. That's enough for me to think he'll be alright.

"Ah, now," the dean says. He stiffly lowers himself down to his knees and inspects the near-corpse at our feet. He peels back the eyelids to inspect the dying man's eyes.

"Who is he?" I whisper my question.

The dean glances at me, pulls a face. "Not sure I recall his name, I'm afraid." He sits back on his haunches and gestures to me. It's all light conversation, all brevity. The death means nothing to him. One less prospective Hunter, sure, but also one less mouth to feed. "What are you doing out here, Mr Jones? It's raining. You'll catch a cold."

"Trying to find God," I say, more bitterly than I mean to.

A droplet of rainwater slips over my eye. My hand is shaking. I tease my finger off the trigger. Vaguely I'm aware that I'm holding contraband but the dean says nothing about my gun.

"The chapel?" the dean questions. Either he didn't hear or he doesn't care for my dig. He sniffs and waves vaguely into the night. He's no longer looking at me when he says, "I'll take you, when you're done here."

I blink. "When I'm done here?"

Now he looks. "Go on, Mr Jones. Be a good lad. Put the poor thing out of his misery."

I freeze, not because I haven't heard him, but because I have. There is no mistaking the cadence, the tone, the enunciation: the dean speaks clearly and truly, and in doing so imparts on me a role.

I don't even think about saying no to him. It is not an order, but it's also not a question—I am to be this suicide's executioner, and I don't even know his name. Sweat prickles the back of my neck despite the cold. Is this my punishment for having a gun? I'm too much of a coward to ask.

I have killed *teras*. I have killed monsters pulled from myth. I have never killed a man.

Why does it feel like the worse sin of all, even when I see in his eyes the desperation and the pleading? He wants the pain to end. I have a gun. I can end it.

What kind of coward am I that I can't ease his suffering?

"Mr Jones," the dean speaks slowly. I glance up, realising I've been shaking. The look on the dean's face is as if we're at a party. He smiles, gives me an encouraging nod, and gestures back down to my task as if all that's before is a game of chess.

It's my turn. I am frozen.

"What's his name?" I say again, but I am relieved when once more the dean expresses his sincerest apologies for forgetting it. Good. Thank God. It would only make this harder.

This is a game of chess. It is my turn to move. I put my finger on the trigger. I pull.

Checkmate.

The shot rings out, echoing tenfold in the grounds as it rebounds off the buildings. Somewhere beyond London's bounds, I hear a screeching cackle—some *teras* call I don't recognise, except it is monstrous. Feels fitting when I look down and see the obliterated brainpan of my fellow student.

"Good lad," the dean says. He stands with a creak and a sigh and mutters something at the grass stains on his legs. When I'm not immediately on my feet, he comes around to help me up. I don't want him to touch me, but I can't stop him; my traitorous body leans on him for support. "Rough business that, for your first night. But you did right by him. Nasty fall he had."

"I suspect he jumped," I say, and then realise how stupid I am being. My shock from the first trial compounds with this, suddenly, and I close my mouth.

The dean doesn't correct me, but nor does he admit his mistake. He slips an arm around my shoulders—too familiar, too fucking familiar—and I am led onwards towards the chapel.

"Did right by your brother too," the dean carries on, like nothing has happened. "Thaddeus would be very proud of you."

Once I might have debated that. But I don't know anymore. I don't know the truth of Thaddeus Jones, and I never will, because my brother is dead. And maybe he was a monster, in the end—maybe that's the truth of how the University trains us—but he wasn't always one. He was a good man. Sometimes.

And I can stay a good man.

Sometimes.

LESSON THIRTEEN

The University's chapel is the worst place to pray to God.

If you look past the main flaw, it is a very beautiful room. Limestone walls and a domed ceiling, with twelve little arched windows sitting up in the drum. Ribs climb from between the windows and converge in a beautiful circular fresco of a dead *scylla*—which then ruins the whole beauty of it, because it reminds me again of this chapel's flaw.

Which is this: a massive centuries old *scylla* carcass is embedded in the room. It is a long dead creature, but it upsets me to look at, because it is forever locked in an open mouthed scream.

"Act of God," the priest tells me at the expression on my face. Father Veer is forty, fifty maybe, by the salt-and-pepper hair and well lined face. He seems good natured, but I can't relax. Not with this thing bearing down on me. The priest says, "Died out at sea. Some good men found it after the waves dumped its body out near Kent. But it is a good reminder for all students. Satan's *teras* can be killed, no matter their size."

The sight of the *scylla* makes me think of nothing more than the nearness of death. Not the grace of God.

Eerily humanoid, its massive upper half rears high above me. The *scylla*'s ribcage slumps around a supporting beam, confirming to me that this church was renovated around this monstrosity. Its skull-less spine crashes off to one corner, so the whole church is awkwardly spaced around the *teras'* death. There is no forgetting this beast. This so-called Act of God.

The *scylla*'s lower half is a preserved, dried-out husk of octopus limbs. Blanched legs arc and twist in the air, touching the ceiling at odd angles. Candles and melted wax seep over it. Each one of the legs is capped with an open-mouthed fish head sneering over rows of sharp teeth, forever petrified in the moment of its death. But death is a funny thing, and petrification has a kind of life to it. Looking at it, even from this angle, scares the piss out of me.

I sit down in a pew and ask the priest to leave me to quiet contemplation, and I stare up at the creature. The only thing I'm grateful for is that its head is missing—stolen, I am told, before the body arrived. At least it means I don't have to meet its eyes. But I still have to pray before it. The altar to God is sequestered beneath its mass. I hate how much sitting before it looks like worship. How much it feels like it. But this is a church—there are crosses. There is a priest. No devil can lurk here, can it? I squeeze my eyes shut and beg for God. Then I open my eyes and I'm at prayer before this beast of Satan.

There is nothing peaceful here. God is no where to be found.

I'm up and out of the chair before I can stop myself. Nausea broils in me—if I vomit over the carcass, will I have desecrated the church, or shown brass to Satan?—and I have to steady myself on the wall.

The peace I was hoping for here never comes, and I

decide it was never the place for it. I was just being foolish, assuming I could find God here.

Before I manage to stumble out of this damned place, the priest's hand finds my shoulder.

"Stay," Father Veer says.

"I. . ." I swallow. I don't have the right words. Denying him feels blasphemous, especially after tonight. Would he still be touching me if he knew I was a murderer? Would he still be touching me if he knew I lust for men?

Irrational, extreme thoughts swirl in my head as he guides me to sit in a pew. He squeezes in beside me. His action, I assume, is meant to feel securing and friendly, but I am trapped between him and the wall. I finally take stock of him. Blond, strong jaw. He doesn't look like a priest. In this candlelit murk, he could pass for an older Leo. And just like that, I think about kissing him, how Judas kissed the Lord, but this is a true blasphemy, not just an approximation of one. I resolutely turn away and wring my hands.

"You are the first of your cohort to come, you know," the priest whispers. "That surprised me. Truly surprised me. Usually. . . well, some true believers find me before the trials even begin. But after the first one, there's always a sizable flock here. Tomorrow, I expect there will be many of you. Not tonight."

I don't know why he's rambling, but I have no true cause to stop it. His voice is a lullaby at this moment. It might as well be God himself talking to me; I listen, enamoured.

"Whatever plagues you should plague any good Christian. But the state of our world demands such things. Think of yourself as a Crusader. An Agent of God."

This talk might have worked, if I wasn't so aware of how eagerly my body wishes to sin. I can't pretend I was made perfectly, but neither can I pretend that God instilled desire in me he did not wish me to follow. I reject the belief that I am being tested. It should not be my fault that God made men so beautiful. In the same vein, I cannot pretend that the University is God.

He did not make these trials. He did not set *teras* loose in this supposed haven to kill us. Those were men. Humans.

"Dean Drearton," I begin, and then stop myself. This priest belongs to the University as much as he belongs to God.

I don't think I can trust him, so I say nothing.

Father Veer sighs with an understanding he doesn't actually possess. "Yes. The dean did tell me of the incident, as you settled. And if it is an absolution you come for, child, you have it. As I said: the state of our world demands such things."

I realise he thinks I am here for the almost-suicide, and not for the general terror and rage I hold for what is happening here.

Limbs at awkward angles, half his skull caved in—

No, don't think about him. But it's too late, and I'm already speaking, soul craving the absolution the priest spoke of.

"He jumped. He would have been a suicide, in hell. But I shot him. I made him instead the victim of a murder. Does this liberate him? Make him worthy of heaven? Was my gun an extension of God's hand and will, Father?"

I sound snarky, and desperate, and pleading all in one. What started as a rejection of the priest's words became something else: a wish for his approval. For any exoneration he can pass on to me.

"Of course. You freed him from pain and from the gates of hell alike. Truly, you walk in our Lord's image. And I imagine you will continue to do so, both through these trials and beyond. You will bring God's justice to the creatures of Satan."

I turn to look at him, half thinking he's taking the piss.

How broken a soul would I have to be to hear this drivel and think it righteous? I'm almost glad to be cynical. But I figure I can't afford to make an enemy of the church, not when I so often need the comfort of God. I smile, I sit for as long as I can take it, yet my mind is elsewhere, already on tomorrow.

"Do you know. . . what comes next?" I say, in my best approximation of a dutiful son of Christ. "If I pray, will God reveal to me the trials, and what I must do?"

The priest smiles at me, but only with his lips. There's a deadness in the eyes, a grey-storm of something I can't name. I shiver when he reaches out to touch my shoulder.

"Pray, my child," he says. "God will give you strength."

My question goes unanswered, which is an answer in itself. I thank him without meaning it, and leave.

ॐ

THE CIGARETTE IS sweet and biting. I love the bitter burning of it and breathe deep and slowly. Leaning against a pillar outside of the chapel, I watch as the rain falls. From here, I can see the disconnected accommodation buildings, and the patch of grass where I killed a man. The body isn't there anymore. I squint, thinking maybe the shadow of his flesh has blurred into the darkness, but when a flash of lightning cracks overhead, he's gone. It's as if he was never there. And the rain has aided this spectacularly; all the blood and viscera is being washed away.

Stop thinking about it, Cassius. Stop fucking thinking about him.

A shadow stumbling towards me snaps me out of the memory. I stand as relaxed as I can make myself, smoking slowly, trying to not look out of place. The shadow is someone tall and broad, wrapped in a raincoat. They stop when they see me, mutter something, and then storm forward under cover. When they shuck the thing, I curse—it's Peter Drike, because of course it is, God has it out for me.

He manages to make me feel like I've just done something incredibly stupid. Gloating, obnoxious leer. Roll of his eyes. He's a little shite. He greets me with a raise of his chin and a sneering, "Sodomite." Then he shoves forward—goes well out of his way to walk into me, so he can spit at my feet and shake off half the water on his coat.

But he's here for church and God and I find the dichotomy between his actions and his faith exceedingly funny.

"Love thy neighbour and all that," I mutter.

He shoves me, very easily, against the stone. I have to bite the end of the cigarette to keep it flying out of my mouth.

"Keep scripture out of your filthy cock-sucking mouth."

"Why? There's plenty of room for both."

He shoves me harder against the wall and then seems to realise he doesn't know what to make of my reaction. I really don't mind men stronger than me shoving me against walls. So we stare at each for a long time, and then he spits again—on my shoes this time—before decoupling and stalking into the chapel.

I look down at my shoes, which are probably still blood stained, probably still harbouring the gore of the suicide I killed—*The Lord our God is merciful and forgiving, even though we have rebelled against him*—and now I have Drike's saliva mingling with it all. I move and hold my leg out in the rain until I assume it's washed away, smoking until the cigarette is pure ash, then I hastily light another, covering the precious flame from the wind. I smoke that one more slowly, more sullenly, trying to savour the taste of it and its burning. I attempt to lull myself to a false sense of peace. Of course, I fail.

Drike isn't my problem. Not really. This place is. The state of the world is.

What is there to do? I have two nights at best, if we're to believe the dean, before the next trial. Another day of rest. Another day to vomit out our fear and depression, and rise to the next awful thing they throw at us. God, they could spring the trial on us tonight, if they wanted. But I have to believe they won't. I have to take these two nights and use them, if I'm going to survive. For Thaddeus. For my mother. For the emptiness that is my father.

There is no other safety than London. There is no other future for me than here.

The resolve is nice, and it grounds me. My mind goes to Thaddeus' letter, sitting neatly beneath the boards of my room.

1. Python. Gun's useless. Dead: 32
2. Use for trials 2, 4. Library in centre. Massive willow. Courtyard. Meléti helps for a price. Dead: 1
*3. Plant from 2 is a **toxin**. Be careful to*

I CRAVE an essay from my brother. From any graduate. I want to know what they went through. But all I do now is recall the second and third lines.

I don't know how many have died in our trial, but I can't afford to care. Number two. Library. Meléti helps for a price. And only one died.

If God can't reveal the truth of these trials, perhaps Thaddeus can. If my brother stumbled across something in the library, then I will take it.

Briefly, I consider going back to the rooms and rallying

the motley lot of us together. I want their company, because we're already bound by the horror of what happened this morning. But no one is giving as much as I am. They are all, already, so determined to be alone, and I'm simply too exhausted to worry about charisma. I could crawl back to them and sleep, or bicker through the night, watching the rain, wondering if all of us are going to die.

And I couldn't stand that. I'd go insane. If I can return to them with even the tiniest bit of insight, it will be enough.

Massive willow. Courtyard. The University is labyrinthine and strange. I recall I haven't seen a single student beyond the cohort desperate for a place. No first years, no seconds, no thirds. I decide I don't want to encounter anyone anyway. Not Blood Hunters, certainly, but neither students. There seems something about their status, now: a dark and unsettling certainty of what they've done to secure their place.

I decide right then and there that if I am to die, it'll be once the Jones family were secured in London. Preferably much later.

Without a map, I am left to either scale the buildings for the vantage of height, which seems a sure-fire way to snap my neck—to end up sprawled and gasping in the grass, limbs at odd angles, face caved in, *no, don't think about him*—or to wonder through the halls. It doesn't sound good, but I hate impotence more. So with a final drag on my cigarette, I stub it out beneath my feet, and turn to my right, facing further into the bowels of this place.

The University, as I've said before, is maze-like. But I am not sure this does it justice. It is disorienting, and if I believed more wholly in magic, I would assume it was a spell of haziness that falls over me whenever I walk its halls. I think neither God nor Satan has a hand in this, but some bastard novice architect; none of its design makes any sense.

I orient myself before I walk away. The main hall, where I

first entered the University, I believe is the original mass of stone. Then there are the towers and rooms for accommodation, which are scattered and disconnected buildings to the west of the hall. The chapel sits down a covered outdoor corridor. If I were to go left from where I'm standing, I would return to the great hall, where we eat. To the right, then, will take me further into the University proper.

I walk from the chapel down a stone corridor that then splits to my left and right around an enclosed colonnaded garden. The rain patters down mercilessly on sad looking shrubs and something that might have once been a tree; it is a gloomy garden. No flowers. No colour. Exits trail off from this garden to the left, right, and straight ahead. I choose the one that is brightest—only the straight path has torches burning, and besides, this path will take me deeper. As I walk it, the chill sets in, and even out of the rain I shiver as wind barrels down this corridor. Then I am well and truly in the bowels of this place. Darkness swarms like a plague.

Still, there is no one, but that doesn't change the shiver that splits down my back. The instincts in me that flare wild around *teras* suddenly spark to life. I flatten myself against the wall, my heart hammering for no reason.

You're paranoid. Anxious. Cut the crap and focus, you fucking cur.

I can't tell if that's my own self hatred speaking, or Thaddeus', but it does the job. I centre myself, breathe. Peeling myself from the freezing wall, I walk forward with my body tense and my hand securely on the gun. The next corner I turn startles me with sudden brightness. Countless candles dribble wax onto the stone floor. The walls are bright; torches burn in sconces, their flames fluttering with the wind but, spiritedly, never go out. The light is so overwhelming after long stretches of darkness, there might as well be a thousand lamps burning in front of me. I feel exposed, but I push forward anyway. It is so cold I expect the wall to open up into another garden, but instead there is only a large room to the left, and another stretch of corridor heading straight. I peek carefully around the bend, bracing myself for people, conjuring an explanation for my presence here if I am asked. But there's no one.

There are, though, a dozen coloured lamps in glows of amber and blue and red, coalescing on the walls with bright hues, split and cut like the scales of a snake. Great tomes sit open and unattended.

Unexpectedly, I laugh.

This is a honey-pot for a scholar. A beautiful room, rain outside, leather-bound ancient books sitting unattended, waiting to be consumed. It almost feels like the devil knows me, and I am frozen with fear and excitement and a lack of understanding at what I'm seeing.

Until the pages move. I see them turn one by one to the next page, a seamless movement, without flesh to do it. *Strings*, something in my head tells me. This is an automaton display, meant to. . . to entice students. . .

I sound weak even to myself. And then, brief as anything, as bright and illuminated as lightning, I see—a woman. She sits around the tomes. She is studying. There is no grand or awful devil pulling strings, just a student; in uniform, scanning pages. She glances up at me, and I know her gaze is dazzling even when she is washed out and faded like a ghost.

I blink. She is gone.

My hands shake with the absolute fear of a man who has simply dealt with too much in one day. I feel my legs buckle. I want to scream, if just to ease the sheer insanity of this place, but I stop myself. Or rather, I don't think my body has the energy for it. Slumped against the cold stone of the wall, I let it seep into my skin, wait until my cheeks are burning.

The library. Get to the library. Meléti will help for a price.

It is the only mantra that will get me to move. I forget what I saw, or try to, because I have no space in my head to rationalise one more impossible thing tonight. I pick myself up, I square my shoulders, I walk past the strange alcove without another glance to my left.

As soon as I'm in the next stretch, relief pricks at my head and a great weight removes itself from my shoulders. I breathe deep, realising only now that my lungs can stretch that there was a great heaviness on them. Spots burst in my eyes. Briefly, I'm forced to stay myself with a hand splayed on the wall.

For many minutes, there is nothing but stone. I walk. I decide which way to turn. But I'm operating purely on instinct. Anytime I feel the pressure of another uncertain, suffocating place, I circumvent it, or turn away. If my gut doesn't like it, I change direction.

The only indication that I'm not walking in circles is when I move towards the wind, and find myself, inexplicably, where I'm meant to be. It is a quadrangle, with a covered walkway around the grassy centre, which is dominated by a tree that is surely ancient. Its long limber arms of the willows scraping the ground. Unlike the front of the University, which is lush and bright, this area seems almost uncared for. Dry, patchy grass covers the square where I assume students have sat for years. The rain plummets hard, turning much of the balding areas to mud. The willow bends with the wind, and I shiver. All of this is revealed to me through muted and distant torch light. Two torches burn by the doors of a room on the far right of the quadrangle building. How they're surviving in this wind, I don't know, but I am glad for them. I am about to step out when a jolt of lightning burns overhead. For a split second, the courtyard lights up—sun struck, incandescent— and I see a figure moving slowly from a door straight across the grassy square. Near to my right—too bloody near—a door closes.

"Well?" The voice nearest to me speaks. It's deep and ragged. I watch a figure in a black Mackintosh coat and Hunter tricorn cross the square to the willow, not caring about the rain.

Eager to hear, I drop low and move into the quadrangle's walkway, body pressed against a pillar closer to the willow. I am grateful for the night and the shadows; I'm not seen.

The figure across the way shouts back. "Runner. Got out by the western gate."

From close to me there's a scoff. "God. Every time. They don't listen."

The man's accent is thick and northern. Glancing out from behind my pillar, I watch as beneath the boughs of the willow a tiny speck of fire burns as a cigarette is lit. Footfalls slap over, muddy and wet, as the other figure—same silhouette, if leaner, with same tricorn hat—moves to join the other.

"Give me a puff," she says.

"Fuck off and get your own. Tobacco farms are barely importing anymore. Stuff's golden."

"Don't be an arse," she says, unbothered. There's a beat of silence as the cigarette is presumably passed over to her. The smell of tobacco wafts towards me, and I breathe it deep, in hopes the second-hand smoke will settle me like a cigarette of my own would. I try to ignore the mention of the tobacco farms and a failing crop—that reality is too terrifying for me. I miss laudanum. I wish I had that hazy release now.

"What's the compass say?" The woman says after a while.

There's a shuffling of wax-covered coats as someone rifles in their pockets, then a sharp snap as metal is opened. I glimpse only the shine.

"Due west," says the man. "She's a *xenos*, right? Probably heading to Ludgate. Newgate, maybe, but Ludgate's closer."

"Guard might stop her," the woman mutters. She doesn't sound at all convinced.

"Come on, Payne, don't be fucking daft." A boot crunches, wet and hard, and the burning end of the cigarette disappears from view. "Let's go. Don't have all night."

I press myself to the wall, fearful they'll swing by me, but luck is on my side and they leave through another exit. I hold myself there for a moment and then I say a quick prayer for that runner. Two Blood Hunters are after her. She has no chance.

That's two of my cohort to die outside a trial, as far as I'm aware.

Confident that the way forward is clear, I skirt around the covered walkway to the other side, where the woman Blood Hunter emerged from. Every few metres, a set of double wooden doors sit. I can see no lock on them, but they won't open for me. They're practically seamless. I move to the next door, for the sake of it. Try it. Fail. Again. A creeping sense of impending failure hangs over my head. I have seen too much today. My nerves are fried. My sense of control and calm is frayed beyond belief.

Even if I enter the library, who's to say it'll be empty? And if not a professor, or a Hunter, the University's students surely will tell on an un-initiated upstart trekking inside—let alone come to learn the University's precious information.

I swallow and look to my right. At the far north of the quad sits another double door, only these are massive arches with wrought iron decoration that shoots out of the hinges in florals and arrows. It is obviously my destination. I move towards it, and then stand there in silence for five achingly long seconds, hand hovering over the door.

Do it. Hurry up.

With both hands, I swing open the doors.

They yield. At first, there is nothing. I was bracing myself for darkness, or the spitting to life of torches in sconces, but it's already lit.

I blanch, bracing myself, expecting company. I see no one. No *teras* launches itself out of the doors.

I force myself to relax, but my breath is still coming in sharp.

The library is an expanse of books. I'm assaulted by the sight of them: four levels of book-lined walls and rows of bookshelves. On the ground floor, a circular station is set up for a librarian (who seems, thankfully, absent). Flush against two giant windows is a marble statue of a woman with Herculean iconography: she wears the skin of the Nemean lion. She holds in her hand a real spear, made of iron or some metal. I don't know if the statue depicts Omphale, or some University Huntress emulating her, but the effect is the same. I am amongst culture. I am here for the future.

Two staircases flank the statue and curl up to the left and right to the next level.

I crane my neck and look up. A bowled roof with rafters like the underside of a boat is painted bright. There are clouds, angels, cherubs: an onslaught of Christian iconography that still seems out of place in an institution meant to fight creatures from pagan myth.

I give an airy, breathless laugh. My heart beats fast, but it is happy, this time: a thrill of another sort. It is like the latent academic in my heart is stretching, waking up, and it's not the honey-pot trap from earlier this evening, but a lifetime worth of study. For the first time since the horror of today, I can *see* myself here. I imagine finding a nook, hunkering down to study. Perhaps with Leo. Perhaps even with the others. I fancy that I can see myself as part of this world.

Then, my heart stops.

"Ah," says a deep, echoing voice. "I was wondering if someone might come and visit."

LESSON FOURTEEN

There is a scream behind me that makes me spin, and I'm met with the faces of my roommates—all of them, all of them here.

"What the hell are you doing?" I seethe. Leo is at the front of them; I see a crumpled bit of white paper in his hand. Heat and shame assault my face. It's a little betrayal, a tiny one, but I hate it all the same.

"That's *mine*," I say.

"We heard a gunshot," Leo says, defensively. The paper crumples in his hand. "And I saw you hiding this the first day. This says library, so we—"

Real anger flashes in me. "Oh, I *fucking* knew you were too good to be true. You still don't trust me, do you?"

Leo looks hurt, then furious. "I—"

"Shut up, shut *up*," Victoria says. "How have either of you *not seen that thing?*"

I blink at her. "What thing?"

"Hello," a voice says. Behind me. None of my roommates speak.

I freeze. Then I catch movement in my periphery.

I jolt into action, spinning with more force than is strictly necessary. With the same fluid movement, coat tails flying out behind me, I whip Thaddeus' gifted pistol out and point it at the thing's head.

Scattered shocked noises edge out of the others. A tense, still silence follows them up.

My eyes take a moment to adjust, to take it in. At first I see bronze skin, dark eyes. But where skin can sometimes take on a translucent quality, to reveal veins or blemishes, there is nothing like that here. The material of its flesh is opaque. Solid. My eyes drift to a wound in the creature's chest; I see layered clockwork in an open cavity, long bronze tendons exposed in a forearm. I blink. I realise I am holding metal to metal: a gun aimed at the head of an automaton.

"Weapons are not permitted in the library," it says with a jolting, echoing voice.

"Why in God's name do you have a gun?" Victoria whispers. "Did you steal it from the trial?

"Be thankful that I do," I tell her, and ignore the rest of her question. I don't peel my gun away from the automation. I look it over. The automaton's chest is made up of rib-like strips of bronze for, I assume, a technician's ease of access. I search for a voice-box: a black, repurposed music box, perhaps? But there is nothing.

"How's that possible," Bellamy murmurs, suddenly beside him. It isn't a question, really. More a statement of uncomprehending.

I don't know what to say. I am struggling to stay upright. Adrenaline is a constant in my blood today, and I am seeing spots at the edge of my vision. Everything is too bright. Slowly I manage, "Automata aren't like this."

"I saw the *Silver Swan*," Victoria says. She creeps forward into my view, keeping her distance from the thing ahead of it. Clearly drawn to it, compelled in a fascinated way. Leo comes closer to me, but Silas and Fred are gripping each other with extreme intensity.

Get it together. You're their leader, you have to keep that position.

I was worried about them slipping out of control. Leo brought them all here, managed to wrangle them together despite being a *xenos*. Something like jealousy sparks in me. Something like fear follows closely behind.

"Automata are London's fascination," I call out. "Machines that are self-operating. Clockwork."

Victoria supplies the Greek translation with a little flourish. "Acting of one's own will," she says. She has a joy about her, a thrill at being in this machine's presence.

Silas scoffs loudly. "It's not 'London's fascination'. Britain has been long obsessed with the Hellenists, even before their myth bled into this world. But they're not the only damn source, you know."

"Well, who'd have thought you had a single opinion in that quiet head?" Bellamy mutters.

Fred steps forward, eyes a warning. "Stop it."

We lapse into uncomfortable silence and turn back to the automaton. My aim falters momentarily as I consider it. Its face is a mask, fixed permanently with a faint smile that in the right light might be comforting, but now has a terrifying edge to it. Gears turn in the oval openings that serve as its eyes. Fake eyelids jar to a close and spring open once more.

It is a poor approximation of a human and extremely uncanny.

"This isn't something London could dream of," Leo murmurs.

He is right, of course.

Silas, braver now, says, "I agree. Machines that can speak?" He sounds different — scared, maybe, or unsettled enough to make his voice raw with hostility. But then he says, "No, I know my myth. And look at it. This isn't a swan. This is something that can talk."

Bellamy laughs, buoyed by Victoria's calm. "What are you saying?" But then he locks eyes with the automaton and his smile dies.

Silas pulls away. "I'm saying there's *automata* in myth. Talos. Ones made by Daedalus—and given voice by quicksilver. Hephaestus' workshop."

No one says anything. Perhaps the thoughts are brewing in all the others' minds like they are in mine. I put the gun down. It suddenly seems silly, holding it up to something that wouldn't die from a wound. More than that, though, I know both Silas and Leo are speaking truth.

The machine has stayed unnervingly quiet all this time, bronze metal gleaming in the library's light. It's waiting, I think. Either used to this outburst from new cohorts, or in need of instruction to continue.

"You're a *teras*," I whisper.

I glance at Leo, who smiles at me faintly even when the others baulk. But I can't parse the expression; whether he experiences disgust or interest, I'm not sure.

"What?" Victoria asks. I see Fred ready herself, centring her body to attack. I ignore their reactions, in chase shock finds a footing in my already exhausted mind.

"Daedalus and quicksilver," I tell the automaton. "That's why I couldn't find your voice-box."

"I have no voice-box," the machine says soberly. "But I have a voice."

I grimace. "So I hear."

No one else speaks for a time. There is a tension that can't be explained by our situation, exactly. It isn't about the true brutality of the trials, it isn't that we've been caught. If we are right, and this *automaton* has manifested the way the other *teras* have, won't that change the world? Won't that change London, and the University, and the nature of what we are meant to be fighting?

Did Satan tear a hole in the world, or did God? An ambivalent cosmic force? Random happenstance?

"Tell us," I whisper. "Tell us where you're from."

The *automaton*'s head clicks to the side, unnaturally fast. Its impassive mask stares at me blankly before its neck resets its position, springing upright too quickly.

"Perhaps we should begin with introductions," it says. It steps backwards, bronze legs clanking along the floor until its whole body comes to rest against the circular service desk. The machine folds itself onto it, the way a human would rest. But there is nothing relaxed about its posture. Has it been programmed like this? Ordered to act human when it was anything but?

For some reason, it only makes my skin crawl.

Victoria steps forward, hands clasped near her chest. "You have a name?"

The *automaton* looks towards her. What happens next makes my head spin. The machine opens its mouth. I hear the name, hear it say *Meléti,* but see in my mind's eye the Greek:

μελέτη

It is emblazoned, etched in fire in my mind, then my human brain scrambles to assign meaning to what it has seen. I groan and hold my head, and when I right myself the image is gone.

Meléti, from the paper my brother left for me. Meléti. "Study," I translate automatically, after seeing the Greek. Well, what was in a name, after all? Everything, apparently. This *automaton*'s entire purpose is laid out in its title.

Bellamy's face has an ashy, green tone to it. Either the alcohol from earlier this evening is making him nauseous, or he is sobering up enough to be terrified by the machine in front of him.

"Victoria." He says it firmly, beckoning her to retreat. When she doesn't, he speaks it again, more harshly, growl tinging the edge, "Victoria."

"Stop it," she insists, waving him away. "It's fine."

"It's as bad as the bloody *teras!*" He shouts it, barrelling forward to rip her back towards him. Victoria yells, tearing herself free. She shoots him a fiery look as she recovers.

"That you think this a matter of benevolence or malevolence says much about your people," the *automaton* says. "I am Meléti, built to house knowledge. You are trespassers on University property. You are not initiated. You will leave."

I am scared, but I'm not stupid. I trust Thaddeus Jones and that bit of paper more than I do this thing. And if my brother says *Meléti will help for a price*, then I believe him. I just have to know what I have to pay.

In any case, this day has screwed us all over. And coming here, for me, was meant to be about taking back control. To turn heel and walk back into the rain empty handed simply is not an option.

"You have information, though," Fred says. "Information that could help us. We could. . . beat the trials. Strategise for them."

Meléti blinks, one eye at a time.

Fred says, more firmly, "You hoard this information. We need it."

Meléti considers her for a long time. "It is not for you to have. You are not initiated. You will leave."

"What?" Leo laughs. I think something in him has snapped, because he runs his hands over his face. I see in him more of what I sometimes catch a spark of; the unsettled, angry part of him. The fear, the rage. "You are something out of myth. Something made by the hands of Daedalus. A legend. And like out of some nightmare, you and your kin come into our world and wreak havoc. You are sitting on information. Sitting on it." He barrels over. He grabs the *automation* by the neck.

"Leo," I say, more calmly than I feel. "Leo, darling, stand down."

Leo does, almost immediately, to which Bellamy snorts. "Fucking *dog*."

And Leo is so overwhelmed and so close to breaking, I watch him lunge at Bellamy and tackle him to the ground.

"Stop it!" Victoria shouts.

Now I see Leo truly; every tightly wound part of him, everything he carefully packed away. Leo Shaw is furious and angry and wild. He has been raised amongst monsters and he will do whatever is necessary to win. I should be scared; I'm not. I think I want him more than ever, if just for the impersonality of it—the roughness, the near-violence. He is angry at the world, and I am angry at myself, and when there's no room for softness, it means I won't lose myself to emotion. Cursing, I loop my arms under Leo's armpits. I heave, and I'm acutely aware of how bloody weak I am, because the man is *built* and I am not.

"Leo," I say, straining. "Leo, you're angry. Stop it. Stop. Work with me here. I need you."

And Leo stands and spits over his shoulder, decoupling from my touch without another word.

Whatever he's marinating in, I leave him to it.

Calmly, as if nothing just happened, Meléti says, again, "You are not initiated. You will leave."

"No," I tell it.

The *automaton*'s head snaps towards me. I see in its void-like eyes a shimmer of something. In a human, I might have called it annoyance. But this thing is something else. God, my hands are shaking.

I reach into my pocket and light a cigarette. My packet is damp, from kneeling in the rain to kill a man—*Gods, Cass, don't think about that!*—but the cig still takes a light. I inhale deep. The nicotine hits my system and the anxiety pops inside me like an overcooked pea.

When I'm calm again, I realise no one has moved or spoken for that entire stretch of time. So I fill it.

"Thaddeus Jones. Hunter. You knew him."

A whirring buzz of cogs turning in the *automaton's* mind. "Yes."

"He is dead now."

"I am very sorry to hear that."

Dull, bland, no emotion. It makes me furious to hear it from this thing's mouth.

Don't rise to it. Just keep speaking.

"He was my brother, you see. And he told me of a Meléti. He said: Meléti will help, for a price."

There is no response. I let the question sizzle in the air between us, and take another drag of the cigarette. Then when there's still no answer I ask, "What is your price, Meléti?"

"Weapons are not permitted in the library," Meléti says.

Fuck that, all sense in me says—but the *automaton* repeats the phrase incessantly, so I fold, and take out the bullets and skid the pistol out the door.

"Thank you, Cassius Jones," it says. I flinch at hearing my name. Then it spins to Fred. "Winifred Lin, weapons are not permitted in the library."

"Yeah, well, tough luck," she says.

The *automaton* rights itself, flinging off the desk in one fluid arc, and closes the gap between us. In one moment, it bound silently across the floor.

Bellamy stumbles back with a gurgled scream, and the others flinch, myself included. Save for Fred, who somehow saw it happen. She moves herself into a defensive position, knife drawn and raised to slash.

The *automaton* ignores the weapon and tilts at the waist. Its smooth bronze face hovers close to Fred's.

She doesn't step away, but I watch her eyes. They scan, incredibly quickly, up and down the creature. Assessing gaze, looking for a weakness. She says, "Intimidation is the mark of a weak man," but there's an edge in her voice, tension wound tight. She'll strike it if it moves, but I'm not sure she'll be quick enough.

"I am no man," Meléti informs her. "Weapons are not permitted in the library."

Fred stares at it for a while. No one speaks, but Bellamy starts tapping his foot frenetically. His anxiety is palpable. It wears us down, including Fred. She sighs and curses, and dashes the knife across the floor. It skids out of the library's doors. With both weapons outside the library's bounds, the door shuts.

"Oh, great," Bellamy mutters.

Meléti continues, then, as if there's been no pause in conversation. "My price, Cassius Jones, is this. I have no desire nor want for material items. You must trade something else of value."

"Like what?" Fred asks.

"You must trade something else of value."

There's a brief moment where no one says anything. Victoria has given up, a little bit; now that she knows this thing is a *teras*, all her earlier interest has sapped away. She tends to Bellamy, who seems close to vomiting up his guts. Fred is poised still, tense and angry. Leo's got his arms folded. He looks so tall and golden in this light, the brawn of him making him statuesque in this place. He is unhappy. He looks at Meléti like he wants to snap the thing's neck.

"Study."

I turn; Silas has propped himself up against the wall. He looks the calmest amongst all of us, but I see him nursing the wound at his side. He looks paler, pallid. "It's name is study, isn't it? Doesn't take a genius to figure it out."

"Oh, well, why do you bloody tell us then?" Bellamy snaps, not realising how much like a nonce it makes him sound.

My eyes meet Silas'. Though we clash occasionally, he understands. We have the same mind. I nod in agreement. "It wants information."

Silas winks at me. "Got it in one, Mr Jones."

I smile at him and press my own side asking silently if he's ok. He nods, lying straight to my face—but there are more pressing matters.

Information. It's too dangerous a game to be playing. This could be a trial in its own right. What happens when I offer something unsatisfactory for the *automaton?* Does it gut me with its inhuman speed? Part of me curses myself for coming here at all.

What else can you do, Cass. Thaddeus' letter said to come here. And it's true, isn't it? This library, the knowledge contained here, is likely going to be our only chance. Sometime in the coming days, we'll be thrown into another trial. We'll likely face *teras.*

At least one of our cohort died tonight outside the trial, and another was being hunted by graduates. It doesn't bode well for our future. I don't really want to consider it, but the likelihood one of us will die is awfully strong.

I look up at the *automaton.* "Alright," I tell it. "I'll play."

It spins to me with great interest, eyes bulging out of its head. I tense as it approaches, every animal thing in me winding taut, readying my body to flee.

"What do you offer, brother of Thaddeus, named Cassius?"

I hate that this thing knows my name. I should never have

revealed my link to Thad. I am reminded, so suddenly, of the folklore of fairies, and distantly wonder if they have been pulled forth into this world. I've heard rumours of places like Ireland, where great infestations of the Folk have caused chaos. But what kind of power can a *teras* hold if it has my name? What sort of punishment can it bring down on me if I do not please it?

Unsteadily, I clear my throat. "I have information. About the *teras* outside of London's walls. My brother Thaddeus and I encountered a *teras* that could not be categorised under London University's cataloguing system. It was a hybrid. Which suggests. . ."

I trail off as I consider exactly what it suggests. I recall bringing the thing to the dean, the sudden change of subject as my brother was punished for bringing me along on his Hunter route. The complete lack of acknowledgement for what we had encountered—a hybrid, a creature *never before written about in myth*, a spontaneous development.

I'm going to be sick. "God," I say. "The *teras* are evolving. That's why they had an open call. That's why they want the very best of us."

"I still don't get it," Bellamy says. He's angry, but it's a quiet broiling now. There's fear in him, too. "Why don't they just throw all of us at them? They could send us out right now, cannon fodder the lot of us."

"Because they would lose London," Silas whispers. "As much as you lot might like to think you operate here freely, the University rules this place. The church, too. They are meant to be in control. The University can't lose face by letting too many of us die in an obvious sacrifice to the *teras*. So they put us here. Let us die, as we fight to get a spot." He makes a noise and sighs, like all this is boring him. "You Londoners are probably used to it. You give up tiny freedoms until they snowball."

Victoria turns to me. I see her mouth *the letter*, and I shake my head, urging her to keep all talk of the University's ultimatum to herself.

Bellamy spins. He's sweating out the alcohol now, and he's out of Victoria's grasp before she can stop him. "It's a fair system! As fair as something like this *can* be. I'm not defending the University, but this is war. It's war. Humans against those fucking monsters. And that means people are stuck doing jobs they don't want to do, because the alternative is the death of the human race. So, yeah. Us Londoners *do* have freedom."

It's Leo who scoffs. "If you think anything about this is fair, you're blind. Consider it for a moment, *really* consider it. You got lucky. Maybe a few others born outside London made it in, but only because someone in their family could do something the University wanted."

Bellamy gestures wide. "What about the workers?"

"What about them?" Leo asks, growing frustrated. He frowns and uncrosses his arms to gesture right back. "Maybe London would twist a little for the people already in London —for the people who are integral to the city's survival. For workers, like the toshers who work the sewers, or the miners who get ferried back and forth out of London for coal and gas. They're far more integral than a bunch of entitled asshats who sit behind the wards and eat and contribute nothing else."

The three of us who know that this treatment is at an end grow quiet, which is stupid, because our rapid silence gets the *xenos'* attention. I'm aware of Meléti watching all this with great interest, but I can't stop it.

Leo looks at me. "What? What is it?"

I want to say *nothing, nothing that concerns you.* Instead, I look to Victoria. She slides her eyes away and shrugs.

"They'll find out eventually."

I grit my teeth, and when I get nothing from Bellamy, I give it up and tell them.

"Londoners have an ultimatum. For all of us here, only those who manage to graduate from the University will be able to keep their families in London proper. If we fail, anyone who has lived with us is booted, unless they themselves are graduates." I swallow and try not to fiddle with my hands as I deliver this. I keep expecting the *xenos* to laugh—a taste of our own medicine. But they are silent and waiting as I say, "London will be a city of useful graduates or workers and nothing more. The *teras*' evolution, the growing lack of resources. . . it's all part of the same horrible thing, isn't it? London needs to become a military base. It can't remain a simple haven."

Fred makes a noise and nods at her brother. Silas shrugs in response. "Told you."

"What?" I ask.

Fred puts a hand to head. "We're from a farm," she says. "Farm for London. We get a retinue of Hunters and Healers, to protect the crops, and most of it goes to London. But we keep hearing stories. Farmlands being abandoned. Either the entire Hunter squad gets eliminated, or the University is pulling them out. But they were just rumours. Hadn't happened to us. Still, when the Call came. . ."

"You couldn't pass up the opportunity," Leo finishes for her. They share a look, something I think is only for another *xenos*.

"Truly, I'm surprised London bent for so long for the disenfranchised few who needed the city's good will to survive," Silas says.

"Yeah, yeah," Bellamy spits. "Shut up. You're in the same boat as us now."

Before any of this can spiral further, Meléti whirrs beside us. Bellamy jolts with a sharp, "*Jesus*," at the noise.

"Thank you, Cassius Jones, for this bit of information. But it will not be enough to access the information you seek."

I sneer, but keep my gripe to myself. I let it eavesdrop thinking this would be enough, but contention and gossip are not information, really.

"Then what?" I say, folding my arms. That itch for laudanum and nothingness flares in me again. "What do you want from me?"

"Something personal, Cassius Jones."

I tense. I don't like where this is going. "Like what?"

"Your brother gave me the memory of seeing your father return broken from the sea."

I am dazed, suddenly, and horrified. Vulnerability swarms into me, and any bit of peace I was encroaching towards evaporates. I look around at my fellow applicants and hate how naked I feel. This is not theirs to know.

Wrestling back any semblance of control, I say, "A memory, then."

"Yes," Meléti says, with a tone approaching cheerfulness. "Something you don't particularly want to give up."

I stare at it, and realise its danger is this: offering too much of oneself to a *teras*, even one so seemingly innocent, given charge of the information, might compromise me. It is information for information—the deepest secrets of the University offered for my own.

Very smart, Dean Drearton. Exceptionally cruel.

I rack my mind for a memory, something not too horrible, but enough to sate this creature. And when I find it, I nod to myself, resigned.

"Alright," I tell it. "I'll pay your price."

❦ 15 ❦

RECORDATIO

"**G**et up."

Cassius snapped awake. The light was harsh, a blaring white after the snowfall. He was in his house just outside of Hull, a little shack he shared with his brother and parents. Didn't know what day it was. Knew it was morning, at least, but nothing else. Something was burning in the distance, and the smoke made him scrunch up his nose. Disoriented, he blinked once, but he didn't get up quick enough. A hand closed around his shirt and hauled him to standing.

"I said *get up*."

Cass clamped his mouth shut, swallowing a yelp. The urge to lash out ran through his mind momentarily, but it was quickly quashed. Striking his father would bring him nothing but a world of pain. He was still sporting the bruise from his father's last ill-managed flash of anger—Cass wasn't in the mood for any more aches.

He raised his chin. At twelve, he wasn't nearly as tall as his father or Thaddeus, so he had a constant crick in his neck, a constant strain to appear taller. But it didn't take much to make him feel small. Just one look; the withering, disappointed stare of his father. The man's coarse hair was shaggy, and the bags under his eyes told him he'd slept poorly again. He smelled like whiskey, fish, as he always did, and the general unclean scent that clung to everyone in this town.

Cassius wasn't sure what was going on. Sleep still hewed to him, making him groggy. But when Mr Jones put a finger to his lips and a hunting rifle in his hands, Cassius grew cold.

He knew what all this meant. Something was outside. Broad daylight usually deterred *teras*, but not always. Whatever was out there would have to be fought.

He shook. He was horrified. But this was life, outside of London. Cassius' father was a fisherman, but there were terrible creatures to be found at sea, and he always trained Cassius and Thaddeus to fight. Cassius just wasn't very good. Not like Thad.

But he had no time to think about that now. Cass carefully positioned himself against the wall of the small shack. A poorly fitted curtain hung over the window. He stood next to it, trying to spy the creature through the cracks.

On the opposite side of the shack, Thaddeus was crouched on the ground, knife in one hand, pistol in the other. He'd been awake longer than Cass had and should have had a better grip on the situation than him. But Thad was shaking. Cass knew he hated this. Thad was sixteen, raised his whole life outside the protection of London, and he was good at Hunting, when he had to do it, but Cass knew he wished for something different.

Cass grimaced and glanced away. Mr Jones caught his eye. Cassius' father was staring at him, assessing him as he sometimes did. It was all part of his training—sizing him up, seeing if he was scared. *Only a fool ignores their fear*, he sometimes said to Cass. But a greater fool let it overwhelm them. Adrenaline ran molten hot through his veins. If he could utilise it, stoke the burning fire just enough to centre him, he could slay this thing in no time. These were, of course, not his words nor his feelings. He was regurgitating everything he'd ever been told, in case Mr Jones was angry today, and wanted to hit him.

His father saw right through him. Still staring, he got up and knocked Cassius' shin.

"What, boy?" Mr Jones hissed, risking whatever was outside hearing him.

Cassius felt his face crumple, both out of fear and a dark disappointment. He bit his tongue. He couldn't reply.

"Focus," his father ordered.

Cassius nodded frantically, clutched the rifle and looked back out the window. Sweat beaded on his forehead and ran down his back. He tried not to urinate on himself. He'd done that once. Got beaten for it.

It was times like these that Cass liked to pretend he wasn't scared of death. But the truth was he felt it: a yearning in him, a need to stay alive that felt more vital than breathing. He didn't want to die to his father's anger. He didn't want to die to a *teras*. He didn't want to die in a rundown town outside of Hull without a taste of the world beyond.

He didn't want to die at all.

So when the window beside his head smashed in, he screamed. Something closed around his neck. Cass thrashed, still screaming, and put his leg on the sill for leverage. The grip around his neck loosened. Cass stuffed the curtain against the broken window, but the hand still grabbed for him; long fingers curled through the curtain fabric trying to find his flesh. Cass cocked the rifle. The curtain blocked his view. It didn't matter. He shot blindly.

There was a howl of pain. Someone cursed.

Cass lowered the gun. Blood was in his ears. But someone

was outside cursing. Over the panic he heard herself, in shock, asking, *what kind of* teras *swears?*

Thaddeus shot up, knife and gun pointed towards the window. "What's—"

A new force burst through the broken window. With a screech, the curtain tore off its rod. Two hands folded the curtain over Cassius' gun and clamped down, heaving. Cassius held fast. The muscles in his shoulder strained against their sockets, but if he lost that gun Mr Jones would beat him bloody. Then a man roared and dragged him forward. Cassius was twelve—he had barely any body weight to stay grounded on a good day. When the force outside pulled, he couldn't resist. He was dragged over the windowpane.

Cass screamed, at first from the fear bubbling up and over, and then from the pain: a white-hot flash of it over his abdomen where shards of broken glass had sliced his stomach. He hit the snow with a thud. Cass rolled, wriggling backwards away from his assailant. There was blood in the snow, little drops of it. He reeled away with a choked scream, catching sight of dark boots, a figure towering over him, but the snow was blinding bright. He couldn't pick out details; he needed to get away.

It was then he realised the rifle was out of his hands. He struggled back in the snow, feeling around for it.

Just as he grabbed the rifle, a gun cocked above him.

Cass froze. His heart was in his throat. At this point he knew it was pointless to struggle. He jutted out his chin and squinted up at the man above his. He tried not to cry. He failed. Tears welled hot in his eyes.

He didn't want to die.

"For God's sake," the man said. He took his finger off the trigger and hefted the rifle from Cassius' hands. Cass tracked its arc; it landed well out of arm's reach in the snow.

He didn't hesitate. Cass spun on his belly and crawled towards it.

"Cassius," his father called. His voice was calm.

Cass didn't listen to him. Whatever this was, whether it was real or one of his silly games, he wouldn't face it without a weapon.

But seconds later, something grabbed both his ankles. Cass was dragged back in the snow with a scream.

He turned over and kicked whoever was holding him. Now that he was on knees, he could get a good look at him. The assailant was white, about his father's age; a big man, bald-headed and broad. He had the burnished skin of a farmer. Cass realised belatedly that he'd shot him; a bleeding groove in his cheek proved that. Cass didn't recognise him, but that didn't surprise him. This nameless town was more a pit stop than a home.

"Would you stop?" the man shouted, Midlands accent slurring with his anger. Cassius hadn't stopped kicking, but he abruptly did now, when his father nodded at him. The assailant let go of Cassius' ankles gladly and stood, muttering under his breath. "You owe me, Jones. More than we agreed."

Her father put up a hand, eyes fixed on Cass. "Later, York."

It was a momentary bulwark against this conversation, but it worked. The big man stalked away, still cursing.

Cass tucked his legs closer to himself, hands splayed in the snow. In the back of his mind, he knew what had happened. His father had hired someone. Not to kill him, not even to maim him. But to show him and Thaddeus the value in his training. In staying strong against all the world's invisible dangers.

He wanted to be wrong and he hated that he wasn't. Even at twelve he had already seen too much of the world to know Mr Jones was right. Curse that part of him that was still a child: he wanted his father to love him, but he was certain this was as close as he'd ever get.

When he looked up, his father had his arms crossed. Thaddeus stood with the knife slack in his hands.

"What was that?" Thaddeus asked. "I thought it was a fucking *teras*."

Mr Jones ignored him. "You should have moved faster. Both of you. If that was *teras,* you'd be dead."

With a little bit of bravery, and a little bit of sullen stupidity, Cassius muttered, "You were no help."

It was the wrong thing to say. Mr Jones stalked forward. Before Cass had a chance to understand how greatly he'd overstepped, his father slapped him hard across the face. The sting was immediate. It blossomed over his days-old bruise from the last beating he'd taken.

Cassius shifted his gaze to Thaddeus. They locked eyes. His brother was the favourite, but it didn't do much to stop Mr Jones' anger. Not for the first time, he met his eye and urged him, hoped Thad could feel his urgency in his blood: Thaddeus had a knife, and a gun, and Mr Jones had his back turned, the rifle scattered somewhere in the snow. It would only take the right kind of will. The right kind of force.

For God's sake, Thad, do it, he wanted to scream. *Do it for us.*

He said nothing. Cass bit his tongue so hard it started to bleed. He broke eye contact with Thad, and in his periphery, watched as his brother put the knife away, put the gun back in its holster.

"You really think you have the wit to survive this world, boy?" his father hissed, finger jabbing towards his face. "You think you have what it takes? My whole life has been *teras*. There's not a human alive who remembers the world before. So you better believe I am doing this for you. For you to live! I won't have you being a faggot. Hear me? Weak, fucking fairy."

There was no mention of Thaddeus, but there never was. Cassius was the undesirable, the mistake. The boy who was too weak for a world like this.

Their father spat over his shoulder and sniffed. "Your mother's scavenging. I need to fish. Boat's leaving in an hour."

And just like that, he was gone.

"Need help getting up?" Thaddeus asked. *A test is in its own right.*

Cassius rolled and got up. "I'm fine," he lied. He wanted to cry. He wanted to yell that Thaddeus was meant to protect him; meant to realise the threat of their father and take him out.

And then where would we be? Dead, or dying. Another broken body to be eaten by monsters.

That is the last thought I have before I wake.

LESSON SIXTEEN

Immediately, I vomit. My mind splinters and pain floods my body; great throbbing pulses of it, making my hands spasm, my body convulse. Hands are on me—I flinch away, screaming—there's a danger in the softness with which they caress me. It could be anyone; Bellamy, Victoria, or someone closer to a stranger, and I might debase myself by crawling into their lap and weeping. Just for a moment of peace. A moment of affection.

I can't let that happen. I can't let them see me slithering and desperate and in pain. I roll away from the hands and the vomit and let my cheek, slick with tears, rest against the cold of the marble floor.

"Cassius, hey, hey," Bellamy sounds panicked, and there's a disconnect in my mind about him calling my name and sounding distressed, because he so often doesn't care. We are barely friends, aren't we?

"What happened?" Victoria screeches. I look up in time to see her do something incredibly brave and incredibly stupid. She beats her fists down on Meléti's bronze body. I gurgle out a *no*, because I half expect the monster to snap her pretty neck. But the *automaton* just waits there impassively for the extreme human emotion to wither away.

"You have made a mess in the library," Meléti says.

I laugh, disbelieving, and wipe the vomit from my mouth. "Seems I did."

In all this commotion, I don't notice what the *xenos* are doing. What Leo is doing. The ever-present anger that has kept him alive this long, the thing that has meant he's survived all this time in a world trying to kill him—overtakes him. I hear a scraping noise and when I turn, Leo is by the statue of Omphale, tugging out the iron spear clutched in her marble hand. His eyes are wide, and he's not looking at me. His eyes are for Meléti.

He's going to kill the thing.

Leo raises the spear, hefts it high, poised like a javelin. Through his shirt I watch his muscles tighten. I see everything in slow, excruciating detail. He slams forward with the spear. It leaves his grip, travels through the air. Meléti turns to look at it; seems to have a ridiculous amount of time to assess its direction, realise it will be hit, and move out of the way.

The *automaton* darts aside. The spear clangs against the marble, skidding sharp.

Leo pants, ducks low, and slides across the floor to reclaim the weapon.

Meléti blinks at him. "You have damaged the library," it says. "You will leave."

"Like hell I will," Leo spits, but as if by magic, the library's doors are swung open from some unseen force, and then Meléti charges forward. It shoves Leo out with one hand. Leo flies through the air, eyes wide and bulging, and manages to haul the spear before he lands and the doors slam shut.

This time, the spear doesn't miss its mark. Meléti hasn't had time to right itself. Instead, it raises a hand, as if it might compel the air to stop around it. Bronze tendon, dorsal muscle, bone—all of it explodes outwards with a sharp screeching whine as the spear tip shoots through it. The *automaton* barely reacts, even as sparks fly. There's no shudder of pain, no reaction. It merely pulls the spear free with its other hand, walks to Omphale's statue, and replaces the spear in her hand.

I stare at the door. I think on what Leo just risked. And it's the first time I realise how insane empathy is. This is the first time in a very long time someone is caring about me, without concern for themselves.

You're delirious. He needs you for the trials. He needs your insights.

But I don't want to believe that. Not when Leo was enraged and gambling his life away to strike a *teras* with a spear.

"Enough," I cough. I struggle to stand. Bellamy comes and helps me up.

"Good man," he whispers, with three pats on my back. The closest I'll come to affection from him, I imagine. "Good man. Feeling alright?"

I give him a tight nod and turn my attention to Meléti. "I gave you what you wanted. I paid your price. Now it's your turn."

Meléti blinks at me and moves to clean the mess I made after hurling up my insides. But as it works, finally, without another moment of hesitation, it says, "What information do you seek, Cassius Jones?"

I wrestle forth my memory of the paper Thaddeus left me. The third point on it, in particular.

*3. Plant from 2 is a **toxin**. Be careful to*

· · ·

"WHAT PLANTS DO you have at the University?" I ask, and then curse myself. "No, wait. How many questions do I get to ask?"

Meléti doesn't look my way. "However many it takes to clarify the information you seek."

Perfect. "Then: is there a greenhouse on the University's campus?"

"There is a greenhouse. It is not for students. It is protected."

"Protected," Victoria repeats. She folds her arms, shuffles close to Bellamy. "By what?"

I can guess, but I wait in case Meléti replies. It reacts like it hasn't heard her, which I imagine is some sort of stupid stipulation about who paid its required price.

Sighing, I repeat Victoria's question. Meléti whirrs, "By its protectors. It is not for students."

"Fucking useless," Bellamy spits. He rummages around in his pocket for a cigarette and tries to light it. Meléti spins to him and informs him smoking is not permitted in the library.

Bellamy's eyes flicker to me, then Victoria. "Fuck this. Sorry. But," and he puts both his hands up, cigarette taking priority. Meléti lets him out. I strain for a glimpse of Leo before the doors close, but I don't manage it.

"I'm sorry," Victoria whispers, flushing red. "Sorry for him."

You shouldn't be sorry for something he's done, I don't say. I just shake my head and touch her shoulder.

"What information are you trying to figure out?" Silas asks. He hasn't moved from his place at the wall.

"Thaddeus' paper says we'll encounter some kind of plant in the second trial. Says it's a toxin."

Silas nods. "Ask about the toxic plants in the greenhouse, then."

"Meléti. Are there toxic plants outside the greenhouse?"

"No."

I know it's not enough to hope, but a spark ignites in me. Perhaps the next trial will take place there.

"Which plants in the greenhouse are toxic?" I murmur.

"Only one," it says.

"Show me."

I don't see what it's done with my sick—thankfully—but when the *automaton* stands, the marble floor is scrubbed clean. Then it whirrs and turns and leads me up the staircase to the second level of the library.

It is overwhelmingly bright, all the light reflecting off the marble of the first floor. Up here, the floor is made of a deep wood. The boards creak as we walk across it, like something old groaning, disturbed in its sleep. Sconces line the walls with fire light. Rows upon rows of shelves stretch up to the ceiling. Meléti leads us to one, and then extends its body in a terrifying display; its torso spins violently like a corkscrew and separates from its legs, which then push upward with upsetting velocity until the *automation* is towering above us, thin and eerie in it inhumanness. It plucks a book from high above, and when it returns to its normal height I realise it has returned something that's barely more than a bound series of handwritten notes. There's no title. No author. Meléti opens the manuscript with speed to a particular page.

Botanical notes adorn the page. Green stems, fern-like leaves with toothed edges. Flowers like a cluster of white-headed acne on a cheek, curved and umbrella-shaped.

Hemlock.

"What are we meant to do with this information?" Victoria whispers beside me.

I shrug at her and take the book from Meléti's hands. "I don't suppose we are allowed to browse at our own leisure?" I ask it.

"You are not initiated," it says, as expected. "I am unable to leave you alone."

Part of me wants to tear this damn page out, but Thad's letter said we'd need the library for the fourth trial—let alone the years of study I'll have to endure should I make it in at all.

Which is still, surprisingly, something I want.

I hastily read the notes. It describes hemlock in great detail, and then its effects on humans. Respiratory failure, nervous system attacks, causing tremors, paralysis, muscle damage. The page gives me a fatal dosage—for humans. . .

And for *teras*.

I slam my finger onto the page. "There. Silas, Fred. You ever heard about this?"

I wonder if there are farms across England, generating gallons of the stuff. But the siblings just look at me like I'm mad and shake their heads.

"Would've been mighty useful to know that," Fred whispers. "But I've never heard of London farming this. Maybe somewhere else. Further north, or. . . " She trails off. Her fingers glide across the page and land upon its fatal dose. She glances back to Silas, then to me. "But does it work for all of them?"

Meléti acts like we aren't speaking, so I turn the next page and read thoroughly. The book uses the University's classing system of the *teras*, which was generated by an early University Scholar, Stefan Albitz.

Teras are ranked in tiers, from F to S, where F denotes the lowest rank—make no mistake, though, these beasts can still kill. The *cerastes* that hid from the *manticore* was this rank. The *manticore* itself would be an *S* tier. Incredibly deadly. Incredibly fast.

There are a few crosses next to affected *teras*. Of course, the *manticore* is not amongst them. But hemlock can apparently destroy the gastrointestinal tract of a *cerastes*, so there's that.

"Alright," I say. "This is in the greenhouse. I don't know what the next trial is, or even if it will involve this plant, but Thad wrote it down. So if we see some, let's grab it."

"For what?" Fred asks.

"You saw the page, I'm sure. It was burned. Your guess is as good as mine."

No one replies to me. Mentioning this note was apparently a bad idea, because some unspoken anger settles over them, a tenseness even the damned *automaton* seems to notice.

"Shall I take the book from you, Mr Jones?" It says.

"Hang on." I try to memorise it. I ask Fred and Silas to memorise it, too.

Cerberus Class, Arion Class, Nemean Class, Stymphalian Class, Caledonian Class. I can't remember their dosages. The *automaton* prompts me again, and Silas and Fred are looking at me unhappily. All this over a note. I worry I've squandered this opportunity, and try one last time to get the dosages in my mind, but when Meléti prompts me a third time, I give it back without another thought, thank it, and walk down the stairs.

"You're not going to address it, then?" Silas asks before I can wrench the library doors open.

"Oh, no, I plan to address it," I say, pulling them wide. Bellamy startles, cigarette barely more than a burning stub. Leo is on the ground, knees under his chin. He scrambles to rise when he sees me.

I look back at Silas. "Just don't want to have to repeat myself."

"What did you find?" Bellamy asks, and I briefly tell them.

"Though it seems my brother's letter has made you all hate me," I finish.

A pause. No one breaks it, for nearly a minute. It's still raining outside. I look around for the gun that was thrown out of the library's doors. Leo proffers it from his coat.

"Thank you," I say. He nods. "And my brother's letter?"

This promotes an agitated rustle. Leo looks down at his hands—really, what was I expecting? He was too good to be true—and says, "What have you done with the rest of it?"

I laugh, but no one else is laughing with me. They're all eager to hear, all agreeing with Leo's line of questioning. So I sniff. "That's all that was there. I swear it on my brother's rotting corpse. It's the only help we have."

"You didn't tell us soon enough," Bellamy says. "Jesus, Cass. Aren't we friends?"

I stare at him, because it's a very good question. But then I think about the way he acted in there. The concern he had for me. And I'm ashamed immediately.

"Of course we are," I say, and light a cigarette of my own. "But my brother used his dying words to get me into that room, and I wasn't sure. . ." I trail off, because I don't have much of a good excuse. "I'm sorry, alright? I know I pitched the whole working as a team thing, and then I've gone and pulled this, but now we all know as much as each other."

If it was done to me, I would be furious. But I am hoping the nature of these trials means this lot will band with me despite the stunt I pulled. Fred and Silas keep exchanging looks, and I don't think I've done anything to have them hating me quite so much—but neither can I fault them for not trusting me.

"Why didn't you just ask us to come with you?" Victoria whispered. "You didn't have to lie about running off to church."

"I didn't lie," I say. And then the flash of the dead man's body, lumps of viscera, broken bones. . . I swallow down my bile and sigh. "The gun I have. That's from Thaddeus, too. I took it and I've had it on me all afternoon. And when I left the wing, I heard something."

"Screams," Leo offers. He glances at Fred and Silas. "A gunshot. We heard them, too. Thought maybe the second trial was starting. That's. . . why I went through your things."

I pretend like he hasn't already admitted to spying on me as I found this letter beneath the boards in the first place, and continue the story. "I heard a thud, first, before the screams. A student jumped from his tower room," I say, far too calmly.

Everyone freezes.

"What?" Victoria's hand flies to her mouth. "He killed himself?"

"He tried to." I dig around for the gun and open the barrel for everyone to see my five remaining bullets. "He wasn't quite dead yet, you see."

"You killed him," Fred says. I can't tell if it's respect in her voice, or a resigned sort of disgust.

I shrug. "In the sense that I pulled the trigger."

"Cassius," Victoria says, and nothing more.

I look her in the eye. "The dean found us. Not a single word for the dying man. Just told me to put him out of his misery."

I close the barrel with a click.

"Jesus," Bellamy says, reeling away. "*Jesus.*"

And because I'm already speaking, I can't seem to stop myself.

"When I went to the church, I found no solace there." I leave that thread hanging; I'm not sure where God sits for these people. "So I thought about the letter, and I came here. And then I saw Blood Hunters. Someone else has done a runner. So that's two of our cohort dead outside of trials. Three if you count the boy who confronted the dean."

Bellamy rubs his face, and Victoria turns to stare at the

rain. Fred grabs her brother and says they'll see us back at the rooms—they want little to do with me. I know they don't trust me. Leo is the only one who maintains his eye contact. Stormy expression. I don't care about Fred or Silas' opinion.

I do care about Leo's.

We walk back in relative silence, Victoria and Bellamy ahead of us, sharing a cigarette, arm in arm. The lit cigarette bobs forward through the dark corridors.

I feel Leo next to me. Feel his heat, the sheer size of him. The urge to link our arms assaults me, and I do something idiotic: I let my bare pinkie finger graze the backside of his hand, and then I flinch away as if I was burned even though Leo doesn't move.

If he notices, he does me a great service by saying nothing.

"Are you upset with me?" I am compelled to ask.

"No. Not at all. I know why you'd hide such a thing. We are strangers."

I blush for no reason other than shame. He's right, but I feel badly for it. I'm a hypocrite for telling them all we need to work together, and then for hiding such a note.

But Thaddeus is your brother. Not theirs. And it's all you have left of him.

"Are *you* upset with *me*?" Leo asks suddenly. He gestures for my cigarette before I can answer, and I'm stunned into handing it over. He breathes in, holds it, coughs madly into the crook of his arm. Shaking his head, he hands it back to me.

"Still can't get used to it?" I ask.

"Disgusting stuff. No offence."

"None taken," I say, though after one more puff I stub the thing under my foot, worried that every pore in me is leaking out the scent of tobacco.

Back at the tower, there's not much else to do but sleep.

It must be past midnight by now, and we have no idea when we're meant to be awake. The Lins are nowhere to be seen. Probably asleep. No one makes the effort to chat. It's been too long a day.

Victoria and Bellamy go to bed together, without any pretence of heading to their individual rooms. I say nothing, because I cannot blame them, and because I am, admittedly, jealous. Everything in my body is tense and unsettled. For plenty of people, I'm sure that would be enough to feel absolutely no lick of lust. Well, I envy those people.

Something about the horridness of the world means I crave to lose myself completely in another. I get so wrapped up in the sin of it, the layered transgressions I make against God—I cannot marry my lover, my lover is a man—that I briefly forget none of it really matters, in the end. What use is there in getting worked up about my so-called sins when living to thirty is a luxury? Hell is here. Hell is on earth, clawing at London's walls. And if I can live a little happier for taking someone to bed, why shouldn't I do it?

So this time when Leo says goodnight, I say wait.

He waits. He looks at me like I'm about to tell him something secret. And it is secret, in a way—my desire. I like to think I'm not this kind of person. But when I voice my question to Leo now, he will know exactly what I am, and what I crave. Even before he's touched me, that's a vulnerable position to be in.

The alternative, though, is letting every rabid thought from the day eat away my peace. I won't sleep tonight. I *need* to sleep tonight.

"Do you want to. . ." I say, and I flush immediately, because I'm a coward. I gesture my head towards the closed door of my room. "Would you like to have a drink with me? In my room?"

I tack *my room* on the end, as if it isn't the most important part in all this. The private, liminal space of *my room*. The door that we can close. The illicit things we might do to one another. Leo glances between the door and me, and the look in his eye darkens. There's an open yearning in them, a hunger. I wonder if he has the same qualms as I do about sin and men, before I realise God's kingdom beyond the wards is broken. It is much easier to overlook so-called misdeeds when death is a near certainty.

"I'd like that," Leo says, with a small smile.

We are alone in the corridor, but I still make my footsteps as silent as I can. I have a latent shame in me, if that wasn't obvious. I fear being seen; I fear being known. Thus I lead Leo to my room, half brimming with anxiety, and with lust. We cross the threshold. In the dark, I stumble over to light the lamps on my desk, and then at my bedside table.

I want this. I also never want to be touched. I want to be fucked like an animal. I want to drag my virginity from the gates of hell.

My head is a mess and my heart is hammering against my chest. I'm so obviously on edge, Leo gently touches my shoulders and asks, "Everything alright, Mr Jones?"

"Just splendid, Mr Shaw," I say, and then I crumple. I hate the way I sound. It's too standoffish. Too deflective. "Leo," I say. "I. . ."

"You don't have to say anything," he whispers. And then he gives me an out. He cocks his head and smiles. "It's only a drink."

Of course. I nod. "Only a drink," I say with a smile I don't feel. Disappointment rumbles in my belly—which is stupid! Half a second ago, I was nervous enough I thought I would throw up. Half a second ago, I wasn't sure I wanted this. But when he looks at me with that gentle smile, and the touch, I want him. To be beneath him.

Leo closes the door. I go to my knees by the hollow floorboard and take out the other bottle of liquor stashed away there. Once it's in my hand, I take a long swig from it before I hand it to Leo.

"Cass," he says, worriedly, half-scolding. "Calm down."

"Perfectly calm," I say, and then I stagger up to standing and drape myself between the desk and the window.

He smiles—he knows I'm lying—and drinks deep as well. Then he comes close, to put the bottle on the desk. We lock eyes for a moment before he retreats near the bed.

"Have you done this before?" he asks me, without looking at me.

It is not such a simple question. "Yes," I say. I feel the urge to explain myself, as if I'm in trouble, but I swallow that. "Yourself?"

He glances at me. "Yes." Then he smiles a little, not sheepish, but confident.

Something in me unwinds. The admission itself makes us co-conspirators, harbourers of queer desires in a queer little world.

I tell myself I won't smoke another cigarette, but I have a man in my room, and the door is closed, and that is intimacy to me. A private room and a private moment, and no fear of my brother catching me, or the look my mother will give me, or my father trying to cave my face in. So before I can register how nervous I am, my shaking hand lights a cigarette, and I move to the window to smoke it. Leo sits on the edge of the bed, leaning forward. It still groans with his weight.

The only light is from the lamp on the bedside table, and the other one I have going on the desk. It's muted; everything is baked in terracotta glow, slight earthy redness. Only parts of Leo's face are lit. Cheekbones. Part of the sharp jaw. A tendon in his neck that keeps tensing and untensing. Shadows are our friend tonight.

"Why are you so nervous, Cassius, if you've done this before?"

I don't know how to answer that without opening up my body and pulling out all my insides, like a haruspex, as if Leo might parse from them an explanation regarding the mess of my life. I laugh a little and shrug, turning back to the window and the dark rain outside. "I don't know. I think, perhaps, because when it ends, it ends. With men in London, I mean. We rarely, if ever, see each other again. But you and I will probably be colleagues."

"If you're worried about your reputation. . ."

"I barely have any of that. Honestly, I'm not sure if it's what people think of me, or what I think of myself." And then, because I worry how much of a turn off this conversation is, I look back at him over my shoulder. "But I wouldn't have invited you in if it wasn't what I wanted."

I know I'm inconsistent. That's faith for you; it messes you up. It's always in conflict with what I really want. I turn to the window and smoke the cigarette unhurriedly, letting the tobacco-calm wash over me. I'll need to restock, soon, from the University's dwindling coffers. I stare out at the pitch-black night and the rain and the silhouette of London in the distance.

There is no mirror in the room, and the window glass is fogged up by the rain and the mist. It means I have no chance to meet my own eye and talk myself out of this. No chance to find something disgusting in my gaze. I have only the rapid beating of my red-hot heart, and the heat curling around my groin. Only desire. A raw and eager thing.

When Leo stands up, the bed releases him with a springing whine. I don't turn around. I wait, holding myself tensely, eyes on the cigarette as it smokes away to nothing. Leo's arm wraps around me. It's not an embrace. His hand, rough and calloused and sun-kissed, skims over mine. He plucks the cigarette from my fingers and flings it out the window. I watch the tiny burning end as it disappears into the dark, drowned by the rain.

Leo grabs my hips and spins me. My lower back smacks the stone, but my shoulders, my head, my neck—I'm half bent out the window. The cold refreshing night greets me. I fill my lungs up with it, exhaling the last of the smoke and replacing it with petrichor. Rainwater drizzles from the awning onto my forehead, my hair. Leo's hands are on my hips, palm of his hand grinding into my pelvis like he's fighting me. Then one arm snakes through the window, presses the wetness of my shirt against my back. He climbs between my legs, leverages them apart. I don't stop him. I spread myself wider.

I look up; he is backlit by the lamps, only the high bones of his face and the whites of his eyes are gleaming with the light. I can barely see him, but when his lips split open, his teeth catch the glow. He leans in. I lean too.

He kisses me. It's an inhale of a kiss; I smell the deepness of him, the golden amber, the leather of old books, the sweat. I am flooded by it. My hands tangle in his shirt and I fancy I can feel our hearts matching time, entangling themselves in a dance. He pulls away to look at me, and I am so thankful for the darkness of the room. I am embarrassed. I have a priest in my ear calling me a sinner, and a devil on my shoulder desperate for the intimacy. For the love.

God, is it such a sin to want to be loved?

He kisses me again, forcefully, pushing our faces together. Teeth skim my lip, sharp, biting. He drives me against the desk; ink bottles clatter against one another, chair scraping against the floor. Leo kicks off his shoes and I put my hand to the back of his neck to keep him from pulling away—we keep kissing, our hips grinding impotently against each other. I feel the tenting in his pants, feel my own groin throb in response. Leo grunts; I look, I see his eyebrow quiver, eyes closed tight. His hands are inescapable things. His grip is so strong, when he moves me there's no fighting it. We stumble back from the desk and the window, blindly moving toward the bed. Leo's hands go to my shirt. I go straight for his pants. I unbuckle the belt, move to the buttons. He tugs my shirt free and throws the offending thing out of sight, moving immediately to kiss my bare neck, my chest, and I lose the purchase on his pants. He takes my hand in his, moves my arms high to grip his hair. I am pulled into him, eager for this closeness, and then I'm tugged down and we're on the bed, a messy tangle of limbs, panting. On top of him, I look down to see his face cast in red shadow. Both his hands go to my hips, keeping me still above him, and he thrusts up against me, a desperate little grind. He is straining in his pants, now. Those buttons are probably killing him.

With a grunt, he spins us so my back is on the bed, pulls my legs apart in the same motion. Gone is the cautious tenderness; he's hungry and he's using strength to his advantage. Flush against my groin, he hastily undoes the buttons. I kick my shoes off behind his back. Before I'm done, he's kissing me again, tugging my head back with a firm, possessive grip on my hair.

I make a noise, a little moan—I can't help it—and he surges forward, one hand pulling hard, wrenching my neck back, the other splayed on my chest, and I buck my hips like an animal, eager for him to take my pants off. Leo gives an insistent tug and I arch for him, shielding my face because now it's only me straining in my drawers, and the muted lamplight is too much, and then Leo doesn't stop with my pants. My breath hitches as he hooks two fingers on the waistband, pulling them just low enough my aching cock is freed. I squeeze my eyes shut, hands on my face. Leo pries them away and kisses me, shuffling out of his own pants as he does. Desire is stronger than my embarrassment. I reach down and arch my back and slip the drawers free, holding Leo in a kiss. The other man runs his hand over my trembling belly, and takes me in the palm of his hand, just once, just enough for me to cant my hips. Then before I know what's happening, he pulls both my legs over his shoulders and folds himself over me, cock spilling onto my belly as he reaches for the bedside table and the oil top-up for the lamp. He coats his fingers, eyes on me, and I know he wasn't lying when he said he's done this before. He coats himself, goes to coat me, but I don't like the feel of that. Wordlessly, I push his fingers aside and reached for the other, his cock-filled hand, pulling it towards me until it's lined up.

We look at each other. He pushes forward.

"God," Leo moans on entry, "*God*," and it's the most beautiful prayer I've ever heard. A blessing and a begging all in one. He pushes deeper and it *hurts* and I'm tensing around him until he's all the way inside, moaning high as I adjust. I feel him quiver inside me.

"Cass?" he whispers, and in answer I kiss him and gently move until he moves with me, until I feel him building pace and I'm reeling with every rebound, every thrust, pleasure popping like starbursts behind my eyes.

I am a mess. I go to reach for myself, and Leo's hands snake through mine and wrench both my arms high until I'm stretched out beneath him. Weakly, desperately, I thrust, trying to grind myself against his belly. I am swollen, leaking, eager; Leo thrusts without stopping, until my mind is blank and frustrated tears prick the corner of my eyes, and I whisper my own prayer up to him, to Leo, the closest thing to divinity I have ever touched. *Please, please, please.* I want the oblivion. I hook my feet behind Leo's back, and then I beg for him to touch me, and when his hand wraps around me I curve and moan and arch. Leo empties himself into me. We lock eyes. Connection and a closeness, a communion between the two of us. I come quickly after, my consciousness briefly ejecting itself, to float in bliss above my body.

He looks at me, for a long while, eyes heavy. And we don't speak. There's nothing to say, really, nothing that can be said. It is a perfect and protected moment. Why sully it with words and hopes and fears?

Leo leans forward. We kiss. And then we let sleep take us, a suspended limbo between the moment of pleasure and the horror of the new day.

Part of me hopes I don't wake up.

17

LESSON SEVENTEEN

But I do, of course. And when I wake I am alone, as if nothing happened the night before. The sheets beside me are mussed up and coldly damp. Leo is long gone.

It's still early when I wake. No bells have rung. Out the window, it's barely light. It's tempting to roll over and go back to sleep, but I force myself up onto the cold boards, just to read the books they've left us up here in case something useful is hiding there, or in case all my knowledge of Latin and Greek has simply escaped from my mind.

Mainly, though, it's because the nerves set in the instant my eyes open, and when I try sleeping, the only thing to get my mind off the trials is the thought of Leo fucking me. Of the sweet pleasure and the release. I realise belatedly it was one of the first times I've ever fucked in a bed. No back alleys. No awkward, half-standing sessions. A bed. A closed door. I put my head in my hands because I can feel the flush on my face.

Don't you dare. Don't you dare get attached.

This is not a good coping mechanism to develop.

So, as I said: I get up, and dress—in uniform, this time. It looks good on me, though the vest curls oddly around my hips, and something about the get-up makes me appear five years younger. I spend a few minutes trying to put my hair in some style that won't make me look so damn young, and then decide there are more terrible things to be worried about today.

Before I can spiral, I step out of the room, and wish we had a pot of coffee up here. I expect the sitting room to be empty at this time, but I hear the boards creak with weight. Peering in, I'm surprised to see Bellamy on the ground, arms around his knees and staring into a warm, crackling fire.

"Morning," I say.

He jumps, sucks in a startled breath before he glances back at me. "Morning."

I creep in without another word, and now being awake seems silly. It's too cold, and I could use the sleep. Studying random texts for the sake of it is a fool's errand. But now that I've announced myself, I can hardly leave Bellamy here. I take a seat by the window and search through the books. There's Plutarch's *Rise and Fall of Athens,* a translated copy of Apuleius' *The Golden Ass,* Virgil, Horace, Ovid, Catullus, Varro. I fiddle idly with Catullus, just for the fun of reading something about sodomy before the sun has fully risen.

"I couldn't sleep," Bellamy says suddenly. His voice is heavy and croaky, deep drawl seemingly stuck on something in his throat. I freeze when he says it, because the tone makes me feel like I've done something wrong. I wonder how long he's been awake. I wonder if he heard the noises Leo and I made, the squeaking betrayal of my bed. Would that be the end of this friendship? I already pushed it far yesterday, when he learned about Thad's note.

But Bellamy doesn't turn any accusing eye on me. He just

slumps sadly into his hands. He hasn't bathed, by the look of him; sweat, the smell of liquor, a general sense of despair.

I close the book and move to the floor. "What is it?"

He glances at me, shrugs. He doesn't have the words, so I try to supply them for him. "The trials?"

"Of course," he scoffs.

I ignore the tone. "Did you. . . have a dream?"

Bellamy swallows. "No," he says, but I think he's lying. "Just kept laying there. Looked down, saw her in my arms, and thought. . ." he shakes his head and looks away from me. "I don't know. I don't know what I was expecting. I think part of me thought they'd be academic tests. Not physical. Not *teras*. And now, what the hell am I meant to do with that? I have to accept it, because I can't leave. But that means eating a fat load of shit about the goodness of this place." He sniffles, mumbles something I can't quite catch. "I mean, Jesus, Cass, am I a fucking idiot? I really thought the University was *good*."

It's so easy, seeing everything in black and white, morality laid out in simple to comprehend categories. I can't fault him, and I don't know what to say, because part of me thinks the same. But another part doesn't. Whether it's shock or a general apathy, I almost expected this. Then I sit back on my haunches and think of Bellamy's words. *I saw what this place did to Thad*, I think of saying, to explain why I'm not so affected by it. But Bellamy's elder sister graduated, too. Perhaps she was more stable than Thad. *Nothing in this world is as easy as 'good' or 'bad'*—I also don't say this. I think of God, who is goodness incarnate, and all the bad, twisted things humans have done in His name. I think of the chapel on campus, and how seamlessly the Church can intertwine the horrors of Satan with the *teras*, how every graduate of the University can be made agents of Christ in the same vein.

Bellamy has spent so much of his life in London, I don't

think he has the capacity to comprehend the weight of the University's betrayal. The *xenos*, and me, and even Thad—we know human nature. The nastiness in it. The capability to put oneself before all others. But Bellamy, Victoria. . . they trusted the institution that promised protection. I worry that Bellamy is going to crack, and this close to the next trial, I'm sure that will kill him.

"It's because you're a good man yourself," I tell him, hand on his shoulder. He doesn't move away, which is how I know how low he really is. "And good men think justice comes before all, for everyone in this world. You saw the University as a protector, and a necessity, and maybe it still is, even with what we know."

"But if they're willing to do this," he said, "what else have they done?"

That stumps me. I take my hand away and stare into the fire with him. I change tactics, because I need him focused, and maybe a soft and gentle lie will make him feel better. "That's why you need to secure a place—cause if you don't, you forfeit it to some soulless bastard. We can't have any more of them running this place."

"Maybe soulless bastards are the only ones who make it."

I turn; Fred is leaning against the doorframe, arms crossed. She is in uniform, which for women is a grey pleated skirt over stockings, though Fred is wearing a pair of her brother's pants.

I say nothing to her comment—what am I meant to say? —and in the silence, I watch in my periphery as Bellamy slowly straightens himself. I know him. I know he's determined to rid himself of any sign of physical weakness. Hand to God, he is regretting speaking to me this morning with anything other than his usual confident drawl.

Fred sniffs, and gestures vaguely to the window. "Second trial. Hemlock. Is that all we have?"

I shake my head, thinking of Thaddeus' paper. "It said *plant from two is a toxin*, but not that it had anything to do with the trial itself."

"I agree," Silas said, appearing out of nowhere. His face practically materialises over his sister's shoulder, which is upsetting and haunting this early in the morning. "BUT I think we will be doing our future selves a disservice by not taking some today. If we see it."

With that sorted, we gather the rest of our little party, and walk to the Great Hall. As we go, I recite the classes affected by the hemlock. Cerberus Class, Arion Class, Stymphalian Class, Caledonian Class. I hope we face none of these today. They're all D tier and higher, making them formidable enemies.

"Alright?" Leo asks me when we're outside and crossing the field, and it's such a benign little sentence I almost start laughing. I look at him, I see the face he makes when he comes, and I immediately turn away.

"Peachy as always, Mr Shaw," I say. He gives me a nod. He says nothing else.

I wish last night had diffused the tension between us, but it seems to only be worse.

"Down three this morning," Dean Drearton announces, as if it's eggs that are missing from the kitchen. "Two *xenos*, which did *not* surprise me—no offence to our lovely applicants from beyond the wards, but you do have quite a lot less to lose. Which is to say, there was one Londoner who exited the mortal coil last night. Now, I know all this is a lot. But London—and the entirety of England—needs graduates who are willing to do what it takes. We need protectors, the very best of the best. Please focus. These trials are only a taste of what you'll face should you graduate."

I cross my arms. *And we can't be bothered wasting time training up the worst of you.*

"Today," the dean continues, "will be the second trial for this cohort."

We are gathered, as expected, in front of a dazzlingly large greenhouse. It looks to be nearly a hundred metres long, though I can't see most of it from this angle. The greenhouse is deep into campus. We were escorted here by Blood Hunters—the same ones who killed the runaway, I imagine. Thankfully, no one bolted on the walk over. I am not in the mood for seeing more death.

On the walk over, I could see the building had two dome-shaped pavilions; a colossal Victorian-style greenhouse, green-cast iron. Up close, the glass is slightly frosted by the humidity, dewy droplets obscuring much of the inside beyond a vague green haze of plant life. If there are *teras* waiting inside, I can't see them. But there are plenty of shadows. A dozen places for beasts to lurk. And the *automaton* said the greenhouse had protectors.

"Our last trial focused on individual survival skills. But this test will be for groups. Pre-picked, of course. Your roommates."

A shudder runs through us all as early alliances are either secured, or threatened by sleeping arrangements. I thank my own damn self for cutting a deal with the dean, even if that will come back to haunt me. A *manticore* is S tier. It took out a whole squad of graduate Hunters. What the fuck was I thinking?

No time to panic now. You might die here, and never have to worry about that.

I take a deep breath and hold it. Victoria and Bellamy step a little closer to me, and the *xenos* move towards one another. I'm wary of that. I give Leo a glance, because a divide in our team will bring nothing good for any of us. If anything, fucking should have made us closer. I give him a nod. I'm relieved when he nods back.

Trusting is difficult enough, but I hope to trust him.

The dean's voice booms loud. "The trial is this. Imagine a town beyond the wards is being harassed by *teras*. They're quick, they are hard to pin down. Your duty is to *not* to simply exit the greenhouse. You must eliminate the *teras* threat."

A few panicked murmurs rise up that the dean resolutely ignores. "Of course, you will have weapons. And yes: I am aware that, for some of you, Hunter is not the mantle you would choose, should you secure a place in the University. Not every one of you needs to fight—but we do expect a basic level of survivability for all our graduates." He pauses, rather dramatically, though I'm not sure if it's put on, because his voice has a quaver in it when he next speaks. "Times are changing, you see. The University's role may shift with it. Artificers may need to work harder and quicker, on the field, to get our Hunters back in action in a timely manner. Scholars may need to consult onsite. We cannot have these disciplines vulnerable. Understand? Good," he claps his hands before any of us can reply.

Leo leans close to me and whispers, "You were right. This will be a war college soon."

I don't want to think about that. Something in my body packages away my terror. I feel, suddenly, close to nothing. Not the bitter cold. Not the misted rain. Not even the heat of Leo at my side. Whatever primal urge to live that sits in my gut is shutting down everything else, making sure I don't lose myself to panic. I check the pockets of my uniform. Thad's gun, with its five remaining bullets, sits at my right. The sparker is at my left. I pat them down. I check them again. I do this for several minutes, as the first group heads into the greenhouse.

We wait. I see Peter Drike and some crew of his—room-mates, or people to terrorise, I'm not sure. He grabs one of them by their neck and hauls them close, aggressive, whispering in their ear, only to shove them away again a second later.

There's no commentary. We aren't told what happens, but there is, once again, screaming. It's muffled only slightly by the distance and the glass, faint cries like banshee wails rippling through the air.

When my name is called, I am jolted back into the present. Fred moves first, dragging Silas forward. I linger, because Leo lingers, and as he steps forward, he asks me to describe hemlock.

I do, but I look up at him and I think: God, I don't want you to die for a plant. Even if it screws me over in the next trial, don't you dare lose your head now for a *plant*. But instead, I reach out, grazing the side of my pinkie against his hand, and my heart swells with ridiculous joy when he doesn't flinch away.

"Best of luck, Mr Jones and co," the dean calls. Fred looks back at us, lingering on me for a moment too long, and when I nod, she shoves open the greenhouse door.

We are assaulted, immediately, by a muggy humidity. My body shivers at the change, shrugging off the cold for this. All of us gather around the entrance, tense and unmoving. Butterflies flit about in the air. A droning buzz of insects makes for ambience. There is no other sound, though we strain to listen.

"No hemlock in this room," Silas says. "Far too hot."

"But probably *teras*," Bellamy mutters. "So let's not be daft."

Tree shaped cast iron columns run to the ceiling. The plants here are tropical.

To our left is a table practically devoid of weapons. We are only the second group to move through, but it seems the first lot took liberty to strip us of anything useful. There is a tiny percussion handgun—ridiculous in size, as if for a child—but it is old. It takes powder and it will be no use in a fight against *teras*. I review what's left, and I'm surprised that most of the long-range weapons remain. A flintlock, like the one I used to use on hunts, is sitting there. That one I do take, just for the comfort of another weapon. But when I check its barrel, it only has one shot.

"They took all the close-range weapons," I say. "We need to look out for some."

"Not sure it did them much good," Silas mutters.

We turn to him. He stands over a patch of blood; a great deal of it, near the end of the room. This pavilion is separate; there's a door at the end of the room. After a minute of tense canvassing, we relax. No *teras* in this room—as far as we can see. Whatever made that bloody mess is long gone. There's no human body, either, which is a relief.

But who knows how long that luxury will last.

"I'll open the door," I say. Most of us are weapon-less, and besides, this humidity is making me sweat. I ready the flintlock gun and put my hand on the knob.

Do it. Do it.

I have to trick myself into opening it, wrenching it back at the same time I shove the flintlock through, half my body shielded by the door. Nothing rips the gun out of my hand. Nothing attacks me. I strain to hear; ever so faintly, in the distance, I hear a wheezing. My body reacts; gooseflesh ripples up on my skin. I carefully open the door all the way and it betrays me by whining loudly. I pause. The wheezing keen doesn't stop.

Psalm 22 is in my head, echoing in the voice of my father, who used to genuflect to the cross we had in the hovel. Everyday would be the same utterance, perhaps one taken too literally.

He would say:

DELIVER *my life from the sword, my precious life from the power of the dogs.*

Rescue me from the mouth of the lions; save me from the horns of the wild oxen.

I will declare your name to my brothers; in the congregation I will praise you.

AND I THINK my father believed, in some regard, that the Lord would step in personally. That an angel might come to rid this forsaken land of the devil's work. But as I step into this greenhouse, and the psalm spills into my head, I think Dean Drearton is another lion to watch out for.

"Alright, Mr Jones?" Leo whispers. It's a kindness, to get me to move before the others realise how distracted I am.

"Of course, Mr Shaw," I whisper back.

One by one, we filter in, until all of us are lined up along the wall. This room is cooler. Gone is the uncomfortable, overbearing warmth. We stay fixed to the wall, freshly tense. There's chatter somewhere—I crane my head for birds, and see none—and then a metallic scraping makes me jump. I turn in time to see Bellamy dragging a metal pipe from the ground. More blood is splattered over it.

We wait in silence, gathering courage. At this point, I have to wonder if this trial is about nerves. I am still sweating, despite the change in temperature. Beside me, Victoria has grown ever paler. She clutches to Bellamy with a fierceness that turns her knuckles white.

"Cassius," Leo whispers. I jump at the sound. He nods down the hall. I follow his eyes, scanning for whatever he's seen, flintlock gun raised.

"No." He comes around me, one hand on my waist, right arm pressing gently against my face as he points.

Tiny white flowers, fern-like leaves. I exhale and say aloud, "Hemlock."

Fred nods. "I'll get it."

Silas moves half a step forward with his sister but gives up as she creeps forward along the path, body pressed low and shielded by a line of conifers, geraniums, ferns—a beautiful backdrop for violence. She shudders to a stop, on her knees, hand on her mouth. Fred scrambles backwards and spins to us, eyes wide.

Leo and I give each other a look, but we move forward nonetheless. The lot of us, an impotent army, edge forward and help Fred up from the ground.

"*Teras?*" Silas asks.

Fred shakes her head and points. The path splits left and right around another set of trees, and a small patch where the hemlock sits. To the right lies a bloody mess. Two people are gathered there.

A girl I don't recognise has her hands covered in blood. It goes nearly up to her elbow, the white shirt completely drenched with it, as if she's stuck her hand in someone's body. I scan, looking for the wound, and can't find one.

"Help," she murmurs, not looking at us. Her eyes stay on the boy beneath her. He isn't moving, but I don't see why until I edge around the girl sobbing over him. Several deep gouges have opened up his stomach. Skin split open, flesh pulled apart in red strings. His stomach is exposed. He is holding his organs. Intestines spill out of his arms onto the dirty floor. I am hit with a freezing shock—Thaddeus, Thaddeus, *my brother,* my brother holding his guts, an armful of his organs, God, he's dead—and I turn away violently. I will myself not to throw up. Pray. Pray again.

My God, my God, why have you forsaken me? Why are you so far from saving me, so far from the words of my groaning?

"He's dead," Victoria says. She moves to squat beside the weeping girl. "You have to get up. Don't you want to live? You have to get up."

"No, no, *no,*" the girl screams. Suddenly it isn't silent sobbing. Her body heaves with grief; her body can't contain it, and it spews out of her in a pitchy scream.

We back away and tense, waiting for the *teras* that did this to emerge. It doesn't.

"This is ridiculous," Bellamy croaks. He lets the metal pole fall to his side. "Where is the damn thing? Aren't we meant to kill it? Hey," he drops down beside Victoria, tries to get the sobbing girl's attention by snapping his fingers in her face, "Hey, did you kill it? Did your group kill it?"

"Stop it," Victoria mutters. Her own voice starts to rise into a sob. "For God's sake, Bellamy, *stop it.*"

Bellamy mutters something in his flat voice—all the vulnerability from the morning has been swallowed, apparently—and he pushes away from Victoria. I know he's on edge, but he's letting it leak out of him.

Fred gestures her head towards the hemlock. "Alright just to grab it?" she whispers to Silas.

"It's only poisonous if you ingest it," he informs her, without looking away from the sobbing girl. Fred moves and squats to wrench it free, and Silas says, "But I suppose there's no harm in—"

Two screams sound. One is a great, triumphant cry that curdles, croaking and clicking undercutting the tone. The other is human—I spin in time to see massive destructive claws tear into the girl's face. In the same instant, the *teras* is gone. Victoria screams and staggers back. Blood gushes as half the girl's cheek sloughs off. Her hands hover in front of her torn face, screaming, *screaming*, and all of us are caught by shock. For too long, we simply don't move.

The next swooping attack goes for Fred.

I watch as the *teras* emerges from the trees. It is huge, coming up to one's navel, its wingspan the size of a tall human. Its body is muscular and feathered, a malformed buzzard, overly large. The talons are deadly, just great, hooked toes that dive at Fred's face. And the head—God—I jolt away and raise the flintlock gun, but the thing is too fast.

Harpy.

It has the head of a shrieking woman, hair whipping around its pale face; its mouth is open wide and when it screeches, a thin, flat tongue emerges. Fred rolls out of the way, torn out hemlock in her grip. The harpy dives again. Talons flex over Fred's head. This time I'm forced to fire. Either my shot goes wide or the harpy dodges, too quick for me to see. It shrieks and shreds up Fred's arm. Silas wrenches the pipe from Bellamy's motionless hands and screams, charging for his sister. The harpy masterfully darts and weaves, and it's clear to me Silas is still affected by his wound. Three great overhead swings later—enough to deter the harpy for a moment—and he clutches at his side. The grey vest grows sticky with blood.

"Get to cover!" I hiss.

I run to the left and hunker low against a tree. Thin scratching branches snap against my neck as I push close, catching my breath. The others move similarly, except Victoria, who weakly pulls at the wounded girl's arm. She is sobbing, gripping tight to the dead boy.

"Leave her," I hear Bellamy hiss, and my stomach twists—not at the decision, but at its necessity. What kind of man am

I becoming if ensuring that girl's death doesn't make me flinch? It's barely been three days.

Leo rushes in beside me, panting. He fixes me a look, then his eyes wander to the girl.

"She wouldn't survive," he says. I hate that he says it. "Out of the wards, I mean." He swallows and I think he's done, until he says, "You have to be willing to walk away. To protect yourself. Like you did with Thaddeus."

It's a gut punch. I'm not sure he meant it how I'm taking it—how soulless I am becoming, how cruel and hardened—and I try to look at him with a stony, accepting expression. But I can't hold it. Something flickers in my eye and Leo touches my shoulder and squeezes.

"Live, Cassius Jones. Don't sacrifice yourself for a girl who will not appreciate it."

I look back at her. *She's mourning*, I want to say. *She's in shock. Someone she loves is dead.*

But even now, with her face wounded, she won't leave the body. I don't know how I can help her.

There is nothing, in the end, that I can do. The harpy swoops out for an easy meal. I quake and spin against Leo's side. I think he keeps watching. There's one final scream, and then the wet sounds of raw stringy flesh tearing from the bone. Leo barely makes a sound, like he's used to this.

God, I hate that. I hate that more than anything.

"Have you faced one before?" I whisper to him.

"No. Not exactly. There was a summer where they lurked around Southend. But they really were just after food. Anything that was left out. Animals. Bread. Fruit. They'd swoop in and take it. Lived most of that summer inside."

"How did you get them to go away?"

Leo grunts, face creasing in apology. "We didn't. They left of their own accord. Got bored, I guess."

"Okay," I say calmly. I feel anything but. "Any suggestions?"

Leo says, "No."

"Okay," I say again, less calmly. His eyes are fixed on the harpy and its meal, as if he has a duty to watch the girl be consumed; as if by living, it is now his burden to bear the dead.

Well, good luck to him: I have no such convictions. If my last reaction is anything to go by, I have processed my brother's death not at all. Not one bit. And I can't afford to lose my mind right now, because when I scan the greenhouse and spot Fred and Silas whispering to one another, and Victoria and Bellamy with their hands over their ears, I wonder if anyone else has a plan.

I rack my brain for harpies. Any goddamn mention of harpies. Hesiod wrote about them. Apollonius, too. And Ovid. I know what they look like. I know they're tormentors —they played with King Phineus, stole his food, made his life hell.

"Pretty sure the texts say nothing more than what you lived. The bastards love to torment," I tell Leo. "And they're fast. Faster than the wind, by some accounts."

"Yeah, I know that much," he murmurs back. "How are they beaten?"

I swallow at that. "In the texts? The gods intervened. I don't know. They're just ravenous. Do you have any food?"

He looks at me like I'm mad. "Oh. Slipped my mind at breakfast, Mr Jones. Usually I ferret half a loaf away. *No*, I don't have any bloody food."

Snarky little—I don't like this side of Leo Shaw. It's profoundly upsetting to learn, after giving your body to someone, that they can be a right ass in a situation that requires calm.

He does not apologise. "Well, then, the hemlock?"

"No. It needs to be ingested, first of all. And 'harpy' wasn't on that list. Cover me," I whisper to Leo, and I offer him Thad's gun. It is like giving part of myself away. Surely Leo must know that; anxiety and disgust and fear all swell in me, and it seems disproportionate to the act. I hand over the gun. Leo takes it. Thaddeus screams in my brain that I'm a fool, that Leo won't give it back, that I am weapon-less save for the single shot in the flintlock gun. Leo looks at me, brows furrowed, and I wonder if he can see something in my eyes to make him worried.

"What are you doing? Take it back. There's only one shot in that gun."

"I know." I swallow; I have the urge to tell him I'm not stupid. "I'd prefer you have more shots to save me when things go south."

"When," Leo repeats, without intonation. He doesn't try to stop me. Do I have a right to be irked by that? I am so close to leaning in, to feeling the sweat of his brow against mine, the firm press of his lips to mine. I can all but feel the warmth of him as his leg touches me, hip to knee, impossibly intimate. I want comfort. And then I hear the happy sounds of a monster devouring flesh, of a sternum cracking from the weight of the harpy, and the wafting acrid scent of blood, metallic in the air.

I don't know what comes over me. Suddenly I am creeping out of the shrubbery, flintlock gun raised. I have exactly one chance, and that knowledge is a burr in my gut.

Somehow, over the sounds of bone cracking and flesh tearing, it hears me. The twisted face spins towards me. Its lips, which are sunken and flat, are peeled away from its sharp, blood-covered teeth. They drip with gore, and the depth in its eyes gives me pause. I aim, I ready myself to fire, and then—

The harpy speaks.

. . .

18

LESSON EIGHTEEN

"Horresco olfaciens tuum putridum odorem,
qui sicut sanginem alterium putet."

I freeze. I do not shoot. The harpy is looking at me, mouth open, tongue wagging—*speaking* to me. I try to take a deep breath and I fail and splutter, and I wait for it to launch itself from the body. I step back. It steps forward. A heavy taloned foot slaps onto the ground, slick with blood.

Desperately, I translate. *Horresco.* First person singular. I shudder. *Olfaciens*, present participle; smelling, to smell.

Tuum putridum odorem, the reason the harpy shudders.

I shudder to smell your putrid odour.

Qui sicut sanguinem alterium putet.

Which stinks like the blood of another.

I swallow hard. I killed a boy last night. I put a bullet in his brain. And like Orestes, I am polluted by that sin.

Euripides, in my ear: *"For there is no escape from miasma, no hiding from the gods, no avoiding the judgement that is deserved."*

The harpy takes another step. Up close, its body is foul with sweat and blood and gore, rotting from its mouth. Its feet slap through a pool of blood at its feet towards me. Hastily, I translate, to rid myself of the pollution that interests it.

I don't know why I just don't shoot. But now that it's spoken, I have to speak back. Call me stupid—I don't care. I say, rather poorly, "*Mandatum datum a meo superiore secutus sum.*"

I have followed an order from my superior.

"*Si non paruissem, punivissem.*"

If I had not obeyed, I would have been punished.

The harpy opens its mouth and cackles. Its head turns unnaturally, like an owl's, until it's staring at me with a twisted neck and glistening eyes. "*Cuius mandata secutus es et cur non curo sed modo te id fecisse.*"

I am momentarily stumped by the length and speed of the sentence. I need a fucking dictionary.

Cuis mandata.

Whose orders.

Secutus es—perfect participle of *sequi*, to follow. *Secutus es*—you have followed.

Et cur non curo.

And why (you followed them) I care not.

Sed modo te id fecisse. Fecisse, perfect active infinitive of *facere,* to do. *Fecisses,* to have done.

Whose orders you followed and why you followed them I care not, but only that you did it.

When I do not reply quick enough, the harpy chitters happily, a staggering sound, a haunting sound. Something primal in me quivers. My body knows itself to be prey.

"*Vivo ut te concelebram et prosequar, quod mihi voluptatem dat.*"

Vivo. I live.

Ut te concelebram et prosequa. Ut, in order. *Concelebram* is trickier. It can mean celebrate, to make known—but in this case I suspect it means frequent. To haunt. *I live in order to haunt*—and *prosequar,* to hound, to pursue.

I live to haunt and hound you.

Quod mihi voluptatem dat. Voluptatem, pleasure.

Which gives me pleasure.

"What the fuck are you doing?" Bellamy hisses from the bushes. The harpy spins to face him, then back at me. The spell is broken; it stops its slow approach and rears up with a screech, launching off the ground and into the air. Talons outstretched, it dives for my face. I point the flintlock gun and fire.

The harpy screams, a primitive and near-demonic sound. An arterial spray of black blood blasts my face and my mouth. I taste the metal in it, and something else, how I imagine sewage. Rotten, putrefying meat coursing in the beast's blood. I howl and stagger backwards, blinded, and around me I hear a shot ring out, then the sound of a metal pole landing, then curses. The harpy still chitters and shrieks. When I finally wipe away the blood, the harpy is gone. Leo has the gun raised to one of the cast-iron columns. I look up to see the harpy preening, digging in its own flesh with a talon and sucking at its wound.

"Shit," Bellamy says. "Shit."

Victoria is crying, I think—I don't turn to check. But Fred and Silas have slipped out of their cover to join us.

"That was very stupid, Mr. Jones," Silas informs me. "It's playing with its food. You're only doing what it wants."

Intermittently between his words, I hear the arrhythmic chittering and suckling of the harpy tending to its meal. The noise keeps sparking my anxiety. I can't keep my eyes on Silas. They keep drifting up to the attacker overhead.

I wet my lips. "If we can get out of this with information—"

"We need to kill it," Fred says sharply. "Not let it toy with us. Not let it tear us to shreds." I notice now, for the first time, what the harpy has done to her arm. A deep gouge is in her shoulder and forearm, where she raised it to defend herself. A trickle of blood streams from the wounds. Silas looks furious—like it's my fault.

"Can it speak English?" Leo whispers. I shrug, unsure. All of us huddle closer, luring Bellamy and Victoria out momentarily. I keep my eye on the harpy as it suckles at its wound; one eye lolls towards us, watching carefully.

"It's too quick," I say. "The wings are a problem."

"Well, we have no net," Bellamy says. "What do you suggest?"

"I'll distract it. I'll keep asking questions. But the metal pole—Fred, you need to bludgeon it. Victoria, Bellamy—you need weapons. Go find some."

They hesitate, and then peel off from the group. But I watch as the harpy's eye follows them, and then it launches from its place to circle the separated prey.

"Careful," I call out to Bellamy, and then I lose sight of both them and the harpy, and have to run around a corner. Fred darts ahead, pole raised, and I hear her grunt and Victoria scream. The harpy's talons wrench at a fistful of Victoria's hair. There's an awful tearing noise. Horrifying, like the scalp itself is peeling from the skull. Then a blow lands. There's an affronted *oof* as Fred swings and the pole collides with the harpy's belly. It lets go, squawking, and dives again. Victoria dodges ungracefully, sprawling in the dirt and rolling. Blood weeps from her scalp. Bellamy is screaming; it's pandemonium, chaos. The harpy spins in the air, talons flexed; skin is caught, peeled, flayed from flesh. Bellamy howls as part of his forearm is ripped free.

Leo shoots from behind me, and everyone screams, then; the bullet goes wide, nearly hitting Silas.

I breathe deep and shout, "*Quomodo huc mundo veneris?*"

How did you come into this world? I demand an answer. I

pray for it. The harpy pays me no mind. Fred swings wildly with the pole.

"*Fera innaturalis, tibi praecipio ut audias!*"

The insult gets its attention, so I hurl another. "*Turpi femina!*"

The harpy screeches and caws, furious, and turns all attention to me. I repeat my question: How did you come into this world?

The harpy looks at me, seething, hovering high and out of range of Fred and her weapon. It spits and moves to circle above me, unnaturally wide eyes focused on me at every turn.

The harpy screeches, mournful and twisted:

"*Tractus sum huc.*"

I have been drawn here.

"*Ego sum Canis Iovis, spirita venti.*"

I am the hound of Zeus, the spirit of the wind.

Then, with laughter, "*Miasmam olfacio et merentos molesto.*"

I smell miasma and torment those who deserve it.

"*Inclusus sum hic, sed epulum datum est.*"

I am trapped here, but given a feast.

I shake my head at it. "*Cur non discedis?*"

Why don't you leave?

Something like a mournful wail sounds, a soft and distant cry that seems to echo from the opposite side of the greenhouse.

"*Iuppiter me non audit.*"

Zeus does not hear me.

"*Sorores meae me non audiunt.*"

My sisters do not hear me.

For a second, I feel sorry for it. And then it plunges for me. I am surprised by my own tranquillity as I watch the unnatural jaw open, sharp stained teeth bearing down on me. Thaddeus, in my mind, tells me to wait. To hold. Hold.

Distantly, my heart pounds; throbbing in my chest, adrenaline swamping me. I go near blind with it.

Then: I move.

"Shield your eyes!" I call to the others.

Someone asks *what*—I have no time to answer. A second before those talons rip into my face, I drop to my knees with the sparker I've pulled from my pocket. I raise it. *Click.*

Intense, radiant light. Through my eyelids, I see a flash of white, and when I open them I'm still somehow struck by a dazzling afterimage. The harpy drops, panicked. I see it blinking, head convulsing as it twists, trying to shake itself out of its blindness.

Fred rushes in. She drives against the bird, slamming the pole across its head. It squawks weakly as something bodily snaps. Blood oozes from part of the skull where it's matted and red. Still, the thing tries to fly away. Once it flies, we'll have lost it—so I jump onto it. My arms wrap around it. I feel muscle rolling beneath feathers, oil-slick with blood and gore and grease. The *teras* twitches and spasms, screaming at me, a torrent of Latin and gibberish and pained cries I don't quite catch. Its chin is wet, half caved in. The talons scrabble up to my arms and my belly. The harpy tries to gut me. Instant, white-hot pain scorches through me. I howl and writhe with it, hands losing purchase, sliding down to grip the ankles and wrench its claws away from me. My stomach is slick with wet and heat, and my head is buzzing—I don't know if I am gutted, I don't know if I will look down and be my brother, propped up against a tree, intestines in my hands. Fred puts the pole around the harpy's neck and chokes it. Then Leo comes, cocks the gun, and shoots the harpy in the head.

It goes slack sluggishly, as if it is desperate to hold on. I watch as life filters out through the tiny hole in its skull, a slow crawl of blood and gore seeping free. I watch its eyes. Our heads are so close together, I can't help but see when the life leaks out of them, until it is empty and dead, and nothing more than a foul-smelling corpse. Then, almost immediately, the air is lighter, the tension gone. But it's a deceit of my body. Spots crowd my vision until everything I see is a star scape. Cold douses my limbs and seconds later I am freezing, shivering. *Shock*, some part of my brain informs me soberly. *You're going into shock*. And on the back of those words, I feel pain for the first time; sharp, stinging fire. With shaking hands, I pull my vest away from my body. It's torn to shreds and bloody. My shirt beneath it is the same. My belly, too. A gouge divides my navel. Other desperate scratches line me.

"God," I whisper, and then I am on the ground.

Here it gets foggy. I have only impressions; of the greenhouse in a blur, foliage and flowers an ill-defined bloom of colour. Someone yells my name, then several someones, then hands are on me—everyone is so warm, I could go to sleep in their arms—but then I am shaking.

My mind starts to come undone. I fancy it is my soul, unpicking itself from the flesh, hoping to fly through the greenhouse and out, up into the dreary English sky. I think of Corinthians, and Paul, and the second coming of Jesus, and the transformation of this mortal flesh into a glorified body. When I might taunt death.

Where, O death, is your victory? Where, O death, is your sting?

But then the sharp, hissing pain flares along my stomach and I think: the sting is right fucking here. Death is a moment and a state, a finality. It is the state of *dying*—the long drawn-out act of it—that is definitively worse.

"You're not dying," someone—Leo?—tells me. God, am I speaking aloud? Am I rambling?

"I'm in shock." I know I say that one out loud, because Leo agrees with me, and a different kind of burn blazes in my belly at his agreement. He swims into view, face soft and indistinct in my fuzzy gaze. But I can still tell he is beautiful.

I reach up and manage to graze the side of his cheek with my finger, before he moves it away. Swats me away like a fly. I think.

I hear only snippets.

"Do. . . the harpy?"

"I'll carry it. The dean might release another, for the other groups. And him?"

"Shock, I think. Only, I don't. . ."

Sound flits around me, too quick to catch.

"Close your eyes," Leo whispers. Someone starts humming. I don't know if it's me. It feels familiar, as old as my body, so I start humming too. A song comes to mind, a little lullaby my mother wrote. Dactylic hexameter, like the epics.

> *Somnum cape, parvule, sub tegmine alarum Dei*
> *Protector est, et semper te custodit in pace*
> *Et tenebras immanes, quas daemones parant*
> *Lumine suo, Deus exsuperat et vincit omne malum*
> *Sleep, little one, under the wings of God,*
> *He is the Protector, and always keeps you in peace*
> *And the immense darkness, which demons prepare*
> *With His light, God surpasses and conquers all evil.*

❧ 19 ❧

LESSON NINETEEN

I dream that my insides are turning black and thick like tar, as if rot has taken hold of me and eats at everything good in my body from the inside out. I dream that when I die and they cut me open, no blood will spill. Only putrefied organs will leak from my skin. And my heart will be swollen and black, and that's the thing that kills me in the end. Not the decaying of the rest of my body, but the size of my heart—so large it can never be held by anyone.

I wake covered in sweat, half tangled in a white bedsheet. White light half-blinds me—it's morning; sunlight glaring through grey clouds in that gaslight way. I try to sit up—and searing pain floods along my stomach, forcing me to collapse onto the pillows. My gut burns. I have been stripped of my bloody vest and shirt and wrapped in bandages. A bit of brownish blood has stained them. Experimenting, I press on my stomach—and regret it. God.

I writhe like that for what seems like an hour, hating that I'm awake, cursing myself for not shooting that fucking harpy right away.

"A Healer came to see you."

I crane my neck up. Leo stands propped against the door-frame. He's not looking at me. He fiddles with Thaddeus' gun. He is still in uniform, though without the vest and the shirt half-undone. His sleeves are rolled up, bunched around his thick forearms. I can see his collarbones, the divot between his pecs. His hair is wet like he's bathed. I look at him and I shiver, and it's not from attraction, but a sense of awe at the sight of him. At his beauty. I push myself up slowly, wiggling back until my back hits the headboard.

"Are you stealing that gun?" I murmur, only half-jokingly.

Leo glances at me and spins the barrel closed. "Nothing's too badly damaged. They put a poultice on you, which explains the smell—"

"Very fucking rude, Mr Shaw."

"—and then they were gone. All they said was the harpy kicked your guts. You'll have a nasty bruise."

I scoff. "To complement the nasty scars?"

"Oh, I think they might turn out quite pretty. Give you a bit of an edge, Mr Jones. An allure."

I ask, "Am I in need?"

And he looks at me, devilish smile tweaking at his lips. "Can hardly hurt." He slips into the room now, hesitates, turns back to gently close the door. Then he goes to his knees by my side and offers me Thaddeus' gun.

"Only three bullets left," he says. He drums his fingers over it, then lets go of it entirely, placing it in my lap. I try to catch his eye; he looks away. It hurts, in an odd way.

"What is it?" I ask.

Leo shakes his head.

Because I am eager for the answer to be yes, I quip, "Worried about me?"

He looks up, just briefly, without a smile, before he stares out the window. "I think I expected you to be different, that's all."

I freeze, because I'm not prepared to learn all the ways I'm lacking. But he continues with, "What kind of fool flings himself on a harpy? It could have gutted you. It could have ripped you to shreds."

I set my jaw. "If I hadn't, it would have flown away."

"And what if it had torn out your stomach?"

"Are you *actually* angry with me?"

He shuts up, jaw slamming closed. "It doesn't align. Your actions, I mean, with what I imagined a Londoner to be. Every tale I've ever heard pegs you lot as little lords in your ivory tower—that kind of man would have run."

I swallow. "I ran from the *manticore*."

"Mm. That you left your wards at all says something about your character."

He stares at me as if I'm unreal, an assessing glare trying to sort me out. I don't know why that rankles me.

"What I am now, I wasn't always," I say. "I never said I was born here, Mr Shaw. You made the mistake of that assumption all on your own."

His gaze softens greatly, almost immediately, which makes me feel more ill. "That makes you respect me more, doesn't it?" I ask him.

"Of course, it does. You can't blame me for hating the people who sit and languish in safety whilst the rest of us are struggling to live."

"And what do you plan to do when you graduate, Mr Shaw? When you have a home in London, when you become one of us?"

He doesn't answer. His throat bobs, and that's it. I half expect him to tell me he's going to burn it all down.

"What was it like?" he says instead. "Outside the wards for you, I mean."

I sigh and look out the window. "Shit." He waits for me to continue. I shrug. "Really, it was shit. You would know. You barely sleep. You scavenge for food, or try to farm, or you steal from Londoners. You know," I say, thinking I'll leave it there. But it feels good to speak on something that feels so secret. Victoria and Bellamy don't have the same taint Leo and I have. I feel it, in my soul, like a wine stain that only keeps spreading. A residual anger I keep thinking is going away, until I linger on what's happening here. The rage at my situation. At the helplessness of it. My hands shake, and I reach for the bedside table, fumbling for a cigarette. Leo leans forward and lights it for me, and I breathe deep looking into his eyes, taking him in. When I exhale, I glance away and say, "We lived near Hull. My father was a fisherman. He'd be gone for long stretches, and then would be drunken and angry whenever he was on land. Then an incident at sea rocked him. Completely decimated his crew." I look down at my hands. "He never sailed again." I think about saying the rest and can't bring myself to give it voice. Of those who survived and still had the will to speak, they claimed an *argos* rose out of the sea, its many eyes not hollow or empty, but full. Full of a stretching void that seemed to reach for them, a dizzying, hypnotic stare that ate sailors' voices and minds until they were husks of their former self. Whether or not I believe it doesn't matter. My father never spoke again, but neither did he beat us.

"Anyway, it meant we struggled for a year. He was a liability. Don't look at me like that. He isn't a good man." I look up at the ceiling next, because anywhere is better than Leo's eyes. "That's why Thad did the trials. London was laxer, then. As soon as he had a spot in the University, we were allowed to live here. So I've been here since."

Silence swamps the room, and it's awful, because I don't know what he's thinking. I feel the urge to defend myself bubbling up; I've just woken up from a fever dream, my gut near torn to shreds, and I must explain why I'm not as bad as the other Londoners, not as bad as everyone who accepts the terrors that happen to other people, so long as their own hide is safe. I grapple for a reason why I deserve Leo's pity more than he deserves mine. Which is bollocks, obviously. I am, perhaps necessarily, uncomfortable by his questions. I look down at my hands again. So free of calluses. Of scars.

"I got lucky," I whisper. "It's all about luck, in the end."

"It is," he agrees, "and also the machinations of an institution hellbent on maintaining its importance. But that's a conversation for another day."

He mutely gestures for the cigarette. I don't question him, not when he breathes it in and holds it so long I know it must be scorching him. Not when he splutters and coughs and shakily hands it back.

"Do we know anything about the next trial?" I ask.

He makes a face and shakes his head. "We have a few days." He won't elaborate. When I push the covers back to stand, he appears at my side and lays me back down. His palm is on my shoulder. I can feel the roughness of it; a flash of him in my mind, above me, head lolling, sweat on his brow. I shiver and glance away.

"Well?" I prompt. "Aren't you going to tell me about *your* life?"

Leo stares at me.

"No," he says, rather firmly. Misery cracks through his near even tone. Then he pushes to standing, hesitates, and kisses me very gently on the forehead. "Rest," he says, and then is gone.

I WAKE AGAIN NEAR SUNSET, and when I stumble out towards the sitting room, I hear only the Lins. I do a Very Bad Thing, and press myself up against the frame to listen to them. They are still a mystery to me, and they never talk freely. I fancy that if they're speaking to one another, I might learn something useful. Which should tell you something about myself: I am not as good as Leo thinks. I *do* want to protect my hide. I have been willing to let the rest of the world suffer whilst I get a good night's rest. I've been doing it for years.

So what will it matter if I eavesdrop?

"Because you're wrong, that's why," Silas mutters. I hear a book slam shut, and Fred sighs. She murmurs something indistinct back.

Silas goes, "What?"

And Fred laughs in that tired, overwhelmed way, when you're suddenly sick of an argument and would rather implode than continue it. I hear the strain in her voice when she says, "Go on, then. Tell me why I'm wrong."

The floorboards creak. "Apart from the fact that coming here was *your* idea in the first place, Fred, they have Blood Hunters. And they're real, and they're thorough, and frankly *they are better than us.* Than you. Whether we like it or not, that *manticore* nearly killed me, and I'm barely holding on as it is. You try and leave with me in tow, and I'll be the thing that kills you. I won't have that."

"*That's* what you're worried about? No. We'll figure it out, we'll—"

"I'm not bloody done," Silas says in the smallest, fiercest voice I've ever heard. The window seat groans as someone sits in it. "Listen. This has been years in the making. Us getting here, I mean. And you cannot tell me that it's *really* worse than out there. What are you hoping to do, Fred? We go back, and we're still working for the bastards. Toiling everyday, handing over most of what we grow for these people—only we're massively less safe than if we stay put."

"All this," Fred says, voice high, "everything that has led us here was because we were operating under the assumption that things were *better behind the wards*. But it's the fucking same, Silas. There are still *teras*. And the people—this institution!"

"Listen to yourself!" Silas yells. It's the first time I've heard his voice go high, gain such volume. "And then think about me. For one second. I know that's selfish of me to ask, but Fred, you're brilliant. You're a fighter. You're physical. If you think you can spend your days on that God-awful farm without going insane, then I am jealous. But I'm not like that. I want the books. I want the knowledge. I want to be something, and I can only do that if I'm here. But even then, if you choose to go alone, I know you'll regret it. Not because you've left me behind, not because you'll be hunted until they kill you, but because I know you want it, too. You want to be more than their farmer."

"I want," she says, "to live happily."

"Well, that's nice. But it's a pipe dream. The closest you'll get to that is here."

Fred makes a noise. "If we stay, we'll only be their fodder. You ever seen an old Hunter?"

Frustrated, Silas groans out, "Then declare something else!"

"But it's the only thing I'm good at!"

For a moment, they're both silent. Someone sighs, there's an ambient creaking of the boards, and the wind tapping against the window.

"You're getting ahead of yourself," Silas says gently. "We haven't even passed yet."

"No. I mean. . ." another sigh. "I know. I know. You're right. I just thought, once we were here. . ." she trails off, and no one says anything more for a time.

Having waited long enough, I creep back to my room, and make a very loud show of grunting and swearing and slamming my door closed so they know I'm coming, because I'm a bit pathetic and embarrassing, and I'm trying to offset the guilt of eavesdropping.

As I round the corner into the sitting room, the entire scene is peaceful, as if the siblings have been reading in silence for hours.

Fred's entire arm is wrapped tight in a bandage, and Silas is by the window with his legs up on a stool—though he immediately drops them and sits straight when I enter.

"Alright?" I mumble.

"Fine," he says, rather stiffly. "How are you feeling?"

I shrug. Truly, I'm not too sure. Between Leo's visit and my guts nearly tumbling out of me, I could certainly be better. "Standing," I say eventually, "though I'm not sure for how much longer."

"Sit, then, you fool." Fred moves to clear away a pile of books from the seat beside Silas, and I amble over to it.

"Glad you're alive," Fred says with a small smile.

I smile back. "Where are the others?"

"On a fool's errand, trying to find some clue for the next trial," Silas mutters. "Though we're not faring much better."

Books are scattered around them. I give Silas a questioning look.

"Victoria thought we should look through them. Actually read them, you know? She said the University has done very little for the sake of doing it, that they don't care too much about our intellectual capabilities unless we can apply them to killing *teras*, and that unless these books are here for decoration, that there might be a pattern to the ones selected for the tower."

Well, Victoria has a point, doesn't she.

"She's with the others?" I clarify.

Fred makes a face. "She. . . she didn't seem quite so. . ."

I frown. "What?"

"She's a bit of a mess," Silas says. Fred stands up and kicks his shin. "Ow, what—*stop it*. I'm right. She can't handle these trials. The harpy barely scratched her, and she—"

"—is having a very normal experience to what is happening to us," I cut him off. God, I hate righteous people. I hate it when empathy is frowned upon. Refusing to absorb any of Silas' sulking, I gesture to the books. "What about the other rooms? Other students, I mean. Are their books the same?"

The siblings exchange a look. "Only a few." Fred pushes them towards me: *Metamorphoses, the Aeneid,* Varro.

A short, bound manuscript I've never seen before.

I go for it immediately. "Have you read it?"

"It's in Latin," she says. "My knowledge is. . . rudimentary, at best."

I nod and take it. It looks to be mediaeval in nature, complete with illuminated letters, drawings scrawled in the margins. It's entirely handwritten—and the scale of it upsets me when I know that every other room on campus has one, too. But it is dated to only a few years ago.

From my brother's trial year.

It's also, notably, not Classical Latin. Dean Drearton's name is signed beneath it.

I read aloud:

De Disciplina Venatorum: On the Training of Hunters

The best young people have been trained to protect us from the *teras*. Soon however, with London flourishing as the crown of England, we must face the truth. Our rule is unable to grow forever. And so only the most select students should be trained. And in doing this the true nature of each student will be laid bare.

Optissimi adulescentes ut nos ab *teras* tuerentur exerciti sunt. Mox tamen, Londinio florente ut corona Angliae, veritatis ferri debetur. Nostrum imperium sine fine crescere non potest. Itaque discipuli selectissimi solummodo formari debent, et hoc faciendo vera natura cuius discipuli patefacientur.

All students must be taught how to defend us against the *teras* threat, whether he chooses the mantle of Hunter or not. Not only on account of the safety of he himself but also on account of the safety of the University, which might soon need Scholars and Arcanists on the field if it is necessary to wage war.

Omnes rationem defendendi nos contra periculo *teras* discendi sunt utrum ordinem Venatoris eliget an non, non modo propter salutatem ipsius sed etiam Universitatis quae si nobis bellum agere necesse est mox in campo Doctores et Astrologi exiget.

And so the trials will test the mettle, skill, and determination of each student in a safe environment.

The first two trials will test the student in a simple way, so that Teras in levels F to D can be conquered. The more powerful teras will only be involved if the strength of the student is more important than the number of graduates, as is happening. By the same logic the remaining two trials will have teras in levels C to S. These should be completed by brute force alone.

A student should not be punished if he has prevailed through sheer strength, but shown urbane and intellectual methods of conquering which might lead to victory without injury and death.

These Teras can be: stunned, tricked, blinded, distracted and other things as passed down to us in the stories. For example, Nemean Teras, whose flesh is unable to be penetrated by sword and is only able to be killed with a great amount of hemlock, or ensnared in a trap, and also take as an example the Stymphalian teras which always move in a flock, a most grave source of danger.

Itaque simulacra pugnae constantiam, peritiam, et fortitudinem animi cuius discipuli in tuto loco explorabunt.

Primae duae simulacrae in simplice modo discipulum tentet ut teras in gradibus ab F ad D vincantur. Potientiores teras solum implicabuntur si fortitudo discipuli est gravior quam numerum graduatorum, ut fit. Eodem ratione reliqua simulacra teras in gradibus ab C ad S habebunt. Haec vi sola perfici debent.

Discipulum, si puro fortitudino vincat, non puniendum sed monstrandum urbanos et ingeniosos modos vincendi, qui ad victoriam sine iniuria aut morte ducant.

Hae teras possunt: obtundi, fraudari, caecari, distracti et cetera ut in fabulis traduntur. Exempli gratia habe teras Nemeanae, cuius caro cum ferro non penetrari potest et solum cum magno cicutae aut interfici potest, aut in occulto laqueo illaqueantur, et quoque habe Teras Stymphalii, qui semper in grege moveantur, gravissima causa periculi.

. . .

Separating the birds and defending against their beaks and distracting them while the head or body of the bird is attacked is a way of killing [the birds] which could be tried.	Separans aves et contegens contra rostra earum et distractans eas dum caput aut corpus avis petitur est modus occidendi qui temptari possit.
However, since many of these methods are only taught from the second year of University, students must be given appropriate weaponry, and both a place and time that is appropriate so that these trials are true examples of ability.	Quoniam tamen multi horum modorum ex secondo ordo Universitatis docentur, discipulis arma recta et locum et tempus rectum dandum est ut hae simulacra sunt vera exempla ingenii.

WHEN I'M DONE, the siblings are staring at me. Fred collapses back into her hands with a half-muffled scream she then tries to play off by running her hands through her hair.

"Why would he write this down and hand it out to us?"

"To prove he's not trying to trick us," Silas whispers. He rocks forward, picking at something on his hand. Whatever book he'd been reading has since been discarded at his side.

I put the manuscript down. "It's a test in its own right, isn't it? There's no way we could have known about the hemlock without my brother's letter—unless we'd read this. The dean is ensuring we have all the necessary skills and resources to make it through to the end of this. To test that we're not so scared that we'll overlook information that can save us."

"Fucking terrible," Fred grunts.

"Could be worse," says Silas. "And anyway, we've got more of an idea now than minutes ago, and I call that a win."

He says all in such a deadpan way that I almost laugh, because of how much of a lie it seems.

"Nemean Class, then?" Silas says, nearing cheery. "It would make sense, given the hemlock."

I want to believe it's that simple, but I'm nervous, and can't trust that there's no other horrible thing hiding in this trial. "If it is, and even if it isn't, we need to find a way to make it ingest the hemlock. And then we'd need to hide for, what, half an hour? A full hour? Who knows how it would work in a creature that big." I pause, considering. "Hell, we might not even have enough."

Silas claps his hands together. "We need an Artificer."

"Besides the Blood Hunters, I haven't seen a single graduate on campus," I mutter.

"But a Healer came to the room," Fred says. "For you. For me. They must be around."

I think, briefly, of what I saw on my way to the library that night. Before the Blood Hunters, there had been a flicker of something. I'd thought I'd seen something in the hall, studying—

You say that aloud and they'll put you back to bed. Don't be an idiot.

So I say nothing, naturally. But Fred, at least, is right. Graduates are around—unless that's some other masterfully hidden lie on Drearton's part. Still, even if we do find an Artificer, I'm not convinced of how they will help us.

So I ask, "And what would we get this Artificer to do? We can't use a syringe."

He shrugs. "That manuscript had hemlock down as a method. Which means they've done it before."

God, he can be snarky. He's right, but the *attitude*. "Fine. A wild goose chase through campus." I put a hand to my head, and I know I sound like a right little bastard, but I do hate that Silas is right. There's nothing else we can do. We are operating on the assumption that the hemlock will be useful to us. Now we must find a way to use it.

"Let's find the others," I say. "See if they've found anything."

"COME ON, PETER, YOU DICKWAD!" A sigh. "Go on, give it another kick."

A percussive ramming sounds, echoing down the stone steps leading to the top of the tower.

A door opens beside me; a woman sticks her head out. "Cut it out," she hisses. Her face is bruised, battered. A cut runs down her cheek. I assume there was more than one harpy for the dean to set loose in the greenhouse by the talon-width of that cut. "We're trying to rest."

"Sorry," I say, though I'm not the one doing anything.

We're by the east tower on the opposite side of the college, since that's where all the commotion is. Most prospective students are recovering, from the looks of it, though a few are lingering around the base of this tower, eager to know why Bellamy Taylor and a bulky *xenos* are pounding on Peter Drike's door.

I edge up the stairs. Victoria's nowhere to be seen (good for her—this is embarrassing) and Bellamy's yelling for Peter's attention as Leo's trying to kick the door in.

I ask, half yelling, "What the bloody fuck do you think you're doing?"

"Saw Drike leaving the library," Bellamy mutters. "Bastard knows something and he's not sharing."

Well, we didn't share either, I don't say. Drike is just prioritising himself, and whatever crew he's shacked up with.

"Stop it. Leo, stop it." I edge between Bellamy and Leo, who is sweating, and furious, and *God*, he can be an idiot. He looks at me and his expression slips into something sheepish. I force myself between the pair and knock—firmly but politely—upon the wood.

"Peter? It's Cassius."

"*Fuck off, faggot,*" comes the muffled reply.

"Charming as always." I glance up at Leo again. His face is lively with renewed fury. I reach out and touch his hand, and wait until it looks like the urge to pulverise Peter Drike is contained.

Sighing, I glance back at the Lins. Silas' stare is firm, and I fancy he knows what I'm thinking of doing, because he gestures to the door and nods. I turn back and say, very quietly, "Peter, we know about the third trial."

A scoff. "*Bullshit.*"

"Nemean Class," I say, and nothing more.

There's a pause, then a shuffling, then the muted noises of people discussing something, then the far-less-muted noises of the same people fighting. The only clear noise that filters through is someone moaning, "*Ow, ow, fuck! Fuck, you bastard, alright!*"

Finally, the door unlocks, and Peter Drike is standing there, same old obnoxious sneer on his face.

"Why you bothering me, then?" he grunts.

"What did Meléti tell you?" I ask.

"Fuck off." He tries to shut the door—one hand splayed, breathing hard, Leo stops him. He steps over the threshold into Peter's room, eyes dark. They stare at each other, both about the same size, both angry in the physical way I think all tall, broad men are by nature—they can afford to be what more delicate bodies cannot: rage with force behind it, rage tethered to a vessel where bodily violence is possible. I am pretty fucking brittle by comparison and God, I think I'm jealous. Peter Drike shoved me against a wall like I was nothing. Leo Shaw can stand there and hold his own and not look one bit scared.

"He asked you a question," Leo grunts. "So answer it."

A smirk, a look back into the room to someone out of sight. Peter rolls his shoulders, quirks a brow. "*Xenos* cunt."

Leo punches him square in the nose.

Blood spurts immediately. Peter stumbles back from the door, which groans wide, revealing a mismatched group of people standing in wait behind Drike. Several are cowering— a woman, two men—and the other three square up, reading to shatter Leo's face in return.

"*Shit!*" Bellamy practically squeals, arms high. His torn-up forearm is bandaged. "Nope, no fucking way." Then he's gone, rushing down the stairs out of the way. I don't blame him, but I can't turn tail. Not when Leo stood there for me.

I take the gun out, cock it, and point it at Drike's head.

The effect is immediate, in both the faces of his roommates, and the air around me. There is at once the bare-bones horror of having a gun to your face: of realising all that strength and brute force means nothing with a tiny bullet hurtling toward your skull. And around me, in me, I feel my own body shift with the power the little gun affords me.

"Christ," Drike mutters. He makes some gesture and turns his back on Leo and me—a bold statement, I think, that he's not scared of us. He collapses on their window seat equivalent, which is covered in paper notes and a scattering of books. I think they've torn pages out, to write on or maybe for the fun of it. Drike makes a show of shoving the pile onto the floor, opening his hands with false showmanship. "Sit, then."

"No, thank you," I say, and lower the hammer on the gun before I put it away. "This will be quick. Just want to know what the damned *automaton* said."

Drike turns to the others—he must be hurting them, from the way half of them flinch—and hisses through his teeth. It's a signal and it sends them scattering until it's only Leo and me facing Peter Drike down.

"You said Nemean Class before," Drike says, when the final roommate's door shuts with a click.

"That's my guess," I say. I don't want to give too much of my hand away, in case he has nothing to offer.

"Don't know anything about that."

Leo breathes deep, expands his chest, looks very, very good for a dazzling moment as he looks Drike up and down. "Are you sure about that?"

Drike meets his gaze with vitriol. He grinds his teeth so obviously his jaw protrudes, like he's about to spit on Leo's feet. But he changes his mind at the last minute; sits upright and sighs. "Meléti didn't say anything like that. Didn't name the class, or the tier, or what to do. Just told me where I could petition graduate students on campus."

"Where?" I say—too desperately. Drike acts like an oaf, but he has a brain, and he catches my tone, my over eagerness.

He quirks a brow and snorts. "Oh? You want that information, do you?"

I slam my jaw shut, but I know the damage is done. "I've given you the next *teras* we'll face."

"Yeah, and you gave away the single bargaining chip you had. Not my fault you're too stupid to play the game, Jones."

Before I can say anything, Leo's hand is in my pants. I freeze instinctively, because that primal instinct in me is filled with relief and interest—I think my soul is a whore; I think I don't know how to love without using my body—and I look up at him to see he's not looking at me. He's grabbed the gun from my pocket, re-cocked it, aimed it at Peter's head.

It doesn't have the same effect. The shock is gone. Peter

was expecting this, I think. He laughs a little, rolls his eyes in an obvious taunt.

"You won't," he says.

"Cassius has already killed a man on the University's grounds," he says.

Drike's smile quirks—not because he believes it, but because he doesn't. His eyes slide to me, and I see in them a calculating, disbelieving scepticism. I am the lithe, delicate queer Drike's been teasing for years. I am the man who's never fought back when he's shoved me against a wall. But I killed a man—that much is true. Drike doesn't need to know the circumstances. He just needs to believe it.

"It's true. Under the watchful eye of the dean, who so gladly throws us all to the *teras*," I say. "I pulled the trigger. You might have heard it, before you went to pray the other night. If you think something as shapeless as morals will stop either one of us from pulling this trigger, I advise you to make your peace with God now."

"I'm not telling you shit," Drike says.

"Then most of us will die tomorrow."

I'm horrified that I sound so sure of it, but I'm right, aren't I? The trial behind all these sadistic little games is this: navigating an institution run by neurotic academics, seeking information from lost tomes and fragments, never knowing if your information is correct or valid, never being able to verify it. That is academia; that is the study of the ancients. Only, in our world, a lack of sources can easily mean our deaths.

Drike snarls, but there's an exhaustion in his eyes, his face. He hasn't moved from the couch. I wonder if the trials, and the truth of them, is hitting him the same way.

"By the library," he says. "There are doors. You must knock. Automaton mentioned Janus, so," here he kicks the pile of books and loose pages on the floor, eventually revealing an old volume of Varro. He picks it up and waves it at me. "Was hoping something about it was in here."

"Thank you," I say. I can figure out the rest—I know about Janus. The distinct Roman god with no Greek equivalent. The god of gates, and transitions, and portals. I grab Leo by the arm, and he relinquishes Thaddeus' gun immediately. We turn to leave. Drike clears his throat before we step over the threshold; before we step through the portal to the campus, away from Drike's realm.

"What are we meant to do?" he says, in barely more than a whisper. "Tell me. Please."

The last word is a plea. Leo grabs my arm firmly, a squeeze that says to drop it and let Drike flounder. I'm almost petty enough to do it, but I'm not sure I want to be the man that lets this place condemn us to death.

"Nemean class teras are susceptible to hemlock," I tell him. It is the only lifeline I offer.

Bastard doesn't even say 'thank you' as we leave.

LESSON TWENTY

Varro's *De Lingua Latina* is in our apartment, because of course it is. I feel no joy or sense of genius when I pluck it from the shelf.

"Explain it to me again," Victoria says. I don't know where she's been, and I don't ask—she says she found no further information, but I secretly suspect she wasn't looking. Her eyes are puffy; not sunken in from lack of sleep but inflamed from crying. I won't comment on it, and no one else does.

All of us are back in the sitting room, in a circle again, with a new wave of melancholy washing over us. Sleep feels distinct, our desire for it like a dream, but none of us can afford to rest with the next trial so close. My gut still aches, and I have to shift awkwardly to keep my body from complaining. Every so often a sharp jolt of pain reminds me how close I came to being torn open.

Bellamy and Victoria are together on the couch, those she looks put off by him; hugging herself close. The Lins are hovering by the wall again, Leo by the fire. I've wrenched Varro free from the shelf and stand in the centre of them all.

I heft the book in my arms. "If we assume the Nemean

Lion is the next *teras* we face, and we know it's susceptible to hemlock, then Silas is right. We'll need to find a way to administer it. And yes, Bellamy—even if it takes a good hour to take effect. It might be our saving grace."

I turn to chapter 7, and scan for the reference to Janus the index promised me. The book is old and dusty, with that worn-in smell of age and ink.

"So we knock on this door, and what?" Victoria asks. Then she sniffs and readjusts. "We need weapons. I need—I need a gun. Or an axe." She fiddles with her hands to hide the welling tears in her eyes. She's panicking. I'm so useless I pretend I don't know what's happening.

"We knock on this door, and a graduate opens it. Drike said we have to petition them, to see a graduate." I know they're about to ask 'how' but at this point, I know as much as them. "Here," I say, before anyone can speak. My finger on the passage, I read it aloud.

COZEVI OFTORIESO. *Omnia vero ad Patulc(ium)*
    commisse<i>. laneus mm es, duonus Cerus es, du(o>nus Ianus.
Vew(i>es po<tissimu>m melios eum recum . . .

O PLANTER GOD/ arise. Everything indeed have I committed unto (thee as) the Opener. Now art thou the Doorkeeper, thou art the Good Creator, the Good God of Beginnings. Thou'lt come especially, thou the superior of these kings. .

"AND THAT MEANS WHAT, EXACTLY?" Fred asks.

"It's a prayer. A Salian Hymn. Janus is an elusive god; there's not much written about him. But you see here, he's referred to as the Doorkeeper."

"And the *Good Creator*," Silas whispers. "Perhaps a god of procreation, or crops. But it's a threshold—"

"Yes! Liminal spaces. Intermediary zones. Transition from one place to another; a *portal*."

I don't mention the other thing: that I saw *something* that first night, like the shade of a student studying in the halls. Bellamy rolls his eyes anyway. I slam the book shut. "We have to take it seriously," I tell him. "Because we already had one ritual to get here, and they took our blood. To track us. If this institution is serious about it, we must be too."

He puts up his hands dramatically; Victoria carefully implores him to calm down. We're all splintering—not that we were particularly close beforehand. Still, I can tell it's getting worse.

Silas and Fred. Bellamy and Victoria. They are established pairs.

I don't know about Leo. I don't know about myself.

"We don't have time to sit around," Leo says finally. He pushes off the mantle and nods at the door. "Come on. Before it gets dark."

It's not raining this afternoon, but it's overcast. The grounds are empty and cold, the grey-tinge from the fuzzy sunlight sets everything gloomy, and a wind bites through all of us as we walk. I take Varro with me, but I haven't smoked enough today, and the craving hits me. I press the volume against Leo's chest and he takes it without a word; just a gentle smile.

By the time we're in the courtyard I've smoked my cigarette down to a stub. I hesitate entering it, in case we come across Blood Hunters—not because we're not allowed to be here, but because they unnerve me. I know they are always here. I know they can always find me.

"Which door?" Victoria prompts.

I bite my lip and point to the one on the left side of the

quadrangle, where I saw the Blood Hunter emerge. "Try that one."

We all go before it like supplicants, and even if Bellamy wants to laugh, there is a ritualistic feel to this gathering. And now that I'm looking, each side of the door bears Janus' two-faced head, one face staring in each direction. There are two of these decorations on either side of the doorway.

"Knock," Fred says with bravado, though her arms are tightly folded against her chest.

I lean forward and rap three times.

Nothing happens. Because, of course. It would all be too easy if anything happened.

I sigh and gesture for Leo to hand me the Varro volume.

"What are you thinking?" he asks, handing it to me. I flip to chapter 7 again, and read aloud the same passage I read the others, first in Latin and then in English:

O PLANTER GOD/ arise. Every-thing indeed have I committed unto (thee as) the Opener. Now art thou the Doorkeeper, thou art the Good Creator, the Good God of Beginnings. Thou'lt come especially, thou the superior of these kings.

AND WHEN AGAIN THERE'S no response, I reach up to the Janus ornaments and fiddle with them, thinking they might twist or turn, but they're only decoration. Then: "Fuck it."

I knock again, endlessly, for close to half a minute until a lock clicks and the door opens extremely reluctantly.

The glinting whites of an eye grow from the darkness. I can make out nothing else beyond the silhouette of a leather tricorn hat and the deep shadow it casts across the rest of the face.

Whoever it is grunts out, "You are not supposed to be here."

"Bullshit," Leo snaps. He kicks the door wide; very little light pours in despite this. We are met only by an illuminated shadow—a long dark coat, a wide tricorn hat, pale skin and that one eye poking out from underneath it. Leo isn't fazed. He says, "This is exactly what we're meant to be doing." Here he grabs Varro from my hands and shoves the volume forward, over the threshold. Immediately, half of it is subsumed in darkness. Leo flinches and pulls back.

"What," he says—not a question.

Behind me, I think I hear Bellamy swear and step away.

"You are not supposed to be here," the voice says again.

"An Artificer," I say. "We are here to petition an Artificer."

No reply. Leo hands the volume back to me, and I wonder if he's squaring up to haul this doorkeeper over the threshold. But he seems reluctant to reach over the threshold, and instead he hovers, practically vibrating with frustration. I almost reach out to comfort him, until I remember the others are behind us.

Silas nudges me aside without apology. "Meléti said we could petition a graduate."

The eye flicks to him, and the image of the doorkeeper—of this sullen and reverent figure, watching us from the dark—shatters. The doorkeeper sighs and the eye blinks out as their head dips forward in a bow.

Muffled, but barely concealed, we hear, *"Fucking automaton piece of—"* The door opens fully. "Fine. But you step over and that's it, okay?"

Leo walks forward without a single care for his own well-being. The flesh of him ripples and shifts. Shadow on him looks like ink in water, undulating in patterns over his skin. He gasps and shudders to a halt, and when I try to prompt him he doesn't answer me, just looks back; expression buried in the dark.

"No way," Bellamy mutters. "Victoria, *don't you dare*."

I turn in time to watch Victoria wrench her arm free of him. She gives me a look I can't parse—she's unhappy, still, but I don't know why—and goes to cross the threshold when Bellamy pulls her back.

"Don't," he says, voice low.

"Let go of me," she whispers. Her voice buckles with emotion. "Bellamy. *Bellamy.*"

He's holding her, and holding her *tight*, I realise. Enough that the way she's straining against his grip has got to be leaving a mark. I flinch—I feel ill.

"Let her go," I say—plainly, because I'm surprised at him, surprised that he isn't listening to a woman he claims to love.

Bellamy's eyes flit over to me and he blinks rapidly. His grip softens and Victoria stumbles back against me. I put a hand on her shoulder. She's staring at him, and she's shivering, and *God*, have I missed something? I can feel her trembling.

"Victoria," I whisper, but she spins away, brown hair half over her face. She crosses the threshold before I can ask her what's happening.

Fred has her arms crossed, and she's looking at Bellamy very differently, now: with a kind of reproving, dark scrutiny he very much deserves. She crosses after Victoria and her brother follows at her heels.

"What was that?" I hiss at Bellamy, but he ignores me like I'm his conscience; without looking my way, he storms after the others.

Which leaves me in the cold afternoon, Varro volume clutched in my arm, and what else can I do but step over the threshold?

A warbling crowds my ears. Pressure pops, like my head is

under water, and I'm forced to blink rapidly as my eyes adjust to a sudden shift in the lighting.

My body shivers involuntarily—not from the cold but from an abrupt and overpowering nausea. The dark room I expect to find is lit up: golden glow of a hundred candles, saturated light, tapestries on the walls. It's a circular stone room small enough like it's sitting at the base of a stone tower. I spot a sitting chair and a straight-backed wooden one at a messy desk. Papers, a quill, ink, and an open compass sit on it. A bottle of laudanum, too. Directly opposite the door we've entered from is another, plainly wooden exit. Positioned in the centre of the room, on a round handwoven rug, is some metal contraption I have no name for. Its bottom half is a tripod, but then it explodes into an array of brass appendages like an orrery, but instead of solar objects, vials of blood are suspended and moving in relation to one another. Each vial is labelled, and of course I recognise them. Every one of us put our blood in one of these as we crossed that other threshold, onto the University grounds.

My eye stays on the blood orrery, where some vials jerk and move, and others remain stationary. I can't be sure what it's for—whether the blood needs to stay moving, or if it's something worse, like a tracker, or a map—but it at once disturbs and compels me.

The only other thing that gets my attention is the presence of the doorkeeper.

He is a Blood Hunter—the same Blood Hunter I saw the night of the first trial, meeting his partner beneath the willow to hunt a runaway. The gruff northern accent aligns with my memory, but he doesn't look how I imagined. His lips are sunken and thin, and his skin is pockmarked: first from acne, many years ago, but again from old scars, running thin and knife-like across his cheeks. He looks to be in his forties, but is probably younger—at least bodily. He has one of those faces where exhaustion flavours him with deep-set, hollow eyes, a haunting thousand-yard stare, an expression devoid of any joy and life. He is old in spirit. His soul seems practically haunted.

From the other door, I hear commotion. Or not *commotion*, but *noise*. And I'm shocked to hear it—shocked when I realise that I haven't heard the bustle and ambience of a city since coming onto campus. I'm hearing now the muffled signs of life. The indistinct sounds of the thing this campus has been missing all along.

Students.

I don't know what comes over me. All my fear calcifies into exhausted bravery: I storm forward and wrench the door open. There is, again, a great darkness like a sheet separating this room from the rest of this building. But I can see form-less shadows moving, and I can hear more clearly their conversations. As if said entirely for my benefit, the words: *"Should see one of the Artificers"* pierces the veil with a stark clar-ity. Without thinking, I go to step over the threshold.

A rough grip hauls me back. I stumble, and the Blood Hunter ungently slams the door closed. He stands between me and it, and grimaces.

"Stupid," he says.

"There are students in there," I say, dumbly.

"Yes, well done," the Blood Hunter snorts. "But you're no student."

We stare at each other. Over his shoulder, I see Leo shift, frowning at the orrery whirring in the centre of the room.

I go to tug the door open again and the Blood Hunter grabs my wrist. He's big, I realise—the bulk of him is drowning in the black Mackintosh, but he certainly has size. I grunt and reluctantly let go of the handle.

"But can you take us all on?" I say with a confidence I don't feel.

He snorts, and then lets out a full-bellied laugh. "Oh, Lord. You're Thaddeus' brother, aren't you? Yeah. Same unfortunate nose." (I flinch. I like my nose.) The Blood Hunter flicks his finger across it and shakes his head. Then he wrenches the door open. Leo makes to step forward and the Hunter tuts, hand raised.

"I wouldn't," he says. He sniffs and hacks and moves toward a tall wooden wardrobe, but when he opens it there are just hundreds of little wooden drawers from floor to ceiling, with golden letters imprinted onto the wood. He moves immediately to 'J', plucks out a vial, and pulls a pipet from his coat. Uncapping the vial—*my* vial—he draws up a few drops of blood and moves back to the open door and its foggy visage.

"You watching?" he clarifies, knowing full well all of us are staring. Then he squeezes the blood free.

It spontaneously combusts.

There's no other way to describe it. The blood hits the barrier and is instantly engulfed in a fire so bright I step back.

"*What the fuck*," Bellamy whispers. I glance at him; he's open-mouthed and staring. Victoria has her arms crossed still, and she frowns at me when we lock eyes.

She steps forward and tears Varro. Waving the volume dismissively in the air, Victoria says, "So we're stuck on this side until we pass. Got it. Let's not waste our time thinking about that when we have a fucking *Nemean Lion* to survive in the morning." She looks back at the Blood Hunter, who is smiling at her, for some reason. "You're the Doorkeeper, aren't you? *Ianus, ianitos*—there's no cult of Janus, it's just *you*, monitoring the passage between the testing ground and the real University."

He stares at her, not unkindly, but also not like she's spoken some great revelation into the world. "Well, yes. Did you come here expecting to find a god?"

"We came here," I say slowly, "for an artificer."

"Is this another trial?" Silas asks.

The Blood Hunter glances at him. "No."

"Then I don't see what the problem is."

A cock of the head, a sigh. "I am not supposed to help students win any trials."

"Fuck this," Fred says. She nudges me; I know what she wants. I oblige, because I'm getting desperate, and tired, and *God*, have you forsaken me, truly? Why can't we catch a break? I reach into my pocket and cock the gun at the Blood Hunter's head. Fred raises her chin. "What about now?" she says.

It feels different to pointing the gun at Peter Drike, or a *teras*, because this man is smiling. Not, I think, because he feels truly invulnerable—but because it would be mutually assured destruction. I pull this trigger, and what? At best we face tomorrow, and are torn apart and eaten, a gory meal for a monster. At worst, it will be a quick death: the dean won't let us leave. It will be an execution.

My face must show my hesitation, because the Blood Hunter gestures at me. "Why d'you think you're meant to petition an Artificer, Mr Jones?"

I flinch. It feels so much like a question that'd be lobbed to you in school. "So we don't forget how much we need the resources of the University. So we are beholden to this place."

It's an obvious answer. It doesn't appear to satisfy him. The Blood Hunter takes a deep sigh and walks towards the barrel, and I let him: I let him get close enough that all he has to do is gently push my wrist until I'm aiming at the wall.

"It's creative, I'll give you that. Resourceful, too. But it's not the only way to beat this trial."

I think of the hemlock. It's the only advantage we've got. I know what he's saying: that we have to be prepared to improvise, that inevitably there will be a time in our careers where we'll have no information, no resources to fall back on, and we'll have to fight a *teras* on instinct alone. But why should I let myself die when I know a way to survive?

"Well, it's the way we're going for," I mutter. The others are getting agitated. I see Leo looking at me, rolling back his shoulders, ready to fight this man if he has to. I don't look his way, in case I'm his trigger. "My brother was half eaten by a *manticore*. I plan to stop it. To kill it. It's still roaming out there, you know. Feasting." I step closer, so the Blood Hunter can see the sincerity in my eyes; the fear, too. I want him to see me as an honest man. A stupid one, maybe, but honest. "I can only do that if I make it out of tomorrow's trial alive."

A small smile softens his features. "Lad, you're not killing that *manticore*." He sniffs, sighs. For a moment, I'm certain I've lost him. How am I meant to know whether he even liked Thaddeus? But something shifts; obligation, I think it must be. Whatever it is that pushes him to relax, he's still reluctant. "Alright," the Blood Hunter says. "I'll let you petition an Artificer."

He steps towards the door. Silas unfurls his arms and tries to ruin this one good thing by saying, "Thought you weren't allowed to help us."

"You sure you want to question me, lad?" the Blood Hunter shoots back, just before he steps through the veil. "Don't touch a fucking thing."

⚶

We wait in cramped silence, all of us spread out as far as the tiny space allows.

The first thing any of us does—naturally—is to touch things we aren't meant to. I move to the desk and promptly pocket the laudanum. Bellamy immediately goes for the orrery, but it just whirrs out of his way. Its lower tripod half extends rapidly until the vials and whatever strange map they're following is high above any of our reaches. I'm surprised that Bellamy gives up, and even more so that Silas takes his place as resident chaos-causer. His are more scholarly efforts, though. He starts digging through pages, but when I hear him swear I know they're all in Latin.

"Cassius," he calls, begrudgingly, and I go, because I'm petty and enjoy knowing more than he does. But then I have to contend with the embarrassment of not knowing what it's written in. It's not Latin. Not Ancient Greek either.

"Aramaic," I mumble—because I think that's it. "Sorry, Silas. Don't know that one."

He makes a face at the pages and I leave him to it. I almost go to Leo. He looks at me and mouths, *Are you ok?* I want to mouth back, *Are you?* but I think I know the answer. I nod at him and smile and promise myself I have all tonight to mope about him. But Victoria is by the door to *our* campus, arms still folded, back to all of us. With Bellamy preoccupied with opening the tallboy filled with our blood, I need to use the opportunity to speak to her.

She flinches when she hears me approach, half turning. Her eyes are raw and red, bitter look making her lip curl.

"What's happened?" I ask. "Beyond, you know. The trials." Because it's more than that—or I assume so.

She scoffs. I brace myself, expecting her to send me away. But she drops her arms and rocks forward until she's stumbling out of the door. If she were to open her mouth now and howl—let out the most tortured cry—I'm not sure I'd even blink. I realise I'm hovering at the threshold, waiting for her to scream. Victoria doesn't. She wanders to the willow and stares up at it. I follow after her, vaguely aware of the pain in my stomach and torso. I put a hand to it and wonder vaguely if it's nausea or the harpy's claws making me feel this way.

"This is going to sound ridiculous," Victoria says very seriously when she hears me approach, not looking at me, "but I don't think I was prepared for how hard this would be."

That last bit she says in a quiet voice, and when she turns to look at me, it's with searching eyes. Victoria is hoping for solidarity. And how can I not give it to her? She looks at me, rosy cheeks, sunken eyes, pinched expression as if bracing herself for a mockery. I killed a fellow student. I nearly lost my mind speaking to a harpy.

"Victoria," I say breathlessly, half laughing, "I'd think you insane if you were handling this at all well."

Here she gestures to me, and back into the room. "Everyone is—"

"Collectively about to implode. Holding on by our fingertips. But you. . ."

She makes a face like a disappointed grimace and spins back around. "But I'm worse. I'm slipping."

I glance back at the room. "You're handling it as well as anyone. That wasn't what I was going to say."

"No?"

"No." I think about reaching out to her, and stop myself when she instinctively tenses. "What's happening with Bellamy?"

A scoff, a muttered word I don't quite catch. "He's just an asshole."

I press my lips together and think about what I want to say for a moment. Bellamy has always been impulsive. Capricious. A bit of pressure, or stress, and I think he could very easily slip into aggression. "What did he do to you?"

"Nothing," she snaps. She spins back. "Really. Nothing. That's what makes it all so awful: I suddenly can't stand him. I can't stand any of this. I can't stand myself. Do you understand that? Something in my—my *head*, or my *heart*—it just wants to give up. I want to—I don't think I can—"

In the last moments of her awareness, Victoria's body

carefully lowers her to the ground, where she promptly becomes hysterical. I go down with her. I notice her knuckles clenching, the grinding sound of gritted teeth, and I realise she's trying to hold back.

"I thought," she shakes her head; I let her cry into my shoulder. Her voice muffles and the tears soak through the fabric and I can hear her trying to speak, but it's coming out choked and—

I hold her. I hold her and I rock her and I try to find a rhythm that feels safe and calming for the both of us.

It only takes a few moments before she swallows it. I know she has more tears to cry, but I equally understand there's little point in shedding them. We have more trials to get through. More death to contend with. When she sits upright and dabs at her cheeks, I offer her my hand and we stand together.

We arrive back in the room just as the veil ripples and resolves into the Blood Hunter—and another.

"Really, the *proper* processes—"

"—both know there's more to it than—"

"—not *difficult* to—oh."

The Artificer—I assume that's who she is—is not quite what I expected. She is tall and waifish with an anaemic wash over everything; her skin is bloodless, the warmth of her hair is washed away. Her eyes are the most troubling eyes I've ever seen. They are set deep in her head, and low, uniquely hooded; dull and hardened. She gives us all a once over and shifts, turning to the side, which only makes her body look even more insubstantial.

"You're all here," she says with pursed-up scrutiny.

The Blood Hunter clears his throat. "Right. Mr Jones, this is—"

"Don't," the Artificer snaps. "Don't say my name. I was never fucking here, was I?"

She doesn't wait for his reply, just walks over to his desk and sits herself on it. When a beat of silence passes, she starts gesturing impatiently to the lot of us. "Well?"

"Nemean Lion," I say hurriedly, getting right to the point.

She sighs heavily, tries to catch the Blood Hunter's eyes. "There's no weapon that will—"

"Pierce its flank. I know. But we're not trying to get through its flank," I say. "Unless you have one of its own claws." (She stares at me like I'm an idiot, but that's how Hercules skinned it. Whatever). "I need to get into its mouth."

She frowns, and says, "Letting it eat you is the easiest way," and kicks off the table before I can say anything. There's commotion on our side immediately.

"Hey—"

"What do you—"

And she's ignoring us, murmuring something to the Blood Hunter, until all at once she's yelling. "*I can't!* God, I'm not an idiot. Every *bullet* has an artificer's signature. They'll know. Immediately, they'll know."

"Then tell us how you beat it," Leo says.

The Artificer stops and turns to him. I feel, ridiculously, jealous of that stare, because whatever she sees in his face makes her hardened gaze soften. She folds her arms. "We didn't. . ." she gestures outside. "It wasn't like this."

The Lins exchange a glance. Fred says, "No *teras?*"

"Not B tier. That didn't really start until. . ." she gestured to me, and I knew she meant Thaddeus' year.

I glance away. "How long have you been graduated?"

"Long enough. I'm not here for small talk." A sigh. It sounds defeated. "Tell me what you have."

"Hemlock," Silas says.

The Artificer raises a brow. "Okay. And your plan is to

feed the Nemean Lion hemlock, and wait until it goes to sleep?"

As a chorus we say, "Yes."

I amend this with, "It's the only advantage we have."

"No, no. It's a fine one," she says. "How much of it do you have? They'll starve it. Send it out ravenous. If you had any meat. Or a corpse—"

She stops herself, perhaps realising we're not on the field; we don't have an abundance of bodies around us. Except, perhaps, the bodies of our fellow students.

Victoria and I lock eyes. She quivers; I think she hears me, somehow, or has the same thought.

"Where do they take the corpses?" Victoria whispers. It's the first time she's spoken since we were outside. Bellamy moves to her immediately, and she holds him back with her hand. "I suppose they feed them to the *teras*?"

"Yes," the Artificer says. She does not elaborate. Momentarily, a heist unfolds in my head: whatever dark pits our bodies are discarded in is on campus. We could spend the night finding it, fighting back the hungry *teras*, stealing a body of a dead comrade to feed the lion tomorrow. It falls apart easily, but for a moment it's almost pleasant thinking of all the ways we might survive this. All those impossible ways.

"We don't have time," Fred says gruffly. "Whatever you're thinking of, we face this thing tomorrow. So it can't be anything that takes more than a few hours to put together." She rubs her hands over her face. "Christ, I don't know. We don't know anything else. We don't know where we'll be facing this thing, what the landscape will be. . ."

She trails off, likely aware of how harrowing it is to hear how many unknowns we're meant to face tomorrow.

"Just make it drinkable," I say, gesturing to Silas. He nods and roughly pulls out the hemlock from his knapsack for the Artificer. "Maybe a salve. We'll figure out the rest tomorrow."

"What, staring down the lion?" Bellamy scoffs.

"If you have a better idea," I start. "Hell, *any idea*, I'll take it." And he shuts up, obviously, because none of us know what we're doing.

So we hand over our saving grace.

The Artificer looks down at the bunch and nods. "The *teras* that are vulnerable to this—it doesn't take much. This should kill it."

"Should?" Leo prompts.

The Artificer stares at him. "At the very least it will be so sluggish you probably won't die quite so easily."

Leo concedes with a murmur. "Good enough."

"I need two hours. Maybe three," she says. She looks to the Blood Hunter, says, "You owe me, bastard," and steps back through the veil.

Within moments, she's gone.

No one speaks, except the Blood Hunter. "Go on, now. Sod off. You can come back in two, but I'd prefer if you gave me three."

He's kinder than I thought, I realise; but maybe that's a front. He's hunted down another student. He won't hesitate to do it again.

I keep catching myself slipping, thinking there is beauty and hope and friendship in amongst all this. I know that if I let myself feel any of it, it will kill me. If I let my guard down, it will kill me.

And Cassius Jones must live.

LESSON TWENTY-ONE

Everyone splits after that. It's almost time for the dinner meal, but I tell the others I'm not hungry, just so I can have a moment on my own.

Almost certainly, I'll regret that later. I must make sure I eat something before tomorrow, if I have any hope of surviving.

Maybe if you're thin and lanky it will go after someone else, some part of my brain spits out.

Don't you think it's incredible how, even in a situation like this, I can be so worried about how I look?

Victoria, Bellamy, and the siblings head off—not together, notably, but in pairs. And Leo waits for me, like I'll be changing my mind.

I struggle not to meet his gaze, because in the moments where I can feel him looking at me, it dawns on me that what I'm feeling isn't anxiety. Or at least, not anxiety alone.

When I think of tomorrow, when I think of the potential of my death, I feel, irrevocably, ruttish. I don't know—I told you earlier, it always seems to come out of nowhere. Right before something awful. My body knows, and it responds with no easy coping mechanism; no detachment, no simply shutting down of the nervous system. Instead, it practically orders me to fuck. To have every anxious thought railed out of me. My gaze slips to Leo, and then I remember the laudanum I tucked away, and who knows. It's probably better to lose myself in the oblivion of substances than beneath that man. I know myself, you see.

When we slept together, Leo asked me if I had done it before, and I'd told him of the men I let touch me, and never had to see again. Leo thought I was worried about my reputation; that in fucking me, I would be so ashamed of myself, I might never look him in the eye again. But that wasn't what my concern was.

Too much of sex, too much of comfort, and too much trauma. Should I sleep with Leo too often in these circumstances and I know I'll think I love him. And I can't afford to do that—whether it be a love conjured by hormones, or in truth.

Not because I'm scared of love. But because I am not here for me. I am here for my family. On God, I am here to make sure my mother lives comfortably. Duty before men. Duty before cock—God, it should not be so difficult.

"I should pray," I tell him, and he nods at me quietly.

"Do you need company?"

The urge to say yes nearly overwhelms me, until I acknowledge what kind of company I desire from Leo Shaw. I can't bring that desire into a house of God. "Are you a godly man?"

He leans himself against one of the courtyard pillars. A little breeze moves through his hair. "For you, I could be," he whispers. At this point, I think I would be forgiven for reaching out and kissing him. He looks so damned lovely; and hungry, too. I know just by looking at him that he shares my desire, and I want to be wanted so badly I feel my resolve slipping.

BE ON YOUR GUARD; stand firm in the faith; be courageous; be strong.
1 Corinthians 16:13

"No, Mr Shaw," I tell him, my hand flat on his chest, over his heart. I feel the rapid beat of it. He raises his hand, gently envelops mine with it.

"Alright, Mr Jones," he whispers with a smile. His tone betrays him, though– and I'm not quite sure he's trying to hide his disappointment. I think he wants me to feel it.

God, he's good. Or perhaps I'm simply a slut. I almost cave and tell him 'later', but I'm a good, brave, and strong Christian boy, and I smile back at him instead, slipping my hand away so I can walk to the chapel.

Because I refuse to take it on hallowed ground, I uncap the laudanum when I'm out of sight of Leo, walking back through the shadowed halls. I don't have much of it, because I want to stay awake; just a finger dip I rub into my gums, a few drops down the throat. My body convulses with the bitterness, but within seconds the euphoria hits me. Muscles I wasn't aware were wound so tightly start to release.

The chapel is beautiful at night. The doors are open—I think they must always be open—and candles burn from within, warm glow pulsing its welcome out into the afternoon. I stagger in still high and stumble into a pew. I think part of me forgot there's a giant *scylla* carcass fused to the chapel's walls, because I keel over at the sight of it, but I manage to land well on my knees in a crumpled pile resembling prayer. Though it still looms there, though I'm still knelt before it as if in worship, I mark my words very clearly. I mark them for God. And I say a prayer on my knees, though my words quickly slip into outright begging. My skin burns with shame; the shock of this place hits me like grief does, in layered waves, never truly going away. When tears threaten to spill, some image of Thaddeus comes to me unbidden, and that does it. That's enough for grief to burst through the bulwark. I sob. I have to press my lips together hard to stop making a sound, but *God*. God. What kind of place is this? And what have I gotten myself into? If I'm wrong about the trial tomorrow, have I damned us all? Have I damned Leo?

I rock back into my haunches and uncouple my hands, pressing the butt of my palms against my eyes. I feel—filthy. By now, it's obvious that I'm uncontrollable. I smoke, and I drink, and I lose myself in laudanum. I have sinned. I will sin again. I've fucked. I've taken pleasure in another man. If Leo wants me tonight, I will let him fuck into me until he's spent, because I enjoy it. I've enjoyed myself, writhing beneath him —and my brother is dead. And people my age are dying. And this place wills it so.

I realise that I'm shaking. I'm not making sense. Every-thing I want, really—objectively—has nothing to do with the horrors happening in this institution. But it is the only thing I'm meant to be able to control, and I let my groin rule me. So that feeling of filth crawls up my spine; I can hear the devil chattering in my brain.

If only to feel the touch of God, His forgiveness, I stand and shove myself into a confessional.

"Father," I say, but I don't think he's there. So I wait. Within a minute, I hear the door of the priest's booth groan open and shut. The wooden seat creaks as it takes his weight.

Old indoctrination sparks in me. The urge to be cleansed of this filth fills me up and I don't wait for the Father to invite me to speak—another of my sins to list!—and in fact, before he can say anything at all, I begin.

"Bless me, Father, for I have sinned. It has been months since my last confession. And I have. . . sinned so wholly I fear there's no coming back from it. No hope for my immortal soul." I pause, I inspect my hands. "I lust for my colleagues. I lust for men. I crave them, even now. Even—" I make a noise. "Even in amongst all this death and this fear, I still feel the urge to seek them out. I think you'll say it's the stress, but I know what I want. I know, in my heart of hearts, that loving men is a sin because of how good it feels. And nothing on this earth should feel so close to heaven. Is that blasphemy?"

I wait—there's no response. Briefly, I consider no one's next to me, until I hear the creaking of the chair. And when another moment comes with no offer of rosaries or penance, I think: Cassius Jones, you have fucked up. You have bared your soul to an agent of the institution who does not care if you live or die. Who will gladly add your sins to its arsenal should it need to put you in your place. You have gone and whored yourself out again, thinking God is watching.

But by now, I'm starting to wonder if God even cares.

"It is not a sin to love," says the man in the booth. I start, I'm so shocked to hear it. And then I choke. I know that voice. I *know that voice*: I've had it moaning in my ear. It is not the priest sitting there, listening to me spill my heart out.

It's fucking Leo Shaw.

"You bastard," I hiss, beating the partition separating us. Furious, and nervous, I curse silently, squirming in the relative privacy of the booth. *Bastard! Fiend!* I'm ashamed he's heard me so vulnerable, awfully nervous Leo Shaw has heard something that lets him see me more truly. I've gone and shattered some fantasy, tainted his lust for me.

Another part of me is fearful in a more base way. Fearful God will strike me down. Sinning outside His house is one thing, but letting an impotent lover do as he pleases? Letting him act as a priest, adopting a mantle he has no right to? I knock my head against the back of the confessional. "Bastard," I whisper again. "That's not—I don't. . ." I sigh, rubbing my temples. My cheeks are burning. I want to tell him: *This is* my *place, you blaspheming devil. My religion. My God. If you are faithless, so be it. But don't taint mine.* Instead, all I manage is, *"Don't* mock me again."

There's a groan as the wooden seat is released, and a moment passes where I don't hear him. I assume he's left, stormed out or sulked, I don't care. But then the door to my booth creaks open.

Leo looks at me forlornly

"I mean it," he says. "It is not a sin to love."

"Leo," I say, "what are you doing?"

He doesn't answer. He just walks in and closes the little confessional door behind him, and something about that, something about being this close to a man who's been inside me, who I have had carnally, who I lust after—the weight of the sin feels immense. This is a holy space.

I shouldn't be feeling what I'm feeling. Heat flooding my groin. A twitch. This isn't—what I wanted. I wanted—still want—absolution. I sigh and readjust myself. "Why did you follow me?"

He looks at me and flinches. "I don't know. I thought. . ."

"You thought?"

A defeated sigh, and then his confession true: "I wanted to. That's all. I wanted—"

He cuts himself off, perhaps realising he has propositioned me and then stalked me as I ran to God. And I think he is about to proposition me again. And I think the act of defiling myself on holy ground will be yet another sin God cannot forgive.

But I don't think I can stop myself.

Leo is looking at me, heat in his eyes, hungry. I shift and turn my head to stare at the wall.

"You've heard all my sins," I whisper.

"They're hardly sins," he says.

I snort. "Really?"

He moves. I can see him; the shadow of him, pressing forward in the cramped booth. I can all but feel the heat from him, and I go dizzy with a terrible kind of arousal, where I'm scared of what I'm feeling. Of the intensity.

Leo knows exactly what he's doing. When I gain the courage to turn to him, his eyes rake over me like my flesh is an altar to be desecrated. I am meant to keep myself a temple to God, and I keep letting other men in. This will be no exception, because Leo bends over me, arms pushing against both narrow walls until I'm trapped beneath him, until I have to arch my neck to look up.

A smile quivers at his lip. Barely more than a whisper he says, "Do you want to know what true sin feels like?"

God.

God fucking save me.

The way he says it, the way he looks at me, shoots straight to my groin. I feel my cock fatten, and my confession burns in my brain: lust is my greatest sin. I'm too weak to stop it.

I am too weak to *want* to stop it.

Leo stands straight and steps back. "Get on your knees," he says.

And I am a good boy, so I do what I'm told.

I go down ready to worship. I forget that my entire torso is covered in bloody bandages; the promise of pleasure is briefly enough to expel any latent pain. Leo's eyes glaze over with lust and want. He reaches into his pants, face creasing up with happy surprise. I don't think he expected me to do this. Hell, I shouldn't—I know I shouldn't. But I think it is obvious by now.

I am not a very good Christian.

So when Leo takes his cock out of his pants, I let out a little moan. Leo's finger grazes beneath my chin as he raises it, thumb edging against my lips, rubbing over my teeth.

"Open," Leo whispers. I open dutifully. He's so hard it must be painful; head red, swollen, dripping pre-come. I open wider. Leo presses the head of his cock on my tongue, and I taste him, tonguing up into the slit. Leo jerks forward, seizing with a groan, and presses into me fully. We moan together; I am suddenly so hard I have to move. I dig the palm of my hand against my breeches, grinding up for the friction, even as the material strains and starts to hurt. My focus is on Leo, on the staccato noises, the heavy grunts he's making. I stare up at him, at the way his face twists, religious in his ecstasy. And I let him fuck my mouth, every snap of his hips making me choke, each thrust another blasphemy.

I reach up to brace against his thighs, then snake around to the swell of his arse, gripping hard.

He grabs my hair and fists it—*fuck*, I am completely at his mercy. He whispers something I don't catch, and then he's coming suddenly, pumping down my throat and moaning, saying, *"Holy God, Holy God, Cass, fuck,"* and I swallow and pant as he pulls out of me. But shit, I need it now—need him to put his hands on me. I'm so hard I will probably fall apart from the slightest touch. Leo reaches down and drags me to standing, kissing me hard. He's crowding against my body, inhaling against my lips like he's trying to catch his breath by stealing mine. His hand moves down my torso and he palms my erection—God, prayer has never made me feel like this. God's love has never made me feel like this. I want—

"I want you," I say, and Leo's lips quirk up in a grin, and then God intervenes.

Just as Leo crowds me back against the confessional's seat, spinning me, hands tearing at my pants, we hear it.

Footfalls on the marble outside, and a voice—Father Veer's, curious as he calls out, "Is someone. . . seeking absolution?"

Leo puts a hand on my mouth. We go quiet, but then the priest's footsteps start up again, and he's going to open the door and find the two of us tangled up in sin. I feel Leo make the decision. His body tenses and he presses more firmly against me; my erection throbs in his hands.

"Yes," he says, fumbling me. I try to bite the flesh of his fingers to keep my eager moan locked away; I'm not sure if I managed it.

In any case, the priest says, "Very well." He walks to the booth, he opens it, and settles in, and all the while Leo's hands are touching me.

So I am trapped in Hell, or a Heaven so tainted by my filth it has become this—suspended between the back of the confessional booth and Leo's work-broadened body, with his big hands palming me and his cock growing hard again against my backside.

"*In nomine Patris et Filii et Spiritus Sanctii, Amen,*" Father Veer says. I shiver when he invokes God's name, fearful that if He wasn't watching before, He certainly is now.

Leo parrots my earlier line, and manages to sound devout in a way that, if I didn't know him, I would never question that he was Christian. "Bless me, Father, for I have sinned," he says. He doesn't know what comes next, doesn't know the formula ingrained in me, so he just says, "I have committed the sin of sodomy," with a low growl.

"I see," Father Veer says. I can't parse his tone—my mind is elsewhere, my mind is focused on bucking up towards Leo's hand. "But God's love is infinite and His mercy is without limits. You are here seeking forgiveness, my son. That is the first step towards repentance."

"It would be," Leo says. "But I know I'll do it again."

Christ, this is the act that will plant me securely in hell. I want Leo to plunder me, but I will make do with the friction. I try to fuck my cock up into his hand, but he lets go suddenly, putting both hands on my hips to lock me in place. Against my neck he mumbles, "Did you hear me, Father?"

"I heard you," Father Veer says. He shifts in his seat—discomfort, maybe, making him move. The priest clears his throat just as Leo grazes the sensitive head of my cock, so my moan is slightly muffled.

"Everything alright?" the priest says

"I'm bereft, can't you tell?" Leo says. Cocky bastard. "Can barely. . . keep it to myself. How upsetting I find it. How incapable I am of stopping myself."

He's taking the piss now, and I should be furious, but I'm quivering and bent over. Leo starts working me with an intensity, and I am braced against the back wall, sweating, desperately canting up—but the angle is terrible, and I barely have any power to my thrusts, so it's up to Leo entirely. He does the job with an almost cruel ease, wrist rapidly stroking, breath hot against my ear, cock straining in his breeches against my backside.

"Son," Father Veer says. "Whilst I. . . cannot condone or approve of such behaviour, I will still offer you God's love and mercy. God prefers you focus on the *teras* threat. He will overlook this, if you destroy the beasts of Satan."

Leo pauses in his movements and I swallow a groan, burying my face into my bracing arm. I need it, I *need it*. I arch my back for his attention, but his hand doesn't move.

"It's this place," Leo says. There's a change in his tone that gives me pause, but I'm barely thinking beyond what I want him to do to me. "I don't want to die without knowing what true pleasure is. I want to have as much of it as I can. I want to fuck as much as I can. Can you blame me?"

A sigh, the kind of noise I expect of a man who truly doesn't give a shit. Not what I expect from a priest. "I'm not here to pass blame on you. Only forgiveness, if you're seeking it. But it seems. . . that you're not."

Leo touches me with renewed speed and I arch into his touch so far I lose my purchase on the wall. I bend so I'm half collapsed on the confessional's seat, one hand over my mouth, and—

God.

Nothing ever feels. *Like this*.

"Oh, my God," Leo breathes as I come suddenly over his hand. "*God*. I'm definitely not."

I want to moan and have to bite down hard on my own arm as I quiver and nearly topple forward. My legs twist inwards, knees buckling, and almost immediately the clarity of what I've done hits me. It's not long before I'm bludgeoned by shame. Leo's hands disappear. I look over my shoulder—pants around my ankles, cock dripping, an absolute mess of a man—and watch Leo lick my cum from his fingers.

"Sorry, Father," he says. He opens the door to the booth just as I hike my pants up. "I didn't mean to waste your time."

The booth smells of sex and sweat and sin, but I'm too ashamed to stick around. When Leo leaves, I leave with him, head bowed, cheeks flushed, and back turned to God.

For any Christian reading, it isn't that I've decided to hate the Lord. I want the embrace of the Church and the absolution that comes with prayer. But I want, too, my body. I want to use it. I want to feel something with it. And there's nothing quite so perfect as giving myself to men; of having the beauty that is men touch me.

And I don't think I can admit it's a sin. Certainly not when the act is tender, but also not when it is rough, debasing. It's all love. It's all love for *my body*.

Perhaps I don't feel guilt for what I do. Perhaps I feel guilty because it is expected.

LESSON TWENTY-TWO: NOLI DORMIRE DUM IN SPECULIS

I stop Leo outside the great hall; one yank against his shirt that makes him slow down.

He looks back at me and exhales, small smile on his lips. He thinks—or expects—that I want to kiss him. That after what he's done to me, I'll want him to take me right here.

Which I do. Of course. *Of course*. But I've decided to be angry, and that takes priority over anything else. Leo starts crowding me back towards the wall, and I know if I let him do it, I'll lose my resolve. I'll lose any kind of backbone if he presses into me. So I flip him. One foot hooked around his ankle, shoulder barrelling into his chest, and I ram him back against the wall.

He exhales noisily as all the air is punched from his lungs —but it's still fun and games for him. He smiles at me, teeth glinting in the fading sunlight, and he shifts and breathes and adjusts his hips against me. Something twitches in my pants —I ignore it. God, I ignore it.

"Never do that again," I tell him, gesturing back to the chapel. "Never."

The glint in his eye fades, and he cocks his head, inspecting me. "You liked it," he says.

"Yes." I can admit that much. Crowded close to him, I can feel the heat from his groin doing things to mine. He makes me ruttish, like an animal. And I can't afford to be like this. Not tonight, not before what comes tomorrow. What we did should have calmed me. It should have been enough to satiate me. But it didn't.

Don't think about it. Focus on the teras. *Focus on the lion that's going to rip you open tomorrow.*

"But that—wasn't right," I say. "That wasn't the kind of man I want to be. I believe in God. I pray to Him. And even if I'm not *good* at it, even if I want you, and will let you have me, we should not have. . ."

I sigh. I don't know if I can get my point across when I came so hard. The filthiest thing I've ever done, and the least moral thing I've ever done, and I loved it.

"Cassius. . ."

He looks at me strangely, then. Teeth glint, lips widen. I brace myself to hear him say: *"Why? I am only trying to fuck you."*

He doesn't need to respect me, if that's all it is.

What else would it be?

I settle my jaw and wait, but Leo raises his hands to my shoulder. "I won't. . . tempt you like that again," he says. "At least, not when you're on holy ground."

It's fucking pennies, and I dive to snatch them up. I exhale against him, edging forward until his breath is hot on my face, my neck. I press my lips to him and somehow I can feel his intent in that kiss alone. His hands aren't on me, there's no tenting in his pants—but he wants me.

I pull away, trying to subdue the fluttering in my heart. How much I love being wanted.

Perhaps it's pathetic that the smallest bit of respect makes me glad, but I will take what I can get.

"Come on," I say, and grab his hand—before immediately letting go of it. Far too intimate. I remind myself this is nothing more than carnal comfort. We are trying our best not to die, and sex is a decent way to stay sane.

So don't lose yourself to him. It's only sex. Focus.

Maybe if I say that enough, it'll get through my damn skull.

The great hall is stuffed with food and drink and light, with all our surviving cohort revelling in a feast.

Sure, they are all eating like it's our last meal, and getting drunk to forget the slaughterhouse we walk to tomorrow. But it's *nice*. It feels close to what I expected, coming here. A University with no monsters on campus. A community bound together by more than fear.

It's never been done up like this—visually, I mean, not even to welcome us. So decorated with candles and flowers and food that it feels like a funeral feast. A grand farewell to see us all off before we are inevitably torn to shreds tomorrow.

More than that, it seems like a waste. London is not overflowing with food. That is part of why these trials exist, part of why we're all competing for a place and the safety of our families. London has luxuries, but not like this. Even the food supplied to the University isn't usually so excessive.

But, as Horace wrote, *Carpe diem, quam minimum credula postero*. And I need a good meal.

Leo and I slip in and take our seats with the others. They are all waiting, halfway through their meal, and I can't help but feel like their eyes can see more than I want them to. That somehow they can smell Leo on me, or my scent coating his fingers. Really unfounded fears, born from a kind of shame (though shame is doing a really poor job of stopping me from fucking men).

No one says anything, of course. Not about us, anyway. I immediately light a cigarette and take a few heavy drags, slowly catching up on the conversation. The hall is cold innately; somewhere deep in the stone, in the building's marrow, it simply leaks heat. So when someone moves and shuts the outside door, I'm grateful. It gives me a chance to warm my bones. I shake out the latent worry, and the leftover drowsiness that always hits me after orgasm, and try to take comfort in tobacco.

"Stop drinking," Victoria says when Bellamy pours himself another glass of wine. "I mean it. Tomorrow, you'll be—"

"Gutted, most like," Bellamy says with a sniff, half his mouth full of wine and meat. "So what's the point in being sober for it?"

I don't know what's happened in the hour or so since we last saw each other. Why Bellamy expects to die tomorrow, why Silas is sitting apart from Fred. I settle awkwardly at the table, and I can *feel* the way the tension sits between us all.

"We're not dying," I tell Bellamy. He glares at me and drinks deep with a childish defiance. Victoria unfolds her arms and ends up drinking herself, jaw working as she repositions herself. Her body angles slightly away from Bellamy.

"Sure," he says.

I sigh and pour myself my own drink. Beneath the table, Leo's thigh grazes mine, and I have to bite my tongue to stop myself leaning into it. And then I tip my head back and scull the drink and grimace as my oesophagus lights up, burning with the alcohol.

"Shit," I say. "This is strong."

I've become so used to watered down wine that I'm shocked at the drink's potency. I take another gulp and welcome the soft unwinding power of it, marvelling at how quickly my muscles relax. It feels good. Nice. I could see myself getting very drunk tonight, and facing the Nemean Lion hungover and half-dying.

"Definitely numbs the pain," Silas murmurs.

"From the *manticore?*" I gesture to his side.

"And every damn movement since."

I sigh. "We should have petitioned a Healer, too. Maybe—"

"No," Silas cuts me off. "No, don't worry about me, Mr Jones. We would have only been allowed one—and I'd much rather secure my spot in this University than worry about a flesh wound."

Fred quietly sips her wine, which to me says 'flesh wound' is a massive understatement for the state of Silas' body. But the problem is I agree with him. If the *Ianus* Blood Hunter had told us we could only choose one, in every reality I would have chosen Artificer.

"You're right," Fred murmurs suddenly. "This really is very strong."

"Party," Bellamy says deadpan.

And then I suddenly regret drinking. Awareness settles on me like something freezing and sharp; I see the hall, how drunk everyone is, how relaxed, and I think: surely not.

Surely they would give us this and mean it. Surely they would allow us a night to ourselves; they will make good on their promise, and give us the trial tomorrow.

Because, so far, everything has been fair and true.

"Don't drink," I say.

Leo notices how I've stiffened. "Cass," he murmurs, cautious and testing. "What is it?"

The doors are closed. All of them, from every angle. I could have sworn—they were open, weren't they? When we walked in? Or do I. . .

The alcohol's effect is quick and strong. When I push

back against the bench, wood scraping along the stone, and stand, my vision immediately swims. "Do *not* drink," I say.

"Poison?" I hear Leo ask. He believes me instantly—I love that—but no.

"No, they just want us to relax. With our guards down."

Fred makes a sound of annoyance, and I can hear her whisper something to Victoria, but I can't worry about that. I wouldn't mind being wrong about this. But if I'm right, they'll know about it.

I move to the door Leo and I entered from. Someone closed it, and I was happy about that, because it meant the cold would be kept out.

But it also means—

Something is wrong. Something is—not right. Because when I push against the door, it does not move.

It's been locked. From the outside.

And we are trapped inside.

"It's locked," someone repeats. Who, I'm not sure. For a moment, I am barely in reality. A torrent of emotions threatens to drown me, and I can't breathe, and *God*, this is His hand, and I deserve it, I am damned and full of sin

"Hey, Cass. *Cassius*. Stop it. Calm down. What's happening? What's wrong?" Leo's strong hands are on my shoulder. Usually they calm me, ground me. But I feel so fucking unhinged right now that being touched is overwhelming. I step out of his embrace, breathing hard with my back to the door.

"They've locked us in," I say.

"So what?" Bellamy barks from the table.

"Never let your guard down," I say, but it's Thaddeus speaking through me, throttling me on the back of my head. And in my mind's eye I see him, my brother's ghost. Arms folded, tutting at me as he leans against the wall. His guts hang out, drooping down to his ankles.

"Fell asleep at the watchtower, brother?" he slurs. He is eviscerated and still disappointed in me. As he should be.

I let myself get distracted. I let Leo in my head and in my body and I *relaxed*.

First rule of Hunters. *Never let your guard down.*

"Get up," I hiss at Fred and the others. "Get up *now*. Stop eating. Stop drinking. Grab what you can. Meat, maybe, if it's hungry. And then—"

"What are you bloody talking about?" Bellamy guffaws through a mouthful. And for some reason that's when I know I've had enough. I break a little. As he's sitting there chewing, grease around his mouth, unfocused eyes laughing at me, I kick the table backwards. It hits him in the stomach and he half chokes, half spits whatever he's eating onto the table with a wet plop. Victoria groans, the siblings mutter—they still don't get it. Angry now, Bellamy starts paying attention. But just as he slams the table, scrapes back his chair to stand and spits, "What the fuck, Jones?" I climb up on the table and scream.

Just one long, unhinged scream. It's everything I have in me. A roar, a hysterical, broken noise that says: I am so close to breaking! And God, if you don't listen to me right now, I know I'll lose my mind!

The chatter quiets down—it's hard not to notice someone howling on a table—and I can see Leo in my periphery, staring at me, eyes focused.

"*What the fuck,*" Peter Drike mutters in the crowd; I hope the bloody lion eats him first.

"We're locked in," I shout over their mutterings, "because *this* is the next trial."

Noise goes up, but there's no consensus. They think I'm drunk. They think I'm insane—whatever they think, in the end, what does it matter?

We're too late.

The doors to the great hall grind open.
Something growls from the shadows.

LESSON TWENTY-THREE

The first thing I do is praise God that our table isn't the closest to the door.

The next thing I do is freeze.

I don't know—all my muscles lock up and I am perched high, in the direct line of sight of the *teras* stalking out of the shadow. Conflicting commands race through my brain: run, stay still, drop off the table. Lower yourself down and grab a butter knife—just to feel something in your hand. Just to feel the weight of it.

But then Leo slips his hand around my waist, and slowly but firmly lifts me off the table. He pulls me against him and I can feel the fluttering of his heart at my back. We lower ourselves slowly to join the others.

"No, *no, no,*" Victoria is saying. "What about the hemlock? The Artificer said—we need to—" And it's shock making her babble, and fear, and Bellamy has to put a hand over her mouth to keep her quiet.

There are a few sharp murmurs and hushed whispers. No screams yet. No sound of people being torn apart. I squint and brace myself for an attack. But the thing hasn't even

261

crossed the threshold yet, like it wants an audience, like it's assessing how it can get to all of us in one bound.

All this is a guessing game. I can't see it. And I need to. I edge around the table and scrabble along the floor to the one beside ours—Leo makes a sharp noise that's echoed by the applicants at the next table as I shove into their crew.

"Stay down," I tell them, like I know what I'm doing. I think about asking if any of them has hemlock, but what's the point? There's nowhere to hide and no way to administer it. We will all be ripped apart before the hemlock does its job. "Just stay down."

I edge around until I'm at the table's head, and the angle is enough that I can see into the shadows of the open door.

Glowing eyes glint through the dark of the doorway and canvass the room. Sound is muted on the stone, but I still hear the *teras'* approach. The thud of a fat, hefty paw, the low clicking grumble in its chest. *Pad, pad, pad*, reverberating, echoed in all of our hearts. The great beast crosses the threshold and glows golden. Its fur, impenetrable, refracts the candlelight so that it shines; so that it could be an agent of God if I couldn't see its face, and how misshapen its jaw is. It's not a normal lion. This one is bulky, with visible muscle, and its maw is twisted and swollen, with most of its face distended around giant teeth. And when it opens its mouth and roars, stringy yellow spittle sprays out of its mouth, red swollen tongue lolling out over its teeth.

It is a standoff that doesn't last. Someone thinks they can outrun it: a young man shoots up and dashes to the back of the hall. It's stupid, there's nowhere to go, but fear is in his legs. The *teras* bolts forward, roaring; it leaps in the air, a near vertical ascent, and mid-air above the tables it twists its massive body. When it comes crashing down on the stone, it cuts off the boy's path, already facing him.

He's dead before he knows it. I hear one terrified

choking nose, some frightened instinct that realises he's about to die, and then the lion strikes. A sizable claw cuts across his neck. I have a perfect view of it, I see all the horrific details. Skin, tendon, muscle; all of it sliced open in a way that looks like it's unstitching, a seam falling apart. Blood pushes out of the wound in a spritz, then a stream, and his face grows unnaturally pale rapidly at the same time the glint in his eyes peters out. His head does not come off. Not fully. The flesh at the back of the neck holds on, and he's *not dead yet*. Raspy breathing sounds as the body tries to breathe through the severed windpipe. His hands spasm, half reaching to the throat, playing out the last moments of his dying brain.

The body crumples to the floor in a pool of its own blood. I can't tear my eyes from it. I think back to Watford, I think about sitting in all the gore and those bodies, and Thaddeus' guts in his hands, and the boy whose brains I blew out with my gun, and *God, am I still a good man?*

Adrenaline kicks in before I can succumb to that spiral and it ousts the panic with a numbing focus. The rapid beating of my heart ebbs away to an orchestra of screams. I blink back into awareness and I feel rough hands on my shoulders.

"Cassius! Cassius, for God's sake, please!" Leo shouts at me. Fred and Bellamy kick the table over and drag it to hide us from view. I don't know where its original occupants went. I don't know why the *teras* didn't lunge for me when I was sitting there. I don't know, I don't know, *I don't know—*

Slap.

Sudden stinging pain dances across my cheek. Victoria is breathing heavily in my face, tears in her eyes. "Stop panicking," she pants, clearly on the edge of panicking herself. "Stop it. Just stay here. Talk. We need to—figure out what to—" She pauses to hyperventilate, five or six rapid inhales, before she gets a grip. She lets Bellamy wrap an arm around her and huddles back against the table.

Roars and wet crunches, screams cut off abruptly, rasping breathes that become gurgles as lungs drown in blood. It's picking us off one-by-one.

"We can't stay here," I hiss. "We can't." I risk a peek over the table barrier. Little pockets of students have done the same as us. I can see them huddling behind overturned tables, waiting for the inevitable. But the Nemean Lion has grown momentarily bored. It moves from corpse to torn apart corpse, scavenging, tearing flesh from the bones and grunting. Someone spasms weakly, still alive, and it whips around to them, jaw unhinging and gore-stained teeth biting down into the neck.

I flinch and sink back down. Blood is in my nose. The stench is acrid and everywhere. The animal instinct in me is terrified, shaking; how can I be a Hunter when I am so clearly prey?

"We have to get out of here," I say. Leo flinches closer towards me. He grabs my hand. In one fluid motion, he's brought my fingers to his lips to kiss them. And over my hand Leo just nods, like he'll follow me anywhere. My body relaxes, the adrenaline flooding my heart eases off, and the result is a dizzying wave of nausea.

God, I don't want him to die.

"Do we have to kill it? Or—?" Fred starts. She cuts herself off when a nearby snort sounds awfully close. We all brace ourselves like the flimsy wood can be a legitimate saviour. But nothing attacks. After a beat she continues, more softly. "Or will we forfeit if we leave?"

How am I to know? And forfeit what? There are no consistent rules to this place. We haven't been told if the trial is to survive or kill it. I don't answer, because I don't want to sound angry about how little I know. Still, all of them look to me as if I know more than them. I think about saying: we're the only hope for everyone alive in this hall. But I don't want to bear the inevitable burden when half of them are torn to shreds.

So I clear my throat.

"Plan is the same as it was before," I say. "We get out. Get the Artificer's salve. Plenty of food here. Plenty of bodies. We slather the salve on something, and we entice the *teras*, make it eat it, and then it's done. We've killed the Nemean Lion."

And yes, it's so much easier said than done, but saying it aloud is all I can do. No one comments, but neither does anyone argue. Before I can say anything else, though, Fred, who has been scanning over the table as I speak, suddenly slips out from relative safety. Silas' hands go after her and hover in the air. I feel him ready himself to move, but she's back within seconds, pulling back with her a silver platter of beef.

"In case we can distract it." Fred takes a fistful of medium-rare, marinated beef in her fists. "Don't look at me like that," she says glaring at me. "You're going to make us run for it, and the instant that thing gives chase, we're dead."

I make a noise. "Well, if you have a better idea, I'm all ears."

She holds up the fistful of beef. "I clearly don't."

"Okay," Silas says, exhaling. "What about everyone else in this hall?"

In truth, I hadn't been thinking of anyone else. I am barely thinking of *us*—I just want to get out of here. I don't know how much more of this shit my body can take. But Silas looks concerned, and I think: God, this man actually has a conscience. He might be the only one of us that truly cares for the sake of caring. I am always, inevitably, worried about God's judgement—but am I compassionate? Would I care if it wasn't for my immortal soul?

"Please," Silas says, looking at me, and what can I say?

"Silas," I whisper—God, he is a good man. "We'll come back. I swear it. And you can hold me to it."

He reaches out and grabs my forearm, squeezing it. I meet his eye. He is too good for this place.

I peer over the table. The Nemean Lion tears at a body, pulling free a chunk of flesh from the flank of a girl. It paws around the shredded uniform for the meat. I have to carefully and quickly shut off the part of my brain that registers the body as human. A kind of spotty, distant nausea flares behind my eyes; fear and recognition sparking, saying, *that could be you. Don't let that be you.*

I tear my eyes from the scene. Directly opposite us, huddled against a table of his own, is Peter Drike and his crew. We lock eyes. He's so scared he's showing it, face aghast, breathing hard. I nod my head towards the open hall gates and his eyes go very wide. Slowly, Drike shakes his head.

I nod with more force. *Yes, we're doing this. Yes, it's the only way.* He shifts his body in response. I see his leg, uniform torn apart, near black with the amount of blood that's pooling in the wound. Too much blood. Something vital has been split open. He's dying and doesn't seem to know it yet, and I don't know what can be done. No Healer will come here until we beat the trial, if the harpy is anything to go by. Something tells me I should feel sorry for him, and when I feel nothing, I tell myself it's the adrenaline, numbing the proper moral pull I should be feeling in my heart. Bully or not, it's a terrible way to go.

In any case, Drike's friend has it worse. Behind him, I see someone propped up, and multiple hands pressing down on a shoulder wound that might have destroyed the nerves in her arm. She is not conscious. Hell, I don't know if she's alive.

But staying here will be its own death for the rest of us. And I want to live. More than I thought.

Near the back of the hall, I see someone poke their head out and make a run for it to Drike's table. There's a growl; the Nemean Lion rears up, huffing, interested by the movement. But the girl is quick and she's out of sight before the *teras* spots her. I see her choosing the same plan we have. She crawls to the edge of the table and peeks around, readying herself to dart to the next bit of cover.

"Come on," I murmur, shuffling myself in the same way. "Let's follow suit."

Victoria is breathing hard. I worry panic will make her clumsy, and Bellamy, too. But I can't worry about them, I can't, not if I want to live.

"Fuck this," Fred says. She puts the fistful of meat down and picks up the silver plate it was resting on. Too late, I realise what she's doing.

"Fred," I whisper, a warning. "Don't. *Don't.*"

I am ignored. Fred half stands and flicks the plate towards the back table. At first it slices through the air with a whistle, and then gravity takes a hold of it. Within moments it's skidding across the floor, silver on stone screeching as it moves.

The *teras* reacts instantly. It perks up from the body holding its interest, gory fur dripping blood onto the stone. And it bares its teeth. The silver plate clatters against the table, and whoever's behind it gasps. Out of fear or stupidity or both, they stand and peer over the table.

They lock eyes with the *teras*. The Nemean Lion moves. It launches from standing and propels itself across the hall, landing with a crash in front of the table. A chorus of screams go up. Someone stands and makes a run for it; they are felled instantly by one swipe of the paw, great claws gashing through the sternum. They stagger with a gurgled shock, and they're dead on their feet a beat later. The *teras* ignores them. It craves the hunt again. I see it pacing the table, back and forth. Then it roars and bats it away. The flimsy wood flies across the room and shatters on the far wall.

Hunkered together are three or four applicants. The *teras* screams again.

Then the begging starts.

Whispered prayers to God, to the beast itself, to anyone watching. *Oh, God, please, please.*

"Oh, my God," Silas breathes. "Fred, *what did you do?*"

His sister ignores him. She just grabs his wrist and runs. The rest of us look at each other and launch up within a beat of our hearts. I don't look back. The doors to the great hall are swung wide, inviting, and we just have to get to them; something about crossing the threshold feels safe, even if that's bullshit, false faith. I tell myself to get to the threshold, and everything will be okay.

The background to all this is death. I see none of it, but those cries are brutal.

The sounds of people who know they are about to die. Who have no power to stop it. Who must live on for timeless seconds in agony as they are cut from groin to neck, eviscerated, bleeding out, stop it, stop thinking about this, Cassius, *you will fall apart if you keep thinking about this.*

"Get the door," Leo hisses to me, and any good man would have stopped and stared at him aghast. Because closing this door means trapping this beast in with the rest of them, and what is that if not damning them all to hell? But he's *right.* The Nemean Lion seems to love a chase, and if it follows us, if we don't retrieve the hemlock salve, then what?

Leo is already hauling one of the doors closed. The wood grinds against the stone, a great warning, and the *teras* throws itself around bodily, howling at us from the other side of the hall. I stare at it. It stares back. And then it bounds towards us.

It's in that moment that Bellamy falls.

Maybe it was the wine, or a sole with no grip. I watch him tumble and it all seems inevitable. Victoria stumbles but doesn't go down with him. She staggers to a stop to haul him up. And the lion is bounding towards them, distracted momentarily by their fall.

Leo says, "*No!*" before I've even launched myself off, like I'm sacrificing myself for them, like I mean to die. But I know in my heart—

—I'm not going for both of them.

All the air is knocked out of Victoria's lungs as I grab her around the middle and haul her back. She starts screaming, pleading with me, but she's barely fighting me, too caught up in a sudden wave of panicked tears. *She knows what's coming, and she knows I'm right,* I tell myself. But Bellamy looks up, and sees me, and starts to beg like the others. Says, "No. *Jones*, please. Cassius. Cassius? Don't leave me here."

Voice like gravel, split and broken, a man who knows he's about to die, who is looking his harbinger in the face and pleading with him. The lion bounds forward. I shove Victoria out of the hall, swinging back to grab the other door to pull it shut.

Bellamy manages to stand. He's still looking at me. Why is he looking at me? *Why is he begging me to spare him when the* teras *is at his back?*

"Cassius. *Cassius. Don't—don't—no!*"

My heart twists, just the once.

Not enough for me to kill myself for him.

I haul the door shut.

LESSON TWENTY-FOUR

Victoria throws herself at me with enough force my head smacks against the stone. But that is all the fight she has in her. Her other punches are impotent, weak against my chest; her whole body is wracked with sobs, and she is praying, whispering Hail Marys and Petitions, and then a mantra of *please please please* that slurs together; grief at its rawest, grief that is anger and despair and the urge to claw her skin off, the urge to die to make it end.

I hold myself very still. I don't feel a thing. I promise. I don't feel a single thing. Maybe if I listen very closely, I think I can hear Bellamy screaming—enough. That's enough. Listen to the beating of your own heart. Listen to the life, to Victoria's panic. She's still alive. She's still alive because of me. My eyes drift to Leo. The other man is staring at me, but I can't parse the expression. Is that admiration? Disgust? A confused amalgamate?

God, what will I do if he can't bear to look at me anymore?

"Get the salve," Leo says without looking away from me. The Lins respond with nothing more than silent departure;

they sprint off towards the quadrangle, bodies swallowed quickly by the thick night and the sudden onslaught of heavy rain.

The weather feels fitting at this moment. It is freezing and windy, sluicy rain, and I am backed against the stone with a girl collapsing in on herself, saying prayers to a God who has failed me too many times.

"It would have killed the rest of us," Leo says to placate her. Why is he staring at me? I stare back, unmoving, thinking *what are you seeing in me right now? You called for me to stop; would you have left Victoria there, too?*

"I hate myself," Victoria cries, which comes from nowhere. I flinch and look down at her. Fistfuls of my shirt are wrapped up in her palm, and she's half bent over, crying onto the stone.

"I hate myself. I *hate myself*. What was I thinking? Why on *earth* did I— say those things to you. *That's why you left him.* Because I—"

She thinks confessing that Bellamy was less than perfect made me condemn the man to death. I have to cut her off before she starts believing this true

"Victoria, *no*." I pull her up. She shudders, breathing hard. "I'm sorry. But if I'd waited, I would have damned us all."

"You don't know that," she says, very quietly, and now she's looking at me the same awful way, like somewhere in my skin is a monster. Like I left him there on purpose.

Then she blinks and puts a hand over her mouth. "Oh God. God. I loved him. I swear it. I promise you, Cass, I loved him, I really did, but he was just so. . ."

I tell myself she isn't upset with me. That she isn't scared of *me*, but of herself. I think Victoria Bennet is happy to be alive.

And I think she is glad it wasn't her I left behind.

But when she lapses into a deep silence, I find it worse

than the crying. Because it gives me a moment for everything to settle into place, for the image of Bellamy reaching for me to solidify. I hear the echo of his pleading.

Cassius? Don't leave me here.

And my brother, the actual, soft brother I had before we came here, looking at me with tears in his eyes and guts in his hands. *Cass, we both know I'm not going to make it.*

And I feel myself becoming something I never wanted to be. I feel now what Thaddeus must have felt; a chrysalis, a hardening of the soft body, a necessary shell to grow in. Because if I let myself feel it all, I'll break. It's that simple. I will come undone, and then it will have been for nothing.

So I can't feel this. I can't feel Thaddeus. Bellamy. The boy who I sent to God with a pull of the trigger.

I can't feel Leo: his love, nor this new look he gives me.

I am here for my brother. My mother. Myself.

That has to be enough.

"Victoria," I begin.

She snaps up, suddenly angry. Her eyes are inflamed like a redcurrant has been pressed behind her eyelids. Veins criss-cross in angry havoc, colouring the whites of her eyes. "I dare you to apologise, you bastard. You say those words and I will beat on you until I can't any longer."

Don't feel it. Don't regret what you've done.

I stand tall. "I was going to say that it was necessary. That I could have left you there, too, to be mauled to death. I could have, and I didn't, and I had to make a choice. I bore it, and in the moment I chose you. So you can hate me. I will take your hate, Victoria, because it means you live. It means you live. But don't forget: you live because of me."

"Bastard," she murmurs. She stares at me from under her brow, frowning, and wipes her tears away with the flat of her palm. Then she backs herself against the wall well away from me, away from Leo too. But she does not cry again.

We only have to wait a further five or so minutes before the Lins return, puffing and exhausted but with the salve in hand. As for what comes next, they all turn to me. I regret ever stepping up that first night. I regret a lot of things, then.

Clearing my throat, I nod to the salve gripped tight in Silas' hands. "We need to make sure it eats it all. Get as many people as we can out—" this statement causes a particular kind of tightening in the air, a collective breath being drawn, as if to say, *now? Now you want to get them all out?* As if Fred wasn't the one who sacrificed a whole table of students. As if I was the one who had run first. "—and close the doors. Let the beast die slowly."

I try to frame that last part like a punishment for the *teras*, and not the riskiest part of the plan, but no one says anything about it, because what else is there to do? The hemlock is the only plan we have. We must follow through.

Silas puts his hands through his hair and over his face and that somehow puts resolve back in him. "Alright. Okay. We need—meat. Lather it with the salve. And it seems to like moving prey. So we'll have to. . ."

He doesn't finish.

Moving prey. *Like the* manticore. I distracted that beast by running, then, to give my brother a few more gasping breaths. But this thing is lithe, not bulky like that beast. Quicker. That distraction would be suicide.

Fred bites her nails and glances over to Victoria, who has started to drift, staring out into the rain and losing herself to the lulling rainfall and the night. Leo is quiet, too. Just watching me. I feel—exposed. More naked to him than I ever have been, even after the ways he's touched me, even though he's seen me beg.

I turn back to Silas, because it's safer to stare at that man than anyone else right now. He's the most collected. He knows what we must do.

And I know, of course, where we will get the meat. There is an abundance of the stuff, torn apart, stringy, fresh, just beyond the door. But I can't say this aloud. I'll lose the others, whoever is still hanging on to the sense that we can complete these trials with a shred of our morality intact.

I just put my arms down by my side, very stiffly, grinding my hands into tight fists so they act as tiny weights to ground me. Then I walk back to the great hall.

"Cass," Leo murmurs as I pass, unwinding his arms. I half expect him to reach out and stop me, or to graze his fingers along my shoulder if just for the comfort. But then I'm past him and out of range and he hasn't moved at all.

I am alone as I approach the doors. The others linger back, even though the doors are still securely shut. I press my ear to the wood and wait. My body braces for a cacophony, or pleading. But there is nothing except a soft hum that might have been my own fluttering heart, or perhaps the sound of chewing on the other side of the door. Adrenaline bludgeons back my sense until I feel nothing beyond my duty. I push one door open but it doesn't move smoothly. The hinges groan and creak and I freeze with only a fraction of it open, waiting for the *teras* to come screaming.

I hear more clearly the sounds of flesh tearing. There is a wetness, and a persistent chewing like the meat is tough and stringy. I hear breathing, too; firstly the heavy panting of the *teras* as it eats, happily grunting, but underneath that is an ambient struggling; several humans desperately trying to smother the sounds of their living. I can't see anyone like this, though, so I risk opening the door further.

At once, my body seizes. The visual onslaught is immense and thick. The floors are starkly red with new blood, and smeared with the gore of bodies, of things that had tumbled out from shredded stomachs and bowels, brown or black with their density. A body near the door still twitches and pulses pinkly. The almost-corpse has been torn asunder, stomach gaping. I can't tell who it had once been. I pray I never knew them.

At my feet is Bellamy. I'm certain of it. So certain, in fact, I refuse to look down. I stare at the end of the hall, at the upturned table and a pile of bodies that the *teras* feasts on—the table Fred led it to. I can't see anyone else. They are hunkered down behind tables.

I swallow, and pray, and think, God, there is no way I'm a good man. Because the closest body to the door is Bellamy's. And I need the meat of him. I need to use the man I sacrificed—the boy, really—a friend I left. I need to bend down and drag his lifeless body through the door. I need to slather him in hemlock salve and dance his cadaver about to earn the *teras'* attention. I need to throw him to it and pray he is consumed whole, torn apart and chewed and digested until the hemlock finds purchase in the Nemean Lion's blood. And I can justify it to myself, I can say: everyone else in that room has no chance at living unless you do this. I can say: it is a final 'fuck you' from Bellamy, a chance for his flesh to get revenge. But in this dark and claustrophobic choice, there is also clarity.

My justifications are bullshit. And if I do this, I lose Victoria. I do this, and I lose myself. I am bewildered by the choice, or the lack thereof.

I don't see what else I can do.

So I force myself to look at him. Right near the door. Dead. Bellamy has fallen in a perfect tableau, arm outstretched, reaching for the handle. An arm's length away. He was so close. And I am the reason he is like this.

He is missing one leg. His left has been torn off. Half of his thigh is still attached, but barely. Stringy tendons have plopped onto the floor and pieces of them trail towards the mostly intact lower leg, which is still neatly sitting in the pant leg. The *teras* had given up on him, perhaps when he'd stopped twitching. Perhaps someone else on that other table still lived and convulsed enough to catch the lion's eye. Whatever the reason, Bellamy has been left mostly intact. Which is worse, I think, because he is so close. So tangible. Eurydice at the mouth of the underworld, moments before she is lost forever. *Almost* free. *Almost* alive.

I gently shut the door and go back to the others, the bearer of news that will render me unsalvageable.

"Well?" Silas says.

"You have the right of it. It's the only plan. The *teras* is at the back eating. It's given up on all the bodies that aren't twitching. So we have to. . . make one move."

Fred closes her eyes and steels herself. She takes a deep breath and that is the extent of her emotion. I want her to feel what I feel. Maybe she does. Maybe the guilt is rotting her gut, making her mad, and she just had a better way of hiding it than I do. Part of me—the part that is drowning, and wants to drown with someone else—is desperate to say: the *teras* is eating the people you sacrificed. But there is no point to this pettiness. I will make myself the blackguard; I will bear all their misdirected guilt and anger; I will be a saviour in truth and a devil in the histories. Why does it matter so much to me? I am not a godly man. My faith branded me hell spawn from birth. Why does it matter so much? Why do I care what they think? I am a walking sin; I am carnally depraved. Another mark against my name can hardly hurt me.

But it does hurt. Leo, whispering, *it is not a sin to love* in my mind, Victoria confiding in me, Bellamy exhausted and straightforward telling me *I really thought the University was good.*

Have I become so twisted that I will do this to my friend?

But inevitably I tell them, "There is a body near the door.

It's the closest one and the most intact. We bring it out, put the salve on it, push it back in for the *teras*."

"It?" Victoria ventures, and it's like she knows. I see it in her eyes. The hurt, the fear, the blistering anger that wants to rail down on me.

Weakly, I supply, "Him," as a concession, and Victoria's entire face crumples. She doesn't ask *is it Bellamy?* And I don't tell her *yes*.

Leo turns to Silas and Fred. "Did the Artificer say how long it will take?"

"Didn't ask. Just grabbed it," Fred says sullenly. "We don't have any time. So just do it."

Fred heads towards the doors. I stop her. "It's Bellamy," I whisper, and she pales and briefly closes her eyes. I watch her tense like she's about to turn to Victoria, but she stops herself in time.

"I can help you take the body out," she whispers. "Leo and the two of us should be enough. Silas can stay with Victoria, out of sight, and never have to know."

We stare at each other and I don't know if I can live with that. There's an assumption on Fred's face, a blaming I can hardly stand. But I say, "Okay," because she's right. We don't have time for this.

Bellamy's body will do.

"Leo, with me," I mumble and head to the door. He falls in line and when we are around the corner, he puts a hand on my shoulder and spins me.

"Who is it?" he asks. "Is it Bellamy?"

I don't know what comes over me but I hiss, "Why? What does it matter? It's a corpse. The man is gone."

"A yes, then," Leo murmurs to me, unfazed by my emotion. "You are more ruthless than I thought you were."

"Not ruthless", I say, feeling Bellamy's ghost nestle somewhere in my bones, ready to haunt them for an eternity, ready to keep me in melancholy should I ever surface towards happiness. "Don't mistake me acting as I *must* for acting how I *want to*. And don't look at me like that, I can't stand it. I can't stand you thinking I'm a monster, Leo. You wanted me to leave them both. You were ready to close the door."

His stare is confronting. His eyes are prisms through which light refracts, and with it emotion, and judgement, and a despairing conclusion I hate. For once, I despise the way he looks at me.

Leo says, "Maybe monsters are the only ones to survive here."

That feels grossly insufficient, an easy way of navigating what is happening here. How we are changing. But I'm too exhausted to say anything. I just nod towards the door, wait for Fred to come up behind us, and slowly push on the wood.

The door yawns open once more with that waking groan. I push it wider than it went the last time, trying to be brave, and it comes to a muffled stop as it hits flesh. The dull sound gets the *teras'* attention in the way the creaking door didn't; it looks up from its meal with piercing, blood-drunk eyes. The fur around its mouth is matted with blood. Splatters of it coat its face and ears, and all down its chest is red. It watches us and waits. None of us move. I don't know how well it can see, I don't know if hunger dulls its urges, but I pray to God it finds us boring. There are closer breathing humans hunkered down around it. Why should it care for three more?

I can't signal to the others without moving so I just have to hope they have enough sense to stay still. Cautiously, I lean past the threshold and peer around the door to see whatever's stopped the door.

It's Bellamy's hand. Still attached. Which doesn't make sense because a few minutes ago he was an arm's length from the door. Now he is—here. Right near the threshold. Fingers touching the wood. God. *God.*

He's still alive.

Horror bludgeons me. He's alive, Bellamy is alive, he is still crawling towards the door, still desperate to live—only he's not moving right now. Is he on the precipice? Does he feel the pain of whatever open cavity is causing his blood to flood around him? I can't wait. I can't do this the smart way or the safe way.

My duty now is to Bellamy. I must drag him out, must see he lives a few breaths beyond the room he's fought so hard to leave.

So I say, "*Now!*" and drop to my knees and hope the others follow suit. I wrap my hands around the fabric on his back. Leo staggers over the threshold, half-tripping over Bellamy and the sight of the room. Fred starts gagging at the smell—blood, urine, faeces, whatever other gory substances are crowding my periphery—but she hooks her hands beneath his arms anyway and pulls.

Instantly, the *teras* notices. There's a growl like thunder, a rumble deep within the room. I promise myself I won't look up, won't look this living devil in its face in case I freeze again. We haul Bellamy back, and the body is heavy or I am weak. My heart is in my chest, the beast is growling; I look up.

The lion leaps into the air. One leap is all it needs. From the end of the haul it jumps and I crane my neck. I see its gold-furred flank and blood-splattered mane. Stringy flesh has caught on its claws. An open-throated roar bearing down on me. I see its red-rimmed gullet, smell the stench of rot wafting from its throat. We panic, all three of us, and desperately haul Bellamy back. One arm moves at an awkward angle, and the body isn't budging. I feel him grow heavier and I know that means someone has let go. The *teras* lands. I scream and half fall. Its mutated, massive jaw unhinges and bites down on Bellamy's other leg with enormous strength, and when I scramble back and desperately tug at Bellamy's body, the *teras* just holds fast and growls.

There's only one thing left to do. "Get the salve! *Get the fucking salve!*"

Fred is fucking frozen in fear until Leo reaches over and punches her arm. Her body spasms and moves suddenly, automatically, and with *automaton*-like finesse she reaches into her pocket and yanks the salve free.

"But I don't know—" she says, and I snatch it off her, wrenching the stopper free. Bellamy's—no, he's dead, isn't he? The body's—hamstring has been torn open. There's a fleshy cavity, the stark white of bone peeking through, and I make my decision as I'm uncapping the salve.

I'm sorry. I didn't know what else to do.

I go to plunge my hand, salve and all, towards the open cadaver. I am about to pour the salve when the *teras* lunges.

And I don't feel it. I swear, I swear God is taking pity on me, because I see it all play out as if it hasn't happened to my body. My arm is outstretched. There is a flash; just blood-red teeth, and a wet crunch. When I blink next my left arm is gone. To the elbow. I stare vacantly at it; blood gushes from the torn limb, and the bone has been crunched away awkwardly, so the remains of the ulna and radius sit jagged from the stump.

I have just enough time to pray: *Father, into your hands I commend my spirit* before I shiver, and once shivering, cannot stop.

Cannot. Stop. Shivering. And breathing. Is *hard*.

Oh, God. I think—

But I do not die here. I just remember watching the *teras* chew happily on my arm, and the crunch of glass as its teeth slam through the bottle. There's an unhappy roar, and right before the pain hits me, right before I am knocked unconscious by the lovely combination of blood loss, shock, and excruciating, nameless pain, I think I laugh.

Fuck you, motherfucker. Eat shit and die.

LESSON TWENTY-FIVE

I wake three days later in my bed, dazed and alone. My body finally has a chance to rest, but resting only exacerbates all the aches adrenaline had been staving off. So now I feel the dull ache of the harpy's claws razing against my stomach, a persistent headache from poor sleep and stress, a spasm in my right hip—did I fall? Or is that just a consequence of holding myself stiffly for weeks?—and then there is the arm.

I have a good hour to convince myself to look down. I must have shown no signs of waking, because I have been left completely alone. No one comes to check on me. There are the remains of a Healer's work around me; bloody bandages, forceps, other aborted attempts to stop the bleeding with cotton buds and bloody water. There's a salve, too, but I can't think about salves without thinking about my arm, which I don't want to look at, which I can't stop thinking about, which I have to look at eventually, so *God, Cassius, just fucking look*.

I look down. A fabric sling binds the stump of my arm to my chest. I can't see the stump, I see only the bound white-fabric mass of my arm pressed close to me, but I can feel it: my entire arm, hand and all, throbbing incessantly.

Logically, I know it isn't there. I saw the arm be eaten. It is sitting in the stomach of *teras*, hopefully undigested, hopefully clutching the remains of the thing that has killed the wretched beast. But if I know this, then why do I feel it? How can the entire thing throb and ache like the great teeth of the *teras* are still tearing through it?

I wait for this bout of throbbing to ebb away and then I sit with the feeling, the knowledge that the arm is gone. And I wait for the hysteria or the panic, but it just doesn't come. I think it gets filed away with the rest of the horror. Another mark in the book of awful things that happen here. But it's all I can do to sit there and wait for it to hit, my mind compartmentalising itself to be the soother, ready to placate the part of my brain that loses its grip.

I hold myself in this impossible stasis long enough that the sun is high in my window. And then, when the bell tower rings out for midday, my door unlocks.

It's Leo. I know it immediately by his gait and silhouette, before the light has resolved the shadows of his face. He pauses when he sees me awake in bed, propped up on the pillows. But there's no cry of joy at seeing me, only quiet.

He glances over his shoulder and back at me. Then slips inside and closes the door, stealing an intimate moment for just the two of us.

Leo opens his mouth. I cut him off.

"Is it dead?"

His face goes still and something shifts in his eyes. How he looks at me like this, in bed and sweaty and bloody, and has such a softness in his gaze, I do not know.

Leo smiles at me. "Yes, Mr Jones. It's dead."

Something swells in my gut. It isn't quite pride and it isn't quite relief. I think the hysteria is breaking through, now that sacrifice of my arm means something substantial. I give a great sob and then bite my tongue, but Leo is already moving to me. He goes to his knees beside me puts his hands on my thighs.

"I want to ask how are you, but I think I know," he murmurs.

"Mm," I say. It's the only thing I can say. If I open my mouth I'll just start crying, and for some reason it feels important that I don't.

"When I saw you, Cass, I. . ." he doesn't say anything for a long while, but he lowers his forehead onto my leg and sighs. Muffled by the covers I hear him murmur, "I'm ¬sorry."

I run my fingers through his hair and over his broad back. "For what?"

"Calling you ruthless."

This doesn't help me relax in the slightest. "It's alright," I tell him. "Besides. You meant it."

Leo pulls away, and I'm sorry for it, especially when he drags even his hands back to his side.

"I," he says, "don't like what is happening here. I don't like what it's doing to us. But I don't think there's anything we can do about it. I'm not going back out there. And neither are you. We're the same like that. So when I say you're ruthless, when I say it's monsters who survive this, don't be offended, Cass. Take the compliment."

His eyes have changed again, to something more unpleasant, and he reminds me of the boy I met in the woods, who saw my brother gutted and said he was sorry for the loss of a Hunter. I wonder suddenly if Leo is who I think he is. If the young man I see is perhaps as ruthless as me. If he has survived something similar, out there beyond the wards.

I could ask him. I could watch him lie to me. But I don't want to ruin whatever it is we have. What little comfort I can get from him.

And in truth, I don't really want to know.

"Victoria. . . has asked to be moved to a different room," he tells me. My stomach drops, but it's with an inevitable sadness. I expected something like this. It still hurts. When I don't respond to that, he goes on. "The dean—" Leo begins, then pauses. "Never mind. We'll talk about him later."

"Tell me," I whisper.

Leo shifts and moves back to sit properly on the ground, shuffling so his back is against the wall beneath the window. "He's commissioned an Artificer on your behalf, for a prosthetic. Something about your extraordinary bravery and quick thinking." Leo flashes me a half smile.

A compliment like that from the dean would have once made me ecstatic. And now it feels premeditated and hollow: I want that man to burn in hell.

"Why did they do it?" I whisper. "Why kill so many of us like that?"

Leo's smile fades. He shifts uncomfortably and looks down at his hands, which he holds gently between his legs. "I asked him."

"And?"

Stiffly, Leo regurgitates the dean's reply. "The other trials operated with us knowing they were coming. Even if we didn't know *what* they were, we knew to expect something."

"We're not meant to feel safe," I say. "Not ever."

"No."

I gnaw at my lip. "How long do we have? To the next trial?"

Leo shakes his head. "He didn't say. But I suspect a few days. He said he wanted. . . as many survivors as possible to have a chance." He glances up at me, then. "It's the last one, Cass. One more. One more, and we're in."

And I know I'm meant to feel relief or joy, but I just feel so goddamned tired that I start laughing. Because after that, it's the University, and if the trials were like this, then what will the real thing be? What will the rest of our lives look like?

"I know," Leo whispers, though I'm not sure he does. "But it's better than the outside. I promise you, Cass," he says, like I don't remember that fear. "We'll have a purpose here. And more safety than we could hope for out there."

He keeps speaking like that and after a moment it's practically a lullaby, something soothing he's whispering to himself, to keep his own mind from panicking.

I must fall asleep after that. I have only a fuzzy memory; Leo standing over my head, Leo kissing my forehead.

I don't know how I feel.

Amore et melle et felle es fecundissimus.

❧

"It will come out of your pay, should you ever graduate. Think of it as an advance. And don't worry, Mr Jones. Not a single graduate leaves the University without being cowled by debt."

Dean Drearton is upsettingly cheery this afternoon. I smile at him, and thank him, but inside I am rotting.

I really want this man to go to hell.

I still have not moved from this bed. The dean and the Artificer have come to me, which probably should feel nice, but is probably a favour I will have to repay tenfold. Propped up in bed with the pillows at my back, the remains of my right arm are resting on the bedside table, which has been dragged to the opposite side of the bed and layered with more pillows stolen from the sitting room. This allows the Artificer, a wiry man with brown skin, perhaps five years older than me, to take all his measurements with ease. He wears a tight suit and spectacles, and makes a point of not looking me in the eye. I feel disconnected from everything: this room, my body, reality as a whole. I let him flitter about me, measuring, pressing and prodding, ignoring every time I hiss and groan. The dean watches all this impassively. His eyes are blank and calculating, but his face is twisted in a placid smile. It unnerves me. I try not to look his way.

At some point it becomes easier to close my eyes, and then I'm drifting in and out of sleep for an expanse of time. It's only when the Artificer moves to peel off the bandage that I'm jolted awake by the pain.

The smell is horrible. The salve is bitter and acrid, and mixed with the blood of the arm it smells like rot. But when the Artificer wipes some of it away he says, "Good."

I risk a look down. The flesh has stitched itself together. It's a puckered mess, gnarly and knotted and in a way it resembles a burl on a tree. Bone emerges from the knot, the remains of my ulna and radius, like blunt pincers.

I think I should vomit, but perhaps that's just how I expect to feel. I look at this and it doesn't feel like my body. I can still feel my hand. I feel it twitching, I feel an itch on my palm I cannot scratch. This: this broken arm is not mine. I can't feel badly about something that isn't mine. I can't feel anything at all about it.

I realise stupidly there must be magic involved. Real magic. The wound has been healed in three days, sucked closed around the bone with unnatural speed. I recall vaguely my brother seeing the *teras* in the dark at Watford, Hunter eyes, and I guess I always thought it was pure training that allowed him that. But there is another world at the University, a divide in realities where real students work, and us trial-takers suffer. I should have realised it sooner.

"It's healed well," the Artificer concludes. He pinches the bloody cloth between forefinger and thumb and winces as he lowers it into a burlap sack for disposal. "We can build the prosthetic immediately."

"How long will you need?" the dean asks. He's sitting in the desk chair and shifting every few moments, obvious with his discomfort.

The Artificer shrugs a little, sitting back and removing his spectacles. "Depends on the material, sir. Is it meant for show, or do you want it working?"

I am no fool. I heard the dean—this will cost me. I can't be indebted to this place anymore than I already am. "What's the cheapest material you have?"

The Artificer looks at me with pity, glancing over to the dean. "Well, wood. But I wouldn't—"

"Porcelain and gold," the dean says. "Articulated fingers, the whole works. Get ichor from the *automaton*. And Abraham? Build it fast."

"No," I say. The Artificer, who is halfway out the door with those orders, staggers to a stop. He glances back over his shoulder but he isn't looking at me. I also turn to the dean. "How much will that be?"

"You don't need to worry about that now," says Drearton. "You won't need to pay that off for years, now."

"But I—I don't want—"

"You do," he says. He surges forward and puts a hand on my shoulder. "You want the best. Because if you get wood, it's little more than for show. It'll stop your colleagues from flinching at the sight of you, Mr Jones," (God, what an asshole), "but that's it. This one," he taps the frame of my bed and nods towards the Artificer, "*works*. You won't know the difference from a hand. In fact, you'll have better reflexes."

He's taking such an interest in me that I'm scared. Like the Greeks say, μηδὲν ἄγαν, "nothing too much", everything in moderation—nothing *good* ever comes from gods paying attention. And in this domain, I'd be a fool to think of Drearton as anything less. So to have him sitting at my bedside, personally concerned about the outcome of my arm, and knowing, *knowing*, that he is the same man who trapped the lot of us in that hall and let a Nemean Lion loose—well. Is it any wonder that I'm terrified?

"Why," I whisper. Not quite a question, barely the world itself.

The dean twists his head to look at me and slowly retracts his arm. "Ah, well, why not, Mr Jones? You are proving yourself beautifully. And I think it would be quite a shame to lose you now, when you're so close." The dean uncrosses his legs. "You'd be a great asset, you know. To the University."

I almost ask him another why. Why did you do it? Why did you let it tear us to shreds? But I should know by now no answer will satisfy me, should he even bother to answer at all.

"How long do we have, before the next trial?" I ask. I want to hear it straight from the horse's mouth.

"Four days," he says. "Abraham should be done in two, maybe three. So you'll have some time to practise with it. And I recommend you do."

The dean goes to stand

"Would you—" I begin. I cut myself off because several conflicting thoughts start vying for the space in my mouth. Would you tell me what happened to Bellamy's body? Would you tell me how many of us died? Would you tell me about the next trial? Would you tell me why you do this, why you let all of us suffer like this, just for a chance in your hallowed halls, in your relative safety, forever indebted to an institution who thinks of all its students as canon fodder?

The dean pauses. "What is it?"

"Nothing," I exhale. "Nothing at all. And thank you, Dean Drearton, for all your help."

I put on my most winning smile and he looks at me curiously for a time, assessing it, I think, before he nods slowly and leaves me alone.

When he is gone, I use my right arm to tug out the pillow behind my back. I drag my knees up, put the pillow between them and my face, lean into it.

Then I scream.

I AM a leper for another day and a half. I don't get out of bed, and no one except Leo comes to see me. Even then the visits are short. There is none of the obvious, hot desire he usually awards me. He just puts down my food, asks me how I am, dodges as many questions as possible, and leaves.

Yes, I could get up. I have wandered out three times in total for the bathroom, but each time the apartments are silent. I'm either alone, or everyone is pressing themselves against walls and corners and shadows to avoid me. I don't investigate because I'm ashamed. I have been made their blackguard. My decision at the great hall has put me a step further apart from the rest of them.

No matter that Fred caused the deaths of several. Bellamy was one of us. And he is dead because of me.

That afternoon, five days since the last trial, and two days before the next, I have my first shower. I confront for the first time, too, the mirror.

And I'm not sure if you know what it's like, to walk up to something meant to reflect you perfectly, and see an imposter. Not a stranger—I must make this clear—but something very much like you that isn't quite right. It wasn't just the arm, either, though that was the greatest and most obvious of my differences. Something about my face is wrong. Something about my eyes. My mouth quirked up a little higher on the right. My left eyelid seems lazier, more inclined to droop. My chest seems puffy, entire torso bruised and marked by the harpy's claws. The incisions have shrunk to fine red lines, but still there remained this sense that this isn't me.

I looked so tired and so weak and so bloody despondent that I felt in me the rage that so often fired up in Thaddeus. I realise I am seeing what he saw in me. If this is what I looked like, if this sad little man looked up at Thaddeus with these dreary tired eyes, then no wonder he could never contain his disappointment towards me. It was too much to bear. So much in fact I stalk back to my room, naked, fish around for the laudanum I'd stolen from the *Ianus* Blood Hunter, and pour its contents down the toilet.

(I would come to regret this approximately seven hours later when, lying in bed with phantom aches from an arm no longer attached to me, I couldn't sleep. But in the moment it felt very good. An act for myself. An act of triumph.)

Then I close my eyes so I don't have to see myself again and step into the shower. I wash the remnants of the stinking salve from my arm, and the rest of my body, all one handed, and I didn't realise the extent to which I used the arm until it's missing. I am still keeping a hold of myself here, even when I awkwardly attempt to wrap a towel around myself, even when I fail three times and rush back to my room in case someone has come in since I've showered.

Then I contend for the first time with a shirt.

It's not that I can't get it on. It just doesn't fit right. And it's not just over the arm. Suddenly the way it falls over my chest is wrong, the wrinkles in it unflattering, shadows cutting at awkward angles. The left sleeve droops freely and the whole shirt seems to wilt towards that hanging side, and I can't breathe, I feel the material dragging on my skin, like it's wet, and I'm so overwhelmed by the touch of it I haul it off.

And a whole swathe of horrible insults come into my

mind; I hurl all of them at myself, every molecule of disgust I can muster, just to feel something beyond this numb resignation, the knowledge that I am forever changed. I treat myself very badly for several minutes. I say things in my head I would never dream of saying to anyone else. But all of it feels justified, because I'm a useless fucker struggling with a shirt, and with the simple reality that this body of mine will never be how I remembered it. It is a fact. It is immutable. It will be okay.

But I wish very deeply in that moment to go back to a time where my body was completely untouched. Before the lion, the harpy, the first time a man touched me. Before my father beat me. Before I knew what this world was. I wish I could do it all again and do it better this time. Do it right. God, please—let me be perfect.

"Cass?"

I jolt and freeze. As I come back to myself, out of whatever pit this sudden depression is dragging me into, I find I'm standing naked in the centre of my room, towel and shirt abandoned on the bed. I'm staring at my reflection in the window; the faded, hazy reflection of not-quite me stares back.

Leo comes towards me. I see him raise his hands to my shoulders but I flinch out of the way before he can touch me. I grab the towel off the bed but I don't know which part of my body to hide, so filled with sudden and unfamiliar shame. Towel dropping from my hands, I collapse onto the bed, head collapsing into my hands—hand. Phantom fingers caress my own head, tangling in the hair. I flex them, feel them tug at strands, feel the follicles straining from the pull, and it's all in my head.

How can it be in my head?

The bed groans with new weight as Leo sits down beside me.

"Cass," he murmurs, slipping a hand onto my thigh. This time I don't flinch away; but I keep myself from looking up. Confronting him like this, flaccid cock between my legs, bruised and bloody, one arm down—I feel I am not the man he craved just a few days earlier.

He reaches between my arms and grabs my chin, forcing me to drop my arm. Leo turns my head towards his and he stares at me, opening his mouth several times, saying nothing. What is there to say? He could say anything right now and it wouldn't contend with the things I'm telling myself. I see in his eyes the truth: that nothing has changed, not really. That it's not pity or disgust in his gaze, but care. Concern. But my mind is twisting it all and turning even my own reason against me.

"I'm sorry," I end up saying.

His brow buckles. "God, Cass, what for?"

Bellamy, I don't say. *For my arm. What I did, and how I look like because of it. And I'm sorry that you have to see me. And I'm sorry I can't be perfect anymore. And I'm sorry—*

"I don't know. I just feel it," I whisper over the cacophony in my head. My voice cracks. I don't want to cry. *Christ*. Heat pricks suddenly behind my eyes. My temples ache already, in expectation of a headache. And I speak again, cracking entirely, "I'm so, so sorry."

He pulls away. I hate that. Leo's hand moves down to my thigh where he grips tightly near my knee. "Cassius, you fool. You saved the lot of us. And no matter what they say, I know that."

I tense. I shouldn't ask, because I'm already hurting, and one more thing might be enough to undo all remaining sense in me. I drag my eyes up to Leo. "What are they saying?"

He deflates a little, aware he's walked into a trap. "Cass," he whispers. Then he sighs and drags his hand away completely, bending forward to massage his temples. "Victoria is angry with you. Fred was. . . in shock at what she saw. Silas is a bloody enigma and I have no idea what he's thinking. And beyond that, there's plenty of rumours."

"Rumours?" I prompt.

He grimaces. God, he looks so unhappy and so distraught to be the bearer of this message. "That you shut Bellamy in on purpose."

I did.

"That you did it with glee, as part of some grander plan to kill the *teras*. I don't know. Twelve people died. Several others are probably rotting in their beds. Apparently there is an infirmary beyond the *Ianus* gate, but until we're admitted to the University proper, going through there is death. So."

I don't know what I can say to that. Half of the rumours are hardly rumours, and the rest feels warranted anyway. And yes that is the guilt talking; the rational man in me knows that I took no joy in closing that door, but it feels good in a way to be despised. To see some scathing, internal remarks reflected back at me justifies the way I feel; a reflexive soup of self-hatred.

But underneath all that wallowing is a genuine anger. And if I pull away my misery and self-pity, I see it for what it is.

Fury at this institution. A vengeful delirium roiling low and buried deep, and each new trial is another fan to the flame, each death another reason to feed Dean Drearton to the *teras* he claims to protect us from.

"I want to kill him," I whisper.

Leo looks at me then, a gleam in his eye. "There you are." He leans forward and kisses me, teeth grazing my lip. "I know. I dream of it. But then what? He's not the University, Cass, he's just a man."

"I don't care. It would feel good."

"There are far better ways to feel good," Leo murmurs.

And I can't believe he's flirting with me when I look like

this, when I'm naked, hunched over, missing an arm, scratched to hell and bruised, so I *laugh*. I sit there and laugh and then I push myself back to lie on the bed stretched out. I look up at the ceiling, white with floral cornices, and my heart settles enough that for the first time in days I can really breathe.

I don't know. Maybe it's all okay. Maybe it will be fine. Because he makes me laugh, and I can envision it: years studying together, years learning, making love, graduating.

Leo lies down with me, not looking my way, just staring up at the ceiling. And in that pocket of a moment and a dream for a future, I think I could be happy. Long enough to forget what I had to do to get there.

He reaches out for my right hand. I take it.

"Will you light a cigarette for me?" I ask. I haven't had one in days. "I've been too afraid to try and light it. I think that would break me, you know? Seeing how impossible it is to light a cigarette."

Leo says nothing. But he gets up and lights me a cigarette.

❧

THE ARM IS BEAUTIFUL.

The Artificer returns alone the following morning. He is already in my room when I wake, unboxing the thing as if it's perfectly acceptable to be agitating in the corner of a wounded man's space.

"Right," he says, when he catches my eye. Abraham. "Are you ready?"

The Artificer kneels before this long, tan-leather box with two golden clasps. He snaps them open and the lid pops up, shielding my view. But when he raises it high, and I see it for the first time, my heart nearly stops.

It doesn't look like mine. And I don't mean this literally. I'm not stupid. I knew it wasn't going to look like flesh.

But it is beautiful, inherently. The craftsmanship, the material, the blue shot through the porcelain like veins, the way the fingers droop—how can this belong to Cassius Jones? I'm a rat. I have lived in hovels and a tiny apartment my whole life. Even when I've spent years safe behind London's wards, there is a stark difference between myself and people who grew up here. Between safety and luxury. And I know it is solipsistic self-absorption to think there is inherent dirt in my flesh, but I can't help but shiver at the thought of having such a beautiful item classed as mine.

I have the thought that I don't deserve this. At once, I think I mean losing my arm and gaining this one.

Abraham comes close with it. As he walks, the morning sun catches the metal interspersed between the arms joints. It's a white porcelain, alabaster. Gold connects every articulated joint, and likely runs below the porcelain plates that have been placed on top. And the porcelain is painted in the way fine china is; blue floral decadence, vines my new veins.

Abraham kneels before me and holds the arm high, like a knight offering his sword to a king, which ultimately feels so silly I can't do anything except nod. Yes, it's beautiful. Yes, thank you, please attach it. Abraham's face lights up with my approval. I can't imagine anyone denying this.

Attachment, as it turns out, is not a simple process. The prosthetics I saw outside London were crude but did their jobs, and the wearer was able to slip them on and off with ease. But permanent attachment inside London is possible. Only I never had much cause to ask until now.

"I'm sure it is upsetting," Abraham says far too cheerfully. He puts the prosthetic on the bed beside me and uses both hands to raise my severed forearm for inspection, "but really, having some bone exposed like this is the best for us Artificers. Makes long-term attachment that much easier."

I don't reply, but he doesn't need me to. Without the dean's presence, Abraham is untethered, in a sweet way: the joy for his work is palpable, and he talks endlessly about the process of creation. I learn the arm is the work of four Artificers, and hidden from the eye, their signatures are etched somewhere in the metal or porcelain. I learn Meléti's ichor is the lifeblood of it; and that the *automaton* generates ichor like blood. He drags the bedside table forward and puts the edge of my arm on it. The prosthetic is laid against it, ready for the joining. I rummage in the sheets for a cigarette and raise it, asking Abraham to light it for me. He has matches in his pockets for the joining, and I intend to take advantage.

"Ichor is an interesting thing," Abraham tells me. He wanders back over by the leather box, dropping to his knees to rummage for something. "We can coat exposed bone with it, and it will harden to something like metal. All this without restricting the bone. It can still absorb nutrients, expel waste. It won't die, is what I mean. But it allows us to solder the prosthetic."

The ichor in question is bottled up and looks like liquid gold. When it's unstoppered, Abraham tilts it. Gravity should take over. It should pour from the bottle all over me. But Abraham has to coax it out.

"θέω," he whispers. *I run. I fly.* And the ichor uncurls from its corner of the bottle and gently flows out onto my bones, the ulnar and radius. I feel nothing as it lands, but I watch it once again defy gravity. It acts as if my bone and it are lost friends; the ichor curls around the bone and stops at the puckered flesh. "παύω." *I stop. I cease.* Slowly it hardens. My bone glimmers golden. I am compelled to stare at it; a *teras'* blood is a part of me.

Abraham turns to the prosthetic next and does something

to pull it apart. The forearm splits open, still fully joined from wrist downward. Abraham slips it over my bone.

"Wait there," Abraham says, like I'll run out the window. He returns to his gear and stands tall again with something he informs me is a soldering lamp. It's brass and looks very much like an oil lamp with an extended snout. Abraham lights it, then blows additional air through a blowpipe to increase the temperature. The flame flickers at the end of the snout and when the flame turns blue, Abraham informs me it's hot enough to solder.

He brings the burning snout to the join between the arm and the bone and solders it together. There is more at play here, some Artificer magic I can't see happening, but can feel, because when I next look there is no join whatsoever, no noticeable seam. The arm seems to have fused directly to the remaining flesh. I can't peer at the bone beneath. Nor can I pry it off.

This unnatural arm is mine in truth. It is a part of my body. It might as well be flesh.

I don't know how it works, but it feels like magic; a thrumming that connects what my brain wants to do to the prosthetic itself. It moves in a way that feels supernatural, real but hauntingly so. I tell my fingers to move and they're already halfway through curling. I go to flex the muscles in my forearm, and feel the stretch of them. Somehow I feel the psychosomatic pull to the flesh and bone in the Nemean Lion's stomach ebb away. So quickly my body accepts that this is the arm it was missing, even when I turn it over and stare at the clockwork whirring happening in the palm, beneath the porcelain plates.

"There you are, Mr Jones, good as new."

I glance up at him. I can think of a few choice things to say to that, because there are too many versions of myself in my head, and I think no kindlier for this one—but I let them all fester internally instead. I give Abraham a smile and he accepts it graciously with a little bow.

Then I am left alone.

I smoke my cigarette down to its burning end in the span of a minute and a half, and it's still not enough to quell the anxiety and a broiling panic that's threatening to overwhelm me.

Part of me wants to sleep, but that part of me is a fool. There's no time. No time.

The final trial is nearly upon me. And so is God's judgement.

❧ 26 ❧

LESSON TWENTY-SIX

The apartments are empty when I finally manage to dress myself. My new fingers are confusing; they work but without the tactility, I'm still clumsy. My reflection remains a bane, too; I tried not to look at myself as I dressed, in case I was overwhelmed by this new human staring at back me. And then came the effort of hyping myself up to leave the room itself, hand poised over the door-knob, my mind going, *Cassius, come on, for God's sake.*

After all that no one is around to inspect me.

Outside, I hear collective chatter. Around the corner of the west tower apartments are people. A whole swathe of them. There is more activity than I have ever seen in the yard. It seems everyone who is still alive is packed onto the grass to train. Everyone is physically sparring, or drilling—I don't know which *teras* they expect to battle in hand-to-hand combat, but I understand the horror of sitting still and wait-ing. It feels better to train for some impossibility than sit impotently in wait.

I walk past them, thinking: I need to get away from here. I feel exposed. To my right, a table has been set up for food,

301

since the hall is likely still being scrubbed clean of blood and guts. I make the mistake of veering towards it for a simple meal of bread and butter—my stomach is desperate, I've barely eaten in days—but, God, I feel like I shouldn't be here. That I am not wanted. And sure enough, the moment I go to reach for food, everyone else around the table scatters.

Something curious happens then, a kind of alarm ringing out in the shared consciousness that makes everyone turn their eyes to me. And I can smell it, what I am to them; what I have done holds a contagious power, a pollution seeping through my pores. Everyone is careful around me. In five days, I don't know what kind of mythology has been conjured for me. But the miasma is unavoidable, and my colleagues are Erinyes circling. I wait for them to pass judgement. But no one says anything. They just stare, and that is somehow worse.

I grab the bread and leave, not bothering to scan this crowd for the one person I hope to see.

Thaddeus would be proud. That night we found the hybrid he told me: *If you've managed to kill one, that's the kind of reputation you want to spread.*

Well, how about now? What kind of reputation am I spreading?

And for the first time in what feels like months I recall Thaddeus' letter. It said:

2. Use for trials 2, 4. Library in centre. Massive willow. Courtyard. Meléti helps for a price. Dead: 1

TRIAL FOUR.

By now I know my brother does not know everything,

and I'll never know why he burned away the rest of his note. But where else am I meant to go? Meléti may tell me nothing, but maybe destiny is on my side. I am like my colleagues drilling uselessly on the grass. Moving feels better than staying still, so I move.

I inevitably have to pass by the chapel. Surprisingly it's busy. The priest is leading ten-odd people in prayer. Seeing them all bowed before the *scylla* is something I can't handle today; I have already sacrificed my arm to a *teras*. I don't have the stomach to pray near one.

Perhaps the loss of my arm is punishment for what Leo and I did in there.

(Maybe it was worth it.)

The courtyard is empty, still, and I don't know if that's because no one has found it, or because it feels distinct from the area the dean introduced us to. The only people here are the ones the back of my mind was expecting. Leo, Fred, and Silas stand beneath the willow. Victoria is nowhere to be seen.

The trio speak in hushed whispers, but they're animated. I don't know what they're discussing but I can guess. What else is there to talk about these days? They haven't seen me, so I watch Fred shove a finger against Leo's chest, then the same one into her brother's. For whatever reason, Leo is compelled to look up. Drawn to me, maybe, the way I'm drawn to him.

Better stop thinking like that, Cass. It'll hurt too much when it ends.

"Cass?" Leo calls. The Lins see me, make eye contact with one another, and wordlessly peel away.

"Wait," I call. "Fred—Silas—I wanted to—"

"Glad you're alright," Silas cuts me off. Fred stares down at her feet and eventually concedes.

She steps forward, hesitating, and whispers, "I would have done it, too."

But even with that collaborating whisper, she won't stay. She takes Silas by the arm—he gives me a weak smile—and stalks off.

I stare after them, unsure what to do. We were never close, but I'm close with so few that I feel the strain acutely. And what did I do to earn the ire? Is it Bellamy? Does Fred see how I am at once lauded and feared and think: God, I'm glad no one was paying attention in that hall? God, I'm glad only a few people saw me sacrifice an entire table?

Alright. I'm furious. And I'm barely holding on to myself. I tense my hands into fists.

"Are you alright?" Leo asks. Then, "Oh. Let me see?"

Wordlessly, I unfurl my hands—the porcelain-gold clock-work creaks as the fingers flex. I raise my right arm up for his inspection. He goes to touch it, but stops himself, fingers hovering close.

"Don't want to cover it in fingerprints," he says.

"Why not? You've touched the rest of me."

He flashes me a look, heavy-lidded, and smiles. Uncere-moniously, he grabs it, hauling me into his chest with pure force. With his right hand bracing the small of my back, he encourages me to extend the prosthetic up to the light.

"Incredible," he says, and I pretend he's looking at my face when he says it. "Just beautiful. And it works?"

"Yes." I show off for him, flexing, bending. He looks fasci-nated until he sees my face, which must be bland or telling in some way.

He sighs and pushes me back against the tree trunk. It's the most intimate we've been in days and I don't know how to feel. I don't know what to do given I feel next to nothing when he crowds his body against me. I know I would have gone wild for this before the third trial. Even if I've never felt attractive, I still felt wholly myself.

Leo can't understand this, because I don't tell him. He

looks at me and must think I'm upset about the arm itself, and not what it means for the rest of me, not that my humanity and my mortality will always be in stark contrast to the manufactured perfection that has replaced my right arm. I don't think he would understand even if I did explain it, because I hardly understand what I'm feeling myself. Just that I am not quite right.

"It's an arm," he tells me. "And this one is yours. Do you not like it?"

"It's not about the arm." I don't say the rest and his face hardens with understanding. "Or it is, in a way. It's just another reminder. We must remember we are beholden to this place."

Leo glances down, hand slipping down the bark. I can still feel the warmth of him, but gone is the *heat*, the actual pull between us. I don't want him to touch me, and yet I want nothing more. I am back to impossible contradictions; I just can't bear to be known so intimately right now.

Leo mistakes my discomfort for fear at our situation. "Listen. It's just. . . one more trial. We'll be okay."

I can't stand this.

"What did the Lins want?" I ask, chin nodding in the direction they left towards.

Leo looks as if he doesn't like my question. He leans away from me, hands leaving their purchase on my cheeks. "Nothing," he lies. Then, sighing, "I don't know. I think they might do something stupid."

I recall eavesdropping on them, after the harpy. "They're not thinking of leaving, are they?"

Leo grimaces and shrugs, which is practically a confirmation. Then he pushes away from me completely and steps back. "What are you doing out here, Cass? I'm guessing you weren't searching for me."

Part of me is always searching for you.

I nod my head towards the library and set out towards it, and then Leo makes a noise more exasperated and frustrated than I've ever heard from him.

"Cassius," he pulls my new arm. I stagger to a stop, looking down at the image of connection, of hands holding that I cannot feel. Nausea is sudden and overwhelming and I have to look away. *Keep going. Get to the library. Sleep. Face tomorrow. It's almost over.* But Leo speaks over my attempt at reasoning. "Listen to me. Your brother has been no help. I'm sorry, but it isn't worth it."

I try to tug my arm free. "It's the only chance we have. Meléti—"

"—is not on our side. And your brother." He sighs. "He didn't know what he was talking about. Okay?"

"Wrong. The hemlock?"

Leo pauses. "Thaddeus wrote down *his* experience, and burned half the damn letter anyway. We already know he was wrong. The Artificer confirmed it for us; this year is a whole other test to the one he experienced. I am telling you, the only hope we have is being *ruthless*. We can't plan for this. Not when they're trying to kill all of us."

"Why?" I say. I tug away and fold my arms, feel the hard porcelain through my shirt. "What would be the point? We are here to become the best of the best—that's what they want. London is suffocated by bodies, and the only people it can protect are the ones who make that protection worthwhile. So that's why we're here. To prove ourselves. To earn it. And Meléti is the only source of information we have about what might come next."

Leo laughs, exasperated. He runs his hands through his hair. "What fucking use is there going back to a *teras automaton*, an obvious agent of this death-trap institution?"

"Because I don't know what else to do! And I'm not dying, Leo. I'm not fucking dying!" Because I should be dead by now. Because Cassius Jones has survived this long by pure luck. And if luck is on my side, then so be it. I am barely the same man who entered these trials.

And this man wants to live.

"I thought you wanted that, too," I tell him. "You came all this way—to *live*. You talk to me after Bellamy because you say you understand the necessity of it. But you scare me, Leo, if you think you can go into the trial tomorrow and sacrifice someone to buy yourself time. Which is what happened last time, let's not sugar-coat it. That's what Bellamy's death did for us. It bought us time." I pause. "I don't want you to lie to me and act as if you won't do whatever it takes to secure a spot here. I know—that you would have left them both. Victoria. And I don't judge that; I'll have no leg to stand on if I judge it. But. . . that cannot be your first thought."

I'm scared of him disagreeing with me, or talking back, somehow diluting the importance of what I have to say to him. I'm scared of this ruthlessness he's talking about being who he really is. Scared he is not the man I thought he was. So before he can reply I'm halfway across the quad and pushing open the doors to the library.

It is as we left it. All the lights are on and glowing. The *automaton* is nowhere to be seen, like the first time I stumbled here. But there is someone else, propped up on the table to the right, completely alone. I pause when I see him. He looks up at me, despondent. Peter Drike.

He is walking death. I think I have never seen someone so close to slipping out of life entirely. His paleness is otherworldly, beyond sickness and near translucent. Blue veins criss-cross beneath his skin. The apples of his cheeks are pockmarked red with old acne I've never noticed before. Somehow he looks like he's lost half his weight in the four days I haven't seen him.

And he is, like me, sporting a prosthetic. Only his is not

the porcelain-and-gold beauty I have at my side. His is wood, I think. Leather. His knee still functions, but he has the leg up, spread on the chairs. The joint looks painful, or else it's the shock of it.

I see the realisation written in the wrinkles of his skin, and like me, I know he is contending with the change, too.

"I don't know what to give it," Drike murmurs. He's alone. I wonder if everyone else in his room is dead.

"Peter," I murmur. "Are you alright?"

His face twists and I expect him to shout at me, say something awful, call me a faggot. But the fight drains from him. It's too much energy, being nasty. And he's a shadow of himself, body and soul.

"You don't know what to. . . give Meléti?" Leo ventures. He sighs and rubs his face, and I feel his frustration emanating. Coming here, with him, was stupid. "What will it know? It just knows the books. What can you possibly hope to learn about the next trial?"

Drike stares at him, brows buckling together immediately. *It's his one hope*, I want to say. *Just like it's ours.*

"Meléti," I call. My voice echoes in the library, and I summon the thing. It speeds towards me, frighteningly quick.

"What would you like, Mr Jones?"

"Archives. Diaries, journals, anything from past students completing their trials."

The *automaton* whirrs its head. I think about this coveted, protected knowledge. What price will I pay for learning? What am I willing to give? In the end, this *is* another trial. Another *teras* thrown at us, another chance for the University to press on our necks, to remind us how much we need them. The *automaton* is here for a reason. The University could have made this space public—it chose not to.

I say, "I'll give you another memory. More knowledge."

Another part of myself, another trauma, something intimate you shouldn't have and can hold over me.

But to my surprise, Meléti says, "There is nothing of the sort in the library."

I feel Leo's stare at the back of my skull, that growing *I told you so* on the tip of his tongue. But I feel, too, desperate, the same kind of desperate Peter Drike is feeling. My whole cohort is feeling. In amongst all these books there is no lesson about how to survive this place. Nothing at all in this entire temple to knowledge. Academia is a cesspit for lauding men as gods—is that it? Is that all it is?

So what the fuck am I meant to do? What am I meant to do?

The panic is intense and immediate and I stand there clenching and unclenching my fists, feeling the hot prick of tears at my eyes. I have to bite my tongue and whisper to keep my voice from cracking. "Then how do we prepare for the final trial?"

And Meléti doesn't answer, because what is there to say? Leo is right.

There is no preparing for this trial.

The only hope is being ruthless.

❦

THE INSTANT we are back at the apartments I light three cigarettes. Two of the cigarettes are for me, to smoke one after the other in quick succession, and the other is for Leo. It is the end of my tobacco, and I know I'll regret it later when the cravings hit like a brick, but I'm so—so —*furious.*

No one else is back. These apartments are skeletal and haunted, dark and creaking. I frantically light the cigarettes, new prosthetic fingers struggling to hold the matches. Finally I hand one to Leo, and drag him to my room.

I put both cigarettes in my mouth and dump the matches on the desk. I kick off my shoes. I start immediately taking off my shirt, and it takes forever, again because of the fingers. So I am angry, and frustrated at myself, and frustrated about this place, and wishing I could go back just a handful of weeks to order myself, "Do not come here."

And then what? You might as well have raised the gun and shot mother in the head.

Maybe that would have been better. What has she ever done for me?

It's an impotent feeling and it has nowhere to go except to fester in my stomach. The University feels inevitable. I had no other choice. All this, everything that has happened to me —was there ever any other outcome?

Leo stares down at me, either occupied by the hint of my bare chest or my struggling porcelain fingers, then at his own cigarette. "What are you doing?" he asks and he takes a slow drag. He sputters only once, which gives me time to have my own inhale—both cigarettes at once, a tiny fire in my lungs— and when he recovers, Leo glances back at me sheepishly.

"Cass," he whispers. A warning, maybe. A sad little note, recognition that I'm pathetic for wanting him right now

I've won the battle with the buttons. I throw my shirt violently on the ground. "*What?*"

I'm panting. I can't stop breathing hard.

He comes and he holds me. Wraps his hand around my neck, presses my head close into him. I smell him, sweat, tobacco. I feel the warmth of him. But I can't relax. It feels so much easier to give him my body than to let him see me cry.

I want to pull away. Want him to just fuck me. Want everything to be over, want to sleep and never wake up.

"Everything will be alright," he says, like you'd say to a child.

But it won't be. We both know it. And death feels so much closer than it should.

"All this and we haven't even gotten in yet," I whisper. "Are you scared? Scared that it'll be worse in the University itself?"

He doesn't answer but I feel him tense, and I wonder if I've said something stupid: if none of this scares him, and none of it is as intense as the rest of England is.

And then he says it outright. He takes my hand—the new one, and I can't feel his touch, but I am sure he is squeezing the porcelain hard—and he looks at me with pity, and a bit of hard-to-hide anger. "You would have died out there," he said. "Nemean Lion in the wild? Arm gone? Infection would have festered. You would have died slowly."

I bite my tongue.

He sees something in my face that makes him roll his eyes. "Oh, I am not stupid, Cass. I will be training to become cannon fodder. I know this. But if I train hard enough, I might actually have a shot at surviving. At lasting longer than a few more stressful, horrible years. London has baths. Food. Actual safety."

I open my mouth and he pushes my lips closed with a finger. "And don't say all of those luxuries come from people outside the wards, because I know that. I lived it, and lived it longer than you. You would be a hypocrite for trying to convince me of anything else when you have lived happily here for years. Don't act like you weren't given a choice. You could walk out those wards and never return. Stick to your morals and say, 'I relinquish London's safety, because it is built on the back of suffering.' But you would be an idiot, and we both know that. Your sacrifice would stop nothing."

He puts his hands around my waist. He starts undoing my pants. I let him.

Then he leans in, breath hot against my neck as he whispers, "Neither of us are under any illusion that this place is good. I've already told you I plan to be ruthless. I plan to survive. And I think you're better than me in some regards, Cass—yes, even after Bellamy. Because you were right. I thought you should leave them both. Save yourself." He pauses. "I think you would do well to be more selfish."

Which is insane to me, because I have never felt anything *but* selfish. But Leo is and has always been putting himself first. I realised it the first day we came here—he was using me for information, perhaps is still using me, like I know more than what I've told him—and I think I forgot about that. I saw his desire and his niceness and believed for a moment it might be more than something physical.

He is telling me now, almost outright, that Leo Shaw will always come first.

Any sane man would stop this right here. Would set a boundary and walk away and preserve what little peace was remaining.

"Do you—like me?" I ask. "As a person, Shaw, because I know you like my body."

He looks at me for a long time, contemplating—or formulating, I think. I half expect him to say yes, as if he's worried I won't take my clothes off for him otherwise. But he says, "In all honesty, I don't know," and I like him all the more for it. "But I don't think you know if you like me either."

He smiles like he's caught me in a lie, and I snort. "Tell me something about yourself."

He laughs. "Why?"

"I don't know a damn thing about you. Not really. I can hardly determine if I like you or not."

He plops down on the bed—and this is not, I think, how

he wanted to spend the night. "You know what I think about this place."

"Why did you choose to come here?" I ask.

He grimaces and shakes his head. "You know why."

"No," I say. "I know England is infested. But I don't know why you'd wilfully risk your life for a city that exploits that fear. Even for the luxuries, I just. . ."

He is smiling like we're discussing our happiest memories. Is it a barricade, that smile? A defence against all the hurt in his heart?

"Oh, it's very simple, actually," he smiles, clasps his hands together. "There's no one left that I love."

And I think about his reaction to Thaddeus—my brother with half his insides spilling out of him, how calm Leo was, how nonchalant. What kind of horrors has he seen for that to be nothing to him? Why is he so damn relaxed, even now, even after everything?

I realise very suddenly Leo has never cracked. Not like the rest of us. He's gotten angry. But he's never been close to breaking. And I think I was close to breaking before I even set foot here.

"What. . . happened?" I ask.

Leo shakes his head and a beat passes where I believe he's considering telling me. But then he goes, "I don't think so, Mr Jones." He inspects his hands, presses his lips together firmly; the most subtle admission that whatever this memory is hurts him.

"Alright," I say, and I stop pressing.

What does it matter, the how? They are all clearly dead. And what does it matter, if Leo doesn't really like me? It is better for me if it is just my body. My mind is too unsure, too brittle.

It is better this way.

So I let him fuck me.

I undo my pants the rest of the way and I stand there in nothing but my underwear and my socks. I shiver—there's no fireplace in this room, and the cold is creeping in from outside, but then Leo stands, eyes raking over me, and he slips out of his shirt and his own pants and pulls me against him.

And soon we're both hard, cocks grinding against each other, his pressing into my belly. I run my left hand, porcelain dancing down his spine, and nearly cry. I can't feel him. It's not the same.

"Pin me down," I tell him. "Both hands. Just—pin me down."

Roughly he yanks my arms high and shoves me onto the bed, toppling after me, crushing me: Leo Shaw is stronger than me by far and I am completely incapable of fighting back. Weakly I shove against him, which only rouses him more. He grunts and pushes me into the mattress. My arms stretch out. It doesn't matter that I can't feel with my left hand. I am not being permitted to touch him. I am under his control.

"How should I touch you?" he whispers.

I meet his gaze and smile. "Ruthlessly."

LESSON TWENTY-SEVEN

Bells ring out past dawn like death knells. When I wake, it's in Leo's arms. He's already awake, stroking my hair. It's so intimate that it's concerning. I fight the urge to flinch away, but I know when we have sex, it isn't really about me. I am a body and I am here; that's all it is. But in the morning before this final trial, I still let myself lie there and feel it. I let myself have the fantasy that this is some man who loves me unconditionally and freely, and that it's a decade from now, and somehow we are in London without responsibilities. We exist here in peace and safety. We exist in each other's arms.

But then the bells ring out again and I'm forced to admit how stupid that fantasy is. Gently, I push against his chest to let him know I'm awake. He stops tousling.

We look at each other, squinting through the blackness, and we say nothing in case they're the wrong words. In silence we dress in our uniforms and I think: God, I hope they don't bury me in this.

When I open the door Victoria is in the sitting room. She's curled up in front of a fire she must have made herself.

She's in a fresh uniform by the look of it, and her hair is damp. I assume she wandered in some hours ago to shower and change. And lying here is easier. Her room is haunted like my mind is. It's at once too empty without Bellamy and full of him.

Victoria stirs as I get close and pushes herself up instantly. The look she gives me is withering, until her eyes drop down to my arm. Porcelain glints in the firelight. She glances away, and I can't tell if it's guilt or anger or exhaustion, whether she sees my arm and thinks, "Well deserved, good riddance" or something softer. But her guilt won't be enough to subsume the anger. I know she won't ever forgive me.

"I thought you asked to be moved to another room," I whisper.

"Yes, well," she says, still not looking at me. "I was given a choice." I wait for her to speak. She drags out the silence for a long moment. Then, chin raised, "Drike is alone you see. Everyone else in his room died. Drearton said I could pair with him, if I wanted."

She leaves the real reason unsaid, and it takes me a while, as I muddle through sleep-haze, to understand.

Leo beats me to it. His weight is sudden on the floor-boards and they groan as he says, "It's a group trial." An emotion tinges the words—it's not despair, and it's not fear. I don't have a name for it, but I hear it coating his words. Something that is confirming Leo's thesis to him over and over again; reflexive and full of awe.

It says, once more: the only way through this is to be ruthless.

"Yes," Victoria whispers. She looks away.

A group trial. And Drike is on his own.

My heart tightens. *So you've doomed him instead of yourself*, I do not say. *So you'll damn me for sacrificing one to save many*.

Vindication.

But—I think I'm twisted in a base way. Who revels in something like this? Why does it feel so good to know she suffers like I do?

I rub my face and get down on my knees beside her. She flinches away, dragging her legs underneath herself, makes a noise like a half-formed, "Stop."

I stop. I don't get closer. "Victoria. . ."

"Can we not?" she whispers. "Let's just—not."

A silent scream rages in my throat. It's vanished. Any kind of friendship we had—it's gone. And I know it was never so very close, but it existed. Didn't it?

I stand up quickly because I might rot on the carpet if I don't.

"Come on," I say, and I head for the door.

THE COHORT IS MUCH SMALLER than I remember. The dean clicks his tongue and opens up his pocket watch, sighing.

"Right," he mutters. He raises a hand and gestures, just two fingers, and out of the morning mist come two Blood Hunters. They step out from under the colonnade, back near the dining hall, but they don't come towards us. They split up. I watch them meander their way into various towers, various rooms. We've had an hour to eat and assemble, but not everyone is here.

It takes a while, but soon there are shouts. Then screams. I go completely still as I hear it, and I can feel the dean at my back, watching.

"What," someone hisses beside me.

"They don't wish to complete their trial," the dean says behind us. He's speaking like the delay is a slight inconvenience, and keeps looking over his shoulder for something near the west gate. "And only students or graduates may leave the grounds. You made the agreement when you came onto campus. In the *Phlebotomia.*"

Bloodletting—but not just for tracking us. For a blood bound, an unbreakable covenant. We all agreed, after all, to do this. To complete these trials. And the man did say we wouldn't be able to live within London's wards if we chose not to complete them.

I watch several screaming, struggling individuals be dragged from their rooms. The Blood Hunters have a student each, and those students are promptly restrained by something I can only imagine are Artificer-made shackles, because they both stop screaming and relax fairly instantly.

Someone darts out of a room and legs it first for the west gate before he spots us—then he turns desperately and barrels into a waiting Hunter. But another flees across the grass. There's a whistle. Another Blood Hunter emerges to chase the runner.

"God," the dean mutters. "Ah, here we are. Good, good. Come on, then."

He calls out the last part as weary students emerge; some from their apartments, some from further in campus, near the library. We all make a show of ignoring the screaming of whoever's resisting.

The Lins arrive. Fred looks haggard.

"What happened to you?" I ask.

She shrugs, but gives me a look. "Stayed up all night."

"Thinking of leaving?" I whisper.

She stares right through me and blinks. "There's no leaving," she says softly, and we both turn to watch the Blood Hunters trap our fellow students. Fred puts a hand over her face and exhales into it.

"One more," I tell her, and she nods, gives me a brief and very fake smile.

"One, two—good. Good. That's everyone in your room,

Mr Jones, isn't it?" the dean asks, and when I nod, the dean gives me a grin. "Wonderful. Lucy will take you."

A woman I hadn't noticed before ducks her head as her name is called and steps forward.

"Follow me," she murmurs placidly, and I wonder, if she is a graduate, how she ever survived this place. And that's a judgement based on looks alone, but she seems sweet fundamentally, like the awfulness of these trials never managed to affect her. She is Indian, I guess, and wearing a black bycocket hat with netting draping. It makes her look like a funeral mourner, but it's beautiful. She's in a long wing collar in starch white, covered by a burgundy leather trench with a shoulder cape. A little *S* on her shoulder marks her Scholar— that thing I once wanted to be.

I have barely any time to wonder why we've been handed off to a Scholar. I see other rooms being led out of campus, but no one is heading in our direction. We leave the west gate out of the campus grounds, and I expect more people to run —but what's the point? Hunters of all kinds surge into the green by the west tower on campus and watch us go. They will be stationed there until one of us runs.

We are led up to Ludgate. Most of the streets are empty. I crane my neck to the sky, as if time inside the campus is altered; London is never this quiet. But then we pass a main thoroughfare, and manage to catch sight of a procession. Something I've never seen before. A swelling mass of bodies. I think it's a celebration, but it's a different beast.

Workers, families, all of them are packed tight and shouting. Hunters on horseback or up on buildings, shouting orders in Latin, roughly pulling people to the ground. Violence against the people they are meant to be protecting.

And I realise this is the first round. The first victims of Drearton's sweep through London, evicting any who aren't of immediate use, any graduate families that are simply too large to ride on the coattails of a single graduate. Which means: I see pregnant women and infant children. I see a child no more than ten arguing they can be put to work to stay behind the wards. I see the injured, the disabled, the undesirables that cannot be made to maintain the city, or haven't entered the University, lining up to be expelled. And just before Lucy leads us up another side street away from the crowd, a scream goes out.

It's this brutal and horrified wail that twists into a chant: *Drearton lies! Drearton lies! Drearton lies!*

I see the body of a *teras* hefted high above heads, a Cult of the Rift follower chanting beneath it. It's not a *teras* I've ever seen before. Its body is warped and bulging, an unwell amalgam, an upsetting triptych of *cerastes* and *Stymphalian* and *Caledonian*—rotund body of a boar, sad, useless wings, razor sharp, jutting out of its back, the thin, long neck of the *cerastes*, and two horns that usually protrude from the *cerastes'* head bursting at odd angles in the body.

A hybrid.

In the days I've been on campus, has there been another attack? Another town like Watford obliterated, another new form of *teras* wreaking havoc on England?

I slip my eyes to Leo, and even if he doesn't understand entirely, he nods at me. As if he's seen this before.

As if this is the reason he's here.

But I am thinking: I need to earn a spot here more than ever. I need to learn how to fight these things—properly, under the guidance of trained professionals. Because this world is changing.

And if hybrids can form, what hope do we have?

"Come on," Lucy orders. "We don't have much time. Get in the wagon."

A covered wagon is waiting for us. Two horses and a hooded driver wait at the front. We climb inside only to find there are no windows, save for the tiny barred slit at the back door. It is filled with weapons. Swords, flintlock pistols, ammunition. I immediately fill up Thaddeus' pistol and rummage for another sparker. There is none, so I'm left with whatever fuel remains in mine.

"Mr Jones," I hear called from outside. I get up and press my face against the barred window in the door. Lucy checks the bolt outside and stares up at me, expression blank and uncaring.

"Open this when the wagon stops," she says, and slips a thin white envelope through the bars. It has *Cassius Jones* scrawled on it. No one else receives a letter.

At first I'm not sure if she's abandoning us, but then the horses knicker and the wagon jolts. Lucy doesn't even wait to see us make it through the gates. She turns on her heels and stalks back to the campus, calmly ignoring the growing throng of angry Londoners as they are shoved out of the gates.

LESSON TWENTY-EIGHT

Within three hours, the doors to the wagon are pulled roughly open. Wind barrels inside, buffeting all of us with a freezing sharpness and snow.

"Out," the driver tells us. He is gruff, face nose and mouth covered by a black cloth, and hair jammed tightly under a wide-brimmed hat. "One weapon each."

I take an extra sword, because he hasn't seen my pistol. Leo and Victoria take guns, Silas takes a sword, and Fred takes an axe (though she has two daggers tucked into her back pocket already). We jump out. My feet sink instantly into thick snow.

It will be impossible to run in this.

We are in Nottinghamshire, in Sherwood Forest, where the world is segmented by a thousand birch trees, grey slicing through white. I expect to be led somewhere, to be deposited probably beneath the major oak out of legend, because the University seems to love its rituals. But then the driver stalks back to the front of the carriage with insane speed, quick footsteps crunching in the snow.

"Only waiting a few hours," he says. "I'll be a kilometre or so south. One of you got a watch?" Silas nods. "Good. If you're not there at five o'clock, I'm gone." Then he's whipping the horses to move before I can even open the letter.

"Read it out," Fred whispers quickly, as I'm still tearing it open. She is glancing back at the dense snow, keeps whipping her head to canvass a new angle. I feel the same nervous tension from the others. Leo hovers near Silas and whispers something I don't catch, and Silas nods, frowning. "Yes, I think so," I hear him say.

"We could run," Victoria murmurs, to no one and to all of us. She says it so quietly I think she must not mean it, but I see the Lins give each other a meaningful glance.

"There is no running," I say, in an echo of Fred's own conclusion. Fred nods at me tightly, but Victoria just stares forlornly at the departing carriage, arms crossed tightly across her chest.

"Go on," Fred nods at the half-opened letter in my hand.

I open the rest of it and read it. Aloud. Which is a mistake.

Mr Jones,
I have been very impressed with your assiduity thus far, and I look forward to seeing you blossom during your tutelage at the University.
I think I am most pleased with your understanding of necessity. You do what needs to be done.

(Here I pause because I feel all their eyes on me, this quadrangle stare where they all might be absolved if I take the blame. And for that I skim the rest in my head, without speaking it, which gives me half a minute of shock before I have to defend my hide.)

The rest of the letter reads:

Your final trial will be as much about fulfilling a promise to me as it is testing your group work. Before you worry, Mr Jones, you all survived it the first time. You should have a better idea what to do now.

The last sighting of the teras in question was north-east of your current position (compass enclosed).

P.S. If you need a hint, Mr Jones, it gutted your brother.

— Best of luck, Dean Drearton

God.

God, no.

Something fundamental in my brain gives out momentarily. I think part of me goes missing, or ejects itself from the conscious part of my brain—I just shut down. I keep myself staring at the paper, avoiding those fetid stares from the rest of them, and I already feel like I'm being circled by a pack of wolves.

"Well?" Fred prompts. "Go on."

But I already know what they're going to say. I have doomed them. I bargained their lives away from a set of rooms, for a chance to read a letter from my brother, a letter that has helped us barely at all.

And now we are to fight a *manticore*.

I open my mouth. I close it. So she stalks over and rips it from my hands.

My body tenses and I half lunge after it, until sense stops me. They will find out sooner or later.

Fred reads it and grows pale, which prompts Silas to read over her shoulder. I panic about what to say. *Oh, I never thought we would have to follow through. I thought it would be years from now, when we had training. Yes, I'm sorry I doomed the lot of you, I'm sorry I made a decision on your behalf, but you see, my brother's dying words. . .*

No matter how I frame it, it's selfish. I am at least self-aware enough for that.

Fred looks at me with tears in her eyes. I go to say the first "I'm sorry" of many, but she shouts over me.

"You—you *bastard! You,* who have lived in safety for years, while people like my brother and I have slaved for your comfort! You think you can make decisions on our behalf because of what? Some perceived betterment?"

"No," I say, defensive, and panicking, and God, what have I done?

"You've fucking killed us all!" she howls.

"Fred," Silas hisses, clamping a hand over her mouth. She sobs into his palm, but he grips her there, perked and waiting for the answering howl. "Fred, it's too late. It's too late. It's done."

He looks at me, hurt in his eyes. But he doesn't condemn me. Not even now.

I told you, Silas Lin is too good for this place.

"What's going on?" Victoria whispers. She rips the paper from Fred's hands, who in turn shakes her brother off her back. Fred stalks towards me, jabs me in the chest.

"Time and again in these trials you have made selfish decisions. You have ordered us about like you have all the knowledge—but you don't know *anything!* You don't know anything about this world. "

I can feel myself getting pale. Weakly, I supply, "I grew up—"

"It doesn't matter! You are nestled up in London's bosom and have been for long enough to know it thrives off this arrangement. Did you ever stop to think that maybe the reason the University has *teras* on campus is because it *benefits from it?"*

Silas takes her in an embrace, and I am forgotten. But Fred's words stick with me. Even when I was outside the wards, my father was a fisherman. We lived in a free town—and he was abusive, but it was different to having London's agents watching your every move, the way they would for farmers like the Lins. I back up and risk a glance at Victoria, who has already severed herself from me. Even if she's been here longer than me, it doesn't matter. She hasn't gotten anyone killed the way I have. She didn't set us all up to be mauled by a *manticore*. And I'm scared to look at Leo, but I do it anyway, and I see that he's refusing to glance my way.

We are falling apart before the *manticore* has even emerged

"It was to get the west tower," I say. "My brother died telling me to get there. For the note. He thought. . ."

Thought it would be more useful than it turned out to be.

This does nothing to spark more sympathy for me, and I can't blame them. But neither can I feel anything more than I already feel. Guilt for Bellamy's death is consuming me. Guilt for letting Thaddeus die, guilt for killing that student at the dean's will, guilt for Peter Drike, who right now is probably dying all alone. Guilt for all my sins. What is one more when I am already laden with them? What is one more sin when I am overburdened by self-hatred?

"Okay," I say, sighing. "I signed all of you up to fight the *manticore*, because I had no idea when the dean would call on us, and I was foolish enough to think it would be later in our education. It was before the first trial. I didn't think—he was trying to whittle us down. I didn't know."

No reaction. I tell myself I am fine with that.

I look to the north-east. It's past midday now, and winter is already settling on the sun, muting it. It'll be dark soon.

"I'll lure it out," I say. I turn on my heel and walk before anyone can stop me.

Or before I can realise that no one plans to.

It TAKES a handful of minutes to find the town. It never had a name—it was a little holdout, perhaps four or five cob buildings with thatched roofs, and I never knew it existed, which makes its obliteration all the more upsetting. The settlement had cleared some trees, built a spiked fence, and it's a mess of wood and gore, now. Fire burns in one of the houses. Two others have crumbled. There is no doubt in my mind that a *manticore* has barrelled through them, though if there was doubt, the half-mauled torso of a woman and the free limbs of several others would assuage that.

I am pressed into the snow beside a tree, and I have to disconnect the primal urge to panic. I am reminded of Watford, of sitting in the gore and blood of those townsfolk, which only cascades into me thinking about my brother. Stomach in his hands, pressed against a tree, dying in the snow—how beautifully cyclical it will be if I die here, mauled by the same beast.

But it won't bloody happen. *Be ruthless*, Leo told me—so I will be.

Though first I must do something very stupid. I promised them I would lure it out.

I have no idea where the *manticore* is. Even with the blaze burning at my back, scattering the shadows, I can't see much. And the roaring of the fire means I can't hear it. Without the tell-tale clicking of its scorpion tail, I'll be struck before I can do anything useful.

But I do remember that the *manticore* liked the chase. I bought Thaddeus a few more seconds of tortured breathing by running. So that is what I do now. I pick myself up from my hiding spot and step out into the clearing. And then I run.

My feet crunch loudly in the snow and sink deep. I fight the urge to back myself against the ruined hamlet and the false sense of safety those flames offer. I just run, from one side of the tree-line to the other, and then I pause.

There are shadows there, moving, and a creaking of a thousand birches freezing in the cold wind. I can't tell if the shapes I see are cast from the packed canopy, or if they belong to the stalking bulk of the beast.

It hasn't attacked me yet, so I turn and run back, and I feel stupid, like a bug flailing about in the seconds before it's crushed. I get out Thaddeus' gun, the gun that didn't save him, and my left goes to the sparker, which probably has enough fuel for one more blinding spark, and I think: this won't do anything. This won't stop it. But I am compelled by the inevitability of my death to do *something*, and if that means running about in the snow whilst the people I doomed have a shot at life, then I should do that. Shouldn't I?

God. I really don't want to die.

"Cassius!"

It's Leo voice, pitched in a desperate scream, howling for me.

I spin. Out of nothing but shadow, a tail materialises. Puckered, bulbous, black—the scorpion tail collides with me and I go flying. I am thrown through the air; dizzying and maddening, upside down; there is fire, snow, blood, night. I see a great shadow in the sky. Its wings are spread, bat-like brown skin pulled taught and veiny, and the human-face is open mouthed and screaming. The *manticore's* eyes bulge. And it starts to dive after me.

"No."

I scrabble to my feet, kick off the snow, stumble again. The *manticore* lands with such force I'm knocked to the ground. I think it's on me, that I'm being crushed by it, but it's just snow; an entire wave of it thrown up by the landing.

Tick, tick, tick, like the hour of my doom is approaching, like a clock that can tell me—the tail rears up to paralyse me. I raise my gun. My sparker. I squeeze my eyes and click it.

Intense white light flashes like the gates of heaven. I open my eyes just before it fades to see the *manticore* rearing on its hind legs with a scream. The light hasn't settled; spots of it dance in my periphery, and the whole clearing is visible for half a second before shadow re-consumes it. And in that brief flash I see the others running out of the forest.

A pentagonal attack; the five of us surround the *manticore* before it recovers. Fred is already diving forward with her axe to hack away at its tendons. The *manticore* is screaming. Shots are going off in a beautiful, percussive symphony. One of them gets the fleshy white underbelly and red sprays from the wound.

I have the gall to think this is easy—

—Which is when it all starts going to high hell.

A tail whips overhead. Silas screams. The scorpion stinger buries itself in his shoulder and whips out just as fast. Fred howls his name and carves a chunk out of the *manticore*'s ankle. But Silas is more than injured; he's stunned. The *manticore*'s poison works through him quickly. He drops the sword and sways.

"Fred." His voice cracks. And then he drops unconscious.

I load another shot and aim for the *manticore*'s head. I fire and it screams, outraged more than hurt, hissing and spitting. It swipes out with its colossal paw—a jagged, curved claw rushes down towards my body.

And Leo steps in front of me.

He screams. Claws rip across his cheek.

Flaps of flesh fly in the wind as he buckles, screaming as he lands, fingers trying to touch his face.

I scream too. I scream so sharply there is blood in my throat, and my heart is wailing; I shriek, "Leo! No, God, *please!"* and the only thing that matters in this moment, is him; more than anything I want Leo to live.

I shoot until I'm out of bullets and clicking uselessly. I throw Thaddeus' gun down and yank out the other one I stole and shoot again. It's all desperation. I don't know what I'm doing. I don't know how to kill it.

Victoria throws her gun down and dives for Silas' dropped sword. I run to Leo and put him on his back. He's kicking and howling—I can see his teeth gnashing through the hole in his cheek. Blood is pouring into his mouth and down his face, blood, so much of it.

And if he dies, a part of me dies too.

"Leo, Leo, just breathe, you have to—"

Leo's eyes widen. "Cass, darling," he says, and he grins with blood-stained teeth. "Move, would you?"

I duck.

Leo shoots three shots at the *manticore* before his gun starts clicking empty too. Victoria runs into my periphery, but then her scream fills the air.

One meaty arm flies out and meets Victoria's sternum with a crack. Her cry of pain comes out a broken wheeze as she is thrown; her back meets a tree with another crack and she's out.

"Go," Leo whispers.

I leave Leo and run towards her. The *manticore* spins, colossal body twisting around, kicking up snow in another dusty wave. Its tail thuds three times into the snow. I hear screaming—Fred?—and an unhappy noise from the beast. It lurches around again and kicks off the ground, wings beating in the air. I am knocked onto my back by the sheer force of the gust it produces. I hit my head on a birch tree, not enough to knock me out, but enough that I can't—really see anything—not clearly. Stunned and dizzy I stare up at the beast. It hovers in the air above me and seems to make some decision. I wait for it to take me. I wait for hot blood to pour out of my stomach. But it dives down for one of the unconscious bodies, its taloned feet grabbing hold. It raises the body to its mouth and opens that too-human face.

And then it tears the head off.

29

LESSON TWENTY-NINE

The scream that goes out is haunting. It is raw and it is broken, and it is Victoria screaming for Bellamy all over again, only it's not her. It's Fred. Fred in the snow, hands buried, mouth open, *screaming*.

Even before my vision clears, I know Silas is dead.

"Get up," I say—to myself, or to the others, I don't know. I have to use the birch tree for balance. I only have my sparker. Victoria is still unconscious. I run to her whilst the *manticore* feasts and pull the sword from the snow.

I think I see her breathing. I can't be sure. Because the *manticore* grows bored of Silas' flesh and drops the lower half of his body from its mouth. He is one arm, half a torso, both his legs. Fred howls again, picks up her axe, and runs forward.

"*Fred!*" I scream, stumbling in a chase after her.

The *manticore* is so focused on how she's hacking away that I'm able to skid in the snow. I raise the blade near my face and slide. Snow kicks up around me. I'm so close to the *manticore* I can smell it, I can see the gore tainting its fur, the metallic stench of death, the rot on its breath. And the speed with which I'm moving means the sword catches on flesh and tears. I open up part of the *manticore's* belly. Guts, blood, putrid liquid pours out over my face. I gag on it, on the smell and the thickness. The beast screams, rears up, and slams down. It is pure luck that I'm not underneath it when it lands. But I hear a wet crunch all the same, and Fred's scream turns shrill and then abruptly cuts off.

I roll onto my stomach, still gagging, and drag myself out from the beast. It's wounded, but still alive. I hear it wheezing. Its tail starts clicking and I scrabble up in time to watch it blindly thumping into snow, desperate to kill its attacker. It wheezes and stands, tries weakly to fly. Something vital plummets out of its belly and it howls and drops down after the bloody flesh.

I glance over. I see Fred in the snow. Blood pools around her. I can't see—I can't move—I don't know if she's dead. If it crushed her.

Then, suddenly, there's shooting. I press myself into the bloody snow, squinting against the orange light of the flames. Leo is awake. Pale, and bleeding, mouth exposed through his right cheek, tongue pulsing against hot blood, but alive. He shoots his empty gun in fear.

And then I realise the *manticore* isn't what has scared him.

There is something else in the dark.

I think about running to Leo. About getting up, and moving. Checking on Fred. But I am terrified. I am terrified because something colossal and twisted slouches from the shadows. I see—something.

God. What is that?

The first thought that crystallises is: *chimera*. There is no lion, no goat-head protruding. Not a *chimera* in the classical term then. But a hybrid all the same.

I see:

A snorting bullhead, like that of a *minotaur*, but the body bulges out, like a great deer. I watch it, and I remember Pliny the Elder mentioned the *archils*—an elk-like creature, back legs with no joints. This creature stomps rigidly towards us with heavy footfalls; taller than the *manticore*, somehow, like prehistoric beasts.

Great antlers emerge from the bull's head, but they are —wrong.

Fleshy.

Each prong sprouts into reaching human fingers, an amalgamated hand, and they are twitching.

Its tail is the same as the *chimera*'s—a snake—and a mound that looks like a half-formed head does indeed sprout from its back. The hybrid looks rushed, half-finished; fleshy clay that didn't fire properly.

The *manticore* spins weakly. More blood and gore spurts from the gaping wound in its belly. And then it screams.

The hybrid opens its mouth and howls back, spewing fire and smoke like Cacus from myth, and the *manticore* ignites with a curdling scream, rolling desperately in the snow as its fur singes and melts against its flesh. Burning fills the air. The hybrid stalks forward slowly and tilts its head so the fingers on its antlers can brush against the dying *manticore*. They reach out with tender care to stroke the crying human face, and then with speed they wrap around the *manticore's* neck and *squeeze*.

And all of us watch. It takes minutes. We are frozen as the hybrid chokes the life out of the *manticore*, as the human face squeaks uselessly, throat crushed. Its eyes roll back, milky whites turning glazed.

The *manticore* is dead.

But the hybrid turns to us.

Its fingers retract from the limp neck of the *manticore* slowly. The great shuddering body collapses before the hybrid's feet, and the new beast steps over the corpse with ease, long, jointless legs creaking like the birch trees.

Now I scramble back and manage to stand.

"Get up," I yell to Leo, Victoria. I run to Fred. Her leg is —attached, but mangled. It is holding on by tendons. The tibia and fibula are exposed, cracked in multiple places. And the meat has been bludgeoned into a near paste. Bloody minced meat half buried in the snow.

I vomit. It's so immediate I feel the burning bile in my nose. But then I have to turn back to Fred and decide what to do.

"Cut it off," Victoria wheezes from beside me. She has Leo leaning against her. Half her face is bruised from the impact on the tree and she bends in a way I think some of her ribs must be cracked.

"I'll do it," she says, and shoves me away. She grabs the axe from beside Fred's open hand and raises it above her head, wincing at the stretch.

I turn before she brings it down.

The hybrid is practically on top of us. Victoria is hacking off the remains of Fred's leg. Leo is still gushing blood. There's no way, no way, we'll get out of here in time.

I sit in the snow craning up at this great twisted beast.

"*Siste,*" I say.

Halt.

The hybrid comes to a creaking halt. It twists its head at me, inspecting.

"*Quid dicis?*"

What did you say?

The noise that emerges feels ancient and new all at once: a dozen, overlapping voices, all ages and genders, a coalescence.

I am shaking. The fear that ignites in my body is innate, almost evolutionary. As if an ancestor long ago learnt to fear this thing. I scrabble back and breathe deeply.

I ask: "*Quid vis?*"

What do you want?

And in immediate answer it says, *"Vindicare."*

To take revenge. Or more: *to seek justice. Vindicta* is a ceremonial act. Self-redress by the injured party.

I can feel the others around me frozen and waiting. Victoria has stopped her motion with the axe. Leo's hand is pressed to his cheek to stop the blood, and he's shivering, but desperate to stay upright.

I turn to look at him, and see his awe at this strange creature. When I look back at the hybrid, its gaze drops from Leo back to me, dark pupils readjusting in the bright yellow eyes.

I swallow. *"Contra quem?"*

Against whom?

And I wait in stupefied fear for it to come screaming towards me in answer, but the hybrid just stares unblinking.

It doesn't answer me. Instead, after a minute, it turns and stalks back into the birch trees. The whole forest creaks in answer, welcoming its return, and very soon the shadows swallow it until it's almost like it was never there at all.

"MAKE A TOURNIQUET," I shout, and Leo is ripping fabric from his own shirt for Fred's leg. She's wan, pallid. Probably close to death. She's been bleeding out for minutes, and I don't know what it will take to stop her from dying.

"Need a Healer," Leo says gruffly, tying the tourniquet tight. "Need to get back to the wagon. What time is it?"

But neither myself nor Victoria have any idea.

Silas was the one with the watch.

I rip from my own shirt for Leo's face, but it's fairly useless. I have to tie it awkwardly so the knot sits just above his left brow, fabric dipping horizontally to cover the exposed cheek. He is still bleeding profusely. It is determination and adrenaline keeping him awake now.

Victoria and I help Fred up. Leo is forced to stagger back alone. We debate taking the remains of Silas' body, and I know Fred will hate me when I tell her I am the reason the broken corpse of her brother remains out here.

Instead, as Victoria and I start limping back with the unconscious Fred between us, Leo picks up the axe and stalks to the dead *manticore*. A trophy, like I took that day in Watford. Something to show the dean we have beaten this thing. He goes to the back of the beast and starts hacking, and with ease severs the scorpion stinger from the rest of the body.

"Careful," I call, but he's already wrapping the thing in his blazer. Any venom from that thing paralyses.

He stalks back over. "Come on," Leo says, and leads the way back.

We stumble bloody and broken to the wagon, whose driver jumps down in true shock at seeing us. He helps us climb in, praises us—something about true Hunters, or the future of the graduate class—and drives us back to London with speed. And from there it's a blur. Healers meet us at the gate and take a dying Fred and Leo and Victoria away. I am given a once-over before it's determined my injuries are not worth fussing over. And then I am led onto campus with a Blood Hunter pair at my back, deposited securely by the west tower, and left alone.

There are no congratulations. No ceremony. No feast. There is nothing but the howling wind and a misted rain that starts up quickly. I stay under it and pray it drowns me.

I have seen London's future. I have looked it in the eye.

And it wants vengeance.

30

LESSON THIRTY

"She'll get a new leg," the Artificer Abraham tells me once the Healer is done with Fred. It's been nearly a week. They stopped the bleeding, put that salve on it that healed me, and have left—which I assume is a good sign, but I haven't been in to see her yet. She was so close to death when we brought her back. And I feel nothing about that. I decided I would be the one to tell her about Silas' body, so I've been very careful to not let emotion seep through.

"Make it strong," I say. "As good as mine."

Then Abraham opens his mouth and closes it, presumably to tell me the dean hasn't authorised such use of materials, but I fix him a look. "You will do it," I say.

"It will go on her tab," he says.

I tell myself I am above making decisions for other people —though it's not entirely true. For this, however, I concede. I won't rope Fred into debt unless she wants it.

"Come back tomorrow and ask her," I say, and make sure to lock the door when Abraham leaves.

All three of my remaining colleagues are in their rooms.

Victoria is recovering from three broken ribs. Leo's face has had to be stitched back together. Red, raw lines run across his face. A chunk of the right cheek could not be recovered; they have replaced it with leather.

Fred is arguably the worst. She lost her leg. She lost her brother.

I push against the wood of her door, and it groans open, announcing me to her. She is awake but looks terrible. Dark circles rim her eyes. When she spots me, she pushes weakly against the mattress to sit up.

"You don't have to—"

"I want to," she whispers sharply, then puts her head in her hands. "Sorry. Sorry. I just—can't get the image of him out of my head."

Abraham abandoned Fred's desk chair by the bed and I plop into it, feeling all the gravity of the world in my body. Fred looks away from me but she's tense, wound tight and waiting.

"I—"

She goes rigid, and I cut myself off. I remember Bellamy and Victoria the first day on campus and the way they offered up their sympathies. Sorry feels rotten and clinical all at once. It's an awkward word, and after the fifth time, it's horrible to hear. It feels like reliving the death over and over again.

So I say it plainly. "They brought his body back."

"His body," she repeats, still staring at the wall. "What remains of it?"

"Most of the torso. Legs. Both of his arms."

"Mm," she whispers. Exhales. "And our acceptance letters? When do we get those?"

"Tomorrow. But they won't. . . have your leg ready. I told the Artificer—I wasn't sure if you wanted me committing you to debt, so I told him—"

"Cassius," she cuts me off. I fall silent. Finally, Fred looks my way. "What happened out there?"

I don't know what to say. She was unconscious by the time the hybrid emerged. I don't know if anyone's told her. "What do you mean?"

"You know what I mean. We were about to die. Next thing I know I'm back in London." She turns her body to me and winces with the movement. "Tell me. You have to tell me."

I think about reaching out and touching her hands, but I don't know her all that well. And she is being too cordial to me, after what happened. After my involvement.

"A hybrid emerged from the woods. It killed the *manticore* and meant to kill us. But something in me—I don't know. I spoke Latin. I told it to halt. And it listened."

Her lips come together very tightly. "What did it want?"

"Vengeance."

All the tension seems to go out of her. She glances away. "That I can understand."

We lapse into a silence that feels heavy and meaningful. I see her in the corner of my eye glancing my way. All the sins in the world are on my shoulders and I am meant to start unburdening myself.

A lump grows in my throat and I swallow hard.

Without looking at her I whisper, "Fred. For what I committed us to, for the *manticore*, I am sorry."

There's no reply, so I glance up. She is looking at me blankly. The apology went right through her. She says, "Your decision cost my brother his life," with such careful control of her voice she might as well be discussing the weather.

I want to go to my knees. I want her to tell me I am forgiven. But I can't do that, for two reasons.

The first: I don't deserve it. Simple. I did exactly what she accuses me of: my decision killed Silas Lin.

The second: There is no going back. And absolution of this will not absolve me of everything else. Of Bellamy. Of the suicide. Of my brother.

The only way to survive is to be ruthless.

"As soon as I get my leg, I am leaving these fucking apartments. And I don't think I can stomach seeing you again, Cassius Jones. Not for a very long time."

"I'll have Leo bring the acceptance letter to you," I whisper, and stand.

"I wish we'd never met you."

I know, I know, I know. I can't blame Fred for anything. I can't blame God, who has abandoned me, or from whom I have strayed.

There is only Cassius Jones to blame.

EPILOGUE

The ceremony for the letters is short and sweet. Of the three hundred applicants, half or so are dead. When I think about how many actual graduates there are, I suspect this number will continue to dwindle in the coming years.

Fantastic.

Only ninety-three students stand ready for their letters. The rest are still healing. Rumours circulate about the other trials: another *Nemean Lion*. *Cerberus*, a D tier *teras* for the survivors of a smaller room. Peter Drike was given to a *Stymphalian* class *teras*. C tier, a step above the *python* we faced in the first trial. It was a cruel thing. The *Stymphalian* are man-eating birds. With one leg down, and on his own, it is no wonder Drike did not survive.

But perhaps, if Victoria has joined him, they'd have had a better chance.

It is clear we had the worst of it. I bargained for ours lives and the dean rose to my taunt; I doomed us all. I did that.

Every one of us survivors is broken in some way. There are a lucky few without visible injuries, but most of us have broken limbs, or severed ones. Only four of us have working limb replacements. The rest are waiting for the Artificers working overtime.

I swear I blink and there is a paper in my hand granting me and my family the safety of London's wards—so long as I can make it to graduation. I look beside me to Leo, whose head is bandaged in a way only his right eye is exposed. It lolls over to me and there's a storm in there. So the moment we are congratulated by the dean—all background noise—I go to him.

We stumble out of the introductory hall, that first place we heard Dean Drearton's words before the bloodletting. Leo crowds me against a wall. He can hardly speak with the bandages, but he wheezes out a, "Cass."

He links his fingers through mine and slips open his jacket. I glance back up at him but he's only edging out something wrapped up.

"A gift?" I murmur.

"Weapon."

I don't understand until I've opened it up. And I realise what he wants me to do.

"Leo, I can't."

"You can," he says, voice muffled. "You must. Please." His eye implores me, his hand squeezes hard to keep me here in this moment until I relent.

"And then what will happen?"

He shrugs. "We will figure it out."

I know I am meant to be feeling anger. Or fear. But in the wake of the hybrid, in the ride back to London, I felt nothing. I still feel nothing. I look at Leo, at the emotion in his face, and I can identify the desperation. I understand that he wants it.

But I feel nothing.

"Alright," I say, but I'm not sure I mean it, until Leo hands me the bundle and I think of my father. Not how he is now, but how he used to be.

I think about what I didn't do, and what I begged Thaddeus to do.

How good would it feel to chop the head off the snake.

Dean Drearton's office is past the Janus lock, and without the ceremony—or whatever it is that allows me to pass—I have to wait to catch him. I plant myself in the courtyard by the door and wait for him to meander towards it. I still have my acceptance letter clutched in my hand. He spots me and quirks a brow, and thinks I am there for praise.

"You did very well," he murmurs. "*Manticore*'s head's already being put in the library. Wings, too."

"Shame the tail got damaged," I say.

"Yes," he agrees. "Shame. Anyway, congratulations, Mr Shaw. I look forward to seeing what you do here. And glad the arm stayed sturdy. But if you'll excuse me—"

I take Leo's gift from under my arm. Most of the fabric falls away to expose the thing, and the dean steps back.

I have the *manticore*'s stinger in my hand.

For the first time since the fight, I feel alive. Adrenaline thrums in my blood, and the power—that feeling of total control—makes me near giddy. I have the stinger up against the dean's neck, and he is pressed against the wall. He raises both his hands in surrender, but it's his eyes that give me worry.

There's no fear in them at all.

This is his game, of course. I am a new player.

"Noli esse stultus, Cassius," the dean drawls. *Do not be a fool.* "Pro hoc pugnasti et trucidasti et immolasti."

For this you fought, slaughtered, and sacrificed.

I press the stinger closer and he flinches, which is how I know for certain the threat of the stinger is real. But I think then of how many of us have died. This was a culling.

Slaughter is too chaotic a word. Cull is better. This was deliberate. It was planned.

London is overcrowding, and something has got to give.

The good in me, the thing I wanted my prayers to nurture, whispers, "Nihil boni ex hoc loco nisi mors veniet."

Nothing good will come from this place except death.

And the dean grins like he's won this round before he's even said anything.

"Monstra quae opponimus crescet semper fortior si id destruis quod ea retinet."

And he is right, of course. *The monsters we face will grow ever stronger should you destroy that which keeps them at bay.*

That is the function of this place. This little society. And my function will be cannon fodder unless, as Leo put it, I can learn enough to survive.

"What mantle will you be pledging for Mr Jones?" the dean asks me. I didn't realise I was moving my hand, but I have already lowered the stinger.

I think about what I can do. I can step forward and paralyse the man, and kill him. And this will do nothing, because the University is an institution, and all of London is built around it. I can destroy the wards and doom all of us. I can try to fight.

Helplessness claws at the edges of my apathy until I breathe deep and bury it again. "Hunter," I tell him.

I turn tail and walk back to the apartments.

ॐ

I THINK, in another life, I didn't know who I was. I was doing this for my mother. I was doing it for Thaddeus. And I wanted all these bastards to *like* me. How funny is that? That I was so preoccupied with being liked?

Well, I am a murderer, now. And I can't be sorry for it. As Virgil said: *Flectere si nequeo superos, Acheronta movebo.*

I am not doing this for anyone else but myself.

Not for Leo Shaw. Not for the soft heat of his lips against mine.

But for Cassius Jones.

Because, by God, I want to live.

END

GLOSSARY OF TERAS

AS APPEARS IN THIS BOOK

ANDROPHAGOS, MANTICORE

The manticore is not a Greek monster, but one of Persian origin. It had the body of a lion, face of a man, and a spike-tipped tail, that in some depictions was a scorpion tail. In others, it could shoot arrows from the tail tip.

...the Martikhoras for a choice devours human beings; indeed it will slaughter a great number; and it lies in wait not for a single man but would set upon two or even three men, and alone overcomes even that number... That this creature takes special delight in gorging human flesh its very name testifies, for in the Greek language its means *androphagos* (man-eater), and its name is derived from its activities.

— AELIAN, ON ANIMALS

৩৯৯

ARGOS, ARGUS

From *Argos Panoptes*, a many-eyed giant. In myth, Argos is assigned by Hera to watch over Io, who was transformed into a white heifer by Zeus to shield their affair from Hera. Though fairly benevolent in myth, the *argos teras* encountered by Cassius' father induced madness when looking into its eyes.

And set a watcher upon her, great and strong Argus, who with four eyes looks every way. And the goddess stirred in him unwearying strength: sleep never fell upon his eyes; but he kept sure watch always.

— HESIOD

৩৯৯

Harpy

Also known as the hounds of Zeus, Harpies were depicted as winged women, often 'ugly'. The Homeric poems convey them as personified storm winds, but later they are made birds with the heads of maidens. The most well known story is that of blind King Phineus in the story of the Argonauts, who is punished by the Harpies for revealing the future to mankind. The Harpies stole of defiled Phineus' food, leaving him in constant torment.

On every occasion the Harpyiai (Harpies) swooped down through the clouds and snatched the food from his mouth and hands with their beaks, sometimes leaving him not a morsel, sometimes a few scraps, so that he might live and be tormented. They gave a loathsome stench to everything. What bits were left emitted such a smell that no one could have borne to put them in his mouth or even to come near . . .

— APOLLONIUS RODIUS, ARGONAUTICA

Cerastes

The horned snake. The cerastes had a snake-like body and horns of a ram, either two or four, depending on the myth. It would lure prey by burying its body in the sand and leaving its horns exposed to deceive other animals that a carcass is nearby.

The cerastae carry four-fold little horns; they display them as bait, and destroy the birds they attract. They diligently hide the rest of their bodies in the sand, so that no sign of them is visible saving that part afore-mentioned. By this trick they ambush and kill birds, who have been lured by the hope of food.

— GAIUS JULIUS SOLINUS, DE MIRABILIBUS MUNDI

Nemean Lion

A large lion impervious to weapons. Its hide could not be penetrated. As part of his trials, Heracles was sent to kill the beast as it plagued the district of Nemea. After both his club and arrows failed to injure the lion, Heracles wrestled it to death and skinned it.

> "This was a beast of enormous size, which could not be wounded by iron, or bronze or stone and required the compulsion of the human hand for his subduing.. . Herakles came to the region and attacked the lion, and when the beast retreated into the cleft, after closing up the other opening the followed in after it and grappled with it, and winding his arms about its neck choked it to death. The skin of the lion he put about himself, and since he could cover his whole body with it because of its great size, he had in it a protection against the perils that were to follow."

> — DIODORUS SICULUS, LIBRARY OF
> HISTORY

Scylla

Scylla was a sea monster who lurked in the rocks of a narrow strait opposite the whirlpool Charybdis. She had a fish body, or in some cases, twelve feet, six long necks and mouths, and dog-like protrusions. She was either a beautiful nymph cursed with the form, or was a monster born into a monstrous family. Some describe her body as the result of jealousy by Circe, or by Amphitrite, jealous of Poseidon's love for her.

But Scylla lurks unseen in a cavernous lair, from which she pushes out her lips to drag ships onto the rocks.

Her upper part is human—a girl's beautiful body down to the privates; below, she is a weird sea-monster, with dolphin's tail and a belly of wolverine sort. It's advisable to fetch a long compass, although it protracts the voyage, and sail right round the Sicilian cape of Pachynum, a southernmost mark, rather than to set eyes on that freakish Scylla within her cavern vast or the rocks where her sea-blue hounds are baying.

— VIRGIL, AENEID

Stymphalian Birds
A flock of man-eating birds that plagued Arcadia. They were able to shout out their feathers like arrows. Heracles had to destroy them as part of his sixth labour. He shot them all with his arrows.

"He [Herakles] killed with his arrows on the island of Mars [Ares] the Stymphalian Birds which shoot their feathers out as arrows."

— PSEUDO-HYGINUS, FABULAE

Griffin
A beast with the head and wings of an eagle and the body of a lion. They guarded gold in Scythia.

...a kind of wild beast with wings, as commonly reported, that digs gold out of mines, which the creatures guard and the Arimaspi try to take from them, both with remarkable covetousness.

— PLINY THE ELDER, NATURAL HISTORY

Delphyne, Python

Python was a dragon-serpent who protected the oracle of Delphi. Apollo slew Python when he laid claim to the shrine, destroying it with a hundred arrows.

...the lord Apollon, who deals death from afar, shot a strong arrow at her. Then she, rent with bitter pangs, lay drawing great gasps for breath and rolling about that place. An awful noise swelled up unspeakable as she writhed continually this way and that amid the wood : and so she left her life, breathing it forth in blood. Then Phoibos (Phoebus) Apollon boasted over her : 'Now rot here upon the soil that feeds man! You at least shall live no more to be a fell bane to men who eat the fruit of the all-nourishing earth, and who will bring hither perfect hecatombs. Against cruel death neither Typhoios (Typhoeus) [her consort] shall avail you nor ill-famed Khimaira (Chimera) [her spawn], but here, shall the Earth and shining Hyperion [Helios the Sun] make you rot.

— HOMERIC HYMN 3 TO APOLLO

Cassius' notes on the teras

PLAN
- Research
  vengeance?
- stain!!
- smoke?

STOP
HANGING
HOST
HIM

'ANDROPHAGUS'
MAN-EATER

Name	Tier
HYBRID	???
Manticore Class	S Tier
Scylla Class	S Tier
Griffin Class	A Tier
Nemean Class	B Tier
Arion Class	B Tier
Cerberus class	B Tier
Harpy Class	C Tier
Caledonian Class	C Tier
Stymphalian Class	C Tier
Delphyne Class	D Tier
Automaton class	E Tier
Cerastes class	F Tier

BASTARD

'kind care'
VENGEANCE

FINGERS

- saff?
backwards?

miss class.
Melen = dangerous

355

MANTLES OF THE
UNIVERSITY

SCHOLAR

The Scholar is a rather overlooked mantle. Often demeaned for their lack of experience on the field, the Scholar's role in the fight against the teras should not be understated. During the early years of the teras invasion, which occurred at the turn of the 19th century, the mantle emerged as brave classicists identified the origin of Satan's beasts, and also how they perished in myth. Scholars were thus instrumentable in the creation of the University itself. Without the swift and discerning eye of the Scholars, many of England's people would have perished. The emergence of the hybrid class means the mantle of Scholar is once again extremely significant to humanity's survival.

HEALER

A Healer's duty is the preservation of humanity. For most of the mantle's history, Healers have been expected to retreat injured Hunters returning from patrols. They are aided by the magic that exists behind the Janus Ward within the University itself. However, as the teras fight continues, the requirements of humanity shift. Thus, with Dean Drearton's decision to train jack of all trades, the Healer role requires calm, level-headed experts who are able to perform on the field. Wounds must be treated mid-battle to preserve as much human life —and as many of London's defenders—as possible.

ARTIFICER

Artificers are not one of the founding mantles of the University, though their requirement became apparent in the first decade of the teras threat. Artificers unite technology and medicine, developing practical solutions for those who have been seriously injured by teras attacks. Most commonly, they create new limbs for Hunters who have lost theirs.

These can be simple wooden replacements or incredibly detailed prosthetics—for a price.

HUNTER

The mantle of Hunter is rightfully lauded as the most prestigious amongst all University mantles. Without a doubt, Hunters face the most danger. They are directly responsible for patrolling London and for maintaining outposts throughout England, all with the intention of culling teras numbers and maintaining human numbers. But teras activity is changing, and Hunter numbers are always fluctuating. With the emergence of the hybrid class, the value of the Hunter cannot be overstated.

AUTHOR'S NOTE

This book came to me in a blur in 2021 and sat unfinished until December 2022. *The Teras Trials* was mostly born from an aesthetic: dark academia and Bloodborne. But it quickly became a lot more. I initially wrote this in third person, but Cassius' presence demanded something more personal. I grew up close to Catholicism and must have ingested some of the shame the religion teaches people like me to experience. Cassius is a two-way mirror, at once someone whose desires conflict with his faith, and someone who, in accepting himself, also must relinquish his morality to survive; he must align himself, in a way, with the *teras* themselves. In this current climate where queerness is vilified and so often called monstrous, I hope you can find something in this book to make you feel alive and powerful.

ABOUT THE AUTHOR

Lucien Burr has a background in the Classics and is an author and creator writing dark fantasy stories.

instagram.com/lucienburr

Printed in Great Britain
by Amazon

42660958R00212